PRAISE FOR

REDEMPTION: BLOOD, BROTHERS AND BADGES

"The characters in this hard-boiled tale are each wearing a personal set of ugly psychological scars, and none of them is afraid to show off their marks. Yet all of them—women and men alike—make up for what they lack in resilience and sensitivity with a toughness, a hard and bitter edge that often appears as a near snarl as they face the future. Regardless of what these folks have lived through, they are not cowed, not afraid. While they may be damaged, they still face each day with a rugged—and deep-seated—self-confidence. As a result, the story arc here spins out less like a TV cop show and more like something large, something pure, an experience almost mythic. There could be no other title for this book than *Redemption*."

—**Paul D. Adomites**, Famed Pittsburgh Sportswriter, Author and Baseball Historian

"Ellis manages to blend the wholesome family atmosphere of *Hill Street Blues* with the gritty underworld of *The Shield*, resulting in a remarkable success."

—**Thomas Churchill**, Owner, Blackbaud Designs, "The Senior Private," Citadel Class of '90

"Brian Ellis III is a dedicated father, husband, and son. He is a good man. A quirky, creative, and a 'pleasure to be around' kind of guy. As a man who devoted his life to the military, he sacrificed many things over the years, including a marriage (or two) and his body (sometimes the landings are not always soft). *Redemption* is a small window into that life. . . . The story navigates the many sights and sounds in and around Allegheny County. The author tells a tale of old-fashioned law enforcement, something the modern world desperately needs again. Tommy Spenser is a dedicated detective who has lost his way but still fights the good fight. Life is never easy, and Tommy has one of the roughest ones imaginable. This is one of those books that are hard to put down, and an easy recommendation to anyone looking to read 'something new.' *Redemption* is a fresh take on a familiar story. As a man that has served in law enforcement for over twenty years, this story hits a personal nerve. It is a story of morality, helping those that are helpless, and being a good person. It checks all the boxes. Congratulations to the author, especially keeping me around for the past twenty-five years."

—**Eduard Nogol**, New York Law Enforcement Professional

Redemption: Blood, Brothers, and Badges
by Brian Francis Ellis III

ISBN 978-1-64663-963-2

Portions of this text originally published as
"Redemption of the Irish Rabbi Junkie Detective"
by Brian Francis Ellis III,
Copyright 2019, Melwood Street Publishing /
Ellis & Sons Publishing

Published by

MELWOOD STREET PUBLISHING

RESTON, VIRGINIA
MELWOODSTREETPUBLISHING@GMAIL.COM

Redemption: Blood, Brothers, and Badges

BRIAN FRANCIS ELLIS III

SOME TECHNICAL NOTES

Please allow suspension of disbelief for some of the events and locations. Homestead and West Mifflin in fact have their own police force. It would also be faster to take a trauma patient to any of the downtown hospitals than St. Clair. There is, as of May 2021, no Mercy West Hospital corporation in Pittsburgh, although there is a UPMC Mercy. Although the 20th Special Forces Group does have a staggered process between selection and the qualification course, I cannot verify if selectees would be deployable in such a scenario before being fully qualified in their secondary military occupational specialty (MOS) like the characters depicted. There are also many units in the PPD who deal with specialized high-value-target task forces, which would address such targeted operations as our characters and have leaders in charge with far more seniority and time-in service. For the sake of brevity and to avoid creating a universe of characters that would parallel a George R. R. Martin book, I take some liberties with geography and semantics.

For Roslyn Adams (Cohen) Ellis

January 14, 1941–Dec 26, 2023

Beloved mother, grandmother, sister, and friend

(and the first editor I ever had, at the age of five)

AUTHOR'S NOTE

I began to write *Redemption* during the downtime of my deployment in February to November of 2012. I can think of three culturally defining moments that happened during my deployment to Afghanistan that shaped my views on how the world was processing at the time:

- One of the most scientifically gifted African American men in history, Dr. Ben Carson, saved my son's life in a multiday surgery to remove an arachnid cyst tumor from the base of his brainstem.

- The killings and reprisal protests in Florida of Trayvon Martin.

- The cultural incident on our own compound where certain members of a subordinate unit nonmaliciously burned parts of the Koran to prevent captives from transmitting messages. This was hyped up in US and foreign media and resulted in multiple reprisal killings, including those of US troops, Afghan troops, and civilians. Many American units and key NATO staff who were embedded with the Afghans suffered "green on blue" fratricide killings, murdered by their allies.

Additionally, I write from my own experience as a boy who grew up in Pittsburgh in the 1980s and was brutalized at Allegheny Center Mall in summer 1988. When the cops caught the kids, it was discovered that I was the third one to be targeted that day, and they were just looking for "weak White boys" to beat on.

I reflected on all these things as I wrote the story, but I was shocked to get to page 360 and discover it was rife with my own prejudices. Particularly notable, I had perhaps one or two minority "good guys," nearly all the second-billing villains were Black men, and there was prodigious use of the hateful N-word epithet.

But then I take a look at Pittsburgh today when I visit.

I remember, in 2008, the newscasts of people lining up to vote that showed men from my district holding up Curious George monkeys dressed in suits, mocking presidential candidate Barack Obama. I recall all the times I haven't been able to get into an elevator without someone I don't know trying to have a discussion with me about how much the Steelers suck and how they need to fire "that Black coach."

I also reflect on this:

True to my book, from 2008 to 2012, the minority drug-related violence homicide rate was empirically an issue—but opioid deaths presently outnumber instances of gun-related violence in my hometown. And it's poor White men dropping dead faster than their brothers of color. What difference does any of it make? Dead is dead.

I should also point out that context matters; while Tommy says and accepts fellow cops' use of the N-word, he also calls his brothers "Mick Jews," he calls his partner a "Pittsburgh spic," he calls his ancestors "Irish kikes"; he is worse than Clint Eastwood's Walt Kowalski in Gran Torino with his racial epithets.

Tommy Spenser, protagonist of *Redemption*, is not a recruiting-poster image of an all-American cop. He is an indictment of the failure of trying to live up to the "invincible G-man with a badge" image. His life is a mess; he is buried in a bottle and pills. He is working on another divorce; he uses his phallus as a compass. I could go on.

Had I tried to paint the story PC vanilla and assign him a Black partner in the third act as a way to wipe his slate of prejudice clean, I would have been a hypocrite and untrue to the theme of the book. Tommy's partner in the third act is a person of color, but his presence prompts no real shift in Tommy's moral compass nor the outcome of the story; to do so would be disingenuous and patronizing.

It is not Tommy's job to be morally healed and superior. He will never be one hundred percent. Tommy Spenser is not a John Wayne/Brad Pitt fantasy image of me, as if I were Edward Norton's character in *Fight Club*. Nope, he is a nightmare projection of if I had stayed in a dead-end, one-stoplight corner of town, grown resentful, and never left—if I had given in to prejudice instead of trying to look for the best in others.

Tommy Spenser is not the hero of Pittsburgh. I wake up every day proud that I'm Brian Ellis and not Tommy Spenser. But we must always seek to lean toward goodness and servant leadership, lest we forget how close we are to being hypocrites, to being ignorant, and to being unkind and hateful. We now come to the current day where the world is even more divisive, in the middle of the pandemic and fallout from the deaths of George Floyd and countless others, where rioting, racism, police brutality, and corruption have become the new norm.

I struggled with myself over whether to pull *Redemption* completely from the Amazon sales and questioned whether or not it perpetuated hate and racism. I took an honest, personal inventory of my own ethics and looked at the works of those I admired, like the late Pat Conroy, who also used rough and racist language with morally ambiguous characters but was ethically upright in his personal life and stood on the side of progressivism, civil rights, fairness, equity, justice, and goodness for all people of different races. I'm no Pat Conroy, but I'm also a far cry from Tommy Spenser.

Yes, there are good people in my hometown. But there are many bitter, miserable folks who blame others for their lot in life. If you feel the need to blame an immigrant, or a person of color, for the reason you lost out, throw my book away or take it back to the store.

A final note: The book isn't meant to be a Sunday school how-to on becoming a police officer. It is a character study of one person overcoming trauma and guilt and how he remained functional as a cop, and how a family can suffer continually for generations because of abuse. They say "write what you know"; this is it.

Brian Francis Ellis III
Washington, DC
December 8, 2020

"It is not hard to live through a day if you can live through a moment. What creates despair is the imagination, which pretends there is a future and insists on predicting millions of moments, thousands of days, and so drains you that you cannot live the moment at hand."

—André Dubus, Jr.
August 11, 1936–February 24, 1999

"Change will come to those who have no fear
But I'm not her; and you never were the kind who kept a rulebook near
Weren't we like a pair of thieves? Tumbled locks and broken codes
You cannot take that from me. My small reprieves; your heart of gold
Weren't we like a battlefield? Locked inside a holy war
Your love is my due diligence, the only thing worth fighting
for. The only thing worth fighting for."

—Lera Lynn, *"The Only Thing Worth Fighting For"*

"Out here, there is no good and there is no bad.
To survive out here, you've got to out-monster the monster.
Can you do that?"

—Jeffrey Allen, *Triple 9*

CHAPTER 1

Clarissa Louise Samuels-Hewitt—Claire—came into my life wrapped in tragedy.

It was September, and I was doing my stint in Narcotics over in Homestead, Pittsburgh. We got a call about a domestic disturbance two or three doors down from where we had just grabbed Trevor "Razor" Washington for possession of heroin with intent to distribute.

Normally Razor wasn't prone to making mistakes, but this week, after picking up the stash, he decided to stop off at one of his girls' houses for a Friday-night quickie. Rookie mistake, the kind that a pro only makes when he's blinded by the beaver store: he left the stash in plain sight on the passenger seat. Didn't even need to wake up Judge Scanlon for a warrant. I grabbed the Louisville slugger from my trunk and started whaling on the hood of Razor's car, setting off the Viper alarm.

He came out the front door, pants around his knees and gun in hand, took one look at me, and knew he was fucked. The department would bitch at me for damaging personal property, but now we could add a weapons charge to Razor as well.

My partner, Marco Escardo, carried a tiny Beretta .22 as his backup piece. We often referred to it as the Bette Davis purse gun. He stepped out of Razor's blind spot beside the doorframe and brought the dainty .22 up behind Razor's left ear.

"We have drugs, weapons, and now we have you approaching a Pittsburgh City Narcotics sergeant in the course of his duties with what is likely a loaded and stolen firearm used in multiple felonies. This is more than enough for a self-defense righteous kill. Drop the piece, Razor, if you ever want to smell pussy again."

"The main pussy I'll be whiffing is that fat, ugly spic wife of yours when I post bail tonight, you little narc bitch! Speaking of pussy, where's you get that sissy-ass gun? You been rolling fags on Liberty again, huh!"

Now, Marco Escardo was as cool and collected as they come. Methodical, never prone to unnecessary violence, and far too established on the moral high ground to pistol-whip a high-prize drug suspect. But Razor was still holding the Desert Eagle .50 cal pistol in his right hand, so Marco Escardo was well within his rights to do what he did next.

Keeping the small Beretta on Razor's head, Marco reached with his right hand for the square, black plastic box on his holster belt. He brought the business end of the taser to the back of Razor's boxers, applied the trigger, and launched the twin prongs at their target. The heat and intensity of the prongs made quick work through Razor's tattered underwear, one prong lodging firmly in his sphincter, the other clipping to the base of his rather well-endowed scrotum.

The twenty-eight-year-old self-proclaimed "Prince of Pittsburgh's Drug Scene" soiled himself and pitched forward against the wrought iron porch rails, breaking his nose and biting off the front half inch of his tongue. He twitched and spasmed for a good twenty seconds before Marco turned off the taser.

I looked at Marco with a wry grin. "He's going in *your* car."

Marco became an honorary Spenser brother at age eleven when my eldest brother, Kenny, spared him a sentence in juvenile hall for trying to boost the tires off Kenny's squad car. We figured it had been some petty hood initiation meant to go sideways. No way was tiny eleven-year-old Marco making off with four police cruiser tires on foot. Homeless before then, he became my mother's ward of the courts.

Our grandfather coached him into a flyweight boxer, and Marco graduated salutatorian of Shady Side Academy (our half sister Francine was valedictorian his year). After three years of a perfect boxing record at Carnegie Mellon, he could rise no further than a club competitor, so he headed down to the Federal Law Enforcement Training Center at Glynco and did three years with Homeland Security as a counter-narcotics expert. Afterward, he came back home to Pitt and did the transfer paperwork to the Street Narcotics Unit (SNU) team, also known as the PPD Counter-Narcotics Division, and had been in the shotgun seat as my partner ever since.

Marco slapped a cuff on Razor's wrist and attached the other one to the porch rail. He pulled on a rubber glove—like all good narcs keep in their pockets—and swept Razor's mouth clear of his amputated tongue tip, then gently laid his head so that Razor wouldn't choke on what remained of his tongue, the coagulating blood, or the contents of his stomach, which some tasing recipients bring back up. Marco gingerly picked up the Desert Eagle and checked the chamber.

"Safety was off, Tommy. He had a full mag and one locked and ready. If he squeezed off a shot, we could have him on attempted murder." Marco stood up in the doorframe and sighted the Eagle to the fender of Razor's car where I had been standing a minute ago. I could see my partner's thoughts: squeeze the trigger, no eyewitnesses to the scuffle and shot, just noise at two in the morning. And years of future arrests and paperwork and plain simple energy saved by locking this piece of shit up on attempted murder.

"Don't even think about it. Bag the gun. I'm not gonna give a guy thirty years for insulting your wife, Escardo. If someone were fucking up your car, you'd come to the door with your pistol in your hand, too."

Escardo shrugged, laid the pistol and clip on the hood of Razor's Escalade, and peered inside where my slugger had made a mess of the passenger window. He pulled out a gallon-size baggie stuffed with vials and gel caps. We both quietly nodded in admiration of our catch, at the same time wondering how the fuck Razor was so clouded by a piece of ass that a pro like him wouldn't deliver the stash first.

"Looks like a week's supply, Tommy. DA is gonna love you."

"Meh, his lawyers will say he was set up by a rival. Unless we pull his prints off the bag. Fuck, wouldn't be surprised if he tried to argue that *we* planted it."

Marco opened the door of the Escalade and reached under the seat. He came up with a fat manila envelope, one of those US-letter-size jobs that my ex's lawyers used to send telling me how much I paid in child support for the privilege of being a two-weekend-a-month father. But this envelope wasn't stuffed with paper. It was bulging with money.

"Tommy, why the fuck would he hide the money and set the stash where everyone could see it?"

"Detective Escardo, if you have learned anything in your five years with me, it is that whether or not Mr. Razor was so blinded by a piece of West Mifflin ass that he forgot his custodial duties or some homie put a tip out and set him up is irrelevant. What *is* relevant is we have a gallon of gel caps that will never make their way into the street. And that, my friend, is what us Irish Jew boys call a good day."

Escardo drew out a gravity knife (a slightly more legal version of a switchblade) and slit the end of the package open. Even in the piss-poor Pittsburgh fall weather you could smell the money on the air. Eighty thousand easily, in fifties and hundreds. I put on my gloves and grabbed a clear plastic evidence bag from the back of our unmarked Crown Victoria cruiser. Into it went the Desert Eagle, the stash, and the money. Escardo slipped the full mag of bullets, in a much smaller bag, into his back pocket. Ammunition was handled slightly differently; we would do a test fire of Razor's pistol to not only see if it had been used in any unsolved murders but also to determine if he had been stupid enough to keep the same batch of bullets that produced the kill shot. I slammed the trunk and locked it and heard Escardo on the radio with EMS.

"Central, this is Twelve-Echo-Three. Need a black-and-white and EMS at 410 Diller Avenue. Possession of narcotics with intent to distribute, possession of a firearm while on probation, resisting arrest and . . ." He paused, looking at the growing reservoir of filth in what had once been Razor's underwear. ". . . indecent exposure. Roger, I'll be on the porch."

"Twelve-Echo-Three, this is Central. We just got a possible domestic battery call from 416 Diller. Can you or Spenser check on it till the patrolman gets there?"

"I got it," I said. Escardo had already had his cowboy moment of the night, and while both of us loathed wife beaters, Marco worried me more. After his getting fired up with Razor, the Joe Dirtbag husband of house 416 might be the recipient of a few broken ribs and internal bleeding. Two-in-the-morning domestic disturbances, even in Homestead, was usually white trash getting slap-happy with the missus after knocking off a six-pack of Iron City. This sad fact of Pittsburgh family life was something I'd known since I was three years old.

It was a risk to go it alone, but a calculated one. I seriously doubted that two residents of Diller Avenue were going to confront us with firearms within minutes of each other. Besides, if something crazy happened, Marco was thirty meters away, sitting on an unconscious dealer.

I crossed three lawns and rapped my gold shield badge against the screen door, holding it high to the window, although I doubted the residents thought I was a Jehovah's Witness—I wasn't dressed well enough.

"Open up! Pittsburgh police!"

The husband answered. Insolent, arrogant, cocky, and—like

every asshole in the world who was taller than me—pissed off that the cop coming for him wasn't Tom Brady with a badge or some shit.

"Take a walk, sir. I have enough probable cause to take you in for assault, but I won't tonight because, fortunately for you, we just nailed one of the biggest shitbird narcotics cases in Homestead. I need thirty minutes to talk to your wife. Take a walk. *Now.* And leave your car keys with me. Call some asshole buddy from work to pick you up and give you a couch, or I'm on the phone to Central right now."

The arrogant look on his face faded to shock, then amusement, then meek borderline gratitude that he wouldn't be spending the night in holding next to the dealers, pimps, and other common scumbags. Even wife beaters think they have moral superiority to people like that; they consider their crimes a slightly smudged version of a white-collar offense.

He handed me the keys, grabbed his jacket, and walked off without another word. I reckoned in about six hours he would be back with coffee and probably flowers, begging her to give him another chance, saying how it was wrong of her to get him so upset. I was five years old again, watching my dad tell my mom that he was a changed man and this really was the last time: he was going to get some help.

Wife beaters are so fucking cliché, no matter what generation.

I gently shut the door, then sat down across from the wife. I probably should have waited for another uniform, but I wasn't gonna pull Escardo off babysitting our biggest bust in months.

"My name is Sergeant Tommy Spenser, Pittsburgh Narcotics. I was making a bust down the block when your 911 call came over my radio. Do you need to go to a hospital? You have quite a shiner there."

She sat wrapped up in a turquoise robe, trembling. The first thing I noticed was that she was very pretty. Not Hollywood-model-vogue-glitzy pretty, but pretty. Her hair was long, past her shoulders, wavy and auburn, spiraling into curls at the bottom. She had lovely eyes, teal green, and even though they were shrink-wrapped in tears, I saw gentleness in them. Her cheeks were tracked with pink streaks where her tears had been running. Her mouth was clenched as if she were holding back shouting or screaming.

From the pictures on the wall, I could tell she had a lovely smile. But now a red-and-blue starburst was starting at the edge of her left eye socket. Her jawline and bone structure looked so tender and frail that a closed-fist punch by the bastard might very well have shattered the socket bone. So, despite being a sonofabitch, either he pulled his punch or he slapped her open handed. There are varying degrees of bastards, I suppose. Above her upper lip was a wine-colored speck of a birthmark, no bigger than the crescent moon on a fingernail, and I studied that slight discoloration in order to avoid staring at the swelling already forming around her eye. Everything about her looked delicate. She weighed maybe 105 pounds if she weighed an ounce.

"Nice to meet you. My name is Clarissa Samuels . . . erm . . . Hewitt. My maiden name is Samuels."

Her hands were bony and tiny and did not resist as I took one of them in both of mine.

"Mrs. Hewitt—"

"Mrs. Hewitt? It's 3 a.m. and I'm in my pajamas. You don't have to be so formal."

"Well, what would you like me to call you, then? Do you have a nickname? Do you go by Clarissa?"

She smiled wryly through her tears. "Nobody's called me Clarissa since I was five years old." Her eyes met mine for a second, then looked away as a tear spilled down one cheek. "You can call me Claire."

"Okay. Claire it is. Do you have somewhere to go for the next twenty-four hours?"

The tears welled up again and fell freely like a waterfall. "No."

"Do you want to press charges?"

She wiped a gob of tears and snot with the sleeve of her robe. "No."

"Do you want me to get someone from social services out here, a counselor, someone to talk to?"

"At three in the morning? I don't think so."

"Mrs. Hewitt—Claire—your husband is a lot bigger than you, and it's obvious he is quick with his temper. I don't want one of my uniforms calling me in a month and saying you're dead. If you don't want to press charges, and you don't want to give a statement, and you don't want to go to a hospital . . . let me just get you out of here for a day or so. Maybe you both get your heads a little straight."

"Sergeant, you just said you're a narcotics cop. This is way below your pay grade. What do you care? Shouldn't there be some twenty-one-year-old uniform fresh out of the academy with shaving cuts writing all this down?"

That wasn't a good sign. She had been around the block with this asshole and the police, enough to have grown rather cynical. I didn't have a quick or witty retort. I looked again at the pictures on the wall. My training flashed through my mind, and I could almost kick my own ass: I hadn't thought of clearing the house first.

"Anyone else here I should know about? Do you have any kids?"

"No." She trembled a little more at that. "I don't want to bring a child into this."

"Well, there's got to be family or friends we can reach out to. There's got to be someone out there who loves you and doesn't want you in the middle of this. I'm gonna call up one of our female detectives. Why don't you go get changed, and I'll take you to meet her? Meanwhile, on the drive you can think of someone we can bring you to for a couple nights' rest."

She nodded weakly, almost defeated by the conversation. I watched as she started down the hallway to her bedroom and noticed her trailing small red droplets. She froze, ran her hand down to her waist, and turned around, whiter than a three-day-old corpse in the river. Her fingers came out of her pajama bottoms covered in blood. I caught her right before she collapsed against the wall, and rested her head in my lap. Her pelvic area was slick and sticky with dark blood.

My first thought was that the bastard had raped her, but there had been no overt signs of a struggle in the house, and I saw from the hallway that the bed was still neatly made. I punched 911 in my phone, identified myself, and told them I had been answering a domestic dispute and the victim had passed out and was now expelling blood heavily from her vaginal area. Her pulse was shallow but steady.

I had the bottom half of her robe as well as my suit jacket pressed up against her groin. Her forehead was scalding. I let go for ten seconds to soak a washcloth from the kitchen sink and press it against her forehead.

Kim, the same EMT who had been patching up Razor two houses away, came through the door with her med kit. "Jesus, Tommy, what happened?"

She shed the gloves she had been using and put on a fresh pair. Grabbing a set of shears from her belt, with deliberate precision she cut away the bottom half of Claire's robe and pajamas. Out of modesty I looked away. Kim glanced up at me and rolled her eyes at my decorum. "Snap out of it, Sergeant Spenser. I need a pillow and towels. Get all the lights on you can."

I was only too eager to help. I stepped around them, yanked a pillow off the bed, flung open doors until I found the linen closet and grabbed four or five towels, then ran back down the short hallway. I propped the pillow under Claire's head and helped Kim stuff the sheets under her legs, then flushed with embarrassment again as we bent her knees as if she were in an exam room at the OB-GYN.

Kim said, "Spontaneous miscarriage, Tommy. From the bits of tissue, I'm judging she was maybe two months along. Fucker must have punched her in the gut; I'm palpating at least two cracked ribs. Tell Bobby to bring me lots of saline. I'm gonna have to flush her out on-site to make sure she doesn't go septic on us."

"I . . . I don't think she knew. That she was pregnant, I mean."

"Why didn't you cuff the bastard, Tommy?"

"Fuck you, Kim. I was trying to de-escalate the situation. I figured telling the guy to take a hike and getting some breathing room between them was best." Claire had been sitting on the couch, and he opened the door willingly. *How could I have known what happened?*

"That's why you wear the gold shield, Tom. You're supposed to know better."

I tried to keep from retching as Kim's gloved hand reached in with businesslike accuracy and cleared blood clots and God knows what else from that mess.

"Well, now it's gone from a domestic dispute to aggravated assault." She turned back to Claire Hewitt. "Pretty little thing, too. You poor girl. We'll patch you up." Kim turned back and without looking directly in my eyes said, "Have Bobby bring the bus over in the driveway and get the gurney ready. She's lost quite a bit of blood. She needs an IV and probably antibiotics."

"Where's the uniformed patrol I already called for?"

"Came across a fender bender on the way over here. He's writing a citation over on the bridge. Marco's flying solo to take your boy in to booking."

I backed out of the house to see Bobby's flashing lights from the ambulance already in the driveway. He shouldered past me with a Skedco, as the door was a bit too narrow to bring a full-size wheeled gurney through. A Skedco is a sturdy, plastic, durable brace that rolls up almost like a beach towel and can be used as both a stabilization board and a jury-rigged stretcher, known for its use on the battlefield but getting more and more popular with urban EMS and SWAT teams. Once we had the fluids and lines going and had Claire secured, we three hefted her up and brought her outside. The EMTs got Mrs. Hewitt buckled on the gurney outside the front door, and Bobby looked at me.

"Are you hit, Sarge?"

"No, why?" I looked down. Both my forearms and my waist were covered in her blood. I grabbed up a few of the towels and wiped down as best I could. Marco was already on the way to the station with Razor, so being without wheels or a change of clothes, I jumped into the back of the ambulance and held Mrs. Hewitt's hand, wondering why the hell anyone who considered themselves a man would hit a woman.

■ ■ ■

The sunlight streaked through the windows of UPMC Hospital. It was 5:15 in the evening on Saturday, but the sky was still clear—that point of the day where it goes from blue to reds and yellows to dark. I had fallen asleep in a chair next to Claire and had one hand resting on the thumb break of my .45's holster. (Like her asshole husband was gonna do a frontal assault past the nurse's station; I'd seen too many movies.)

The EMTs had scrounged up a pair of blue flight coveralls for me to put on, and my sharp gray suit—well, as sharp as you could get off the thrift store shelves—had found its way to the incinerator of the hospital's custodial department. I took a shower shortly after I knew she was stable. I was on the butt end of nine days of duty; I had three days off coming up, and I didn't have the kids visiting. *What harm could it do to keep her company?*

More heightened than the physical trauma of the miscarriage was Claire's emotional distress. Sometime during my near-comatose state after the night's activities, the on-duty hospital shrink had come in and talked to Mrs. Hewitt about her late child's brief residency in her womb. The double shock of not knowing she had been pregnant and thusly miscarried had put her into a frenzy of grief and outrage, and the shrink had judiciously put her on a cocktail of painkillers, sleep agents, and antianxiety meds. The stash in Razor's car couldn't have done a better job of propelling her into euphoric bliss.

I heard a familiar voice from the doorway.

"Prince Valiant, the noble knight at it again, I see. Oh, nice overalls there, cutie!"

I looked into the eyes of the hospital's chief trauma nurse, Samantha Knight Callahan, RN, MSN, DNP—former married name of Spenser. Samantha usually worked shifts at St. Clair, which was closer to the house she shared with her new husband. But she moonlighted at UPMC when the chief nurse was sick or called away. I managed a small smile for the mother of my kids.

"Need I mention the irony of the caduceus and that 'cowboy cock' of a .45 in the shoulder holster going well together?" She pursed her lips into a sarcastic smile. Even in medical scrubs after a double shift, my ex-wife still looked fabulous.

I stood up, adjusted the EMT flight-suit coveralls as if they were a dinner jacket, and planted a perfunctory kiss on her cheek. "How are you, gorgeous?"

"I knew you didn't have much of a social life, but really, Tommy? Picking up chicks in the ER?"

"Hardee-har. She was part of a domestic dispute next door to a bust."

"I heard about that. I just got done watching an intern stitch up"—she consulted the clipboard in her hand—"Trevor Washington, a.k.a. Razor. Was that yours or Marco's work?"

"He had a gun drawn. Marco tasered him from behind. He fell where he fell."

"He was cuffed to a chair in the ER waiting room half the night, howling for his lawyer. Cussing you and Escardo and every other honky cop on the planet."

"Escardo is a Latino."

"I guess he was generalizing. Anyways, he needed about thirty stitches from where his face hit the rail. You gave him a true gangster scar. You probably even upped his street cred."

"Why'd he wait so long?"

"Well, he was ambulatory coming in, and it was a busy night. Plus," she added with a small laugh, "you don't piss off my nurses if you want five-star care."

She hugged me around my shoulders from behind. Not a loving, romantic hug like we once shared but one of those hugs a friend, even an ex-wife, gives you when they know you've caught hell that day. Resting her chin on my shoulder, she looked down at the broken, battered, and doped-up shell of Clarissa Hewitt resting peacefully in bed.

"And this one?" she said. Samantha hadn't handled her. Kim's call over the net had brought in not one but three off-duty OB-GYNs—God bless them—wanting to help at 3 a.m. on a Saturday. She had gone straight past the ER bullpen and into surgery. A simple D&C, but they went ahead and did a small exploratory incision and scope to see if the bastard had caused any internal damage. Claire Hewitt wouldn't have gotten better treatment if she were a visiting UN ambassador's wife.

I wondered bitterly if the fact that a Spenser had picked up this girl had triggered an outpouring of attention. My father's name still opened a lot of doors when it came to cops. For once

I was grateful for my father's notoriety, currency normally used up on expensive dinners, expensive hookers, and bar tabs for his former partners.

"Fucking husband smacked her around. Gut-punched her so hard she lost the kid. Kim found a few cracked ribs when we were bringing her in too. X-rays showed mass contusions on her back, so this wasn't the first time he was free with his fists. And I let the sonofabitch go."

She gave me one last squeeze before backing away. "You sent him away because you were protecting her. I know you, Tommy."

"The bastard didn't resist at all, so I thought the sooner I got him out of the house, the sooner I could get her story. Marco was sitting on Razor, waiting for the unis to show up," I said, referring to uniformed officers. "Such a fucking rookie mistake. She was sitting there on the couch, the house was neat, and . . . I couldn't tell what had happened. I let that maggot walk out the door."

"Okay, hotshot, so say you *didn't* send him out of the house. Say you turned your back to him, and the next thing you know, there's a kitchen knife in your heart and they're handing your son a folded flag. Quit beating yourself up like you're three years old again." She raised one hand to my face. She hadn't touched me there in four years. Almost immediately, she drew her hand back like she had touched a burner on a stove. "That little boy grew up. You may have been a shitty husband, but you're a great cop."

"How are the kids?" I said, changing the subject.

"Allan took them camping."

Allan, the new husband. Structural engineer who worked on the municipality's small fleet of river patrol boats checking out the bridges. A likeable guy, but I could never see past the fact that he had been screwing Samantha the entire last year of our marriage—usually when I was out busting Razor and his cousins. Still, he did all right by our kids. And he treated Samantha well.

At the very least, I knew nobody would put their hands on her like that Hewitt scumbag did to Claire.

She bit her lip and looked at me a long time. There was something on her mind, and it wasn't about Allan or the unconscious girl on the gurney.

"Tommy, you know I'm still listed as your next of kin, right?"

"Yeah," I said, vacantly. I reached down and took Claire Hewitt's right hand in mine, absently reading the alphanumeric data on her barcoded wristband, knowing and trying to drown out what Samantha was going to say.

"Doctor Tolliver called me into his office the other day. He asked if I wanted to see your chart. He tells me your lymph nodes are worse and you're refusing chemo. He says you're self-medicating."

"Sick leave doesn't come with overtime, Sammy Pants."

She hated it when I called her Sammy Pants.

"Fuck, Tommy, this isn't about the child support. Don't you wanna see your boy grow up and play college football? Don't you want to see your daughter's dance recitals? You're thirty-five fucking years old. You don't have the right to euthanize yourself! Or is this all a big act to try to garner sympathy from me?"

"Samantha, I'm a cop, and you just said I'm a good one. What fucking good will I do anyone in a wheelchair?"

"What good will you do anyone in a goddamned casket? At least drink plenty of fiber. The Percocet will constipate you. Don't mix it with Vicodin. Or whisky. Or Ambien. Fuck, Tommy Francis, take care of yourself, okay? I may not be in love with you anymore, but don't think that means I don't care about your sorry ass."

She left the room. I sat back down in the overstuffed chair and reached over to again hold Claire's limp hand in mine. At that moment, I felt incredibly sad for her. Part of the fight that precipitated the events of the evening had been about the Hewitt house being in foreclosure. By the time Claire got out of the hospital, there would be an eviction notice on her door from the bank. And while she had been in the hospital fourteen hours, I was the only one being visited by friends and family.

The bruise on her face had started to darken, and I absently brushed back her hair from her forehead, whispering that nobody was going to hurt her ever again.

When she had awakened and was alert enough, she, her doctor, and I discussed where she was going to go. She knew the outline of the tentative plan but mostly stared off into space. Psych did an assessment and ruled she was not a danger to herself or others, though they gave her several Seroquel for sleep. Somewhere in that haze she had the wherewithal to lift a pen and sign herself into my custody.

Both the precinct department shrink and the on-duty hospital shrink took me aside and gave me the speech on trauma bonding, Stockholm syndrome, transference, white-knight syndrome, Florence Nightingale effect—pretty much everything that encompassed what Claire had been through and what, if we were in close proximity throughout her recovery, she might soon project on me. (I probably should have had a better ear.)

Before we could depart, we had to formally review the plan with her. Her doctor, Samantha, Marco, and I joined her in a room as she was wheeled in, staring off at the window. Next to Samantha was a thin redhead in a brown Prada power suit with cranberry checked pinstripes over a tan blouse with a bold, matching berry ascot around her throat.

The lady's corresponding cranberry-colored eyeglass frames made her look cutesy in a comic-book way—as if she were trying to pull off a female Clark Kent look. It was wholly apropos in this case; in my grandfather's eyes, she had been his little "Supergirl."

The power suit was our half sister, Francine Shira Goyevsky, sole daughter of our father, Frank Spenser, and graduate of Yale Law, certified by the Virginia, Maryland, Washington, DC, and Pennsylvania Bar Associations.

Although Francine's proper legal name was Spenser, she used the name Goyevsky, her late mother's name, on her American Bar Association card, especially within the city limits of Pittsburgh. Saying you were a Spenser that practiced law in this town was like saying you were part of the Mafia.

Francine clerked as an assistant district attorney for the City of Pittsburgh on the Victim Advocacy Task Force. I held off on informing Claire that Francine was related to us. Not necessarily a full-court-press deception, but between my ex-wife being her nurse practitioner and my adoptive brother/partner joining us, I didn't want her to feel completely strong-armed by my current or former family.

"Mrs. Hewitt," I began.

"Claire is fine."

"Claire, then. Claire, this is Attorney Goyevsky of the Victim Advocacy Task Force. She took your statement along with my partner when you were first conscious. We've called you in here to discuss the next steps with you. Your house . . ." Tears began to stream down her face as she continued gazing into the distance. "While you were in here, your house went into foreclosure status and the eviction fully processed. You cannot go back to your former residence, else you'll be considered trespassing by the Allegheny County Sheriff's Office. The family court judge has offered to sign you into my protective custody for an indefinite time, with your consent. This wouldn't be funded by the department, but my family . . ." I looked at Marco. ". . . *our* family has a place you could stay till you're on your feet. There's a couple apartments. I'd be right next door."

Claire responded by clicking the self-administering pump on her IV three times. "Just take me to the shelter."

Francine leaned forward and pushed her glasses to the bridge of her nose. "Mrs. Hewitt, the domestic violence shelters have a nearly sixty-day backlog of overflow. Sergeant Spenser's offer is the only thing anyone is offering you right now."

Claire stared back out the window, tears still flowing freely. "My baby's dead. Gone. I don't care what happens to me."

Samantha took charge. "Can the ladies have the room, please?"

Marco, the doctor, and I looked at one another, mixed confusion and trepidation on our faces, and quietly exited to wait in the hallway.

Fifteen minutes later, the door opened, and there was some light conversation and—to my surprise—a few smiles in the room. Samantha pulled me aside and passed me the clipboard with Claire's signature and the liability waivers declaring that she was signing herself into my care.

"You should have led with the fact that we're all related in some form. It put her mind at ease to know that someone's looking out for her. But be careful, Tom. She's a human being; she's not a puppy that followed you home."

"That's fucking rich, Samantha. Lessons from you on how to be compassionate and have awareness and empathy. That's some fucking Oprah Winfrey/Maury Povich–level irony."

Her smiling expression immediately switched back to the oh-so-familiar anger and bitterness I usually stoked up in her disposition.

"You're a real prick, Thomas Spenser."

"And then some."

CHAPTER 2

I signed Claire into my custody, as far as the hospital administration was concerned, and wheelchaired her out to my beat-up 1987 Ford Mustang, black with one red door. Samantha had gotten the Grand Cherokee in the divorce.

I wasn't a social worker, but I felt the girl was my responsibility, seeing as how I had let the bastard who assaulted her walk free. But Pittsburgh police had caught up fast with the no-so-gentlemanly Mr. Hewitt at Sharky's Bar in Carnegie. Although assault and battery wasn't our beat, Escardo called in a few favors with the detectives who usually worked the Homestead domestic battery beat, and when they put him in the interrogation box with Hewitt, I heard the motherfucker was crying like a schoolgirl.

Jake Hewitt, an otherwise law-abiding citizen, posted bail two days later and had a protection-from-abuse levied against him. By the time I tracked him to his brother's house in Greentree, good old Jake had decided to jump bail and get the hell out of Dodge. Having been recently unemployed and dumped by the local Greentree Millwrights Union, he drew the last of what was in his checking account. I gleaned from a few snitches as well as his internet search history that he had headed to Seattle to find work on a fishing trawler as a deckhand and mechanic.

I decided to let him go. Who gave a fuck about a piece-of-shit wife batterer jumping bail? It wouldn't bring back a dead baby or undo the damage to his wife. If he was freezing his ass off on a fishing boat and he wasn't beating on some poor girl in the Pacific Northwest, good riddance.

Part of me felt I should drop Claire at the nearest halfway house or find out where her relatives were and get her to them. Go home, fix a drink, catch up on the DVR, and close the book on Mrs. Clarissa "Call me Claire" Hewitt. But that part of me was my dad and my brothers. I could hear the old man now, in all his hypocrisy as a lifelong card-carrying member of the order of abusive husbands: "Dumb broad should have gotten the hell out of there when the thumps first started coming." But my brothers would have at least made sure the girl was somewhere safe. *That* part was passed down to us through our mother.

■ ■ ■

Retired deputy commissioner Frank Spenser never again laid a hand on my mother after the night I came back from Little League to find him passed out on the sofa with a bottle of scotch pooling at his feet. Brady was pitching a doubleheader the next day and working extra hours with the coach. My mom was in the kitchen, holding a bag of frozen vegetables against an eight-ball-size hematoma on the side of her face.

With the same Louisville slugger that I smashed into Razor's whip twenty-seven years later, I busted my old man's jaw and the orbital bone around one eye socket, broke four ribs, and whaled the bat against his leg, shattering his kneecap so badly he would walk with a limp the rest of his life. But he never drank again nor raised a hand to my mother, ever. The official story to the police was that I was still warming up with Brady at Little League practice when the "unknown assailant" attacked my dad. No mention was made in the police report of the condition of my mother's face, nor were any charges ever pressed against the old man for what he did.

I don't think it was the first-class ass whooping from his eight-year-old son that sobered him up; it was being taken off the street as a homicide investigator and relegated to a desk for the rest of his career.

For a long time after that, my brothers didn't talk to me—out of shame, it seemed. Kenny was a bit older than us and already out of the house, but it hit Brady hard. Brady and I are twins and had been looking out for each other since we were tots. Once, when I was five, I got between Mom and the old man and took a beating so bad that one eye swelled shut for a week. Brady was the smart one of the two of us; I was the one who thought with my fists. If it had been Brady who took out the old man that night, you could bet he would have had his getaway plan and alibi already laid out. And Frank Spenser would have been in the grave.

■ ■ ■

From the hospital, Claire and I headed to my apartment over the family gym.

Born Mikael Ivanov Rosencoff and affectionately known as Papa by me and my siblings and Mickey by everyone else, my maternal grandfather managed prizefighting boxers when there was still smog in the sky over Pittsburgh from the steel mills. He started out over in Churchill at an Italian gym, but when the owners started paying protection money to the local racketeers, my papa made a move of brass balls. He borrowed against the house and bakery he owned with his brothers to pay for the old Point Spring and Driveshaft warehouse on Melwood Street. Over several months, he paid Irish and Polish and Black demolition crews off the books and under the table to turn it into the gym he had envisioned.

When all the naysayers were talking shit that the bank was going to foreclose any minute, my papa held a pro tournament on opening night that covered feather through heavyweight divisions, dubbing it the Steel City championship. Open registration was fifty bucks a fighter, a pretty chunk of change (worth around $800 in 2012) in 1941, so he attracted a lot of rich steel magnates who were sponsoring up-and-coming fighters, and the bookies went nuts. In five hours, he made the monthly mortgage payment and cleared a thousand dollars after concessions, staff, and paying the fighters and referees. In five months of business, he'd paid off the building.

He turned that little strip of Pittsburgh into a boomtown, but he never forgot his roots. He kept the same modest little house he had always lived in with my nanna, not even two blocks from the gym, and when Alzheimer's and dementia took my nanna at eighty-seven, he lived the remaining eleven years of his life in the little set of bachelor apartments he had built above the gym for coaches, trainers, and visiting fighters. It was there I found him the morning of October 9, 2009, when he didn't answer the phone and the daily regulars couldn't figure out why the doors were still locked. He had the sheets pulled up to his chin as he always slept, and I wept like a baby when I saw the picture on his nightstand was of me, him, Kenny, and Brady the day Brady and I graduated Metro Police Academy.

I wasn't alone in my weeping. All the men and the handful of women he had coached over the years turned out in droves as my brothers and my mom and I sat shiva in the little efficiency; we eventually had to open the somber festivities to the entire gym to accommodate all the mourners. Primanti Bros, Papa's favorite Pittsburgh restaurant, donated two truckloads of catering for the wake. His procession of pallbearers was a who's who of boxing legends and Pittsburgh celebrities. His gloves from boxing in his late teens to his early thirties were bronzed in a showcase by the door, and there was an empty stool next to the judge's booth that his cane, now gilded, still rested against.

Papa had named the gym Mickey's, and after he died, we decided to leave the corporation's name intact, with one minor modification: since he had been more of a dad to us than our useless drunk of an old man, we commissioned the gym "Mickey & Sons" a year after his death. Each of the brothers was a shareholder, and we bought out our mom and uncle for their shares.

When shit started to go south in my marriage with Samantha, I moved into Papa's apartment above the gym, leaving everything nearly as it was when he was alive. I wound up buying bunk beds for me and Thomas Junior and a crib for Allie; both kids were barely toddlers when their mom and I split. Kenny and Brady never mentioned it nor charged me a penny's rent.

"Your sister's nice," Claire said as we made the drive from UPMC. "Smart lady, smarter dresser. I knew who she was before the nurse said anything."

"How'd you know she was my sister?" I asked, a slight grin forming on my face.

"Because I'm not a complete idiot." She chuckled from under the bundle of blankets in the passenger seat. "Everyone was nice. Funny coincidence your ex works in that hospital."

"She doesn't always work that one. She's on rotation there sometimes."

There were three studio apartments above the training areas and fighting rings. One was mine, formerly Papa's. One was for guest fighters and coaches coming through for events, and one stored spare gear and promotional stuff. From the streets, the primary set of stairs and the hallway to the studio apartments that made up the roofline ran in an enclosed corridor exterior to the main part of the building that housed the gym, heavy bags, fight rings, and workout machines. The interior catwalk leading to the doorways that faced into the building and overlooked the inside of the gymnasium was originally meant for emergency fire exits.

A handful of regulars were wrapping up their workouts for the night, and I heard catcalls, unsolicited advice from the benches, gloves hitting canvas, guys talking shit to other guys, and a steady snap of jump ropes smacking against concrete. Nobody paid any mind to me escorting my guest up to the loft, except for a few instances of "Hey, Coach Tommy" or "Hey, boss."

As Mickey got older and weaker, we had installed an elevator lift at the end of the row of apartments to bring him up to the catwalk after he trained the fighters downstairs. Before he passed, we'd discussed remodeling and making the catwalk an actual observation balcony.

"Okay, here we are," I said cheerfully, supporting her around the waist as we stepped slowly on the suspended platform to the set of studios and she steadied herself on the handrail. I fished in my pocket for the key to the apartment next to mine. It had a queen-size bed for the visiting guest fighter and two daybeds/couches in the living room for the trainer and cornerman. I intended this to be Claire's place, but as I handed the key to her, she shook her head.

"Can I stay at your place?"

"Claire, I'm not sure that's such a good idea."

"Tom, I just . . ." She heaved a choked sob, leaning her head on my shoulder so I couldn't see her eyes. "I just don't want to be by myself right now."

"Sure. My son and I have two beds over in this side, over here. I'll just stay on the couch."

"It's your place. You tell me where you're comfortable. Thank you. I just want to go back to sleep."

So it was on TJ's bunk bed that I temporarily set up Claire Hewitt while she was still lethargic and riddled with grief. The woman had lost enough inside of a week, and I'd be damned if I was going to say no to her.

My mother lived a few streets over and, though in her late sixties, was still sharp as a tack and kept the books for the gym as diligently as she had done for her father when she was nineteen. She hadn't so much as raised an eyebrow when I walked past her office with the 100-pound bundle of battered housewife cradled in my arms. She was used to moments of charity clouding judgment in the Rosencoff-Spenser boys, and I think it pleased her that we were so different from our father.

Still, after I tucked Claire in and made sure she was comfortable before venturing off to speak to my mom, I found myself looking down at my shoes the same way I had after I introduced my father to my Mickey Mantle–edition line drive.

My mom peered at me over her glasses, then went back to her ledger. “The mother of your children called. She told me we might be having a guest.”

“Did she now?”

“Is our guest on anything?”

Having been a cop’s wife and the mother of cops, my mom had plugged wounds, passed incriminating documents, ironed shirts, and made matzo ball soup for a variety of snitches, informants, loan sharks, debtors, thugs, conspirators, and corrupt politicians as well as a smattering of Dad’s drug-addled hookers who made up the unofficial intelligence network of the Pittsburgh criminal underground back in the day. Nothing would have surprised her. However, in the business her father had built, she had one golden rule, regardless of whether she was a silent partner or not: no using on the property. This went from the general anabolic athletic steroids favored by up-and-coming boxers to marijuana, meth, speed, cocaine, and everything else under the sun.

All of Papa Mickey’s fighters had been natural muscle; jump rope and sparring had built his legacy the last seventy years. Hardened dealers, even some of Razor’s crew, would run at the sight of little Mrs. Spenser swinging open the doors to Mickey’s gym with a shotgun bigger than she was, “sweeping away the riffraff from the porch,” as she called it. And they all abided. To give a cop’s family any sort of grief was a death knell, period. To fuck with a woman with three cop sons and an ex-husband who was a retired deputy commissioner . . . well, that was just suicide.

Razor and his boys kept their rivals away from Melwood Street and made sure their transactions happened across the bridge.

"She's on some painkillers from the doc, but other than that, no; she's just a beat-up young lady who needs a place to stay."

Mom stood from her desk and put her glasses down. For the thousandth time, she reminded me of Golda Meir. Not in actual looks but in the dignified way she carried herself. Such a little lady, someone's grandma you just wanted to scoop up and hug, but at the same time she exuded an air that she was not to be trifled with.

"And how's my best boy?"

I laughed at that. She called all of us her best boys.

"Tamas—Tommy, your ex-wife tells me you are neglecting your appointments."

"She talks too much. And I don't earn from a hospital bed, Mama."

"Fah! Money is not why you do it."

"No, Mama? Then why do I do it?"

"You have a demon in you that you are trying to outrun. You think that part of you became your father the night you protected me from him. That's why you live in that little apartment when your ex-wife lives in your house with her new husband. That's why you take care of someone else's wife whose husband is just as much of a bastard as your father was. That's why you went Narcotics. You think you can save everyone. And you think if you can run fast enough, you can outrun death."

"But you're proud of me that I'm a narcotics cop."

"I'd be proud of you if you were a garbage man."

I smiled. "Goodnight, Mom."

"I love you, Tommy. I've loved you ever since I first felt you kick."

This started a straight-man routine she had been bouncing

off me and Brady since we were old enough to talk. "How'd you know it wasn't Brady kicking?"

"You always kicked twice as hard."

"Goodnight, Mom."

"You'll see the doctor tomorrow?"

"We'll see. I love you, Mom."

As I walked back toward the stairs leading up to what I considered my home, I was greeted by Charley, the official mascot of Mickey's gym. Charley was an eight-year-old golden retriever we'd rescued as a puppy from the pound six or seven years after our grandmother died, as company for our grandfather. Charley had been Papa Mickey's dog and ever since Mickey's death made a habit of dividing his ownership between me and my mother and the grandkids and the fighters who trained at the gym.

Every evening since Papa's death, he had camped out by the stool next to the judge's box as the fighters sparred in the main ring, and when we shut off the lights to the gym, Charley would crane his head toward the door, waiting patiently for his late master until he heard the door bolt shut. At that sound, in resignation he would climb to the top of the steps to my apartment. We had welded a doggy door off the maintenance entrance for Charley years ago, and as far as he was concerned, he had the neatest doghouse in all of Pittsburgh.

I refilled Charley's food and water and climbed up to my apartment. My guest was sitting up on the sofa and brightened a bit when I came in.

"Hi," I said.

"Where exactly are we? I remember the hospital, and what we talked about, but not much else. I would have made some coffee, but I didn't want to be a snoop."

"No, it's fine. I'll make some," I said. "We're over near Schenley. My family owns this building: Mickey & Sons gym on

Melwood. You were in and out. I didn't know who to call. Your house is, um . . ."

"I know. All I remember was talking a little with the doctor and in your car. How long was I in the hospital?"

"You were in and out of consciousness for about four days." I absently stared into space as the kettle boiled and then poured two steaming cups of water into some instant coffee grinds. I turned and handed her a mug. She giggled slightly—a welcome sound in that lonely apartment—when I grabbed a bottle of Hershey's caramel syrup and squeezed a good amount into my cup. When I proffered it to her, she smiled and shook her head. "Just sugar is fine."

I continued with my report on her stay at the hospital. "They were monitoring you for shock and, um, depression. You lost a lot of blood in the incident, you spiked a high fever, and they ran a lot of fluids through you. You didn't eat much on your own; you actually lost seven pounds, which for such a low body weight to begin with isn't good at all. Your ex—I mean, your husband's family—wasn't very agreeable, and, well, I couldn't find anyone on your side nearby, so that was when I pitched to the doc, and you, to bring you here. Temporarily, of course. Until you get on your feet."

She didn't say anything, so I went on. "My mom keeps the books for this place; she might look in on you from time to time, but she's just being nice. There are fighters in and out all day training, and we usually close up around nine thirty. No one will bother with you, but the door here has a break-in bar on it if you get spooked." I pointed to a two-by-four piece of steel that spanned the width of the door and the hooks to hang it on, then gestured to a small suitcase of her things I had packed before the bank had gotten to the house. "I grabbed your purse and your cell phone too. I talked to the sheriff's office and made a few calls. Most of the things we could identify as yours are in a storage locker across town."

I handed her the key. She managed a small smile and resignedly set it on the coffee table in front of her. "You seem like you've done this before."

"I just did what I would want someone to do for me if I was in trouble."

She placed her mug next to the keys, covering her face with her hands as the first sobs seized control of her body. She cried, more like wailed, for the better part of an hour. I didn't try to comfort her or take her hand; I simply sat beside her, keeping a good two feet away on the couch. When her sobbing stopped and her breathing was shallow and steady, I covered her up with a blanket, went into the bedroom, and changed into sweats and sneakers.

I turned on the main light in the gym and started jumping rope and worked out on the bags while Charley watched, keeping his vigil next to the empty stool. When I came back upstairs, my guest had found her way back to the bunk beds. I stood under the jet spray of the shower for a good twenty minutes, then slipped on another pair of sweatpants for modesty's sake. Grabbing a pillow off Thomas Junior's empty bunk, I headed for the couch and quietly shut the door. I did not jump in shock at the fact that my partner was sitting at the kitchen counter.

Marco had his own set of keys to the gym and was probably wondering where the fuck his partner and supervisor had been hiding for four days. Being a dependable partner, he had already found the Johnnie Walker Black Label and two jelly glasses. He had his jacket off and looked like a 1930s bartender. In addition to the affectation of his little Beretta backup, he also wore classic "cotton club" shirtsleeve cuffs, the kind that went around your upper arm. I didn't know where the fuck you even got those these days. He looked like he was going for a Latino Paul Newman à la *The Sting*.

"My sergeant is not widely known for being Santa Claus. Nor for bringing his work home with him."

"I'm coming back tomorrow. I called in with the captain."

"Are you kidding? He nearly threw a party. You haven't taken vacation time in months. Did you hear Razor is gonna walk on the drugs and his lawyer's gonna post bail on brandishing of a firearm and illegal ownership of a pistol while a felon? He'll probably knock the firearms charge off the sheet due to illegal entry because we had no probable cause to enter the property."

"Since when is a tipline not probable cause?"

"Because we didn't have line of sight or witnesses on any goings-on at the house. The car, yes. But once we set foot from the street to the house property line, defense is calling us cowboys."

"Prints on the bag?"

"Nope. Nor on the gel caps or vials. No prints on the cash, so we seized that. We tried to raise the bail amount on the weapons charge. That fucking defense lawyer of his did a tap dance and a half. Threw a fit about police brutality. IAD wants to talk to you, but as far as they're concerned, everything we did was textbook."

"What do you mean 'we,' Kemosabe? I'm not the hot-tempered spic that tasered a suspect," I said.

"Eat my greasy taco shits, you Mick Jew-boy." We clinked glasses. He downed his drink and stared levelly at me. "Boss, what the hell are you doing with the assault victim in your bed?"

"Sometimes people just need help, Marco."

"It's not on us to get her *that* kind of help. We just make sure people walk the line and stay out of trouble."

"To protect and serve, my friend. What if it was someone beating on Inez like that?" I asked.

My partner's eyes turned to stone. "The motherfucker couldn't be identified by his teeth when I was through with him.

But the woman in the other room's not your wife, Tommy."

"Neither are you, you little Tex-Mex shitbird, but I look out for your sorry ass." We both laughed.

■ ■ ■

The next morning, I went into general holding at the Allegheny jail. I surrendered my gold shield, my belt, tie, and my service department Glock 9 with my Intratec TEC-38 backup to the guard desk. What Samantha affectionately referred to as my "cowboy cock" .45 was an affectation, a near duplicate of the Army sidearm I had carried in Bosnia, but I usually kept it locked up if I wasn't expecting trouble. It was currently unloaded, fieldstripped, and disassembled on my kitchen counter, waiting to be oiled.

After the weapons and explosive-residue detector scored no hits and issued no beeps, I strolled through to pretrial confinement. My suspect was already in the interview room, much more alert than the last time I'd seen him. He was in an orange jumpsuit as a formality, but he and I both knew he had already been processed; his lawyer's office was just registering the paperwork and accompanying the county clerk.

I wanted ten minutes to fuck with him. To add a bit of flair to the moment, I even wore my yarmulke. Razor didn't seem to notice the clear, surgical, latex gloves over my hands.

"The Irish rabbi's little kike son. Detective Tommy. What brings you to my palace on the river?"

"Hello, Razor. I came to talk."

"Y'all heard they let me off on the drugs and I'm gonna walk out this door soon?"

"Oh yeah."

"So technically youse is violating my civil rights. This harassment."

"It could be. It could also be just two men talking."

"I'm listening, Officer Tommy."

"You were set up. Who hates you enough to do this? I've been tracking you so long that I know in my gut you're too much of a professional to keep your stash in plain view. That's methhead-tweeker levels of error. You have lieutenants and street soldiers for distribution. And why would cash and product be in the same spot?"

"Two men talking. Hypotheticals?"

"Completely off the record. I don't even have a pen on me."

"So, a friend of mine, in the same line of business, would say—this is a friend, mind you—it could be one of two things. It's a setup for a hit on me. Death by cop. They expect me to react same way I did. Or . . . *or* it's a setup on *you*, Mr. Tommy. One user of product to another. Course, I just dip my hands in the jar from time to time. I don't ride the dragon of death like you do. Took a few bullets back in '99 and just used that as an excuse to try every drug under the sun, didn't you? And here you are, Tommy. Narcotics. Talk about a fucking hypocrite! I hear, though, you've weaned off of heroin these days, just sticking to pills. Tragedy, really."

I felt a shudder down my neck, and my skin burned behind my ears. I grasped the underside of the steel table welded to the floor because at that moment I felt I just might fall off the earth.

"Shit, Tommy. I never thought a White man could get whiter, but yo' ass just did, nigga."

I looked over at the two-way mirror. The light was on, exposing the chamber and showing that nobody was watching us.

Razor started rattling off in reverse chronology. "August 2012, Percocet, two bottles, Old White Tower Diner. July 2012, six fentanyl patches, Allegheny Center Mall. June 2012, three bottles of Tramadol, an IV bag of morphine, and an IV infusion kit. May 2012, no activity; all the brothers thought you were shot again because you were an alternate on the SWAT team roster, maybe chasing an adrenaline-junkie rush, but your cell phone ping ended up putting you out at Harmarville Rehabilitation Clinic. Fuck, that didn't work out too well, I guess. Otherwise, you score Oxy from the street hookers you use for snitches. I hope at least you double-bag your pecker."

His street drawl was gone now, and I could have been talking to an Ivy League law club chairman or a litigator with twenty years' experience. I closed my eyes, and instead of the staleness and antiseptic of the Allegheny jail, I imagined the mahogany and cigars of Pittsburgh's Harvard club—rich leather seats, the way the hubbed-spine books' pages felt like bond certificates in your hands. Razor in a three-piece Tom James suit instead of prison overalls. I went to this place in my head because it was all that kept me from throwing up in a panic attack, allowing Razor to look down on me even more.

"But I hear now you got another addiction, a little pet project: little Irish redhead from Homestead that her man uses as a punching bag—"

BANG. I grabbed a good length of his dreadlocks and smashed his nose into the steel table. I reached into his mouth while he was still dazed, jammed two fingers in—both to gag him so his tongue would come forward as well as to prevent his jaw from coming down to bite—and pulled at the threads of his stitches. Brown scabs and blueish-red blood came drooling out, an early Jackson Pollock abstract spray on the silver steel square of the visitor's slab.

He was about to scream for the guards but then squinted up at me and chuckled. After spitting, gagging some more, and wiping the messy substance on the long sleeves of the white, thermal underwear he wore under his prison orange scrubs, he swallowed back the rest of the blood, even though it looked like it was making him ill. After a few more gulps and sucking on his teeth a bit, he finally spoke.

"So, you see where Internal Affairs might have created a

scenario to observe if you'd take the bait dangled in front of you. Guess it's a good thing your brother lets his twin be a junkie. And that leads us back to me. Someone's trying to take me out. So go and be a fuckin' *cop* . . . and find out who."

I stood and gathered myself, smoothing out my jacket, then studied the steady mess of Razor. He looked like a *Walking Dead* zombie, a bib of bright-red blood making an upside-down sunrise on his prison jumper. I reached into my sportscoat and tossed him a clean handkerchief, like offering a Band-Aid for a sucking chest wound.

"If you want to stay here a little longer and have the medics re-stitch you, then you're welcome to say it was me. I could use the paid leave. However, that's probably a tumble-fuck of paperwork, investigators coming in and talking to you, and likely another two or three days here in holding. If you want to get the fuck back home, you would be wise to say you're a heavy bleeder and you slipped, and head back over to UPMC Mercy. I'll let Dr. Kerrick know to expect you."

"Will do."

"Oh, and, Razor?"

"What is it, Detective?"

"Next time you roll up heavy on me, you'd better shoot—and not miss." I was out for blood. I wasn't thinking straight.

"Bitch, you'll never even see it when I take you down."

■ ■ ■

I had Claire spend the night at my mother's under the pretense of a warm, home-cooked meal, good conversation, and the appeal of sleeping in a bed that wasn't dimensionally designated for children. She was only too happy, and slipped out the door with eagerness and a smile, squeezing my hand and looking into my eyes with—what was it?

Those eyes were doing a number on me. My fingers held hers slightly longer than the invisible decorum between us dictated, and a wan, awkward, patronizing smile appeared at the edges of her mouth before the door shut, the kind you wear when you're dealing with shitfaced uncles who piss themselves in the middle of the dance floor at your sister's wedding.

I sent Charley home with Respottek, our lead coach and trainer, for the night. Repo was practically another brother to us, having grown up with Kenny as one of Mickey's boxers in the '70s and '80s. He had been a Navy master at arms (their version of military police) and later a Homeland Customs and Border Protection officer who coached practically for free in his double federal retirement. Charley sometimes bunked with Repo if I had work that took me out of town. Repo didn't raise an eyebrow or ask any questions. I wanted the gym to myself for what I was about to do.

I sent a text to Marco, and waited.

At 10:55 p.m., the door to my apartment opened. I had intentionally thrown off the breakers to my apartment only, while the rest of the building remained lit. I heard a bit of cursing in Spanish and the distinctive thud of both the pocket .22 and Marco's M45 SOC pistol. I knew his next step would be to try to use his cell phone as a flashlight. As soon as he began to rustle in his pockets, I nailed him full force, a linebacker hitting a tackle dummy.

"*Sarge*! Tommy, what the—"

I had one hand around his throat. The other had my Intratec .38 pointed in the center of his head. "Did you rat me out to Internal Affairs, you rat motherfucker?!"

"What the fuck are you talking about?"

"Two weeks ago you had four days off! Then all a fucking sudden we find a drop vehicle with a bag full of drugs and cash! Setting up Razor to look like the biggest goddamned mongoloid in the history of drug dealers that breathed air or setting me up to look like the biggest mutt that ever was because my own fucking partner is trying to rat me out to the fucking *state police*!" I held the .38 steady as I applied more pressure to his throat.

He brought his knee straight up into my balls, and a starburst exploded across my eyes. All the air went out of my lungs. I dropped the .38 and writhed in agony until I caught my breath again. His hand struggled upward and closed on the counter. I heard him cock the SOC pistol, and he fired a warning shot out the kitchen window, shattering the glass. Thankfully, there was nothing but a vacant lot across from our property. He had kicked my .38 away under the couch and out of reach. Dogs started barking nearby. Fucking whole window was gone. I stood up, about to rush him again, and saw the red-dot laser in the center of my chest.

"You fuck around anymore, Tommy, and the next shot is in your pants. I will have Kenny and a SWAT team haul your ass away in cuffs."

"Aww, poor widdle foster kid gonna run to big bwudder because Tommy knocked him on his ass—again. Not much has changed since you were a kid pissing in your pants, running to Rose when Brady and I caught you going through our shit whenever we were home from college."

"Tommy, I fucking swear to God, the next one's in your knee, or your *prick*, if you don't calm down. Are you snorting Oxy again?"

"Where the fuck were you the other day then?"

"The fucking Cumberland Wellness Clinic!"

"What the fuck is that?"

He was red with embarrassment, and angry, frustrated tears built up in the corners of his eyes. "It's a fucking in-vitro fertilization facility in central Pennsylvania. PD won't sponsor IVF, so we had to use Inez's health plan. Her HMO is specific, and we had to go to that clinic first because it's tied to her corporate headquarters. That's where we fucking were for four days. Here." He reached into his jacket for a flyer. "That's all the info. We're trying to have a baby. We made a . . . a fucking mini second honeymoon out of it and stayed at a resort hotel by Penn State because she had daily fucking appointments! Turn the goddamn power on in here and quit beating my ass, and we'll put our fucking guns away and talk."

I went downstairs and threw the breaker to my apartment back on. Marco had used his phone to find the kettle and two mugs and got the coffee going. He dutifully poured a few fingers of rum in each mug once the kettle whistled. Having recovered my gun from under the couch, he emptied out the .38's bullets, spun the cylinder cowboy style, snapped it back shut, and handed the empty pistol back to me.

At that point, the buzzer to the door of the gym sounded. I looked at the security monitor mounted next to the TV above the breakfast bar. A Pittsburgh PD black-and-white with lights flashing, but no siren, sat idling at the front entrance.

I gave Marco the *shh* sign and went downstairs, my gold shield in my back pocket.

I opened the door. Patrolman Suzcyk. Hadn't seen him around before. Probably worked the Fifth Avenue beat. Maybe headed home when he got the call.

"Good evening, Officer."

"Good evening, sir."

I gently held my arm out to show him that I was not a threat or acting out of malice and turned my hip to indicate I was reaching into my back pocket. After a slight, curious nod from Columbo, I produced my credentials. "Sergeant Spenser, Counter-Narcotics Unit. My family owns this building."

His demeanor changed from that of John Q. Law to a puzzled footman. He wasn't quite sure what to do at this point.

"Sergeant, we had reports tonight of what sounded like, ahh . . . sounded like a gunshot?"

"Yeah, come with me." I walked him around the side of the building and pointed up at the now empty kitchen window, a few shards of glass still hanging in the frame. Some bits crunched under our shoes where we stood. I assessed the trajectory and estimated the bullet had gone over the vacant lot and embedded in the hillside beyond. Past the hillside was the rest of the city, and I mumbled a silent thanks to God that Marco's bullet hadn't found an errant path to a kid's bedroom, reminding myself to truly kick his ass sometime later.

"Fuckin' women, right? Can't live with 'em. Well, anyway, my girlfriend's over earlier tonight, makes me a five-course dinner. Beautiful. Chicken à la king, pasta, garlic bread, soup, nuts, crème brûlée. I'm gonna get fat again just talking about it. Anyway, she *forgets* to turn off the goddamned *gas*. Fortunately, the doors were shut to the other rooms. Couple hours after she leaves, I step in and light a cigar. *BOOM!* Fuckin' fireball blows out the window, knocks me on my ass, my head hits the corner of the coffee table, that's where I got this fuckin' shiner, and burns off all the fuckin' wallpaper. My buddy and I are inventorying the damage now so I can call the insurance guys in the morning. You need to come up and have a look?"

"Um, no. That's okay, sir. Who, ah . . . Ya said there's someone else who's up there with you?"

"Oh, my partner, Detective Constable Marco Escardo. Need me to have him come down?"

"Maybe just have him wave from the window."

"Eeyo, *Marco*! How's it looking with the insurance tally? We gonna be able to salvage anything?"

I could hear him trying not to laugh.

"Well, *buddy*, I think your mom's crystal collection is blown to shit, but other than that, the worst damage was to the stove!"

Officer Suzcyk mumbled our names into his radio back to Central and reported there was no need for fire services to be called at that time, then wished us both a good night.

I went back up the catwalk to my partner, exceedingly sorry I had doubted him, and we proceeded to tie an epic alcoholic binge on for the rest of the evening, which may have involved whooping, hollering, several rounds on the heavy bag in the gym, and I think we may have even put on the gloves and gone a few rounds with one another.

Regardless, what started out as an evening of thinking my partner had screwed me over ended as most nights in the Spenser family ended—with combat, alcohol, beatings and brotherhood, tears and laughter. To an outsider it would seem like violence and pure dysfunction. To us, it was comfort, normalcy, and love. Most times I couldn't tell this person who was my partner and kid brother all in one that I loved him without being totally wasted. The Spenser boys never, ever said they loved each other. We barely said it to our wives. We awkwardly said it to our children. Between the brothers, we spoke our love in analogies. From the moment we first played cops and robbers to after we got our shields, it was all tied to being policemen. You couldn't say the word *cop* in our family without a reference to love. Those two words were one and the same in the Spenser dictionary. It was just our way.

I wish I had told Marco I loved him more during the times when I was dry and sober. I wish he'd known how much I loved him, how much of a real brother—blood or not—he'd been, and how truly special he was to me. I wish we'd had more nights left to us like that one.

CHAPTER 3

At eight the following night, we rattled Razor's cage where it hurt. We staged a harassment raid on Little E's jazz club, Razor's legitimate front that laundered the majority of his illegal affairs. The SNU team came in through the back, and the kitchen crew were the first to run out, most of them being undocumented workers. Marco and a few uniformed detectives then started dumping the hostesses' closets. For "hostesses" read "strippers and prostitutes." I figured there would at least be five to seven grand worth of felonies in there—between coke and ecstasy and some heroin needles—to make him sweat.

"Boss, what about the safe in the back of the kitchen?" one of my guys shouted.

"We would need a separate warrant to drill that open. This clearly states plain-view access or simple door access like kitchen cabinets or the hostesses' changing room. We can't hit the safe tonight, even though that's where he probably has his shadiest shit."

Since the customers bolted at the first sign of trouble, the booths were all empty, save for Razor sitting rather smugly near the VIP section. Grinning, I grabbed a bottle of Johnnie Walker Blue from behind the bar and sat down across from him.

He had shaved his dreadlocks off. He was wearing a shark-cut Hugo Boss suit and had gone for a mandarin collar versus a traditional single breasted. He was every bit the erudite-scholar bootstrap entrepreneur, the Stringer Bell versus the Marlo Stanfield.

"Where is your warrant, Detective Sergeant? You gonna pay for that bottle, or at least leave a receipt?"

I surveyed the room as I reached into my suit jacket for the warrant, then flippantly threw it in his lap. "You know, I came in here last week. The girl who sat with me said something about law school. Fuck, I never realized how many nurses and lawyers out there in the tri-state area are gonna be so *fucking skilled* at sucking off a cock." I filled the highball glass half full of the Johnnie Walker Blue, then downed it, screwed the cap back on, and slid the bottle across the table to him.

Razor put his hands up in mock supplication. "Officer Tommy, what happens on my property betwixt two consenting adults—"

"Oh no, genius, that's not what the warrant is for. Open it."

Razor picked up the warrant and pulled out a set of reading glasses that made him look even more like an academic Bond villain. He pursed his lips before a tight smile formed. "Tax fraud? Zoning violations? Fire codes? You really gonna go bitch on me like this, little Tommy? What the fuck does the Narcotics team have to do with any of this shit? At least when your daddy rolled up on my pops, he did it with his fucking fists, and finally with a shotgun. He didn't hide like some little pussy behind some bitch-move bullshit like this!"

I pulled out the TEC-38 and slid it across the table in the same path the Johnnie Walker had traveled. It bounced off his right hand, and he stared at it and me like I was a Martian lifeform speaking in alien tongues.

"Bitch move, huh? Is this more your language? Or are you just another gutless Negro who's all bravado and no balls?" I drew out the Glock and set it on the table. "Count of three, Razor. We go for it. Wild West, motherfucker. Fastest draw wins."

"Y-yeah. And I'm a cop killer. What about that?"

"Oh, there's probably surveillance tapes here. A good lawyer could plead it out. And your rich-playboy pimp ass only hires the best. Never mind those poor girls in the back getting abortions by some back-alley butcher or getting AIDS from your nasty johns you have coming through here. Because you don't even give them basic cost of living."

"Hey. *Hey*, muthafucka, this . . . this shit ain't right."

"Ready, Razor? One, two . . ."

"*Nooooo*!"

"Three." The Glock was already in my hand.

Razor blindly grabbed the .38, screaming, and pulled the trigger roughly fifteen times.

Nothing.

"Do you really think I'd give you live rounds, you stupid fuck?" I used the barrel of the Glock to knock the harmless .38 out of his hands. It went clattering. Marco and the other detectives had rounded up nearly every single one of Razor's crew and hostesses to witness it. I looked around at the crowd, probably on the verge of coming across to them as pure evil, pure racist, or pure sociopath.

"Anyone else want to play mobster with me?"

Razor was weeping on the floor, a pure mess. It was better than the raid. We had toppled the king without firing a bullet. Or so we hoped.

"Boss," Marco whispered over my shoulder, "what's your play here?"

"Take everyone in." I pointed to Razor, still on his knees. "Except him. Thanks, Razor, for your cooperation tonight."

A murmur erupted from the crowd.

"Muthafucking lying white-devil-ass muthafuckas! I wasn't in on this! I didn't help *shit*!"

I turned and motioned to his colleagues and employees shouting and struggling against the officers. "What? I can't hear you. They sound *mad* about something!" I cupped one hand next to my ear, the universal sign for listening.

Razor lunged after us but was blocked by two PPD uniforms as another one cuffed him.

"I'm gonna get you, Tom Spenser! You fucking junkie scumbag phony hiding behind a badge! I'm the fucking grim reaper coming for your ass! You and everything and everyone you fucking care about! Ticktock, motherfucker! Ticktock! Tick—"

Marco and I slammed the service entrance open and got the hell out of there, leaving the line officers to deal with that shit. I hoped Marco didn't see the anxiety attack I was having, or how the pistol was shaking in my hands.

■ ■ ■

My partner wisely advised me to stay away from the precinct and the office and the case files for a few days. I decided to spend the next day with my houseguest. The weather anticipated the blustery and harsh winds that inevitably combined fall and winter into one nasty and awful uniseason in Pittsburgh, but the sun was merciful on us that day.

Whether it was a need for human contact, warmth, or a bit of both, Claire hung on to my free arm while I walked Charley around North Oakland. It was still decent enough weather that we managed to find a table outside at Primanti Bros up by Pitt University, across from the Original Hot Dog Shoppe. Charley sat respectfully by the bench, waiting for crumbs to fall.

She did not wear her engagement diamond anymore, but some sense of Stockholm-syndrome propriety had prompted her to wear her gold wedding band. We played it off when the waitress, who knew me as a regular, mistakenly said, "What would you like to drink, Mrs. Spenser?" But I saw a cloud of pain pass over Claire's eyes, and a moment later she slid the ring off her hand and into a jacket pocket.

"Hey." I reached across the table and took her naked hand in mine. "This wasn't your fault. This isn't on you. This is not your failure. He destroyed all of that. Not you."

She kept squeezing my hand and stared down at the table. "I don't want to embarrass you, but can I take Charley and be on my own for a while today?"

I was taken aback, but I said okay. I made sure she was all right with the directions back to the gym and the apartments, then awkwardly ate my lunch for one, staring at her plate as I considered what I had learned about her.

As it turned out, we had been technically incorrect in referring to Claire as a housewife. Mrs. Hewitt had a master's in fine arts and until recently had been on the faculty of Carnegie Mellon's school of music. She was a flautist and a violinist specializing in instructing students who performed in the chamber orchestra. Her teaching career had come to an abrupt halt when her husband, in a drunken and jealous rage, assaulted a colleague of hers at a performance one night.

The faculty and administration were more than willing to overlook her husband's stupidity; the colleague had refused to press charges or alert the police. But Clarissa resigned from the faculty out of sheer shame for her husband's actions. In the college's bulletin, they farewelled her as she "pursued other opportunities and professional endeavors." Yeah. Taking a punch in the gut from a six-foot-tall, 190-pound asshole—truly a professional endeavor.

Six years of student loans plus a mortgage quickly piled up, and class-A fuckup that her husband was, he soon lived up to expectations and lost his job as well. He had been smacking her around for years, but this turn of events made the beatings continuous, every other night for a good two months. I won't go into the particulars of when they conceived the kid. All I can say is some women are grateful when the asshole gets horny because it means he takes a break from kicking the shit out of her. Makes me sick even to say it.

■ ■ ■

The afternoon crew was already hitting the gym when I got back.

My earliest memory was of sitting in a playpen with Brady while Papa Mickey worked his fighters. Sweat, canvas, and the smack of the gloves against the bags. Then and now, those smells and sounds felt like home to me.

As I walked in and took note of the regulars, Charley made his rounds and perched next to someone in the bleachers. It took me a second to recognize Deputy Commissioner (Retired) Frank Spenser. Dad came down every few weeks and volunteered his time with some of the regulars. Although relatively good with strength and conditioning, Dad was a shitty fighter. Couldn't get his rhythm right and couldn't connect a punch that was solid. Except with women and little kids, I suppose.

"Big Frankie!" I boomed out across the gymnasium, much to his annoyance. "He comes here to be charitable with the little folk. What brings you down from your castle to cross the Duquesne Bridge, Dad?"

He glanced up at me from the bleachers and turned his attention back to the fighters. Thanks to my baseball bat skills, there was a dead spot where his left eye wouldn't adjust past twelve o'clock. If someone addressed him from the left, he had to crane his head awkwardly so that his right eye could focus on them. It spooked the hell out of me, even twenty-seven years later.

"I hear you guys are boxing in Trevor Washington," he finally said as I approached him.

"Yep. Just shook him down the other night at his club. But you probably read that in the daily blotter."

"He's one of Dee's little bastards. Nothing but trouble, those Washington boys."

Danforth "Dee" Washington had spread his seed among the whores and welfare moms of East Liberty back in the 1970s and '80s. Once upon a time, when Razor was still in diapers, Detective Captain Frank Spenser—then acting as the administrative deputy inspector of Metro—put two jacketed deer slugs into Dee Washington during a botched liquor store robbery on Southside. One slug in his calf stopped him. The second shot dropped the Uzi he was holding and took out his L5 vertebrae and about twenty feet of intestine after surgery.

Even after being remanded to desk duty, Dad hadn't lost his nuts for busting hoods and running down a suspect. But with Razor's dad, it was dumb luck. Dad was getting gas two blocks down from the liquor store, heard the call on his radio, grabbed his twelve-gauge shotty from the trunk, and limp-sprinted like Roger Maris chasing a pop fly across two blocks, with his bad leg dragging and one good eye to aim with.

Washington Senior was the last time Dad fired his weapon in the line of duty, though. Big Dee didn't die but wound up in a wheelchair for the rest of his life, shitting into a colostomy bag. Last I'd heard, he had caught HIV from swapping needles and died at the county mission hospital. For all the rules of the street gangster, Razor never hit back against the Spenser family for that. What the fuck did he care? He was shitting in his pants and smearing it on the walls when his pops took two in the back.

That capture of Daddy Washington sealed my father's political career, and he had been some kind of special assistant to the mayor since stepping down from active service. What with the diverse background of our family and all, they took to calling him the Irish rabbi. Mayors came and went, and Frank Spenser kept his office across the hall.

For all I despised the old man, he was big behind the scenes of the bureaucracy. He knew which teamsters union was causing trouble; he knew which state politicians were on the take, which ones were cheating on their wives, and which ones favored little boys; and he knew where a few bodies were buried. More than a few.

"I heard you had a busy couple days. Also heard a couple stashes got light. Pittsburgh hasn't been this interesting since the Penguins in '67."

He wisely left out the rumors of my new housemate. I guess he didn't want to start an argument he knew he'd lose.

"What do you think of some of our regular boys?" I said, changing the subject.

"Sparazza has nothing," he mentioned, gesturing at the nineteen-year-old Italian fighter squaring up against his opponent in the ring. Almost a split second after he said it, Sparazza landed a right hook that knocked his sparring mate to the canvas. He put that fucker down for a ten-count, and both of them were wearing full headgear. My father, for all his political savvy, could talk a lot of ignorant shit. Vinny Sparazza was 23-0-1 as a semipro, and there was talk that he was the new Arturo Gatti.

"Yeah, Dad, but he only beats up boxers instead of his spouse. Makes him a fucking saint in my book, even if he isn't Floyd Mayweather. Good to see you, Frankie. Help yourself to a Gatorade. And get the fuck out of my gym when you're done."

"Tommy, don't start with that."

Here it comes with the "poor me" bullshit. The one thing I hated more than a wife beater was a reformed one who'd found

Jesus and thought he had a pass on sins for the rest of his life just because he went to AA meetings.

Full of piss and anger, I turned around in retort. "What I don't get, what fucking kills me, is how the fuck you went to work every day wearing the gold shield. I guess your wife and kids didn't count under those you serve and protect, huh?"

"A wife beater isn't any less of a man than a junkie, Thomas. Percocet or Demerol or whiskey, a user is a user, and a piece of shit is a piece of shit."

"Fuck yourself, Francis. Now get the fuck out of my gym before I start charging you club dues. Unless you want to put on some gloves and finish what we started twenty-seven years ago."

"I don't see a baseball bat, big man." My father glared at me with almost thirty years of collective hatred, and I wondered for the millionth time what we shared in our genetic makeup, other than a badge and gun. I swear to Christ that dead eye was staring right at me.

I smirked back at him. "That's right, I forgot. It's not a fair fight with you unless it's women or eight-year-olds. Come on, Charley, it's starting to smell like garbage down here." Papa Mickey's dog followed me past the fighters and trainers and up to the loft.

I didn't bother looking back to see if my father was still sitting there. A sad, broken old man posed no threat to me.

■ ■ ■

Before the SOFTIC—the Special Operations Forces Target Interdiction Course at Bragg—was established, it had its nascent beginnings in US combat deployments to Vietnam. In July 1968, the US Army began centralized training in-country. The first official US Army sniper school in-country was established by the

9th Infantry Division. The course duration was eighteen days with a 50 percent failure rate.

Frank Spenser, a captain with the Studies and Observations Group, drafted back into service at the ripe age of twenty-eight, had been one of the graduates.

When Brady and I were sent to the SOFTIC course as part of our trainup run for Bosnia, one of the first things I saw my was my dad's name engraved in brass letters on the wall for having the wartime course record for the longest stalk and evasion in the history of the school". I told the instructors that knowing his lack of moral character and his nature for being a shitbag, he must have found a shortcut.

The class mentor was a decades-retired civilian, a steely-eyed man who looked like he had packed Jesus's chute when Moses was a jumpmaster. He pulled me aside and nearly stomped a mudhole into my chest. My wise ass had no idea that he had been not only Frank's classmate but also his spotter, his battle buddy—the person in the course and in warfare who knew him better than his spouse or his mother.

"Boy," he said, "whatever problems you got with your daddy you need to go to a shrink and work out. We don't certify anyone in this class who doesn't possess the lethality to carry those skills into battle. Your dad stripped down to his skivvies and boots and crawled through Mekong bush like you would not believe with his nose to the ground for four straight miles. When the exercise ended and he revealed his position, he looked like he'd been dragged behind a truck. He may be a shit father, but don't you ever again question what it is we do here. You got a problem with that, you go and pack your fucking ruck and get on the bus back home."

On my first attempt at the SOFTIC course, I failed. It almost interfered with my and Brady's deployment to Bosnia. They let me redo the stalk after the open vote of my classmates, who decided I deserved a second shot. The vote was nearly unanimous. The one vote against me was cast by my brother Brady. I knew, and still know, it was because I had shot my mouth off about our dad in the classroom. The dynamic of our family came with a twisted sense of omertà: we suffered silently and nobly, but to the world we were collective and unified. Any transgression of that line came with consequences.

When Brady was later declared missing in action during Bosnia, Kenny told us that was the first time he'd ever seen the old man come apart completely.

I often wondered if Frank would have mourned me.

■ ■ ■

I had seen her only a few hours before, but still—every time I saw her was a pleasant surprise. The hallway of the little trio of apartments held the foggy hint of a shower, and I smelled soap and shampoo on the air before my hand turned the doorknob. When I came into the apartment, she was down the hall in the bathroom in jeans and a sweater, applying makeup to what was left of her battle bruise. I allowed myself a moment of disgust that it still hadn't faded. At least her delicate, greenish-blue eyes were beaming with enthusiasm instead of the murky fatigue, shock, and sadness I had seen in her all week.

It appeared Charley had taken a liking to her, the way he flopped down by the bathroom sink as she primped herself. *Two-faced little shit*, I thought fondly.

"Are you working at all today?" she asked from the bathroom. She was in the middle of some kung-fu ritual with a brush and a set of eyelash curlers. Her auburn hair was naturally curly, but she had rolled the curls into larger waves with an iron. You would have thought Mickey's gym was hosting the Oscars that afternoon. As I stood in the hallway behind her, she regarded me in the mirror, talking over one shoulder, and for a moment I felt a hint of déjà vu, as if we'd always talked like this. It was intimately familiar, nearly spousal, and I had to practically smack myself out of that illogical train of thought.

Asshole. Don't stare. Don't be creepy. Otherwise she's gonna wait until you're out of the apartment to brush her teeth or piss or do anything. This is the only bathroom in the place.

"Umm, I'm kind of keeping my head down at the moment." I yawned. "Listen, Claire, I don't mean to sound like an asshole . . ."

A bona fide laugh pealed from the bathroom. I hardly knew this girl, but I was in love with that laugh.

"The last thing I would call you is an asshole."

"And you are welcome to stay, but don't you have any friends? Sisters? Girlfriends? Besties? Relatives? Someone?"

A text from Marco came up on my phone: All staff from jazz club released on bond. 47 counts poss substance, 7 counts illeg arms, 137 yrs unpaid taxes total all employees :) Judge not seizing or closing business yet.

She came out of the bathroom, leaned against the doorway, and regarded me hesitantly. It was the awkward pause I had seen in dozens of suspects, witnesses, and surviving victims as they traced backward in their mind's eye and tried to account for where their lives had started to royally fuck up with such speed and runaway destruction.

"Jake kind of made sure anyone who really cared about me stayed away."

"Mom and dad? Siblings?"

"Retired in Florida. We are all from Massachusetts, originally, but my grandparents lived there. My grandpa was a Navy captain at Panama City, Florida. When he and my nana got ill, Mom and Dad moved down there to take care of them. They just never left.

I did my undergrad and masters at Carnegie Mellon, and . . . stayed. And I met Jake. I suppose Mom and Dad would kind of be glad to have me, but you know how it is. How proud would you be to move back in with your folks at thirty-two? I have a sister, a couple years younger, up in Portland, Maine. But she would just be full of 'I told you so.'"

"Were you looking for work? When everything . . . happened?"

"I was giving lessons when I could be alone for a couple hours at a time. I had résumés out to a few high schools and that private school up past Monroeville, near Saltsburg—Kiski Prep? It would have been a pay cut, but it would have helped keep the bank at bay a while longer. I could have also had a little apartment there, to myself. That would have been heaven."

She hugged her shoulders and looked around the living room. "Heck, *this* is heaven. The car's in my name, and I suppose I could send a warrant or writ to get it back from him, but it would probably cost more to ship it from wherever he is in Seattle than it's worth." A long pause. Her eyes darkened with what I could only identify as hatred. "I hope he wrecks it."

"Well, there's plenty of room up here. They built three studios above the gym. We store some old equipment, fight-promotion stuff, in the third apartment, but whenever you feel up to staying by yourself, we'll empty that third one out for the visiting fighters, and you'll be free to take the middle one indefinitely."

She looked down, her eyes brimming with tears. "I don't have much of any way to pay you." She pulled a roll of bills from her jeans and counted, recounted, counted one more time, then extended the wad of cash to me. "Two hundred and fifteen dollars. That's all I've got in the world."

"Keep it. You can pay me back by getting that asshole out of your life and staying alive and not being a punching bag."

As soon as the words were out of my mouth, I regretted them.

All the warmth and appreciation she had been exuding snapped shut, and any credit I had established as being a compassionate human being faded into my usual status as an arrogant, mouthy, know-it-all cop asshole.

"Aw, fuck, I didn't mean it like that." I gently touched her shoulders, and she threw her arms around me and fell apart again, crying for a long time against my chest.

I pulled her close to me and patted her back with one hand.

"I'm so sorry. Who the hell am I to judge you? Look, my brothers and I grew up in a bad scene. My dad, well, he was a lot like your husband. Worse, actually. I'm sorry. I know a good person when I see one. No woman deserves what you've gone through." I guided her to the couch and sat her down. "Look, here's the spare key. It opens the gym door too. This card has the alarm code. There's a pantry downstairs; my mom comes in and cooks breakfast for the morning fighters. Help yourself to whatever. Right now, that asshole husband of yours has a roof over his head somewhere; why shouldn't you?"

For one infinite and silent moment she leaned on my shoulder; then she wiped her eyes and wrapped me in an even more forceful hug. Her face touched against mine, and I felt her tears. She turned slightly so that her lips brushed my cheek.

"Thank you," she whispered, then rose gracefully, collected herself, went back to the bathroom, and shut the door.

Charley raised one eyebrow at me, casting an admonishing look from his vantage point by the bathroom.

"You shut up, smart-ass."

But Charley was right. This situation could get stupid really quick. Two emotionally shattered people sharing close quarters. With the bathroom door still shut, I changed into workout clothes and ran downstairs to the gym to mess around with some of the regulars. I didn't know what had thrown me off worse—the scene with my dad or the scene upstairs. I hammered at the bags and sparred a few rounds, working with the junior boys and some of the senior semipro kids as well.

By the time I got back upstairs two hours later, the apartment was neater than it had ever been in the three years I had lived there, and I smelled a combination of her perfume and soap on the air. A note next to the fridge said she was going into town.

I guessed I had a roommate for the time being.

I downed a fresh mug of coffee and stretched out on the couch with the TV playing the local news. I felt stuffed and lazy from the lunch I had spoiled myself with on our "not-a-date." Having nowhere to be, I pulled a blanket to my shoulders and fell asleep.

CHAPTER 4

That night, I took a shower and went to retrieve my clean clothes in the bedroom. Claire's presence had been so light that I didn't even realize she was back there asleep until I poked my head in. Tiptoeing around in the dark, I fumbled for my clothes with one hand while holding a towel around my waist with the other. But her eyes opened despite my best efforts to be quiet.

Groggy from her medications and fatigue, she whispered, "I see you," dreamily, half awake.

"What do you see?" I asked, turning around and flicking on the light by the nightstand.

She reached out both her hands to me like a child beckoning for a hug. Cautiously, I held my free hand out to her, and she drew it toward her face, running my palm against her soft cheek.

"I see a good man, but when he thinks nobody else is looking, he looks so wounded. So sad." The stupor of the sleep aids the ER shrink had prescribed blurred her words to me, but her eyes had a fervent zeal, like a televangelist doing a revival. "I see you, Thomas Spenser. I always see you."

"And what else do you see?"

"My guardian angel. But he's so sad. Who looks out for you, Thomas?"

"I can look out for myself," I said, managing a cynical grin.

She looked away, and soon her chest sank and rose with shallow breaths, telling me she was once again fast asleep. Against my better judgment, I leaned over and kissed her forehead, and then kissed the hand that was still clutching mine, gently breaking free and folding her palm back to her pillow.

"I see you too, Claire."

■ ■ ■

At four the next morning, my cell phone rang. It was the chief inspector of the Special Investigations Unit, also known as Inspector Kenneth Scott Spenser, my eldest sibling.

"Where the fuck have you been, little brother?"

"I've been going to choir practice. And taking piano lessons. And volunteering with underprivileged youth."

"Get your sorry ass down to the Little E's jazz club. Somebody just took out Razor."

"What do you mean 'took out'?"

"I mean the sonofabitch is one dead nigger. Close contact with a twelve-gauge. His head is gone from above the jawbone. Forensics is still pulling pieces of him out of the wall. Two shooters strong-armed through the door with hockey masks. One used the shotgun on Razor, one sprayed the booth with two TEC-9s. Then they raided the cash drawers and the safe.

"He didn't have any ID on him, but you can still make out the stitches on his tongue. A portable lab scanner just verified his prints. Surveillance video matched his face before they blasted it off. The shooters took out two club girls, DOA, and Razor's cousin Darnell is in Mercy with a sucking chest wound. Nobody else hurt or killed. They specifically focused their fire on Razor's booth. Other customers didn't have a scratch on them. Judging from the security tapes, the shots were going off before they even realized what was happening."

"Why the fuck are you calling me? According to you, my narcotics dealer is dead."

"Because I've got forensics looking at that huge fucking safe. You know, that one you couldn't secure a warrant to get into the other night? It's empty. They used a state-of-the-art bore drill and a two bubblegum specks of explosive on the hinges of the safe, and there's a heavy amount of trace residue of heroin. So not only did someone kill your biggest case, they jacked his entire fucking stash. Now, are you going to come down here, or are you too busy banging housewives?"

Samantha and her big mouth. Though we had been divorced three years, her information network still managed to filter through to both my brothers and their wives.

"Piss off, fuckface. I'll be there in twenty minutes." It didn't escape me that I had threatened Razor's life in front of sixty or so witnesses with a loaded pistol not even forty-eight hours before. Either that put me incredibly high on the suspect list or it was such a galactic level of stupid that I'd never even be considered.

I pulled up to Little E's jazz club at 4:35. Razor and his girls were already bagged up, lined almost symmetrically on the pavement with bloodstained chucks strewn all around the bodies like blue-and-white maxi-pads. Kenny was talking to a couple uniforms outside. He waved me over.

Ed Peters, Brady's deputy commander in Internal Affairs, saw me first. Ed was about my height but built like a frigging truck. Think Kingpin in *Daredevil* if Kingpin went into permanent ketosis and played rugby. Usually we were pleasant enough acquaintances, practically good friends. We scrummed together on the department's rugby team sometimes and ran some charity 10Ks together, but tonight he was all business.

"Tom, I have to debrief you. I heard about the pistol-whipping shit you pulled here on the raid the other night."

"Not without my lawyer, Ed."

"Does that mean you had something to do with this?"

"I've got a stunning redhead and the entire evening workout class at the gym that's going to say different. If you don't believe them, Charley is excellent at character testimony." I nudged my canine sidekick, who was sitting with his hind end flat on the pavement at what could be only described as a dog's military position of attention. He opened his mouth and huffed at the air as if to say to Ed, "Yes, that's exactly right!"

Charley and I walked on past. He had been to so many crime scenes he didn't even need a leash.

"If it isn't the social worker of the family." Kenny approached and extended a hand to shake mine. I passed him a hot coffee instead. Momentarily, he disappeared off to the side, and I heard him arguing with Ed Peters about where to shove his "debriefing."

Charley obediently maintained his stance next to me. "How long you been down here, big Kenny?" I asked when he walked back to us.

He checked his watch. "About three hours."

We stepped over busted glass and avoided shell casings as we went in. Charley diligently sat next to the entrance doors and would remain in one spot until we came back outside. There were about three forensics teams, blood-spatter experts, and those big flashbulbs you see in photo studios.

We sat in a booth that hadn't caught any bullets. I had a good idea of what was coming, why Kenny would call me down here at four in the morning.

"Chief had me on the phone since about midnight. Then I'm mopping up down here. Mayor's office is shitting themselves. Wondering who had enough juice to take out Razor."

"Strong-arm punk trying to make a name?"

"No, little brother. Look at it from the strategic level. This was a precision hit. One hour before closing time, when they knew most of the staff was tired. Thursday night, small enough crowd you can control with two guys. They rushed the door and flex-cuffed the bouncers instead of killing them. Why? They whacked those two girls who were technically civilians. Hookers just trying to turn a buck. Why not shoot the bouncers? Because the entranceway is lit. People walking by see two dead bodies in the doorway, that messes up their plan. So, they zip-tie the front door, stash the bouncers in the coat check, shoot Razor and the girls, back to the kitchen, hit the safe, and escape in the alley, where they had a van waiting. Does that sound like a couple niggers rolling the 7-Eleven for quarters?"

Kenny was a little free with the word *nigger*, I'll admit. However, you grow up in Homestead with your half-Irish, half-Russian Jew family being called Black Irish commie kikes your whole life by African American folks, you develop a little hostility.

"So, you got your brother, who's a narcs sergeant, with no narcotics on the premises, in the middle of what is a clear gangland robbery homicide. You going to dance with me all night with your hand on my ass, Kenny, or you gonna make your move?"

"Pittsburgh doesn't have a task force for what looks like is about to be an open drug war."

"That they do not."

"You just scored top percentile on the lieutenant's exam."

"That I did."

"Your captain cannot wait to trade you."

"Because I don't kiss his ass."

"How would you like to be the lead detective in a provisional unit? Centered on high-value drug targets in the city? There's an empty building over by court of common pleas. Top-floor walkup, three large conference rooms, three offices adjoining each room. Used to house the overfill for the district attorney's interns. Consider it your new office."

"You see more of these happening, do you?"

"I think this is the first power play, and we are gonna see a lot more blood."

"And you're giving me rank?"

"As of 0730 Monday, you are Lieutenant Thomas F. Spenser,

officer in charge, High-Value Target Task Force. You close this whole thing"—he gestured to the carnage and broken glass—"and you'll be on the fast track to inspector within a year."

"I've got minimum time in Homicide."

"But you have a stellar record for the time you were in. I see this being more about drugs, with the homicides being rather peripheral—excuse my irreverence for the dead. This won't be whodunits; you find the drugs, you'll find the triggermen, the guys supplying them, and, most importantly, the guys giving the orders. I need a sharp cop who has ties to the drug scene. You already have your networks of snitches, informants, and players. You've already done your homework, whereas any homicide cop thrown into this is gonna be playing catch-up on the bus."

"Didn't the chief bust your balls for picking your brother?"

"Chief picked you. He heard about you and your partner's escapades over at Razor's, followed up by your Lord Byron act a few doors down. As well as your *Lethal Weapon* act here a couple nights ago. My brother the dumbass. He likes you because you don't kiss ass and you take necessary risks." He looked around the bullet-riddled booth and sipped his Starbucks. "Sometimes wholly unnecessary risks too. Still, I would have loved to be a fly on the wall here when you practically pistol-whipped the bastard. Or sucker punched him at the jail."

"And if I fuck up, Chief can fire both of us and blame you? Can I bring Marco with me?"

"Already done. Your captain was more pissed off at my taking Marco than you."

"That's going to leave a wide-open hole in the Narc division."

"Not if you're doing your job right, little brother." He reached across the table. I shook his hand. "Welcome to the big leagues, Tommy. A bit more pay, and a lot more paperwork."

■ ■ ■

Charley and I drove back home, and I crashed on the couch, pulled the blankets up, and fell back into a dreamless exhaustion. In my semiconscious blurry orbit, I heard my roommate moving around and leaving the apartment, and I felt the weight of Charley leaving the couch as he followed her wherever she was going. At some later point, the creak of weight on the metal gangplank filtered through the gauze of fatigue and what passed for dreams, followed by the unmistakable sound of spats clicking on the ramp that led up to the door to my studio. It was Brady.

Brady and I are fraternal twins. Mom never did the identical dress-up bullshit. It was funny, though: as we got older, we tended to borrow each other's stuff, and we both favored dark suits when on the job. But since working for Internal Affairs, Brady tended toward the Brooks Brothers end of fashion. Pinstripes and pastel ties and all that shit—almost effeminate, though by all accounts from his high school and college girlfriends, his wife, and by proof of his progeny of four kids, my twin was a confirmed heterosexual. Even so, I smelled his flitty aftershave before I opened my eyes; it overpowered the gentle, perfumed scent my housemate left behind.

Keeping my eyes shut, I said, "Christ, if I were on a stakeout with you, I would shoot you by now or die of asphyxiation, Captain."

Although we became cops on the same day, Brady was the political animal and had earned his rank with lightning speed. I was the exceptional Spenser cop—because I was so average.

Brady pressed an icy cylinder of Coca-Cola against my pounding forehead. After I graciously accepted it—some twin ESP must have told him I had a migraine and a half—the kindness turned to good-natured brotherly teasing as he wrapped one arm around my neck and knuckled my forehead with noogies and flicks. "Wiseass makes lieutenant and thinks he can talk all sorts of shit to his big brother."

I shoved him away, cracked open the Coke, and nearly knocked it off in one pull. Brady said nothing about the empty bottle of vodka on the coffee table in front of me and the residue of crushed OxyContin on my fingertips.

"You're my big brother by seven minutes, douchebag."

He craned his head toward mine and the kids' room. "Where's this hot-piece-of-ass charity case all the Spenser family is talking about?"

"Took Charley for a walk, I guess."

Brady leaned against the doorjamb and tapped out a cigarette, letting out a chuckle. "He's your dog, all right. His head is never far away from the pussy."

"Okay, that's it. I can't take your homo cologne *and* the smell of nicotine. Please go do that shit outside." A cigar every now and again was fine. I couldn't stand habitual cigarette smokers, though. Hypocrite that I was, I still had one once in a blue moon.

"Step out with me. We've got to talk shop." He grabbed a boxing hoodie from my fighting days off the hook and threw it over to me. "It's chilly." On the back, in rather tacky, large letters, was embroidered THOMAS "MACHINE GUN" SPENSER. Frank, Papa Mickey, and Repo had all at one time owned identical corner short-sleeve shirts with the same logo. They'd also had a set that said BRADY "BULLSEYE" SPENSER. It was funny and totally adorable to stop by Brady's house early in the morning to carpool and see his wife's tiny legs sticking out of Brady's old boxing sweatshirt as she brought me coffee.

Sarah Costello Spenser was the full name of Brady's wife. Her dad was big in the local teamsters unions. Every blue collar with a lunchbox backed him at the elections. He went way back in history with Dad, too. In Westeros, it would have been called an arranged marriage.

Brady and I stood outside, and I jogged in place, pumping my legs as the icy shards of wind against the nylon workout pants and heavy cotton sweatshirt fully awakened my senses.

"Kenny's lab tech called me. He must have been working them all morning because they got a ballistics match in the database on those TEC-9s."

"And?"

"And they were used in three robbery homicides in Morgantown between 1998 and 2004."

"Morgantown, West Virginia?"

"No, dipshit, Scotland. Of course West Virginia."

He stared levelly at me for about a full thirty seconds. Then he continued.

"According to federal records, they were seized and destroyed by state police authorities in 2006 along with a cache of other weapons and evidence that had made their way through the West Virginia felony court system."

"So, how are two TEC-9s seized in 2004 and destroyed in 2006 used in a murder in 2012?" Neither of us wanted to say it, but Brady did.

"I think we have to face the possibility that whoever is backing the folks who took down Razor are either cops or ex-cops. And I think . . . I *think* they are Pittsburgh cops. Someone with access to evidence and someone who knows how to work the system."

"So, they got the guns across state lines. Have you called the FBI yet?" It was a rhetorical question. No way was my brother going to involve the FBI before he knew what we were dealing with.

"I've got a feeling some of the police work that Kenny's putting you on the job for may be my line of expertise."

"Shit, Brady, I hope you're wrong." Nearly all the captains and lieutenants and senior sergeants were guys (and some women) we had come up with since the academy, guys that

Kenny and our dad had mentored. Internal Affairs was a shit job, and my brother lived with it day in and day out, but the most he had busted before were dirty cops and grifters, not flat-out murderers and armed robbers hiding behind a badge. All three Spenser brothers now had probable cause and an open-season permit to hunt our friends in our own backyard.

"Tommy, what the fuck is wrong with you? Your clothes are falling off, and your primary diet is Oxys and Jack Daniel's and Stolichnaya. Are you on a one-way ticket to die?"

I kept looking at the pavement.

"For as much as you claim to hate Frank Spenser, you sure as fuck mimic his habits." Brady blew out a steady stream of yellow smoke.

"My cancer is back, Brady. Fuck, my cancer has cancer."

"Self-pitying motherfucker. And you figure you're going to jumpstart the process."

"Mmm. Something like that."

About the time Brady was finishing up his second cigarette and I was pulling up the hood of my sweatshirt, watching my breath on the air, Claire Hewitt came walking up to us with Charley in tow. She had a bag of carryout and what looked like fresh coffee. For two. Brady bowed to her like a kingsman on Her Majesty's Secret Service.

"Ahh, this must be the lovely Mrs. Hewitt. Captain Brady Spenser, at your disposal. You make sure to tell me if this disreputable little shit gives you any trouble."

She performed a balancing act with Charley's leash and her takeout, wiggled a mitten free, shook his hand, and smiled. Something inside of me twinged when she did it. The way she'd smiled at me when she went to stay at my mom's had been easy and light. But the way she smiled at Brady just then—I caught a glimpse of the face she must have put on for the world every day with Jake.

"I'm still alive because of this disreputable little shit, Captain." She looked at me, a kinetic spark of concern traveling from her face to Brady's to me as they both assessed my pale skin, sunken eyes, and ill-fitting attire. Finally, she managed another sociable, if somewhat forced, smile. "Have you eaten?" she asked me.

Brady chuckled. "Feed his skinny ass, Mrs. Hewitt. He's falling out of those pants. He thinks that cops get by on coffee and Red Bull." He gave me a playful cuff behind the ear. "I'll see you later, partner."

She was wearing a navy-blue parka and a turquoise knit scarf and matching toboggan cap—new wares for her new life. She must have gotten them at a thrift store on her walk with Charley. It was adorably cute; the pom tassel on her hat was almost eye level with me and Brady. She fit in with the neighborhood as if she had been part of our lives from the beginning, walking my dog and bringing me lunch. More than that, she looked goddamned beautiful on the sidewalk on Melwood Street, amid the uncommonly early chill and light dusting of frost. I imagined holidays and fireplaces, her fingers clasped in mine, her head on my shoulder.

Why the fuck am I thinking this?

She was technically still someone else's wife. But I thought of the events that brought her into my life, and I knew in the deepest corner of my heart that Jake Hewitt never saw her walking up the block on a cold afternoon and realized how radiant she was, and how much of a lucky bastard he was for her having once loved him. And in that moment I knew that giving her a bunk bed in my grandfather's tiny apartment was the first kind thing anyone had done for this woman in many years.

Everyone I loved, respected, and cared about was breaking my balls about her, but I didn't mind.

■ ■ ■

We had the task force up and running in five days. Although I was drawing a Pittsburgh paycheck as a police lieutenant, the task-force rank called for a captain to be in charge, a role I would fill. It was subtly indicated that after a probationary period, I could wear and draw pay for the role of captain if the group was still needed. If not, I would go full-time back to Narcotics as an LT. I didn't mind which way the table broke; it was win-win for me.

Although other detective sergeants were working with us, some who had quite a bit of rank on my partner and some old enough to even be his dad, Escardo rounded out the force as my deputy commander. The shit would roll downhill from me to him to everyone, and that was just how it was. If my brother was right about cops pulling the triggers or actively supplying the crew with busted weapons across federal lines, I needed someone I could trust information with and someone who had the discretion to know what to keep close. If the old boys didn't like that, there was always early pension.

The first thing I did was restrict our filing system. Anything we had to input went on a standalone computer connected to a single printer, both in a locked-down room that was pretty much a vault. The pages saved were put into a safe; the hard drive came out every night and went into the safe as well, and anything on paper not saved in the safe was logged and shredded. Surveillance tapes and notes were kept in the same method. Nothing left the office without a courier who verified the transport.

Our first order of business was to look deep into Razor's crew. I wasn't ruling them out; they might have some shitbird on the Morgantown city court payroll who got them the guns. With Razor dead and his cousin Darnell laid up, someone was still selling the product, and someone was still making the money. Whether it's drugs or used cars, a salesman dies, someone else steps up.

On a mostly uneventful Wednesday night, Kenny came to us with an anonymous tip called in to the main switchboard, and Marco and I headed out.

Our target was a notorious heavy hitter's poker game up near Oakland where we knew at least three of Razor's former soldiers liked to hang out. The caller claimed that there were two kilos of uncut heroin in there and they usually were so blasted by 11:30 p.m. that there would be minimal resistance.

Marco and I hung back in his raggedy, yellow '77 CJ5 Jeep until we saw three of the jokers leave the lounge. Music blared from inside, and I smelled a rich batch of marijuana in the air.

"Hoo-wee, that smells like some good, fine Pineapple Express. You ever smoke that shit during treatment, boss?"

"Nah, man, you know me. I don't play around. I go straight for the federal felonies."

"Hey, fuck it, Tommy. If you're gonna get your throat cut, might as well be as a wolf and not as a sheep."

"Shut the fuck up. You bring that shit up again, I'm gonna start patting you down for a wire."

"Eat shit, dreidel boy."

"After I knock a load into that sweet, thick wife of yours, beaner."

"She'd be an improvement on the bitches you bring home, motherfucker."

Then there was an awkward pause.

"Boss, I didn't mean her. I didn't mean Claire was a bitch."

I bit my lip from what I really wanted to say: *Call her a bitch again, and I will knock your teeth out*. Made me a total hypocrite.

"Marco, it's fucking fine. I just insulted Inez. We can talk some shit, brother. Come on, let's do this."

We crept around to the back of his Jeep and gently opened the hatch to put on our ballistic vests; since we were going in with zero backup, I'd made the call to put our full armor plates in the vests and wear raid helmets and ballistic goggles. Black and sterile of insignia up front, the vests had PPD DETECTIVE in large, bright-yellow letters on the back. Our detective shields were clipped onto flaps on the front left shoulder.

The knock was three short taps in a staccato followed by two thumps. When the lookout craned his head out, he got a face full of my shotgun barrel pointing at him, and I grabbed him by the collar, subduing him so I could pull a set of zip-tie cuffs over his wrists and a second pair around his ankles.

"Fucking crooked muthafucka cops!" he hissed. "Where's your warrant, punk-ass bitches?"

I rolled him over on the ground and put my knee in his chest. "You ever hear of exigent circumstances?"

"Exit what?"

Marco went inside, taking the lookout's pistol, and blasted two shots out the window.

"Exigent circumstances, asshole. You just shot up your bar. We are duty bound to go in now." We left him bound and hogtied and moved in.

As we had anticipated, two shooters came around the corner to figure out what the fuck was happening. I wanted to give them a chance to give up, so my first two rounds in the shotgun were rock salt, which went into their kneecaps. The rest of the rounds in the bore were live ammo. They hadn't seen Marco behind the bar yet.

One guy wanted to live to play cards and deal heroin another day; his Heckler & Koch MP5 went across the bar to the opposite end of the wall and clattered to a stop. The other guy kept a firm grasp on an exotic-looking Steyr AUG, extremely bizarre for Pittsburgh, and I brought the shotgun up to eye level.

"Drop it!"

"Fuck you, bitch!"

"Drop it!"

"Fuck you."

"Drop it! Last warning!"

BANG.

The round from the Steyr knocked me down, and in that frozen moment I thought I was dead.

BOOM.

As his head disappeared in a pulpy red mist, my brain suddenly acknowledged that the wind had been knocked out of me. Marco had popped up from behind the bar and taken him out at nearly point-blank range with his twelve-gauge. That round was all buckshot and had zero rock salt shells in it.

I kept drawing in breaths and coughed up bright blood. I pulled my vest open, still coughing, and grinned with relief at the cracked ceramic hard plate and the impacted round, still smoking hot, perfectly center mass. That would have exploded with momentum and mushroomed into my heart were it not for the vest and small-arms protective insert plate.

Marco did a short preliminary pat-down of the shooter who had surrendered and slapped cuffs on him, then checked the corpse for additional weapons or explosives that the cuffed guy could squirm over to find and use against us.

Marco unloaded and kicked both weapons over to me and helped me out of my vest. Eyes angled up in thought, he palpated my chest for injury. "Feels like two cracked ribs, boss. Don't think you have to worry about the lung being punctured, but you better have Samantha give you an X-ray to be sure."

"Search—" I coughed. "Call for backup and search the rest of the place."

When Marco came out of the poker room, he was happy as a pig in shit. One of the bags of heroin was wrapped in a waiter's apron with the embroidered logo of Little E's jazz club. And the bag had been tucked inside a white straw cover, like a pouch you would buy rice in at an Asian market—or, I suppose, like you'd find in the kitchen of a jazz club restaurant.

We may not have had the murderers, but we had a piece of the puzzle, which meant we had a possible lead.

I would be lying if I said we didn't dodge some more bullets and cut some corners as the weeks wore on. Marco and the team and I were cowboys in the beginning, pedals to the floor, gunning it as if we'd live forever.

Stupid.

CHAPTER 5

Claire was shy and timid around the place at first. She slept a lot those first few weeks. But it wasn't necessarily a depression sleep. I would look in, and her face was calm and peaceful, sometimes with a smile. But some nights she needed Zolpidem, some nights Alprazolam, some nights both, some neither. I offered to continue sleeping on the couch, but she insisted I not be inconvenienced; she was perfectly content with Tommy Junior's upper bunk. So, we would lie there at night, her in the loft bed and me below, and like little kids at a sleepover, we started to tell one another stories about our lives. She did her best when recalling the last ten years, remaining focused around her graduate studies, her music career, her blood family, like she was trying to expel the memory of Jake.

I tried to give her space in our little world together. In the mornings, I would be up and gone for a run, setting a breakneck pace until I threw up at the top of the hill, racked with adrenaline, nausea, and bad memories. When I came back, she was normally up and showered and changed, and she would read the paper at the kitchen bar while I had my coffee on the couch. Then one day she took one of the chairs in the little living area. Soon she was sitting at the other end of the couch.

Come the end of the first week, we started making sure there was two cups' worth in the pot no matter who was awake first. Sometimes in those mornings on the couch I would catch her looking over her book at me. I had taken to just touching her shoulder on the way out of the apartment when I left for the day, and she would reach up and squeeze my hand, nothing more. It was nice to have someone around. In the evening when I got home, she would warm up something from my mom's downstairs grill, or I would be greeted with a bowl of soup. I never asked her to do it, and I don't think it was any sort of sappy, housewife-like affection. I think at first she was trying to kill time.

My brothers' wives immediately swept her up. Sarah or Mandy, Brady's and Kenny's respective wives, would pick her up every other day to go for strolls with their little ones and come by with food and drop off clothes, towels, shampoo, conditioner, makeup, curlers, bathrobes—you name it—by the boxload. Eventually the boxes started stacking down our little hallway.

She was bashful and didn't say much around my mother. I guessed it was a matter of pride; maybe it was intimidating that it was Mom, as the ostensible keeper of the building, who had charitably (albeit passively) signed off on giving her somewhere to live, knowing full well Claire didn't have the means to repay us. Or maybe it was the kind of silence that two women who have borne the shame and secrecy of years of abuse use as communication. But one day, my mom appeared at the door in the morning and asked if the "beautiful redhead roommate" of mine could give an old lady an extra hand in the kitchen. The weather was getting colder, and the morning workout crew had nearly doubled as the guys started to favor indoors versus the track. After that the two women were almost inseparable.

But the residue of Jake Hewitt still hung in the air—a third tenant in the apartment, an invisible ghost. One day, a promising patrolman we were trying to groom for the High-Value Target Task Force ended up testing positive for cocaine. The hypocrisy didn't escape me: the only thing keeping me off the same radar and away from the same fate was that all of my vices currently fell into the realm of "legality." I didn't yell, I didn't scream, and I didn't throw things as I stood talking to Marco on the phone. But when I hung up, I slammed the hall closet door as hard as I could. The room got completely quiet. I turned back toward the couch, and she was white as a ghost, trembling.

She stayed on the couch that night, and the next morning, we didn't talk about it at all. After work, I came home, touched her shoulder, and simply said that I was sorry. She turned around and squeezed me tightly, tears streaming down her face.

"Don't do it again. Because . . . you're better than him."

"Who? Jake?"

"No." She wiped her face with the sleeve of an old sweatshirt of mine she was wearing. "Your father."

I think I was probably the one who turned white then.

"Thomas, you talk in your sleep. And you . . . you cry." She hugged me tightly again. She brushed her lips on my cheek and hugged me closer, as if she would fall off the earth if she let go. I held her, whispering to her the vow I had made to her in the hospital—that nobody would ever hurt her again. I felt her nod into my shoulder, her tears of relief and exhaustion and pent-up grief staining my shirt.

Even though I meant it with all my heart at the time, it was such a naïve promise; I did not know what evils were lurking out there, what hell was fermenting. Right then and there, we were safe in our little bubble, our escape pod, clutching onto one another for dear life. The thing about bubbles, though, is one day you have to step out into the real world again.

And that world, it's got fucking monsters in it.

■ ■ ■

Dr. Tolliver stared at me flatly.

"Tommy, you are concerning me. You refuse to attempt radiation or any chemotherapy protocol. You continue to use alcohol and painkillers as your regimen of therapy. By the latest X-rays and ultrasounds, I see growth on opposite sides of the diaphragm and what appears to be a series of metastasized lumps under your right armpit. I can cut out the one in your armpit, as its growing size and the discoloration of the skin are concerning me. You won't need to be put under. You'll have to lay off heavy exercise or lifting and wear a sling for about a week. For anything else, we need to seriously consider chemotherapy or radiation."

"What's the timeline we're looking at?"

"With the exception of your alcoholism, you are an otherwise healthy individual. You are just starting to show symptoms of stage two. If we start aggressive therapy now, there is a ninety-five percent chance of a five-year survival, which is almost a textbook fact. Others have been known to go for up to fifteen. Most people who last beyond fifteen years of recovery . . . well, at that point, it is a bit miraculous, but it has occurred."

"And without your protocols?"

"Two years. Tops. And that is provided you stop drinking, unless you want to add cirrhosis to the file."

"Any chance of sooner?"

"Tommy, do you have some sort of a death wish?"

"I don't know, Doc."

"Would you not consider the incidents the other night in Homestead and downtown death-wish behavior? Trouncing a reputed drug kingpin's car, knowing he would come to the door armed. Then something out of an Elmore Leonard Raylan Givens novel with a duelist standoff at his club? Finally capping off the fortnight with a desperado shootout at an unlicensed gambling den? How am I doing so far?"

"He's the one who's dead now, Doc. Not me."

The lump removal took two hours. He numbed my arm, and the lump felt like a golf ball moving around on the end of a stick as he scraped, cut, removed, flushed, rinsed, and finally praised the intern who stitched up the job. What he held up to me in the metal pan looked like a handful of that gray modeling clay you play with in middle school. He showed me on an index card the exercises I would need to do and told me the antibiotics I would be on. He mumbled something I missed about a removal date for the stitches.

As his intern left, he scrubbed his hands, and I heard the clatter of tools in the hazards bin. With his back still to me, he heaved a sigh. I followed him from the procedure room back out to his more formal office where he met with patients.

"Tommy, would you consider seeing a psychiatrist?"

"Why would I want to do that, Doc?"

"I'm not a psych specialist, Tommy. I'm an oncologist. A psych doctor could help you through some issues."

"Doc, I am a narcotics cop who shares custody of my two children with a money-grubbing ex-wife who was two-timing me the whole last year of our marriage. Yet she feels justified in violating her and your Hippocratic Oaths to discuss my condition with you, without my consent. My father beat me and my brother when we were still in my mother's stomach, and we were lucky we weren't stillborn or born retarded. These beatings continued until I nearly killed my father with a baseball bat. Through some twisted codependent bullshit, he still ingratiates himself into mine, my mother's, and my brothers' lives. The closest thing to a male role model in my life died three years ago, and I found his body.

"I am afraid to form a loving bond with my children because I might be dying. Or worse, I might become like my father down the road. The only companionship in my life is a golden retriever and a domestic violence victim who is currently living at my grandfather's gym. I am outstanding at my job, and I am slightly mourning the fact that a drug-dealing piece of shit I have been trying to get behind bars for six years is dead, because despite him being a drug-dealing piece of shit and probably a murderer, at least chasing his ass down got me out of bed every morning. And now my brother tells me the guys responsible for killing him might be cops. And I haven't dispelled the not-so-crazy notion my father might be somewhere in the mix of all of *that* whopping load of felonies. What nuggets of wisdom would a shrink have for me?"

"Why don't you wish to live, Tommy? And your ex-wife cares for you, as you are both parents of your children. She came to me as a friend, not as a colleague. When you defended your mom against your dad all those years ago, were you hoping he would kill you? Was your pain so unbearable you wanted to die? Do you feel responsible for your father's emotional state now? His physical misery? Do you think that you're a bad son because you stuck up for your mother?"

I slid his prescription pad across his desk to him. "Percocet. Stronger shit. And something to help me sleep."

"You do realize the irony of a narcotics cop exuding drug-seeking behavior."

"You just pulled a baseball-size wad of cancer out of my armpit. I think it's within my rights to ask for some painkillers."

"My professional instincts tell me I should contact your commanding officer and refer you to a program."

"And that will take a thirty-day board of review. Because despite your spitball diagnoses, I'm not suicidal and I haven't been showing up drunk on duty. I don't piss hot because anything I'm taking is a legal script. You can't prove drug abuse, at least not immediately, and you know it. So it would take four weeks or so for you to establish enough cause to put me in any sort of detox, Doctor.

"Irrational workplace behavior or substandard performance? Don't think so. My partner and I have the best clearance record in Narcotics. I just got promoted to lieutenant. And you know it's better for everyone if you just write out that script instead of letting me try to score on the street. And if you're thinking of calling my brother in Internal Affairs, he'll remind you that you're potentially slandering a decorated fourteen-year veteran cop with an *impeccable* service record. Do you really want to play checkers when I'm playing chess, you little pasty-faced, desk-jockey chancre mechanic?"

"No, Thomas, but I refuse to be your doctor anymore."

He tore off and slid a sheet from the top of the pad back to me.

"That should be enough to see you through ninety days. Or just mix it all with some vodka and down it tonight and do us all a favor. Whether you do it now or in two years, you're still out to kill yourself. And I refuse to be your enabler after this. You have a lot to live for despite this cloud of self-pity you wear like armor.

"My wife is the pediatrician who treats your children. Your family has been a part of my life since your kids took their first breaths. And you know what? You don't deserve them, acting like this. You're a self-absorbed, egomaniacal power junkie who thinks not seeking help is synonymous with being some TV or cinematic 'tough guy.' The only thing that separates you from the deplorables you put away isn't your badge and gun; it's the fact those lowlifes shooting up in the alley don't have any illusions of superiority.

"Walk into a meeting and admit you're just as fucked up as them and your dad. Then maybe you can come back into my office like a gentleman, and we can seriously talk about treating you. But until then, I won't subject myself or any colleague I respect to your borderline personality behavior and your propensity for putdowns and hatefulness. What does it matter if I help give you five years or fifteen years or two months? You're already dead inside. When it comes to cancer, a Narcotics lieutenant dies just as fast as a Liberty Avenue heroin junkie on my ward."

"Thanks for the pills, Doc." I made for the door.

The doctor shifted his tone, nearly apologetic. "Tommy, wait up." He rushed to the doorway, gently bisecting it with his arm to prevent me from departing. "We all have pain in our lives. Why do you insist on letting yours define you?"

I firmly but politely lifted his arm out of the way, managing a sad, resigned smile. "See ya, Doc."

■ ■ ■

When you're an addict, even on painkillers and what most "decent folk" consider legal drugs, the middle of the night is the worst. Having anxiety and an addiction turns the nighttime—a time of recovery and rest for most people—into a living hell.

One night, I forgot to take an Ambien before hopping on the couch and watching a movie on TV. Cold sweats, retching, a flushed feeling, freezing to death one minute and feeling like I was on fire the next. Nightmares, too. I woke Claire up—don't know if it was the screaming or the retching. When I came to some level of consciousness, I was doubled up on the tiled floor of the small kitchenette. She ran out to me and knelt down. A short time ago, I was saving her life. Now I was the victim.

"Tommy. *Tommy*! Look at me. What's wrong?"

I squeezed my eyes shut. I felt her palm slap my face. She was probably scared to death that if I passed out, she wouldn't get me conscious again. White flash of pain. Fire in my stomach. I tried not to put the words *enlarged* and *spleen* together. I was sweating so much fluid that if I pissed, straight powder probably would have come out. Uncontrollable tremors. Twitching so badly it felt like my spinal column would rip out of my back and roll across the floor like some obscene Energizer Bunny. My eyes rolled up in my head, and there was a rewarding, warm blackness to it. I felt the stinging slap of her open palm against my face again.

"Goddammit, Tommy, stay with me. I'm calling an ambulance."

"No," I croaked. "No. Just . . . get me back on the couch."

"You're soaked in sweat and you've got goose bumps. And I don't know if it's sweat or puke, but you stink."

She brought me into a sitting position and clutched me from the back, her inner thighs grasping my glutes like a weight-room machine press, her forearms bracing my diaphragm, my back against her chest; then she backed away with a horrified gasp.

"Oh shit—your wound is seeping. Come here."

Her lithe, tiny frame was abnormally strong as she got under my good arm and helped me stand. She walked me back to the shower where I proceeded to retch in, around, and near the toilet and the trash can. I vomited until I felt capillaries in my face burst from the effort and every neck muscle strain with that uncontrollable thirty-second gag that feels like a blade ripping through your windpipe while an invisible tongue depressor keeps you gagging all the more.

After twenty minutes or so of this performance, she stood me back up, tossing the soiled towels into the hamper. Then I felt the stabbing in my gut as constipation gave way to the violence of my stopped-up bowels, and she obligingly stepped into the hallway while I strained my guts on the commode. Solid, spray. Fire, flush. Solid, spray, flush. Repeat.

She rapped patiently on the door and reentered with brisk efficiency, almost like a CIA clean-up crew in the movies, taking more towels to the floor, spraying air freshener, and discreetly covering her face with a cloth. I briefly thought she might roll me in plastic sheets and finish me off in a tub of hydrochloric acid, so animated and mechanical was she in her efforts. When she was sure the smell of Glade overpowered the residue in the air, she set the can down on the sink, looked at me, and crossed her arms.

"Strip," she ordered, turning the water to the bathtub on full gush.

I stood there, teeth chattering, snot and vomit still drooling out of my mouth and nose. At least I'd been able to wipe my ass clean all on my own.

"Come on, tough guy. Nothing I haven't seen before." She swiped my boxers down to my ankles, and I meekly stepped out. She then peeled off my T-shirt. When it hit the tile floor, it made a splash. "Get in."

I stepped into the tub, hoping to slip under the water and drown. There wasn't a word to define the misery I was in.

I heard her go downstairs to the gym. She came back in with two cans of Gatorade.

"Drink them. Drink one right after the other. You've dry-heaved for the last half hour."

She knelt beside me on the tile, furiously working me over with a washcloth, wincing at the smell of my neglected surgical scar. She gingerly scoured around the wound until the yellowed scabs flaked off and the crisscrossed surgical threading became visible.

"When were these supposed to come out?"

"Um, last week. I thought they were the dissolving kind."

"Do you have any idea how stupid it sounds saying those two things in the same sentence?"

She grabbed a pair of small manicuring scissors and sliced out my stitches, and as the wound opened and pus and dark blood flowed into the tub, I almost dry-heaved again. Careful as she could possibly be, she flushed the area with straight alcohol—we had no betadine—while I bit back a scream. She then scrubbed me down all over with a baby wash I reserved for Allison and TJ's visits. I felt like a dog at a grooming station. The Gatorade sluiced through my stomach. Fire, freezing. Fire. Freezing. I'd pissed myself at least once in the tub. I was glad I'd *only* pissed myself.

She pulled out the drain plug, grimacing at the stain of various fluids. "Stand up."

I did as I was told, helpless and weak. *This must be what all those junkies and dealers I put away feel like when they hit bottom.* With that first clink of the prison or jailhouse door, there is nothing to get them over one more wave.

I wanted to cry but could not produce tears. She climbed into the tub after it had drained and pulled the curtain, remaining clothed in her purple boy shorts and a gray sleep shirt with spaghetti straps. She turned the showerhead on and repeated the cleansing process, only this time the water was steadily hot. It almost felt therapeutic. It was probably the most attentive care a woman had paid me in three years. We stood under the spray, and she wrapped her arms around me to keep me from falling over. Then she cut off the water and patted dry the area around the wound, putting butterfly strips on my raw but now disinfected lumpectomy incision.

She dried off the rest of me and walked me—still stark naked—to the bedroom. When she pulled back the blankets on the lower bunk and pointed, I flopped in. She covered me up. Then she went back to the bathroom, and I heard another wet smack of her clothes on the tile. As the shower came back on, I faded in and out of consciousness.

She came back in wearing a T-shirt and shorts I recognized as the same ones we issued to the junior high kids who trained at the gym, and for a split second I allowed myself to wonder if she had grabbed them earlier or walked downstairs in the empty, dark gym naked to retrieve them from the industrial dryer. She shut off the lights and climbed into the one-foot width between me and the wall.

"W-w-wouldn't you be more comfortable in the upper bunk?"

"Don't get all modest on me. I'm staying above the blankets. You're still trembling."

It felt so comforting to have another human being that close to me. Not erotic at all. I wasn't in shape for anything like that, anyway. Just safe—comforted and safe. I smelled the exfoliating soap she'd used on her face, combining with smells of toothpaste and lavender in the inches between her and me. The coziness of the fleece blankets and layers of quilts made me realize I had stopped sweating and freezing. For the first time all night, I didn't want to be dead. I would gladly have spent the rest of my years lying next to her, inhaling the scent of her facial wash.

I glanced at the alarm clock: *2:30 a.m.* I lay my head back, wanting to cry out of sheer exhaustion and gratitude; I was grateful that I was warm and calm and that I wasn't puking or shitting every last drop out of my system. I felt a much softer but still firm *thwack* from her palm cuffing my cheek as a stupor started to wash over me again.

"Open your eyes. *Look* at me, Tommy."

Groggy, dazed, and half asleep, I looked into her eyes, shocked to see tears pooling at the corners.

"I counted three bottles of Percocet this morning. Two bottles were filled with thirty each, and one bottle had twenty remaining."

"Okay."

"So, just a minute ago I counted sixteen in the one bottle and twenty-seven in each of the other two."

"Okay."

"You think I'm stupid that I wouldn't count from the full bottles? You took *ten Percocets* in *twenty-four hours*! Do you want to die?" She hugged me tightly through the blankets and began to cry that awful, choking cry of hers, that helpless, unspeakable grief. "Am I a pity case? How can you care about the lives of strangers—how can you care about my life but not your own?" She kissed my cheeks, my forehead, my neck, over and over, in frustration and tears. Then she stroked her hand over my cheek, stopped crying, and cupped my face in her hands once more, brushing her lips against mine faintly.

"My guardian angel refuses to save himself."

And there you had the perfect epitaph for my tombstone.

■ ■ ■

When I woke up the next day, I was overwhelmed by the clichéd feeling of being hit by a truck. I honestly would rather have been dead. But I had to go into work. Kenny and Brady were pissed that I seemed to be increasing the body count a few weeks into the task force standing up, despite running down one of the bags of heroin.

Charley had replaced my bedmate sometime during the morning. He was curled over my feet and pawing excitedly at me as if we were late for something.

I pulled on a pair of sweatpants and staggered to the stairwell to let him out to run. Back in the apartment, I found Claire sitting at the kitchen counter. She was fully dressed, two accusatory inkblots of rouge on her cheeks, her hair pulled back, wearing a checkered shirt and jeans, topped off with a pair of hiking boots that looked new. That lingering smell of her facial wash greeted me as I walked back into the living room. I recognized her shirt as the same red-and-black plaid shirt my twin brother's wife wore when she raked leaves. The whole family had indeed adopted Claire Hewitt.

With the contrast of the famer-girl shirt against her lovely but pale complexion, she looked more like she was posing in a Hilfiger catalog. The getup looked a lot better on her than a hospital gown complete with black eye.

All at once, I wanted to take her down to Saks Fifth Avenue

and lavish her with dresses, jewelry, and furs, buy her bottles of musky perfume, make her feel like the princess I saw sitting at my kitchen counter, wearing my sister-in-law's yardwork shirt, sipping coffee. I took note that she had not left a second cup in the percolator for me. I gently touched her shoulder as I reached into the refrigerator, and she did not pull away, but her shoulder remained rigid and did not lean into my touch.

"Tommy, I'm going to the pawn shop and selling my jewelry. My wedding ring, the engagement diamond, a few other bracelets and things. I figure I'll clear about a thousand dollars. I want you or your mom—whoever runs this place—to have it. I think maybe if I am contributing, I won't feel like a leech. I want to stop feeling like a stray cat you all took in."

I took all this in stride, but what was really on my mind was how fucking good orange juice tasted the morning after you've almost overdosed. I wondered if Marco wanted to grab French toast at Denny's with me.

"I talked to your mother this morning," she went on. "I asked her if she could get someone to clear the stuff out from the third apartment to get it ready for the visiting fighters and free up the middle apartment for me. I'm going to be helping out full-time downstairs. I could pitch in with the books and the bank-deposit runs for her, signing people in, in addition to cooking for the morning crew, washing the gear, towels, cleaning up the trainer's room, whatever. In exchange for me staying. I've been hiding out up here for almost a month."

She took another sip and put her cup down, looking up at me.

"While I'm doing that, I will start sending out my résumé and putting together enough cash for a place of my own. There was talk of auditioning me for a traveling orchestra, like the Pittsburgh Symphony, but I don't know how possible that is now. Jake was a goddamned control freak and made it out like I would just be some bus whore screwing every guy in the string section.

He went so far as to call a couple offices of the major musical troupes and say as much."

"That's fucked up. What he did, I mean. That's first-rate narcissistic controlling if ever I saw it."

"Tell me something I don't already know, Detective."

I leaned against the fridge, orange juice still in hand. My head was pounding. When I was sure she was looking away, I downed the two Percocet cupped in my palm and chased it with about twenty more ounces of vitamin C.

"What I'm saying to you is I am incredibly grateful—I am *eternally* grateful for you taking me in and taking care of me. I adore your family and I am very fond of you. I owe you my life. But you've got a lot of shit going on in your life, and it seems like you're in some sort of freefall and you don't really care where you land. Or who you land on."

"That sounds about right."

"I'm coming out of a ten-year prison of abuse, and I can't afford to care about someone who doesn't care about himself." She cleared her throat. "I love it here, Tommy. I feel safe and happy for the first time in a decade. A family of cops, who barely knows me, treats me like one of their own.

"I love how all these tough guys at the gym grab the door for me and call me ma'am when I come in from outside. I love sitting on your couch with a blanket over my shoulders and a coffee and a book and knowing no one is going to come through the door and beat me or treat me like a whore. I love your dog, and I love going downstairs when your mom's cooking pancakes when the fighters finish their morning workout, and that your sisters-in-law, who met me only a handful of times, lent me their clothes.

"I love how gentle you have been to me and that you don't treat me like some tossed-away piece of trash. I see the way you look at me when you think I'm not looking. I love how I can take a walk for thirty minutes and there's not some sadistic asshole screaming at me that I didn't make his dinner. Instead it's you here. Waiting for me. And I know, I'm certain . . . that on some level you have love in your heart for me."

She paused and looked me straight in the eye.

"But I don't love it here enough to watch a good man kill himself in the other room and just be expected to do nothing about it."

As she was saying all of this, I pulled on a clean pair of underwear, a pair of jeans, threw on a clean T-shirt, and was pulling on a flannel and my boots. What did I care about modesty? She had just cleaned up my piss and puke seven hours ago. I snapped my .38 into my backup holster around my ankle and buckled my shoulder holster, then loaded the .45, slipping my badge and cuffs into my pockets.

When I ran out of things to fidget with or focus on like a toddler, I met her gaze. "Are you done?"

"I don't think you would bring me into your home and your life just to hurt me. But the way you are destroying yourself hurts me. And anyone else who cares about you."

"I've been good to you, and if I wanted a lecture, I'd go down to the hospital and talk to my ex-wife."

"Have you ever wondered if all of this, what you're doing to yourself, is part of why she left in the first place?"

"Fuck you, Claire, Clarissa, whatever you want me to call you. You do not get to judge me. You were a whipping post for a class-A psycho when I met you. You get a few weeks of clean sheets and good meals in you, and you have tea with my mom and my sisters-in-law, and you think that earns you the right to dissect my life and tell me what's what? If you don't like how I run my life, go take your fiddle on the street corner for loose change."

"You don't get to talk to me like that, Tommy. And your family says I am welcome here. Like I said, I'm moving next door, and you don't have to deal with me all up in your space. I'll still look after Charley because I think you like that, and I know I do. But don't you dare act like I'm some street-tramp ingrate with my hands in your family's pocket. You brought me here. You brought me into *your* home. *You* were the one who set these terms. You don't get to just throw me away like trash. I have done nothing but been kind to your family, and you, and I have shown you—I have shown *all* of you—my gratitude. But all I'm saying to you is what I see in front of me."

"And what is that, Mrs. Hewitt?"

"Your ugliness is why you're alone, Tommy Francis Spenser. And the next time I find you facedown in piss and sweat and vomit, I'll let you drown in it. You've made it quite clear you don't want anything, or anyone, to save you."

"Thanks for the offer, but I can take care of my own fucking dog."

CHAPTER 6

I slammed the door behind me. *Sanctimonious bitch.* Too bad someone didn't give her the same heartfelt, dramatic lecture ten or eleven years ago. It would have spared her quite a few emergency-room visits.

As I made my way down the catwalk to the main floor of the gym, I took the steps three at a time, and my trail boots slamming into the metal scaffolding made the suspension wires hum like a xylophone. Foregoing my notion of grabbing Denny's with Marco, I ducked into the kitchen, grabbed a to-go box and tin foil, and threw in some pancakes and bacon from the warming pan. I shoved a can of Gatorade into each jacket pocket and shuffled as fast as I could to the exit past the front desk, as if the building and business weren't mine and my family's to take from.

I felt my mother's eyes on me from the recesses of her little office. *I'm thirty-five fucking years old, and she can still peg when I'm misbehaving.* I was running from the shit upstairs, not my petty larceny. Still, I gave her a gentle wave, drew a five-dollar bill from my wallet, and stuck it in the tip jar, making sure she saw it.

Back when Brady and I were at Metro Police Academy and after Mom divorced my dad, I asked her why, when she could have gone anywhere and done anything, she chose to stay in Pittsburgh in a smelly gym that was growing less and less safe to run. She had playfully slapped my cheek, stood on her tippy toes, planted a kiss on my forehead with a smile, and said, "This is home for me. All my boys are here. You're everything to me. Home is everything to me."

As I walked out to my car in the cold air, my boots crunching the leaves and frosted grass, I thought of Rose Rosencoff-Spenser's definition of home, and how close it was to Claire's concept of safety. I pounded my fist, idiotically, against the driver's door. I wanted to run back upstairs and hug Claire and hold her and beg her forgiveness. At the same time, I wanted to pack her meager bit of luggage and put her on a Greyhound bus to Seattle and let her go find that worthless fuckbag of a husband.

And I wanted to collapse to my knees in self-pity at the life I had let go, and cry for the fact that fifteen miles away, someone else was raising my kids, in my house, and that by showing that shit side of my personality—first to Samantha, then to any other woman who tried to love me—I had fucked up whatever shot I'd had at salvation. I didn't just want to die. I wanted to blow my brains out, but I wanted someone else to pull the trigger.

A rotten man would throw her out. A good man would apologize. A God-fearing man would pray for guidance. I was all of these and none of these.

Detective Lieutenant Thomas Spenser got in the car.

Beyond anything else, I was a cop who was late for work.

■ ■ ■

Darnell Washington was out of intensive care but still on several tubes and hoses. The docs had scaled down his painkillers, and he was up for about five hours a day and could talk. Escardo and I came into his hospital room around 2:30. He didn't appreciate the buckled restraints on his arms and legs.

"What's up with this, Officer Tommy? I take two in the chest and I'm chained like a slave?"

"Darnell, while I'm sure you and your dead cousin and the dead whores were just talking about fried chicken and Jesse Jackson and church choir practice and shit, you had three ounces of cocaine in your pants as well as a loaded .357. Victim or not, you're still a class-A fuckup on a string of parole violations, including consorting with known felons—among them your late, great cousin. You want to tell me and Sergeant Escardo what happened?"

"Ain't saying shit. I get up out of here, I'll do my own investigation, nigguh. Double-ought buckshot justice."

"Or," Escardo said, shrugging, "maybe you know the shooters because you green-lighted the hit. Had to be close up to be above suspicion. Your partners botched it and hit you and the girls. Wouldn't be the first time in the history of Pittsburgh a 'nigguh' couldn't shoot straight at something two feet in front of him."

"Fuck you, beaner!"

"Wow. That's fucking original there, Darnell."

"Officer Tommy looked out for my family, kept my brothers and cousins out of jail when dey fuck up. But I don't like your spic ass any. I know it was you tased Razor and fucked him up the other day. Groping him like some sort of faggot, too. My boy put more spics on a slab than fucking Border Patrol."

"I was born at the county mission hospital same as you, fuckhead. Why don't you quit acting like my folks coyoted me from Mexico into Wilkinsburg or some shit?"

"Darnell, take away your racial tensions with Detective Escardo and the Pittsburgh Latino community for a minute and talk with me straight. With you out of commission and Razor dead, who's running shop? Who are the big players now? Who's controlling distribution?"

Darnell smiled under his tubes. "Dis America, motherfucker. Land of opportunity. Sheeyit, Officer Tommy, your guess is as good as mine. Second kid to the cookie jar gets crumbs. And I bet there's niggas all over Pittsburgh fighting for that cookie jar by the time I get back on the block."

■ ■ ■

That night, I returned to the gym after a long day of interrogations and work. Climbing the catwalk up to the studios, I slipped out my pistol, cuffs, badge, and backup holster in succession. I had just laid the tip of the barrel for the .38 snub-nose on the table when the lamp beside the couch clicked on.

I instinctively spun toward the sound, but something told me not to bring the pistol up to eye level. Claire sat on the couch in a terrycloth robe that I remembered hanging on the hook in Mandy Spenser's guest bathroom. She was holding a wineglass containing remnants of a pinot noir.

"Don't shoot, Lieutenant. I'm unarmed."

I let out a heavy sigh and slumped into my chair, setting the .38 on the coffee table with a clank. "What the hell are you doing sitting in the dark in here?"

"It's still my place for the time being, no? I was enjoying sitting in the dark with nothing to be afraid of. But you, I don't think you're afraid of anything. Big strong police officer. War hero. SWAT-team sniper. Oh yeah, whoops." She giggled like an ingénue in a Fitzgerald novel. "I may have snooped through your stuff."

"Oh yeah? You find anything interesting?"

"Only that you have way too many Michael Chabon books for such a solvent heterosexual. Chabon always strikes me as a bit of a pansy who cannot get his shit together enough to decide what he wants. He just dillydallies back and forth. Men to women. Women to men. AC to DC. So, I tried to figure out which of Chabon's alter egos you were. Art Bechstein? Too mopey. Cleveland? Too much self-destruction. Grady Tripp? Too cerebral. You're a man of action. James Leer? Too effeminate. You're a bruiser.

"Perhaps Crabtree, the eccentric who takes in pet projects because he's too ashamed to face how fucked up and washed up he is? And then, voilà. *The Yiddish Policemen's Union.* My very own little yinzer Meyer Landsman. Rights all wrongs no matter the cost. Always gets his man. But his personal life is a fucking train wreck. How am I doing?"

She stood and walked around me at the table, holding her glass with one hand while the other absently stroked my cheek as she completed her perimeter. There was a slight wobble in her gait, and I guessed she had polished off two bottles of pinot well before I'd shown up.

"Do you know what it's like, Thomas Francis, for a woman to be afraid of the dark? To be terrified when a man turns the light out because she knows what's coming next? Fists or fucking or sometimes both. Sometimes he disgusts you so much that you want the fists. Sometimes you need the fucking. But no matter how much you get used to the routine, you still cannot quite get used to being there. In the dark. But when I'm here, in your home, the dark doesn't scare me anymore."

She moved closer to me and tried to guide one of my hands into the recesses of her robe. I withdrew my arm with a violent pull, but the message didn't register in her drunken stupor. Instead, she pushed me onto the couch and sat astride me.

"When's the last time you've just *fucked*, Thomas Spenser?"

"Claire," I croaked. "Sweetheart, this isn't you. You're drunk." I stood, and she tumbled off my lap, drunkenly cursing at me the more aloof I tried to be.

"I'm worth saving but not worth fucking—is that it?" she yelled from the ground. "Or are you just a eunuch down there? You have so many pills in your system that you're just a rotted, broken shell of a man? If I shoot you up first, maybe that would get you off?"

"Claire, please, baby. Not like this. Please, don't be vulgar." I felt a rock in my throat, and involuntary tears stung my eyes.

She stood, opened the robe, and let it fall to the floor. She closed the two fragile emeralds of her eyes where tears had started to well. Her only other colors were the creamy white of her skin, the fiery red of her hair, and the eraser-tip pink of her mouth and nipples. She was completely naked except for a pair of blue Lycra panties. She held her arms out to me, tears streaming down her cheeks. Her eyes opened again. "Look at me, Thomas."

"Not like this."

"I want you to touch me, Thomas. I want you to love me." She stroked a palm flatly below her navel where she'd once carried life.

Anger flared inside me. I grabbed the wineglass from where she'd put it down and poured the rest in the sink. "Why would I want to fuck someone who just called me a train wreck? You're a nasty drunk. You're acting like a whore. You think because I'm messed up and got some shit I'm working through in my life, that this—*this*—is the seduction I rate? You insult me, question my sexuality, call me a eunuch, and I'm supposed to drop my pants, whip out my cock, and be oh-so ever-fucking grateful?!"

She stomped over, grabbed the empty glass, and threw it past me into the pantry where it burst into a kaleidoscope of shards. "You know, for a cop, you're just one big *pussy*! Tell me you don't want me! Tell me you don't love me! You're a fucking coward!"

I curled my fists at my sides.

"Oh, big tough guy. What are you gonna do? Hit a woman too? Like father, like son?"

"You're fucking drunk. I have been nothing but good to you. But if you're going to be filthy like this, then you can go to hell."

"You sonofabitch!" she screeched and then reached for the nearest thing to throw at me next. I walked over to her and firmly grabbed her around the waist. She misread the intent and smashed her lips to mine, groping me as we staggered down the hallway and into the elevator at the end of the series of studios. This was the first time I had been in it since Papa Mickey died. The elevator was foreign without seeing him hobble in and out of it. But tonight, we violently flung each other against the cramped recesses, heaving, kissing, and clawing.

She opened her eyes for a moment and, simpering, whispered to me, "The hot tub. In the trainer's room. Fuck me in the hot tub. Mmm, I want you so bad, Thomas."

We fumbled down the corridor after the elevator dinged at the basement floor. I kicked open the door to the trainer's room where the hot tub whirled and bubbled in the same area as the ice bath.

And with one swift motion I dumped her into the ice bath.

The shriek that erupted from her as her body hit the water was deafening. She screamed bloody murder at me, loud and furious, foreign tongues, an apex of a 1930s Southern Baptist revival, the repressed, silent years of her abusive marriage coming out in banshee screeches. She screamed like a dog I had seen in Kosovo that had gotten clipped by a tank and lived for five minutes, half of it crushed in the shape of the tank tread until I had tearfully pulled out my pistol and put a bullet in its head.

She clawed and screamed for me to pull her out; by then the cold dunk was waging war on her body's willingness to function properly. Purely on reflex, she retched wine through her mouth and nose onto the tiled floor I was positive Coach Lou had scrubbed clean that evening.

When I reached into the icy water, she was still swearing like a sailor, but her body was docile, limp and trembling. I gently lowered her into the hot tub bath and turned the heat on the water tank up. Then I stripped down to my shorts and climbed in behind her, wrapping her in my arms. Her teeth were chattering, and in her eyes I saw a combination of horror and shame-faced gratitude. With the same tenderness and dignity that she'd afforded me the night of my overdose, I bathed her like a child. Grabbing the squeeze bottle of soap, I lathered every part of her, then gently rinsed and caressed her legs and arms and back, finally her chest, belly, face, and hair. She cried helplessly, that black, horrible, wailing moan reminiscent of when I'd first brought her home.

Without another word, I bundled her up into towels from the warmer and coaxed her upstairs and back into bed. I dressed her in one of my T-shirts, and she wiggled out of the wet panties she was still wearing, making me turn around as I passed her a set of her sleep shorts.

I went back downstairs. After I drained the trainer's ice tub, I filled it with clean water and grabbed some clean clothes from the dryer. She was still crying half an hour later when I scooted in next to her after showering and putting on my pajamas. I brushed a few clinging curls off her brow and kissed her forehead, then softly touched her lips once with mine.

"I never said I didn't want you or didn't love you. But I won't take advantage of you drunk, either. Come to me when you are sober and your head is clear."

She stared up at the underframe of the top bunk, her eyes bloodshot. "I was wrong. I'm still broken."

"We're both broken, Claire."

■ ■ ■

At around 1:30 a.m., the tactical team radio on the kitchen bar crackled to life. "Drugstore Cowboy, Drugstore Cowboy, this is Border Patrol."

I had to chuckle at that. Usually call signs are Six for the team commander, Five for the assistant team commander, and then down the line with One, Two, Three, and Four being the squad leaders/squad sergeants.

Not my guys.

I was Drugstore Cowboy—for reasons you could guess. Marco was Border Patrol. Brady was James Bond, alluding to his sharp sense of fashion; Kenny, as the overall director of the special task force, was Nutcracker, referencing both his fancy Victorian dress uniform as a cadet at West Point and the fact that he was a regular ball breaker. Eduard Peters, Brady's right-hand man, was Freddy Kreuger: he was the stuff of nightmares; you would not want to meet him in the dark. No one dared suggest he go with the moniker Kingpin—he looked too much like the actual Marvel character for that.

The next guy under Marco was Sergeant Snopes, who had picked Dark Hawthorne. His parents were both English professors at Bowdoin, both African American, and had done him the horrible disservice of naming him—yes, even on his birth certificate—Colonel Sartoris Snopes. He went through most of his early childhood blissfully unaware of this cruelty, until the first day of kindergarten when he found out his name was not Tori, as his mother had nicknamed him, but instead this embarrassing tribute to a short story by William Faulkner. Dark Faulkner just didn't sound right over the radio, so we went with another great of the English classics, Nathaniel Hawthorne. Just don't ask.

"Border Patrol, Drugstore Cowboy," I responded.

"Roger, we've got a tip about a possible cookhouse and product being moved in and out of an abandoned tenement at the intersection of Seagirt Street and Nimick Place. I've got two plainclothes guys sitting about thirty meters back, but I don't want them getting ambushed. I wanted to know if you want to play a little overwatch."

"Duck, Duck, Goose?"

"Oh, you know I'm up for some Duck, Duck, Goose!"

"Okay, that's close to Wilkinsburg," I said. "It's right up their ass, really. Call Wilkinsburg PD. We're going to need a few of their cruisers on standby half a mile over in case we engage. Have them meet us in an hour at"—I looked at the map on my table and circled the spot with a wax pencil—"Graham Athletic Field. It's five minutes away by car. Far enough that it looks to the scumbags like it's just cops taking a donut break and they won't make the plainclothes guys there either. Bring two long guns, two short barrels, and our tree togs."

"Duck, Duck, Goose, boss. Let's fuck some shit up."

"Quack. Quack. *Quaaaaack.*" I broke the connection laughing, wondering what the dispatcher back at headquarters thought of that exchange.

Three hours later, Marco and I had a clear view of the plainclothes cops sitting in a 1984 Bronco II a half mile from the house. We also had an unobstructed view of the house in our sights. We couldn't have asked for a clearer night, and the ambient light made our night goggles feel like ultra-high-definition IMAX theater. We were both in SWAT-style ghillie suits, basically poncho cloaks covered in stripes of varying shades of brown fabric that hung from our shoulders to our feet, concealing us against the broken fall brush where we hunkered down in the vacant lot.

Marco and I both had M40A1 scoped sniper rifles, one zeroed in on the car and one on the house. Marco was currently propped against a much stronger scope, the spotter's optics, that gave him a telephoto zoom on our undercover personnel.

Somewhere behind us, three cruisers with four cops each stood ready to hit the house if we initiated contact. Since we didn't have a warrant and we couldn't reenact the cowboy antics of the poker game, we had to be patient and catch them committing a crime. That meant witness testimony of an exchange happening or an attempt on their part to physically engage the undercovers.

"How's your houseguest?"

"Shaddup."

"That good, huh?"

"Shh. Work."

"She's got nice boobies."

"I swear to fuck. I wish Mom had left you at the foster home."

"You must *like* her if you aren't talking about her . . . or her boobies."

"You say 'boobies' more than my son, you know that?"

My radio cracked to life. "Drugstore Cowboy, this is UC One. You seeing what I'm seeing?"

"UC One, roger that."

A modernized Volkswagen beetle, white, had rounded the curb a thousand meters downward from where we were, going close to seventy-five, eighty miles per hour and closing in. It was driving erratically. If we let it go and did nothing, it could potentially drive past the UCs and hit and kill an innocent. If we took the UCs off the house to run them down and pull them over, their cover was blown. If we had the UCs flash their lights as a warning to slow down, someone in the house might see it, and their cover was still blown.

We had positioned pop-up tire spikes forward and aft of the UC's vehicle, 600 feet in both directions, for just this type of thing—or to cripple the dealers' vehicles if they tried to flee the premises. They could be triggered by a remote device. The UCs had one; Marco had the failsafe.

"UC One, listen to me very carefully. Deploy tire spikes forward of the house. Can you do that before the vehicle gets to your location?"

"Already done, boss."

"UC One, when they hear the car hit the spikes—and that vehicle's gonna skid—the assholes in the house are gonna come out with their guns drawn. They are weapons-free targets at that point. Your priority is cover of whoever is in that car to safety." I switched channels. "Wilkinsburg PD, in about fifteen seconds, you are going to hear gunfire. Remember Border Patrol and I are in ghillie suits. Watch your sectors. There is a white civilian vehicle in play. Approach on my signal!"

The civilian vehicle hit the spikes. It skidded into a light pole and crashed to a stop. My shooting eye was back on the scope, but instinctively I glanced back to the street. I saw airbags deployed. My heart was pounding, and I felt my pulse in my ears. The UCs approached to the crash side, assessed the situation, then pulled one, two, three scared college-age girls out the rear driver's side door and had the girls crouch beside the car. After a few more moments of effort, they pulled the driver, still limp, out in a fireman's carry. They moved with accuracy and swiftness and didn't even flinch when Marco and I sent the first shots through the assholes coming out the front door.

One, two, three little Indians.

Another member of the crew came out spraying an MPX from the hip in rapid succession, and one of the conscious girls stood up to run. She must have freaked out at seeing us rise from our perch in the field and blow away the bad guys. She never had a chance. I saw the MPX rounds hit her hip first, and then two more blew through her chest—possibly still survivable if they missed major organs; then one unforgiving round punched a baseball-size exit wound through her face.

She dropped right there in the field, her mouth in a silent scream, her hand reaching out to me and Marco for help that would never arrive.

Blinking tears out of my eyes, I racked the bolt on my rifle, ejected the shell casing and loaded a live round into the breech, and zeroed back in on the porch shooter. A microsecond later, half of his head was on the foyer carpet, and the MPX had stopped firing.

"Wilkinsburg PD, move in—I say again, move in. We have civilians down by a white 2012 Volkswagen bug. I say again, civilians down and one civilian DOA. Four, I say again, *four* suspects down in the front entryway. The house is not secure, and the undercovers are blown. Snipers are moving in to clear."

Marco looked at me and nodded, and we shucked off our ghillie tops, dropping our sniper rifles and spotter scopes by the Volkswagen with the undercover officers and trying not to look at the two terrified college girls weeping for their friends. The UC officers were triaging the driver, finding a pulse, and intubating her. One side of her ribcage looked caved in. I didn't have time to beat myself up. All of the young women reeked to high hell of weed and vodka.

It was a fog-of-war call.

Right now, my priority was clearing that building and keeping Marco and everyone else alive. We went in with just our M4 assault rifles, our backup pistols, our black Pittsburgh PD T-shirts, and those absurd pants covered in the same material as the ponchos.

Inside, I dropped my M4 so it was freely hanging on the short sling and pulled my pistol, scanning the sectors of the room. Marco came in close to me, patting my shoulder. I nodded, and we crept in side-step fashion, back-to-back and moving in sync, two partners doing an obscene tango—down the halls, up steps, into doorways, bisecting closets and wardrobes. As we were coming back down, I yelled, "Top clear!"

"Wilkinsburg police, cellar clear!"

"Anyone still alive out front?"

"Doesn't look like it, boss. You guys didn't shoot to wound. We'll get forensics in here to shake the place down and pull prints. Looks like four bags and roughly a million-five in cash, and that's just what we found loose."

"Is the other girl going to make it?"

"Looks like the EMTs got here fast and got her stabilized. They're taking her back to the ball field and calling in a Life

Flight. Our backup guys bagged the friend already, sent her along with the survivor. Figured that was the decent thing to do instead of letting her lie here with these pieces of shit. We have units on the way to the family." With his own hand protected by a medical glove, he handed me the poor dead girl's driver's license, still slick with her blood.

"Okay. One, don't go getting any sticky fingers. We saw there's a million-five here. I'm sure there is more hidden in the house. Wait for forensics. Two, no interservice crosstown bullshit. I am the task-force commander. I appreciate your help this evening, but I want it to continue, and I want complete transparency going forward. When Sergeant Escardo here calls your guys for a report, I don't want any 'Fuck them, they're Pittsburgh cops'-type rhetoric. One team, one fight—got it?"

"Yes sir."

"Okay. Thank you for having our asses tonight."

I felt the collective glare, even though their faces betrayed nothing.

"Listen. I'm going to make sure your captain personally knows the fine work every one of you did. I know the shit with the civilians is rough, but the safety of the undercovers was priority. That car was coming in like a missile, and it was a split-second call. It was my call, and I will back that up under testimony. If any IAD rep comes around bothering you, you shove them toward us."

As Marco and I were going out the door, I overheard the senior Wilkinsburg sergeant.

"Fucking thrill-chasing, pill-popping psycho. All he did was maim a little girl and get another one killed tonight. People been kissing his ass all his life because of his daddy. I hope that whole family gets found out for the incompetent assholes they are. I hope Eddie Peters takes his fucking badge."

Marco wrapped me in a bear hug as I tried to fling the door back open, effectively pushing me off the porch, and looked me in the eyes with a maturity and tenderness that went beyond his years. "Let it go, brother. You're *my* fucking hero. That's all that ever mattered."

The Wilkinsburg sergeant came out on the porch.

"Some sort of problem here, Loo-ten-unt?"

Marco, ever the peacemaker, was already trying to de-escalate the confrontation, inserting his small frame against the hulking, Leviathan mass of the Wilkinsburg staff sergeant. The uniformed cop was at least 275 pounds, all muscle, and I remembered him being a beast of a linebacker in his day. One of the success stories out of W-burg, treated lower than rat trash for crossing over to the blue and becoming a cop.

His hateful glare at me turned to genuine fright and alarm, and he grabbed Marco by the shoulders as I heard screeching tires and automatic rounds start popping off behind me. Pandemonium.

The fucking tire spikes retract after ten minutes. Those fuckers know they do.

The EMS cabs and backup cars had taken most of the strafing, but everyone seemed fine, crouched down behind their doors, trying to return fire as the car sped away. I did a visual check on the EMS crews to make sure they were okay and their oxygen tanks weren't hit.

Commotion erupted on the porch behind me. Marco was cursing up a storm and clutching his left arm. Some bleeding, but from the most part he looked winged.

The senior Wilkinsburg sergeant who had come out the door to continue the fight had saved Marco's life. As he was the biggest out of the three of us, I guessed they had collectively sighted their fire onto him. His last act had been to push Marco out of the way. More than likely, he was dead before he and Marco hit the ground. The coroner later told me she pulled fifty-seven slugs out of him from three separate calibers of weapons. And only one had nicked Marco. *One.*

■ ■ ■

At the station, in the regular work hours of the morning, District Attorney Mike Taradash sat in one corner. A Citadel grad with his JD from Harvard Law and thirty years in the military police and FBI, he pursued the law as "something to do" in his military retirement. He was dressed nondescript—navy suit, white starched shirt pressed as sharp as his cadet days, his only affectation the light infantry blue of his college colors in his tie. Otherwise, he looked like a typical federal agent, prosecutor, or a counterintel spy hunter. At some point in his career, he had done each.

Next to Mike was Francine, having traded her tan-and-cranberry collegiate prep look for something more severe and formal that reflected the decorum of her mentor and the gravitas of the occasion. Slate-gray Prada, surely another spoiler from her late adopted grandfather, black pumps, and yet, adorably, still my one and only baby sister with her well-worn, well-loved Yale backpack. Before the aggrieved family member entered the interview room, she had given both Marco and me a light squeeze on the shoulder and a peck on the cheek. She also placed one of her business cards facedown in front of me. It was our internal code for this room, a subtle way to let me know that nobody was observing us on the other side of the glass—or if they were, they were friendly to our clan.

Fran was in her presumptive role once again as the victim advocate for the DA's office, running interference and trying to de-escalate on behalf of the pour soul who had lost his daughter. The victim advocacy programs in most cities are nonprofit and nonpartisan, but in Pittsburgh it was part of the mayor's community outreach to make victim advocacy and law enforcement a "left hand watches what the right is doing" type of mindset. The fact that Francine was a sister of cops was not lost on a few liberal-class elites, but she had also put away quite a few crooked cops, and that painted her as fair, just, and as impartial as one could get.

Marco had been making eyes at Francine ever since we sat down. (Actually, Marco had been making eyes at Francine since they were both twelve years old, long before he even knew Inez.) Francine had Israeli-tan, nearly olive skin, a strong jawline and forehead like mine, Brady's blue eyes, Kenny's ears, my dad's nose and mouth, and hair the color of pumpkins from her maternal grandfather. Her skin was inherited from her mother; the rest of her features were the Spenser bloodline's.

Ed Peters, Brady's right-hand man, was in the room as well. With the deck stacked—me, Brady, Kenny as SIU commander, and even a blind man could see Francine was family—I wondered if the man across the conference table from us thought he was getting shaken down.

Ed Peters spoke first. "Sir, as Lieutenant Spenser is not a suspect in your daughter's death, there is no reason for him or any of his immediate relatives on the force to recuse themselves from the investigation. The initial ballistics report shows the gunshots came from the criminals our personnel were out there to apprehend."

Malcolm Stafford, age fifty-four. Ex-Navy Seabee. Did three years and out. Been a self-made man ever since. Had a demolition company worth just shy of three million that picked up a modest number of contracts around Pittsburgh. Not at all rich by 2012 standards, not the definition of powerful, but a broken, destroyed man whom I could not look in the eye; his daughter was dead because of a split-second call I made.

Stafford slammed the table. He didn't have a lawyer there as this was the notification, but he'd been screaming about lawyers and lawsuits since we brought him in.

It would never happen. That was why Francine and Mike were there. We would all leave the room, or they would go to another room, Ed would bring in a crisis management specialist, and in a few weeks Franny would come in with a representative from the city's liability team, talking about a settlement. A nondisclosure agreement would be part of that settlement.

"My little girl is *dead* because of that cowboy there!"

"Sir," I said, staring at the steel interview table, "your little girl is dead because she was in a car that was barreling down our surveillance site at seventy-five miles per hour, drunk and stoned out of her gourd. I had my officers lay tire spikes to disable her friend's vehicle in the hopes she and her buddies didn't wreck somewhere and kill *everyone* in the car that night, or wreck into my officers and kill *six* people. There was no good call to make.

"We are being forthright with this information—a privilege, by the way—so prematurely in the investigation process in the hopes that nothing is leaked to the press to reflect badly on anyone involved. But with all due respect, sir, I wasn't the one in a bug doing nearly eighty, high on grass and Stoli, with nearly a 0.15 blood alcohol level. Frankly, I'm surprised they could find the fucking door handle."

"Tommy, shut up!" my baby sister hissed at me.

It has been a practice of my stupid nature that I rarely listened to advice from the women I loved. Wife, sister, or mother, I was perpetually deaf to what they had to say. Instead, I continued: "Perhaps if you were as passionate about her upbringing as you are about blaming someone for her death, we wouldn't all be here tonight."

"*Shut the fuck up, Lieutenant*!" That was Mike Taradash, district attorney, esquire.

"Mr. Stafford." Marco's voice was barely a whisper. "Lieutenant Spenser made the only call he could make. From my vantage point, that car could have crashed into our undercovers and, as he stated, killed six people. Or they could have driven on into the night and done God knows what damage. There was no proper call to make without compromising the operation and endangering even more lives.

"Our intent was to forcibly stop the car and get the occupants away from the area as fast as possible. The backup cruisers would not have gotten there in time. An undercover car chasing after them would have compromised the entire purpose of our being there in the first place. Disabling the vehicle as fast as possible was the only viable option. It was the same call I would have made. And I believe any officer in this room or on that scene would have done the same."

This seemed to appease Stafford a bit, but he was still on the warpath and looked at me like I was Death itself riding the pale horse of the Apocalypse.

"Do you know my baby girl's name? Did you bother to learn it before she was zipped into a fucking *bag*, Detective?"

I cleared my throat. I pulled her driver's license, still stained with her blood, out of my pocket and placed it deliberately on the table in front of me. Beautiful, vivacious, cherubic, blond, white teeth, green eyes, tiny ski-jump nose, elegant curvature of her mouth, forever frozen in time at the age of twenty.

Now this pristine face had a gaping mess of blood, brain, and bone out of one hole in her eye socket, and all the king's morticians and all the king's men in Pittsburgh probably could not put that face back together to avoid a closed casket.

"Esther." I faced him. Tears brimmed in the corners of my eyes, but they did not fall. "Your daughter's name was Esther.

Esther Joy Stafford. A name fit for a biblical queen, but the original Hebrew etymology of Esther also means 'star.' The star of your family. She, um, she wrote all this on her Facebook page."

The dad started weeping softly. He buried his face in his hands.

I pulled out my smartphone and clicked a few buttons.

"She drove a forest-green 2010 Jeep Wrangler you got her as a graduation present. Her favorite color was green—stoplight green, not forest green, but they didn't have that color for the car at the dealership. Her favorite dogs were Irish wolfhounds, her favorite movie was *The Town* with Ben Affleck, she had a 3.3 GPA at Carnegie Mellon, but she, um . . ." I checked the phone again. "She wanted to get it higher to make you prouder. Because you knew she could do a 3.3 in her sleep.

"I'm the reason your daughter is dead. It was my call. But five other people aren't. I didn't mean to trade her life for theirs. But I will be damned if I'll sit here and say I would go back in time and trade their lives for hers."

Ed Peters cleared his throat and turned off the recorder.

"Okay, I think we've heard enough. I don't think Detective Lieutenant Spenser should say anything more without counsel or his PBA rep."

Brady was now visibly annoyed.

From behind us: "He's not a suspect, Ed, just as you said." My eldest brother, Kenny, was standing by the door, arms crossed, glaring at Ed Peters in what could be classified as his best "go fuck yourself" face.

Ed snapped his head around to Kenny. "I think at this point, Inspector, it is a matter of the department's liability. Lieutenant Spenser doesn't speak for the department, sir. I do . . . and *you* do."

Mike Taradash spoke at last. "Mr. Stafford, thanks for coming in. Ms. Goyevsky will see you out. Someone from the district attorney's victim advocate office will be contacting you in the coming days. I'm deeply sorry for your loss, sir. We all are."

Stafford looked at Franny as if she had materialized from a beam of light in the room. He looked from her to us, then us to her, then back again, and made the connection. "What the fuck is this, *A Family Affair*?" He stood up, pointing an accusatory finger at Fran, then at me, Kenny, and Brady. "She's your kin, isn't she? Imagine, gentlemen. Imagine if that woman you all loved—*imagine* if someone hurt or harmed her. What rage would you all feel? What lengths would you go to? I pray to God nobody ever hurts her like I've been destroyed tonight."

Fran gently tapped his shoulder as if to politely nudge him toward the exit.

"Get your fucking hands off me, you goddamned bitch."

Marco nearly vaulted over the table like a track star for a piece of Stafford. Kenny, the former NCAA Division 1 running back, all six feet two of him, grabbed the suspenders of Marco's sniper-suit pants and lifted him off the floor as if Marco were an oversized marionette. My partner kicked and cursed. Brady's restraint of me was a lot less cinematic. He simply crouched behind my chair and wrapped his forearms under my armpits with his fingers interlocking at the base of my skull, my head in a full nelson headlock.

Meanwhile, Ed Peters grabbed Stafford by the forearm and waistband—not violently, not abusively, but firmly—and Stafford was a blur as Ed kicked open the door to the interview room and nearly threw Mr. Stafford through it. Kenny followed, the door slammed behind them, and there was a fevered spike of shouting and screams as Ed handed him off to the uniforms on the other side.

Marco sat, surly and insolent, in his spot on the floor where Kenny had brutally dropped him, and Brady eased back out of his vise grip on me. I shifted my arm around the discomfort of my healing armpit. Taradash remained unfazed, as if mixed-martial-arts battles happened on the daily in the interview room. Franny simply collected her items back into her bookbag, stepping into the corridor to confer with one of the clerks from the DA's office.

Kenny came back into the room and tossed four bullets in clear plastic evidence bags on the table. The coroner had pulled them from Esther Stafford in the last three hours.

"I couldn't find a bag big enough for all the rounds they pulled out of Sergeant Hamilton. This is what happens when you go off like a couple frat boys on a joyriding stunt. Where was my signature on this goatfuck? Where was approval? Tommy had tactical command of *twelve* Wilkinsburg cops?! Where was the interagency agreement?"

"You signed it on day one," I said, barely above a whisper.

"What did you say, *Lieutenant*?"

"You. Signed. It. On. Day. One. Sir. When you granted me and Marco tactical command and *complete autonomy* of this unit, completely free from bureaucracy and red tape of the rest of the department. *Especially* considering the weapons used in the murders may have been obtained by a fellow cop."

"That's the defense angle you're gonna run with for killing a decorated sergeant of twenty years' service and a civilian? You two fucking idiots are suspended for two weeks, with pay, pending the coroner's complete report on *all* bodies at the scene."

"Kenny, that is bullshit. It was a clean operation."

"Marco, shut the fuck up. *Two weeks*, or you'll both be in the fucking gun cage, cleaning SWAT weapons. Give your whole continuity over to Snopes in the next thirty minutes. He's acting team commander. And the next time you want to do some Johnny Rambo sniper shit on the fly, and you don't bring the chief of Internal Affairs in to sign off on it—who happens to be the senior shooter and master sniper instructor of the department—I will arrest you both for dereliction of duty. Get the fuck out of here."

Francine came back in after Kenny slammed the door and gave me a gentle hug and kiss on the cheek. "Let's do dinner with Frank sometime?"

I smiled and nodded.

Brady leaned in and hugged me, head-to-head, the way Samoans and Hawaiians do.

"Brother, Kenny's all noise. I wouldn't have done a thing differently. And about the master-shooter shit, I may be the better shot, but *you're* the better hunter. You would have stayed on that target until hell froze over." That was high praise considering what Brady had been through.

Marco and I looked at each other as he unholstered his gun and set both that and his badge on the table. I did the same with mine in turn, sat down as Marco left, and faced Mike Taradash, the only one left in the room. The DA leveled a gaze at me for a long time, then opened his briefcase and carefully placed both our pistols and badges inside, as if he were handling cremains on a funeral detail. He snapped the case shut, reached into his blazer, and produced two cigars.

I lit his, then mine, and we said nothing for a bit, tapping our ashes into a crumpled Coke can. With the clouds of smoke filling the space, it soon had the feel of a sweat lodge.

His eyes narrowed at me through the veil of smoke.

"You know, Tom, sometimes in this line of work, once in a blue moon, you get to take out some true fucking monsters. I am talking the stuff of straight-up nightmares. So, the car comes around the corner—that's five seconds. The undercover triggers the tire spikes. That's three seconds. The car crashes, ten seconds later the shooters open fire for twenty seconds, and you and Marco engage the targets and make your first kill shots in seven seconds, felling three instantly. You go from nothing happening to scene secured and four perps down in forty-five seconds, Tom, and you're sitting here feeling sorry for yourself? You took four cold-blooded dealers and murderers off the street, one and a half million in blood money, $576,000 in heroin. All of that done in forty-five seconds, Tom."

I couldn't look this man—whom I respected more than my dad—in the eye, because of how ashamed I felt that evening.

"You went up against some vicious fucks tonight. And you made it out the other end. And those fuckers are in the ground." He studied the plastic evidence bag on the table, and my cell phone screen that still had Esther Stafford's profile on it.

Then he got up, grabbed his briefcase and the evidence bag, and shook my hand.

"There's a horrible price sometimes for going toe to toe with evil, Tom. You won last night, but . . . you don't always walk away from a win without a scratch. I think Esther Stafford and her friends did some stupid stuff a lot of college kids do and got carried away, and I'm not gonna gloss it over with some 'wrong place, wrong time' clichés. But I think if there is an afterlife, her soul is fucking laughing her ass off at those dead motherfuckers that she took with her.

"And whatever her sins were last night, I hope to God she is at peace and smiling down, because, fuck, Tom, that poor girl has *earned* her wings. I'm not even going to humor you with any smoke up your ass or warm milk or bedtime stories about Sergeant Hamilton. He did his fucking job tonight and saved you and Marco. I don't care what was said or what happened before that car came up shooting."

He motioned to his briefcase. "It won't be two weeks. I will talk to Kenny. More like ninety-six hours. And, Tom, you were a little too rough on the dad. Yeah, she was in the car, but she wasn't the one behind the wheel. That guy feels just as helpless as you do right about now. At the end of the day, all the bullshit swept out of the room, it still boils down, in his eyes, that the call you made subsequently took his daughter's life. But . . . it's the call I would have made as well."

Finally, I looked him in the eye. "Thank you, sir."

"Tom, for the millionth time, it's Mike." The door closed.

■ ■ ■

When I climbed the steps back up to the apartments two days after the operation had ended and the shooting had occurred, it was past midnight. The night I handed my files off to Snopes, I had slept in my office despite being suspended; there was a lot of stuff to take care of.

I don't know what magic Franny and the DA's office worked, but the settlement was signed before the girl's funeral and Hamilton's memorial service were over. The shootings made the news, of course, but the details of the crash did not. That made me want to snort pills and shoot up even more. Hamilton had a male partner who worked at a law firm in Greensburg. I didn't have the guts to find out his name. Kenny and Marco called on him. Marco took Inez. There was a lot of crying.

I went into the guest fighter apartment with a bottle of Oxy and a bottle of gin and stayed there for about eighteen hours.

When I came to, I took a long shower and changed, then cleaned up the place, throwing out the detritus of my drinking binge and throwing the sheets in the wash hamper, reflecting that despite pills and booze, I had actually gotten restful REM sleep there.

I expected to find the door to my place locked. It was open. I cautiously stepped in. She was sitting up on the couch, the end-table lamp turned on. Ostensibly reading a book, but she looked up several times as I laid my stuff on the counter, set my cuffs and wallet down, and reached for a mug. She said nothing as I put two cubes of ice in the mug and four fingers of scotch. Charley, the little fucking turncoat, was happily stretched across the remainder of the couch, his head tucked in her lap, and she absently petted his ears as she read. Charley steered one eye toward me as if to say, "I like it this way. *You* fucking move out."

"I'm sorry I'm still here. I'll stay on the couch if you want me to."

"I've got tomorrow off. I'll clean out the third room; that will open up the second one for you."

"I thought I'd stay. I saw what happened on the news. I knew that was your team. I was worried about you when you didn't come home." She managed a sarcastic laugh at nobody in particular, staring off absently at my bookshelves, the wall, the dining table. "Your mother, on the other hand, is some trooper. I went downstairs, and she had the same news running on the TV at her desk. I was practically bawling. She never stopped balancing the ledger. Didn't even look up at me, except to tell me when dinner would be ready."

She peered over her book at me, a dozy smile and slight dimples, arched eyebrows. I tried to read the mood of the room. She looked me over from head to toe.

Finally, she spoke. "I'm glad to see there aren't any more holes in you than the last time you went out the door."

Now it was my turn to laugh. "I'm glad to still see you in my apartment."

"Are we going to talk like grown-ups, or are we going to keep dancing around the subject?"

"Neither of us were really acting like grown-ups at all that entire last day."

She closed the book. "I was out of line. I'm sorry for throwing myself at you. But you were mean to me, too."

"Yeah."

"I know there's more that's good to you than there is whatever you don't like about yourself."

"How do you figure?"

"If you were a complete bastard as you make yourself out to be, you would have left me with the ambulance. Matter of fact, you wouldn't have ever knocked on my door."

"Maybe you're right."

"Tommy, can you go one night? Without pills or booze?"

I looked into my mug. "I don't know." It was probably the most honest thing I had said to a woman in three years.

She shooed Charley off the couch. "Come sit next to me."

"I'm fine over here."

"Come sit next to me, Tamas." The old-country name. She must have heard it from my mother. The name evoked the quiet, resilient pride and the love of my dead grandfather, and I pretended that tears weren't about to sting my eyes again for the third time in two days.

"Why?"

"Because I'm asking you to."

I sat down, and she curled against my chest. I inhaled the smell of her hair and skin and soap, ran my fingers through her amber-reddish curls, and a bitter sob choked up inside of me.

"Are you hurting? Am I leaning on your scar?"

"I'm okay."

"I liked waking up in your arms."

I said nothing.

"I'm not going to pretend that I'm not confused. A month ago, I was married. As messed up as it was, it had become a routine. Now I have no idea where he is. I just know he left. And what he did to me . . . What do you get out of having me around here?"

"I know you're safe. I know you like the quiet and that nobody bothers you. I figured I owed you that much. I didn't know he'd hit you so badly. There." My hand touched the waistband of her pajamas, the first time since that horrible night I had put my hand there. Well, not quite there, just along the folds where her pants met her shirt. I felt her jump, but then she clasped a hand over mine. What the hell was the matter with me, nearly crying for the miscarriage of another man's baby, that he had made happen?

"Why don't you let someone make you feel just as safe?" She pulled away from me and stared into my eyes, held a gaze for about a minute of eternity, then nestled her head against my chest.

"How about . . . we just stay like this for a little bit?" I asked.

She chuckled. "I don't want to move."

■ ■ ■

I got up after she had finally dozed off next to me. I thought of carrying her back into the bedroom, but she was sleeping so soundly I didn't want to wake her. I grabbed some blankets from the other room and gently tucked her in right there. Then I sat on the floor, and I don't know what the hell brought it out of my guts, but I quietly started to weep. I knew I was falling in love with her.

I let Charley out to the freedom of the gym and almost had a burst of energy to start clearing out the third apartment, but I peered over to where she was sleeping, verified she was out for the night, and walked softly to the bathroom.

I knew she would be watching the pills, and I knew she would be watching the booze. I didn't want to disappoint her, but I didn't want to just stop. And I didn't want to make her cry anymore. I lifted up the cover to the toilet tank—and taped to the lid were twenty injectable cartridges of meperidine hydrochloride, a.k.a. Demerol. I broke off two ampoules. I picked out a decent vein near my ankle. I tried not to think about the cyclops, bloodied, blown-off face of Esther Stafford that flashed at me for a half second when I looked up in the mirror. I felt a shudder, then I plunged another needle, this one behind my kneecap.

When I was done, I bent back the needles and buried them in the bottom of the trash can. *Yeah, some detective.* I turned off the light and in a moment of weakness bent down and gently kissed her forehead. She didn't stir. I went back to mine and the kids' room and felt the first waves wash over me.

CHAPTER 7

While Marco and I waited on Mike Taradash to press Kenny to reinstate us, I used some of the downtime to hang out with my kids. One day, I took them shopping. I didn't expect my eight-year-old to give me a dressing-down as if he were a psychoanalyst.

"Daddy?"

"Yeah, TJ?"

"Who's the lady living at your place at Great-Grandpa's gym?"

"That's Miss Claire."

"Mommy tells Daddy Allan she's living there for free."

"That's what Mommy says, huh?"

"Why's Miss Claire living at Nana's gym?"

"Well, sometimes we get in trouble, and we're lucky we have friends to help us out. Miss Claire is my friend, and I wanted to help her out."

"Is she going to marry you?"

"No, it's not like that, buddy."

"What happened to all Miss Claire's friends?"

"Sometimes people aren't good friends when you need them the most. Sometimes you're so sad about what got you to where you are that you're embarrassed to ask them for help."

"Mommy says she's paying for it on her back. What's that mean?"

"Never mind what that means. Pick out a toy."

"Daddy Allan told her she didn't know shit."

"*Poop*, Thomas Junior." I tousled his hair.

"Daddy Allan told her she didn't know shit-poop."

"Daddy Allan's a good guy. He loves you just as much as I do. Don't get between him and your mom in an argument. Even if he is right."

"Daddy Allan says you are being a good person. He said you have . . . read-em-ink values."

"Redeeming." I laughed.

"What's a read-em-ink value?"

"Well, you know your sister? You don't like it when Allison takes your toys."

"Nope."

"But what would you do if some kid on your street took her toys? Or her bear? Or was mean to her puppy?"

"I'd kick his butt."

"No, 'cause then you're no better than him. But you'd protect your sister; you'd tell Mommy to talk to his mommy and try to make things right, right?"

"Yep."

"That's a redeeming value. Even if you don't like something about Allison, you love her and you still take care of her."

"Did you not have enough read-em-ink values when you were with Mommy?"

"No, pal, I sure didn't."

"Daddy, if you're in trouble, I'll be your friend if you need one."

"You think I'm in trouble, pal?"

"It seems like all grown-ups are."

"How can you tell? You're eight." I smiled. "Buddy, Mommy and I aren't together because sometimes adults just stop loving each other. It's got nothing to do with trouble."

"Mommy told Daddy Allan that Miss Claire would be nothing but trouble for you."

"Well, my troubles aren't your mommy's troubles anymore."

"Daddy?"

"Yeah, pal?"

"Miss Claire seems really sad. She smiled to us when we saw her, but her eyes weren't happy."

"That's 'cause Miss Claire lost her baby about a month ago. You don't make her sad, but maybe she's still sad when she sees children."

"How old was her baby?"

"It was still in her tummy."

"What happened to him?"

"Trouble, pal. Trouble." I peered into the front of the shopping carriage. My four-year-old daughter was sleeping peacefully next to a teddy bear that dominated the rest of the space in the cart.

"I think Allison liked her bear, Daddy."

"Yep."

"Will you always live in Papa Mickey's gym, Daddy?"

"Probably not. Why? You want a bigger place when you guys visit? Somewhere that doesn't smell like a gym and is full of noisy guys beating each other up?"

"Yeah!"

"Well, Daddy does too. Daddy got put on some real important work. When I'm done with it, maybe I can look for a house closer to you guys."

"Daddy, do you love Miss Claire?"

"I only know her a little bit, pal. It takes a long time to love someone."

"When did you know you loved me and Allison?"

"As soon as I knew you were in your mommy's tummy."

He looked thoughtful. "Who protects you, Daddy?"

"I don't know, pal. You want the job?"

He shrugged and exhaled audibly. "If Mommy couldn't keep you out of trouble, how would I know what to do?"

"How old are you again, Thomas?"

"Eight years, six months, five days. Come on, Daddy, you were there."

"You're eight and a half?"

"Yes."

"Then pick out a toy and quit acting forty."

■ ■ ■

Blackness.

Pain.

Then . . .

Garbage. Disgusting, foul, puke- and shit-smelling garbage everywhere around me.

I didn't know how long I had been knocked out. A thirty-gallon steel trash can toppled over as I rolled to my side. The lid to the same steel trash can on top of my face led me to surmise my attacker had used it to render a friendly love tap to my head as I pursued him through the back alley behind . . . Where was I?

Little E's jazz club. The fuck?

In my pocket I felt a familiar, blocklike totem, like a heavy wallet. My gold detective shield. *That's right. We've been reinstated.*

Marco and I were back on duty. Mike Taradash had been true to his word, and then some; within forty-eight hours of Kenny's decree, Marco and I had our guns and badges back, but we had official reprimands that would go into our permanent jackets if we so much as sneezed wrong in Kenny's direction.

Fuck, how hard was I hit? Why am I back at the jazz club?

It slowly came to me. Marco and I were supposed to interview the staff who had been on duty the night of the hit because a few of them never came back after the shooting. Our task-force guys had rounded up some of the missing employees. One of them had done a runner out the back. I reached for my waist; it betrayed me with an empty holster.

Where is my backup?

Then I heard three rapid shots in succession. *BLAM. BLAM. BLAM.*

Oh shit.

Detective Sergeant Snopes came back to me, bent down, and handed me back my pistol.

"You're slipping."

"Is he dead?"

"Marco took him out—one at his kneecap, one in the upper thigh, one miss. Not bad for a sprinting target. Or considering the shooter has one bum arm. Missed the femoral artery, though, so your body count isn't any higher, which will keep you in Sir Kenneth's good graces."

"Aw, fuck, my head is splitting."

"You know, Kenny is probably going to bury you and Marco under the courthouse. Losing your gun the first week after you get it back? Not a good look at all, boss."

"So, what do we say justified the shooting?"

"Oh, don't get me wrong; he had more than *one* gun on him. Yours just wasn't the one he had in his hands."

I sat there, dumbfounded. "We searched everyone in the interviews."

"Duh, Columbo, how hard did he ring that bell of yours? He probably had it hidden under that garbage can he smashed you with and grabbed it coming out, ambushing you when you came out the door. Then he took your gun to make sure you couldn't come after him."

"No civilians nearby?"

"No. You Spensers are blessed that you're lucky versus smart."

"I should go with you guys to process—"

Snopes jammed a finger in my chest. "Boss. *Go. The fuck. Home*. That's an order."

For once, logic surpassed my usual stubbornness. I did as I was told.

■ ■ ■

En route to the gym and despite my heavy protests, Marco brought me by Samantha's office at Mercy West for an authorization for a CAT scan and a basic assessment by Neuro. The neuro intern was in and out and went into the hallway with Samantha for a burst of heightened conversation. Voices steadily began to rise; I always had to giggle when I heard Samantha putting a wet-behind-the-ears doctor in his or her place. I sat listlessly annoyed in a cloth gown, and she came back into the exam room with my file.

"So, I made a few calls across town to the labs. Your bloodwork from when the district attorney's shooting team took a sample the night Sergeant Hamilton and the Stafford girl were killed came back clean, with minimal trace amounts of your prescription opiates. Everything within the realm of legality, and then some.

"Quite frankly, I'm shocked. I was betting even money it would look like a jigger shaker of Jack Daniel's with a bottle of Oxy crushed up in there. Explains why Taradash got your badge and gun back to you so quickly. And of all the ERs in all the world"—she darkened the lights, shined an exam penlight into each of my eyes, and dabbed at the cuts on my face with alcohol-soaked cotton balls—"you came into mine."

As she continued her exam, I asked, "What was that all about in the hallway?"

She turned to the wall and hit a switch. A monitor screen came to life, and within seconds the screen was divided. One side was a bird's-eye view of my skull as if the top were unscrewed like a cookie jar and you could look down into my brain. The split side was my medical biography, scrolling slowly.

The graphic side of the screen was black and white, so while it was mildly impressive that I was looking at my skull and brain, it was pretty much a dystopian moonscape with topographical lines. Then, almost imperceptibly, the intern had marked a small purple arrow pointing to a white mark no bigger than an ant sitting on the edge of a penny.

"What is that, Samantha?"

"That, Thomas, is a potential clot."

"What do you mean a clot?"

"As in stroke. Aneurysm. Death. Clot."

"You say potential."

"Due to the location, it's hazardous to try to remove it right now. It's close to the brainstem and behind your left eye."

"Is that what the best neurosurgeon in this hospital is going to say?"

"Tommy, never mind Mercy West. The best neurosurgeon at *Johns Hopkins* isn't going to go near your case. You're a recovering lymphoma patient and known substance abuser that routinely relapses and avoids chemo and other forms of treatment and has a history of verbally abusing his providers."

"What about the VA?" Brady and I had served in Bosnia as Guardsmen and deployed multiple times in the War on Terror since 9/11 with the Guard and the Reserves.

"The Pittsburgh VA has a huge neuro backlog. Nobody is going to do anything probably until—"

"It bursts."

"Thomas . . ." Her voice cracked.

"Thank you, Dr. Kerrick, for seeing me."

"Tommy, please, don't . . ."

I gave her a small hug, kissed her on the cheek, but I could not look her in the eye. "Bye, Sammy."

■ ■ ■

Charley and I were running one morning out by Schenley Park. My shoes crunched the leaves and sticks at our feet as they struck the jogging trail. Suddenly Charley yelped gleefully and accelerated until he pulled the slacked line from my hands. He sprinted two hundred yards up to where the path intersected. I soon followed him, panting and wiping snot.

When I got to where the trails cut in a T, he was leaping happily around a female runner whose pink-and-gray spandex leggings outlined an ass that could only be dubbed flawless. Then she stood up, pulled her black fleece polar cap off her head, and there in front of us—cheeks rosy with exertion and red, curly locks plastered to her damp scalp—stood Claire Hewitt. Ever since that night we'd declared a truce, we had politely avoided each other after she moved out, save for a few knocks on the door for a household item she hadn't yet bought, or a text in the middle of the night to ensure that I hadn't relapsed.

Despite my better judgment, I let her wrap her arms around me, and for the first time without drugs or booze or plain self-pity being part of the event, we kissed, and she held it for about ten seconds, spectators be damned. There was a hint of toothpaste in her mouth as her tongue glided over my teeth.

We broke apart at the same time, slightly amused and surprised at the other for having kept it going.

"I, well, uh . . ." I stood speechless.

"I've missed you, you jerk." She dug a fist in the middle of my solar plexus, playfully. Her other hand and arm kept a bear-hug wrap on me.

"I'm the jerk? I'm not the one who—"

"No, for that I am the jerk. *You're* the jerk for avoiding me for three weeks when I've done everything I can to come up with reasons to talk to you."

"Why didn't you just knock?"

"Why didn't *you*?"

"Aw, fuck, I don't know, Claire."

"I've missed you, Thomas."

"I know. I . . . missed you too."

"Shouldn't you be at work? What are you doing on my running trail?"

"More like what are *you* doing on *my* running trail? I usually do this same trail from 5:30 to 6:15 every morning. Marco and I did a double yesterday. I got a late start this morning."

She tightened her laces, stood up, and cupped my face for a soft farewell kiss. Then it grew to be twice as wonderful as the "hello" kiss. When I started to get slightly handsy and rest my palms where her fleece jersey touched the top of her gluteal muscles, she giggled and broke away from me, blushing, face flushed—or stirred. She buried her head in my neck where it met my collarbone as she squeezed me in a hug goodbye and then broke that magnificent embrace. Somewhere in my brain, I crash-landed back from the stars to earth.

"Well then, you should get a late start more often. It means I get to see you."

"Claire, I . . . what are you doing tonight?"

"Hopefully spending it with you. You know where I live! The door's open!" she shouted, smiling happily as she loped about ten or fifteen paces away. She glanced over her shoulder and flashed that captivating smile; then, like a rabbit on the run, she was off.

I stood there a bit longer, still catching my breath and watching her. When she was over the trail and out of sight, Charley and I doubled back. I unclipped his lead and let him bolt on ahead, knowing he wouldn't stop until he got to the door at Mickey's gym.

■ ■ ■

When I got back to the gym that night, I smelled the slightly nauseating, enamel odor of fresh paint from next door to my apartment. I ambled down the hall and knocked on the doorframe. She was wearing a T-shirt and old sweatpants, both spackled in whites and pastels from her paintbrush. She was barely five feet two, and the shirt hung like a dress on her, PITTSBURGH POLICE SWAT SNIPER emblazoned in gold on black. One of mine or Brady's. She had potpourri out to attempt to neutralize the smell of the paint, and soft jazz played from a radio on the floor. She was all smiles. She went to give me a hug, stopped herself, and contorted so that only her lips brushed mine without getting any paint on my suit.

"Spenser family does an early spring cleaning, and you get all the goodies."

"I figured I might as well make it feel like home for as long as I'm staying. Your brothers said I could paint. The girls were here all day, brought me a lot of stuff: some mix-and-match bedding, lots of clothes, stuff to decorate with, some drapes. Lots of food. I could feed an army. I only went to the storage locker to get my violin, my flute, some paperwork and photo albums, CDs, stuff like that. I'll probably donate a lot of my old stuff in there. Sell some of my nicer handbags on eBay maybe. I'm quite embarrassed to say it, but most of your sisters-in-law's hand-me-downs are nicer than anything I had with Jakey-boy. Don't they usually seize all of that stuff anyway? What kind of drug deal did you work with the sheriff when he posted notice?"

"I told him I wouldn't arrest his son for selling pot behind West Mifflin Junior High."

She broke into giggles. "What?"

"Oh, he's not a major player. Nickel-and-dime shit. By the time whoever gets it to him, it's so cut and stomped to shit it's mostly tobacco leaves and pencil shavings anyway. There's more weed in the potpourri you have there. Ha. I think he just does it to piss off his dad. We had him on our books for a month, and any good attorney could get him off with maybe a week in Shuman." Shuman was the juvenile detention center in Pittsburgh.

"So, what did you have in mind tonight?"

"You want to grab dinner? Like regular dinner, before you break into that stuff tomorrow and get about three thousand calories of Sarah Spenser's infamous casseroles?"

She giggled. "Are you asking me for dinner, or on a date?"

"What's the difference?"

"If it's dinner, I'll just put on jeans, and we can grab Japanese takeout up the block. If it's a date, I'll get a shower, put on a dress, and you're taking me somewhere we have to keep that tie on you. County just sent me some paperwork, and I want to celebrate! I'm officially single!"

"I thought it takes ninety days for a divorce in Allegheny County."

"I filed under abandonment. Plus, he's got a felony warrant. He's facing jail time if they ever catch up with him. The assault itself constitutes intolerable cruelty. Jumping bail and heading to Seattle and leaving me with the bank mess with the house is all, according to my attorney, constructive abandonment." She shook her head. "I don't get it. Why Seattle? I mean, I don't miss him *at all*, but if he wanted work on the docks, he could have gone to Baltimore or Connecticut or Jersey and gotten work in the shipyards. Hell, two hours up to Erie."

"Those are all places a Pitt cop can go on a couple days' off-duty drive and ask around. He knows nobody's going thirty-three hundred miles to hunt down a wife beater. Unless he just told his brother to feed me a line of bullshit, but the Hewitt family don't strike me as particularly crafty or original. He probably sold the car straight for cash. His brother has a little bit of savings, say he fronts him two grand. Maybe he gets four for the car from a chop shop if it's worth fourteen. So now he has six grand.

"You get out to a town like Seattle or the more ethnically diverse Tacoma, day labor for a White man speaking English is everywhere. And most places don't ask for social security. Get on the truck or the ship at 7 a.m., load and offload all day, do a Fred

Flintstone at 5:30, and draw your pay at the exit. He knows—no offense—he knows he hasn't done anything a bail bondsman is going to chase him across the country for. After a year or so, he calls his defense lawyer back here and they plead to knock it back from aggravated assault to simple assault plus jumping bail for a first-time offender. He does thirty days at the county correctional farm with a misdemeanor record. Got to love American justice."

I felt sorry for giving her a straight answer. I seemed to have knocked the wind out of her sails. She sank into a chair at the little table that had up until recently been where Kenny Spenser sat his beer in his game room.

"Tell you what," I said. "We do a rain check on the date. You keep painting away, I get the takeout, you come down the hall in an hour, and we will eat where the paint isn't killing our brain cells."

She managed a pensive, forced smile, and what my son said about her sad eyes flashed through my head. She nodded. "Okay. See ya at your place in about an hour."

"'Kay."

"Tom," she said.

I turned around. She held out a small roll of cash.

"What's this for?" I asked.

"Call it what you want. Protection money, rent, room and board, the welcome wagon from the girls, late-night talks, and grateful appreciation. I know you're not going to keep it, so divide it up between your mom and your sisters-in-law. I cannot thank them enough."

"Claire, hang on to it. The faster you get money, the sooner you can get a place of your own."

"Tom, I'm not going to be a charity case. I'm happier living here than I would be in some rattrap fourth-floor walkup in Wilkinsburg, which is all I could afford right now, where I'd have to worry about getting raped on my way back from the grocery store."

"My mom will likely give it to the church."

"I thought she was Jewish."

"She is, but my dad is Catholic. It's confusing, I know. Mom was Orthodox until she married my dad. Plus, all the Spenser boys went to Central Catholic in Pittsburgh. Kenny converted when he married his wife. Brady's not much for organized religion. Christmastime is fun: the kids get a slew of presents between Hanukkah and Christmas day. Mom doesn't take the wafer at church, but every day before she makes breakfast for the boys here, she goes to early Mass at St. Luke's and prays for my dad's soul."

"Why?"

"Who else will?"

CHAPTER 8

The sign said TERIYAKI BOWL in bold letters, and the marquee underneath said CHINESE FOOD 2 GO, but the restaurant seemed to encompass everything from Thai fried rice to Vietnamese pho to Japanese sushi. I grabbed enough sushi and pho for two and came back to the apartment and took a quick shower. I heard her down the hall, singing off-key and talking to Charley. It made me smile and daydream for a moment.

On my iPod, Norah Jones serenaded the room from her second album while I got ready and realized I hadn't prepared for a proper "first date" in over nine years. Meeting women at a bar, bringing them back to fuck a few times, and never calling them again did not count as "dating."

I tried not to think about the ampoules under the lid of the toilet tank and how badly I wanted one. Ever since my crash, I had returned to running three miles before work every day, an hour-long workout sparring at the gym, and I cut myself off after a shot and a beer.

I checked out my scar in the mirror and was impressed with my "nurse's" work. After her emergency first aid, the incision had healed up nicely. I palpated along the diaphragm and felt some hardness but not the prison of pain I was in three weeks ago.

After the case, I thought. *After the case, take a month of medical, go under the kryptonite, and get this out of your system.*

As one of her last acts as a roommate, Claire had gone down to the drugstore and gotten those pill boxes that you load by the week. Apparently, they had them by the month as well. She had put one pill of Percocet in each square for days one through thirty-one and superglued each one shut afterward. She did this for both containers. She left both on the kitchen table with a sticky note that said GOOD LUCK with a smiley face. Next to that, she had left a Sam's Club–size bottle of ibuprofen. With a bow on top.

I opted for my old academy track sweats, which hung rather loose on me these days, worrying my mother. At five minutes to the hour, I put the pho in the microwave and reheated it. Precisely fifty-nine minutes after I had left her place, Claire leaned in the doorway. Blue jeans, black turtleneck, red hair held back with a headband and spilling on her shoulders, with her trademark tiny bit of makeup. Almost at once, I felt apologetic at being in sweatpants and not taking her out. She looked spectacular. More importantly, she looked happy.

"You look cozy," she said.

"Mmm. So do you." We embraced and kissed in a gentler version of that morning's meeting on the trail and held it for a few delightful moments before she broke away again, turning her eyes downward. I didn't miss that slight blush in her cheeks. Her eyes betrayed her as she peeked back up.

"I brought white wine. Actually, Mandy and Sarah brought wine." She smiled. "I figured the options you had here were Gatorade, Red Bull, and scotch."

"And Iron City Beer."

"Couch or table?"

"It's sushi."

"Couch then."

As we ate, I tried not to notice her perfume on the air, or how strands of her hair fell across her face. I tried not to notice how lovely her face was without the bruising of Jake Hewitt's handiwork, the way she laughed, and how she dug the toes of her socked feet between the upholstery backing and the couch cushion as we talked and sipped wine. I tried not to admit I was falling for her.

After we were done and full, she snatched up a tiny paper bag of fortune cookies from the coffee table. She grinned and handed it to me. "Host picks first."

"Hmm." I made a big to-do of opening the wrapper, breaking the cookie, and gazing intently at the miniature slip of paper inside. "An empty bed and whacking off make your romantic life complete."

She elbowed me forcefully. "What's it really say, goofball?"

"Friendship makes the world's poorest person rich. Yours?"

"Ha! We got a double fortune. Mine says the same thing."

I mockingly raised my beer can. "To friendship."

She leaned over and squeezed my hand. "To friendship."

Norah Jones had depleted her playlist, and a five-second count hung on the air. I quickly brushed her lips with mine. She smiled like she was about to whisper a secret to her best friend, then set down her wineglass and crawled onto me. We fell back into that relaxed position we'd shared a few weeks before, her leaning her head on my chest. The throb in my scar was almost gone. She kissed me, a long and loving kiss, and the wine on her tongue threw on long-forgotten switches inside my brain. We kissed like this for about five more minutes, until my hand shamelessly cupped her over her bra, under her sweater. She gently but firmly pulled my hand away and interlaced her fingers in mine.

"Easy, tiger. We have all the time in the world."

"Funny, you didn't want to hear that a few weeks ago."

"Oh, but you were so right. I needed this more. Just this—just being in your arms."

Both of us fell back into our embrace, parting only to breathe and kiss again.

We remained clothed, but somehow that was more intimate than the craziness of a few weeks before. We stayed in each other's arms for a great length of time after we'd stopped kissing.

I held her against me, blinking away tears I couldn't explain. Stress, exhaustion, tension, or maybe just gratitude that she was still in my arms. I looked around at the drab walls of the studio.

"Now I saw how cozy you made your place, I wish you were still living on this side."

"Mmm." She hugged me again, sat up to pour some more wine, sipped her glass, put it back down, and squirmed even closer on my chest. "We could always knock out the wall," she joked.

"Think that would fuck with the plumbing? Your bathroom is on the other side of my kitchen. I don't want to watch you drop a deuce while I'm making my coffee in the morning."

"*Drop a deuce?*" She released a long, hearty peal of amusement.

I stood, gently moving out of her grasp—*Please, God, I don't ever want to leave*—and walked over to the breakfast counter. Reaching up to the cabinet above the stove for the bottle I had come to consider mine and Marco's, I took a long pull and capped the bottle again. "Maybe, if it's not too much trouble, you could paint in here. It's exactly the same as before Papa Mickey passed. Be nice to have it brighter. Feel more relaxed. TJ made a comment about the place when I had them the other day. Nothing mean or anything, but let's be honest: it's simply Great-Grandpa's old apartment with some kiddy beds in it."

She sipped her wine and walked over to the wall. "You should keep the pictures up, though. I like looking at them when I'm over here. Is that the kids' mom? I recognize her from the hospital. She's so pretty here." She pointed to a picture—a little over eight years old but specially computerized and tinted to look antique—of a near Madonna-like Samantha glowing while holding a newborn Thomas Francis Spenser Jr. This wasn't the postwar delivery-room shot; this was maybe a week after we took them home, in a photographer's studio.

"So I am told. The icing doesn't tell you how the cake is on the inside."

"Don't be a jerk. That's your kids' mom. You had to have fallen in love with something good about her."

"I think I like Claire the drug counselor better than Claire the armchair psychiatrist." I walked back over to the couch and reclined, motioning her to rejoin me.

She sat back down and resumed her cuddling position. "And Claire the drunken stripper?"

I chuckled despite the memory of that awful evening. "Maybe Claire the stripper skipping the booze and sticking to orange soda might work."

"Tom?"

"Mmm."

"How come you never ask what happened, or how it got so bad, with me and Jake?"

"None of my business."

"Yet here I am, one day divorced and curled up on your couch."

"No matter what happened, nothing short of your wife trying to murder you justifies hitting a woman. And I am talking gun pointed at your head with her finger on the trigger."

As tight as she was hugging me, she managed to squeeze me even stronger. "Tom?"

"Yes?"

"Why did you bring me here after the hospital?"

"Figured it beat a low-rent apartment in a ghetto somewhere or the shelter."

"But you're a narcotics cop. And you brought a domestic violence victim into your home. You knew nothing about me."

"There was nothing for you to rob from me. Nobody could

hurt me any more than I had already been hurt. I figured what was the harm in giving a good woman a place to stay?"

"I don't feel like a good woman."

"You are, darlin'," I said, pronouncing with endearment with an affected Southern twang as I kissed her forehead

"I think you're a good man, Tom. Maybe I overstepped the line with the way I dropped the hammer on you, but I care a lot about you. I know you didn't ask my opinion. And you didn't ask me to take care of you. But I couldn't turn my back on you any more than . . ."

Any more than I could leave her at the shelter.

"There's a difference, though. I voluntarily brought my pains on me. The booze, the pills. You didn't stand in front of your ex and ask to be a punching bag."

"What do you have, Tom? Cancer? Leukemia? What did you get surgery for?"

"I've struggled with Hodgkin's Lymphoma for years. I guess I thought it was in remission. I mean, I was for a long time. Week that I met you, Doc says I'm in stage two."

"Can it be treated?"

"Yeah."

"Can it go away again?"

"Not without me taking a lot of time away from work. And I cannot do it just yet. Maybe in four or five months."

"You could die in four or five months."

"That's a bit dramatic. I do have *some* time."

"Don't cover it up with the work. Your ex-wife and her husband must make good money. They don't need your checks that badly. I'm sure she'd rather see the kids have a healthy father."

"Okay, maybe I'm lying. Maybe it's not about the money. Maybe I'm scared."

"Of what?"

"That if I stop the job, maybe I'll die a lot faster. I don't have much else to keep me going besides that and the kids."

"Tom?"

"Yeah?"

"Do you want to spend the night? With me, at my place? I've got a big queen-size bed over there, and last night I just thought of you and TJ's bunk beds. And your daughter's little toddler bed."

I felt her body twinge. Panic, grief, memory of a month ago, when the baby she never knew was inside her. *Fuck.*

"A sleepover? Isn't it a little soon for you?"

"Tom, I spent years in a prison of a marital bed. I feel safe with you. I'm going to go back to my place. I'll leave the door unlocked. You want to see me, you come in."

She lifted her head and looked into my eyes, and they were almost as serious as during the breakfast-table lecture of a few weeks ago. Or that drunken rage of hers the following evening.

"I would rather hold you all night, feeling sexually awkward and frustrated, and know you're safe and not popping pills and drinking."

"I don't need a babysitter." I paused. "I-I didn't mean that shitty."

"I think you need *something*, Tommy."

"Go get ready for bed. I'll come when I'm ready. Is that a good enough answer for now?"

She kissed my cheek and stood up. "It's an honest answer, at least. If I see you, I see you. If not, sweet dreams." She smiled over her shoulder—the same dazzling grin from the running trail—one last time before she gently pulled the door shut.

Charley, who had been oddly accommodating the whole evening, looked at me.

"What do you think there, Charley-boy?" I brushed my teeth, let Charley out, and flipped up the toilet tank lid in the bathroom.

I didn't want to take one of the ampoules, and if I went to her place, I wouldn't have the balls to smuggle one over there. If I took it beforehand, maybe there were enough years of Catholic-school guilt in me not to go over at all. But more than I wanted the waves of the Demerol high tide, I wanted the nape of her neck and the feel of her arms around me. Replace one addiction with another.

If only we weren't so damaged. Then we could just fuck our aggressions out.

Sleeping next to her seemed more complicated than regular full-court sex, and either option in her bed was just as dangerous as the Demerol. Being a believer that the more fun sin was the one I hadn't tried yet, I gave in and went over there without a Demerol cocktail. The jazz music was back on; it might have been white noise to cover the hum of the basement generator that kicked on at 2:30 in the morning, just as the scented candle was to drown out the smell of paint and not necessarily to set a scene for seduction. But if I pulled back the sheets and she was in a negligee, I was folding my cards at that point and giving into the need.

I latched the door and crept into her bedroom. She was dressed comfortably in one of my old sweatshirts but not any less appealing for it. I tiptoed, hoping I would not scare the shit out of her by climbing in. Suddenly she flipped on the bedside lamplight, sat up, and her face was incongruous: analytical and businesslike, almost admonishing.

"What?"

"Take off your socks."

"Huh?"

"Take off your socks. You got drawers on?"

"Huh . . . uhh, yeah."

"Drop your pajama bottoms."

"Is this what you would call female sexual empowerment?"

"No, this is called me checking you for track marks." She studied my feet, my legs, did a bottom-to-top sweep like a jumpmaster doing pre-inspection on a paratrooper's rig. With no finesse or gentleness or coyness, she brought back the elastic waistband of my trunks and looked down there as well. When I passed her inspection, she drew my pants back up. Much more gently, she lifted up the front and back of my shirt, tracing old scars and two bullet holes from my rookie-patrolman days. Backing Kenny up on a robbery call—Metro SWAT back then. It had been ninety-nine degrees in July, and I wasn't wearing the hard plate in my tactical vest. Two rounds through and through the side, barely missing my left lung.

She traced gently over the two pucker marks of the exit wounds—or as Samantha had called them, "the two extra assholes" that made me a triple-degree asshole.

"Are you satisfied, music professor?"

"If you didn't shoot between your toes or your ankle, where did you do it?"

"I didn't . . . I didn't shoot up tonight."

"Good. Because I wasn't going to let you stay here if you did it and then went ahead and lied to me about it."

"How long have you known?"

"I found your dumped needles the morning after we'd made up from the fight, when I moved out. I knew you'd have the kids staying over, and I was making sure none of my stuff—girly stuff—was in your place. Didn't want to cause trouble with your ex. I expected *an* empty needle, not eighteen full ones. What would keep your son from lifting the lid?"

"I'm sorry, Claire." I really was. Tears of shame pooled at the corners of my eyes. Not at getting caught but at the emotional pain I'd caused by making her worry. Then my tears began in earnest, knowing I had disappointed her.

"How many are left in your stash?"

I mumbled.

"How many?"

"Sixte— Fourteen."

"So, if I go back there with you and lift the lid, there would be fourteen full needles."

"Yes. I swear to God. On my kids, even. That's all there is other than what you already know."

She sat down and patted the bed.

"You still want me next to you?"

"It was more important that you didn't lie to me."

"What was with all the silliness with the Percocet then?"

"I thought maybe it would be a funny way of guilting you into telling me about the stash. Or getting rid of it."

"Okay. Does that mean you want me to stay?"

"Yes. Just quit thinking that because I'm not a cop or a doctor, I'm some sort of idiot." She curled back facing the wall. I nestled in beside her as the "big spoon."

"Tommy. I'm going to ask you one more thing. Tomorrow night, I want you to leave your door open. I'll leave mine open. Before the count on those needles drops any further, you come over here and tell me when you're hurting. If being next to me doesn't make it any better, then *I* will get the needle and *I* will shoot you up."

"Why would you do that?"

"I'm hoping that if I let you know you're not alone in this, then maybe you will think before you act."

"Why are you doing this?"

"Why did you bring me here?"

"Same thing you just said to me. To let you know you're not alone."

She rolled over, wrapped her arms around me, and held a kiss to my mouth, chaste at first, then long and tender. Before we crossed into making the night any weirder, she gently broke away and put herself back against the spot on my chest that was slowly becoming her permanent headrest. Her red curls spilled over my chest, and she embraced me with a strength I didn't know she had. She lifted her head and looked me straight in the eyes with an intensity I hadn't recognized before. With her right index finger, she poked my breastbone, emphasizing her point.

"Get that through your head." She lay there a long time, quietly. "You're not alone, Tommy."

■ ■ ■

A thudding came from the door. *What the hell time is it? Who the fuck is in the building?*

My watch said 4:15. *Shit.* No robber was going to knock. So that meant something was wrong: one of my brothers, or Marco—or Mom! A ball of panic wrapped around my heart as I rushed to the door. It was Escardo.

"Fuck, boss, when you are the *director* of a new task force, you're *supposed* to keep your phone on you. I called you like thirty times."

Shit. I'd left the cell in my apartment.

"What's up?"

"What's up is I'm fucking worried about you and I thought you were dead."

I hurried back inside Claire's studio and gave her a quick kiss as she rolled over and groaned at having been woken in the wee hours of the morning.

Marco and I went next door.

My partner's Latino tendency for histrionics and drama got the better of him, and he started out with his traditional blend of guttural Spanglish cursing. I didn't quite catch it all, but it pretty much came to "Shit, I must have been sick the day at detective school when they said it's a really good fucking idea to start relationships with the victims!"

"Don't come at me with that fucking monkey language, smart-ass; these walls are thin. She can probably hear you."

"Boss, what the fuck? She is damaged fucking goods. Nothing good's going to come of all this neighborly bullshit."

"Marco, I've never pulled rank on you in the five years we've been partners. But if you don't shut the fuck up right now about shit you don't know, I swear on the Virgin of Guadalupe, I will have you walking the beat over on Liberty, writing parking tickets. You come to the apartment—my stuff's all here, my gun, my badge, my wallet, and my car is parked in front. My keys are on the fucking table. Either I've been abducted by fucking aliens, or I'm next door with her! Get a life and quit poking around in mine!"

"I know you, motherfucker! It doesn't matter what superstore of pussy could be next door; you're still a fucking degenerate junkie burnout who could get us both killed!"

I lost it. Papa Mickey's feet took position, and Frank Spenser's right hook connected with my partner's face.

It wasn't until my punch landed that I remembered the forty pounds or so I had on Marco. Blood burst from both nostrils. His lower teeth bit into his upper lip. He reeled back against Allison's toddler bed, flattening it with his weight. The cheap, flimsily molded plastic frame snapped. Charley, who'd been taking all this in from the lower bunk, shot from the bed and ran down the hall.

Marco lay there. His hand was on the thumb break of his holster. Not that he would ever go for it, not over a fistfight, and then I realized he was fumbling with his detective shield next to it.

He stood up.

"I'm your fucking partner. I'm your mate the last five years. I'm your brother since the day your family took me in. But you are bringing a shitstorm on yourself and using it as a reason to cry in your whiskey and pump painkillers in you."

I stood there. He picked himself up, ripped away a pillowcase, and held it to his face to soak up the blood. Then he took off his detective sergeant shield and slammed it on my dresser.

"Fuck you. I'm not being the helmsman for you while you steer the ship into a fucking typhoon. I'm going to the inspector tomorrow and going back to Narc. Fuck sergeant! I'll be a detective second grade, and I don't care if I ever see your sorry ass again. Adios, fuckhead."

I followed him out to the stairs. "Marco, come on, don't be a bitch. I'm sorry I hit you!"

"Fuck you, Tommy! I didn't say anything that wasn't true. I used to think it was an honor to be in the Spenser family of cops. You can keep it! It's a fucking curse. You humps fucking stab in the back anyone who gives a fuck about you, including each other! What, you think you're better than your old man because you beat up on guys and not women? You're just a fucking mirror of him, you are! And you're gonna wind up just like his ass!"

I heard the bottom door to the gym slam. I coaxed Charley out of the stairwell and loved him up, rubbing his upper flanks near his neck and telling him he was the best boy.

I sat on the steps by my dog for about twenty minutes. Charley was still trembling.

"I'm sorry, pal. Charley's a good boy. Nothing you did, buddy." Eventually he let out a small whine and went back down the hall into my living room.

Even my own frigging dog knew what I was. No big surprise that my partner did, too.

Claire's door creaked open. "Tom? I heard a fight. What happened?"

"Go back to bed, Claire."

"Come back with me."

"No, I'm up."

"Okay." She started to close the door. "You know where to find me."

■ ■ ■

Pissing-down rain was how we welcomed November in Pittsburgh. Ice cold enough to shock the hell out of you. That big wet *glop!* of raindrops targeted directly between my shirt collar and neck made me want to swear worse than someone with Tourette's.

I thought back to how freezing cold October 5 had been, and the surprise dusting of snowflakes around the week Claire had moved in. Back in the good old days, there would be six more inches of snow by now.

Nope. Just this fucking rain.

I knelt down by the bodies on Fifth Avenue. Patrolmen feebly tried to cordon off the area, but no one wanted to stand there looking in this weather anyway.

"How long have they been here?"

"About two hours, Lieutenant."

"No witnesses?"

"Drive-by, white Lexus. No plates, or they were tinted over. Car sped up to the corner, two hundred yards over there. Shooters get out. Shotgun to this one, looks like nine-mil automatic on this guy here. Car pulled up to the opposite corner right there, shooters are back in. Witnesses say it lasted all of thirty seconds. They were wearing blue coveralls, some type of white masks covering their faces."

I grabbed a pencil from the patrolman's notebook case and poked at the empty shell casings. Something told me they might match the TEC-9 brass we found at Little E's.

"How come you called the task force and not regular Homicide?" I knelt by victim number one, who lay facedown.

"Check the ID."

"Alario Washington." I slid on a pair of rubber gloves and, with as much dignity and gracefulness as I could manage on an icy, piss-rainy day in Pittsburgh, lifted up Alario's chin and turned his head to positively match his profile with the license. His eyes were rolled back, so I only saw white. I gently closed the lids.

"Half brother of Razor. The other guy is a member of his crew; first patrolman ID'd him on the scene, said he had cited him six times in the last few weeks for vagrancy, loitering."

"Which translates to dealing. Or he was a lookout."

"So, what do you make, Lieutenant?"

"Shit weather. Shit visibility. Shit conditions. Good time for a pro ambush. Won't get any prints off the brass, I'll tell you that much. Witnesses say anything about bags?"

"Bags?"

"Yeah, bags. Did they pick some off the ground, did they have some over their shoulders, did they grab anything off the bodies?"

"Sir, like I said, it was pretty quick. And most of these folks, they were lying in puddles and staring at pavement, scared shitless. The only accurate and concurrent reports were one Lexus, two shooters."

My right hand started that involuntary tremor like I'd experienced the night we hit Razor's club. Furiously, I pummeled my fist against my right leg, and all three cops glanced up from their clipboards with a mixed look of condescension and curiosity.

"Any of you guys got a smoke?"

The sergeant, who had boxed for Pitt and was a semiregular over at Mickey's, buying gifts for Mom and Repo at the holidays, looked at me over the glasses resting halfway down his nose and passed a pack of Camels. Fucking Camels. *Who smokes Camels but the Great Santini?* I took one, nodded in gratitude, and passed the carton back to him. Cupping my hands as a young rookie (the same one who had called on my place the day Marco shot out my window) obligingly hit me up with a Zippo, I took a long drag and coughed, once, twice.

"My bet is they were moving their stash and got hit. Look at this fucking day. Ten fifteen on a Tuesday morning, twenty-nine degrees, and rain, rain, rain. Did they honestly think anyone was going to fuck with them in this weather? Or that any smart G with a gun wasn't staying in, keeping warm?"

"How much do you figure the shooters got away with?"

"Well, let's say the victims were both wearing backpacks. They'd want to be mobile in case they were chased. How much do our tactical vests with all plates in weigh, Patrolman . . . Suzcyk?" I put the rookie on the spot. That's how they learn.

"I don't know, sir. Can be anywhere from twenty-five to forty pounds, depending on how you load it."

"That's right. So, you're a street kid slinging rock and pipe, and you have to go mobile with all your boss's product; you want a reasonable amount on your back to make it worth your time, but you also want something you can outrun any Pittsburgh piggy chasing you with, too."

"Okay."

"So, take the difference of your two estimates. Fifteen pounds. I think a reasonably healthy, twenty-some adult African American male, provided he doesn't have asthma or some shit, can run day and night till the sun goes down with fifteen pounds of cargo and be none the worse for wear. So, fifteen pounds of product, or fifteen pounds of cash. Or both. Otherwise, what's the payoff in taking down these two ballers in this freezing-ass weather? In the middle of downtown, no less.

"So, we get the first call at seven fifteen. People are going to be starting their commute, traffic's going to be heavy enough so anyone driving like a madman will be shrugged off as some guy who has to make a meeting. No players and Gs out yet—they're still fucked up from the night before. Perfect time for a couple brothers with a sober head to move their stash.

"Also a perfect target for a street jacking. No pylons blocking the plaza. Most every other plaza in Pittsburgh has them after 9/11, but they didn't put them up here. You jump the curb off of Fifth, just drive across the plaza, like they did, and you don't even have to worry about outrunning the cops! After you've done the job, you just jump into the side street, go two blocks down, pull into a parking garage with all the other working stiffs, you switch vehicles, and that's all she wrote!"

"How do you know, Lieutenant?"

I stood watching the rain pelt down on the bodies and the shells dance in the puddles. I thought about the day on the corner with Brady. "That's how a professional would do it." *It's how a* cop *would do it*, I thought.

Then, as if someone were listening to me lay out the scenario, Suzcyk's radio crackled to life. "You guys got Cowboy in your vicinity over there?"

I grabbed the radio off him. "Go for Cowboy."

"Boss, it's Hawthorne. We are over here about five blocks east of you in the old Sears employee garage; it's used by some of the tech companies."

"I know which one you mean. It still has the Sears logo on the top."

"Yeah, we've got the white Lexus here. And we've got the getaway driver, with what looks like a close-contact shotgun blast to the head. Judging by his ID, he was one of the Washington crew's foot soldiers as well. The shooters must have swept him up, found out the location of the drop move. How the hell did he not hit the gas and make a break for it when they got out of the car?"

"They probably gave him a line like they had people outside his family's house and they'd kill them all if he didn't go along with it."

"I've got a heavy smell of bleach all over the vehicle, and the plates are gone. It looks like even the VIN numbers on the dash and under the hood have been burned off with hydrochloric acid. They didn't leave so much as a red cunt hair to go off of. It's gonna take a while to find out what part of the country this car even came from."

"What's that tell you, Tori?"

"These boys aren't Sunday softball league. This is some fucking nightmare fuel."

"Copy. Drugstore Cowboy out." I looked over at Suzcyk's sergeant, the senior officer on the scene. "Have forensics take photos of vantage points and pull the data from any traffic cameras. Police up the brass. The bodies aren't going to tell us anything here other than there's two dead gangbangers in broad daylight on Fifth Avenue. Bag 'em. Get started on the family house calls. In person. I want a sergeant or better. In his blues. Gag the press until the families are notified."

"Lieutenant, these are two drug-pushing scumbags. Three, counting the driver. You want us to call on the family like they're fallen Ranger Regiment boys?"

"I'm not saying weep over the bodies and bring flowers. I'm saying look them in the eyes and tell them we will do whatever we can to find out who is doing this."

"Why would we do that?"

"One, we're cops. It's our fucking job. Two—it's what we'd want to hear if it were our kids lying there."

CHAPTER 9

Inspector Kenneth Spenser glared from behind his desk. When Kenny wanted to chew ass, he called you to his office at 6:15 p.m. In your blues. Whether you were a junior patrolman or the most senior deputy inspector on the planet five days from retirement, you cut your hair, trimmed your beard, and put on the blues. Kenny chose 6:15 to remind you that this was typically the time Mandy set the table and poured his first scotch. Kenny very emphatically never changed the punishment hour for this said fact. If you got a 6:15 appointment slip, you might want to start tweaking to your civilian résumé.

"One of you is my brother, and I will kick your ass from here to next week or I will take your shield, and your rank, right now. One of you is *practically* a brother, and I will kick your ass from here to next week and take your shield. Why are my two finest narcotics cops—who I just put in charge of the highest priority task force in the city—having fisticuffs like a few Liberty Avenue whores the morning we get two very dead drug couriers right in front of the William Penn Hotel?"

"Three counting the driver, sir," I couldn't help blurting out.

"Thomas, I'm about to punt your fucking head off like a rugby ball if you give me any more of that snark, got it? And you too, Marco!"

Neither of us said anything.

"Detective Sergeant Escardo, after you processed Trevor Washington while he was still alive, did you accompany Lieutenant Spenser on any visits to Mrs. Hewitt?"

"No sir."

"Did Lieutenant Spenser's leave of absence in October affect your caseload at all?"

"No sir. He only took four days of saved vacation in addition to the three he had off per the shift schedule."

"Other than taking her statement and applying lifesaving first aid, did Detective Spenser expend any Narcotics Department resources investigating the Hewitt aggravated assault?"

"No sir. If he did do any other such inquiries, it was on his own time, on his own dime."

"Did Lieutenant Spenser show any preferential treatment toward Mrs. Hewitt's case at all, or use your time on Narcotics investigations to run inquiries regarding the Hewitt assault?"

"No sir. After her release from the hospital, I am told he referred her to the detectives who handle assault, and the case was processed through the domestic relations officer in charge. You already know about my part in the interrogation of the husband. Mr. Hewitt still remains absent on bail, and the bail jumper case as well as the assault case are in the hands of the detectives at the lower borough precinct."

"Then, Sergeant Marco Luis Escardo, why the fuck are you sticking your nose in my little brother's life?"

"Sir?"

"Did you try to get ahold of me, or Captain Brady Spenser, or either of our wives on the night you decided to play Sherlock Holmes to the rescue?"

"Sir, I was concerned for my partner."

"What he does on the clock is your concern, Marco. And Lieutenant Thomas Spenser, while remaining a narcissist, binge-drinking, pill-popping fuckbag prone to bad decisions, is *still* an adult."

"Yes sir."

"You called on him at four fifteen."

"Yes sir."

"The Penn Avenue shootings happened at seven fifteen."

"Yes sir."

"And where was Lieutenant Spenser when the shootings occurred, Sergeant Escardo?"

Marco mumbled.

"Sorry, Marco, your spic-ease isn't working too well. Please use English."

"Sir, he was in his office."

"And where were you?"

"Sir, I was late because I overslept after the altercation with the lieutenant, sir."

"So, you go to chew my brother's ass out about remaining focused to duty, and suddenly you are late for a triple-homicide call four hours later? Would that be about the correct statement here, Sergeant?"

"Sir, if I may—"

"No, Mark, you may not. Have you witnessed Lieutenant Spenser injecting himself during duty hours?" (Kenny called Marco "Mark" when he genuinely wanted to rattle him.)

"No sir."

"Have you witnessed him getting into a vehicle or otherwise endangering the lives of Pittsburgh citizens after consuming drugs or alcohol?"

"No sir."

"If I were to piss-test him right now, would I find him above the limit for alcohol on duty or find any substance in his system other than those for which he has a legal authorization from a doctor or traces in his urine that he tried to use foreign chemicals to cover narcotics in the test?"

"No sir."

"Did you have any probable cause to enter Mickey's gym at four fifteen, uninvited?"

"Fuck you, Ken. I've put damn near as many years into

building that place and working with those kids as you have."

"Sergeant, I will ask you again. Were you training a fighter, calling on my mother who had a cat in a tree, responding to a fire, or some other Boy Scout scenario?"

"No sir."

"Then, Sergeant, if you had no probable cause to be on the premises—whose deed is in the name of Kenneth, Brady, Thomas, and Rose Spenser—it doesn't matter if your superior officer was in the next room doing lines of coke off a stripper's ass while she was giving head to the second coming of Osama Bin Laden, now does it?"

"No sir."

"Remind yourself of that fact the next time you want to play Jiminy Cricket."

"Yes sir."

Kenny handed Marco back his sergeant's shield and put the small stack of paperwork in front of him through his desk-side shredder.

"Your transfer back to Narcotics is denied. I put you on the task force for a reason. One of them was to protect this sonofabitch next to you. But there is a fine line between protection and control. You are dismissed, Sergeant Escardo."

"Yes sir." Marco saluted and left the office without looking at me.

"Tom. Please. Sit." He shut the door behind Marco. "I want you to get yourself together. I want you to stop using. Don't give me the dog-and-pony shit that it's all legal. You're still using. If I have to, I will command direct you to a recovery program."

"Yeah, Inspector."

"Don't be a smug asshole. You think I'm going to threaten to tell Ma on you? You actually think Ma doesn't already know?"

"She knows. It's the Spenser family denial we've all been perfecting since we were kids."

"Come by the house tomorrow. Mandy misses you. The kids miss you. Bring your lady friend."

"Serious?"

"Yeah, dinner tomorrow, seven o'clock."

Since I was still in my blues, I thought it fair to stop in on Alario's mother.

The details of my Mustang—plates, red door and all, as well as photos—were in the hands of every dealer's cornerman between here and the tunnels. I'm sure the dealers in Homestead had word on my transfer to Special Investigations before I did. Maybe they released a mass text message. When I pulled up on Alario's block, there was none of the signaling, catcalls, or other testosterone bullshit. No "Five-Oh," no "Pig!" It was deceptively quiet.

Alario's mother was on the front porch. Dressed in her Sunday best past 8:30 on a Thursday, sitting in her porch rocker, looking out at the block. She seemed quite at ease—a Black *Downton Abbey* governess in the middle of junkie-ville, without so much as a switchblade for protection.

"Hello, ma'am. I am sorry for your loss."

"Too many folks wearing black these last few months, Lieutenant. 'Specially among the Washington boys."

"Indeed, ma'am."

"Please excuse me, Lieutenant, if I do not stand. I been walking around all day, standing up to receive folk. Everyone come by. Even the mayor's wife comes by. What's the mayor's wife doing coming by for a Black momma lost her baby who was a thief and a dealer?"

"She's a kind woman. They lost a son to leukemia about ten years ago. He would've been about the same age now as Alario was. She's just one good mother that knows about pain, looking in on another."

She kept staring straight ahead, rocking on the porch chair. "She didn't tell me that. She must be a good woman, because a regular politician's wife would have told me and every reporter in a mile from here and brought a news crew." She looked up at me. "I remember you bringing Alario to me in cuffs the first time he was dealing in front of the Stop-N-Go."

"Yes ma'am. I'm a little older and uglier. But yeah, that was me."

"Had to be close to . . . fifteen years?"

"Fourteen, ma'am."

"All the other Irish White boys from the neighborhood are working the factories and the mills, and you one of them fast-tracking Spenser boys—didn't come from shit, didn't have shit. A cop's family, an honest cop's family, is usually poorer than the convicts."

"Yes ma'am, we are thriftier with our money too. We're not exactly one hundred percent Irish, but they let us fly the flag anyway."

"Women down my church used to talk bad on your family. Like your daddy was raising you to go after Blacks with a nightstick. Mr. Frank had his own devil in him, but he was fair to my boys and my family. Hard but fair."

"Yes ma'am, but . . . I think we would have been cops with or without our dad."

"I'll bet you never brought your momma grief like this."

"No ma'am, but she already had enough on her shoulders." After a long silence I asked, "Is there anything possibly I can do for you, anything you need?"

"I don't need your charity, Lieutenant." She wrapped the shawl around her shoulders tighter and turned one eye, blued with glaucoma, up toward me. “Do you think it’s my fault?”

“Ma’am, he was an adult. He made his own decisions. I know you neither benefit from his enterprise nor lavish yourself in a lifestyle. We ran your financials when we first broke into Razor’s—I mean, Trevor’s—crew. It’s a compliment to call them ‘financials.’ You’re still living on the same street you met me on; you have $617 in your checking account. You have no criminal record. You have not so much as stolen a stick of bubblegum in your life.

“You do not strike me as an enabler. None of Alario’s business ‘connections’ have your name anywhere near them. If Alario or Trevor left you a shoebox full of cash for a rainy day like this, it’s not my business or my investigation. My family has an insurance policy on me; why shouldn’t your kids have done the same for you?”

“Look at you. Lying-ass White boy. You trying to tell an old lady that she done right by a boy who is dead and been in and out of jail since he fourteen. And it’s okay for her to spend his blood money to get away from all this.”

“I meant no disrespect in saying that. But there’s nothing I could say or do that would hurt you more than you’ve already been hurt today.”

“You not going to ask me questions? Ask me who it might be? Who his enemies were? Who was leaning on him?”

“No. Even the police have some class. I just came by to pay my respects. Two of your kin are dead within weeks of each other. Another one is in a wheelchair.” I handed her my card. “When you feel like talking—*if* you ever feel like talking—you call that number in blue ink on the back. Day or night. That rings directly to my cell, which as of this morning I’ve been ordered to have no farther than two feet away.”

She traced her gloved fingers over the card and again stared away across the street, clutching the card as if it were a talisman in the hands of a fortune teller.

"I tried all my life to protect them. But you cannot protect people from theyself, Lieutenant. Good evening to you. Don't you worry 'bout me out here. Ain't nobody gonna rob an old lady who got nothing left to take. The Lord done took all I got."

I took off my white glove and extended my hand to her. "You're in my prayers, ma'am."

"And you're in mine, Lieutenant."

I started to walk back to my car.

"Thomas?"

"Ma'am?" I turned around.

"When you was a boy, maybe nineteen, I saw you fight once. They squared you up against some Black boy who must have had twenty pounds and seven inches on you. But you went ten rounds toe to toe with him. He'd knock you down, you'd get back up."

I chuckled. "Yes ma'am. Chris Tatum. He won by decision that night."

She smiled. "A lot of the brothers lost money that night."

"Why?"

"Everyone bet you wouldn't last one round. You went all ten rounds."

"But I lost anyway."

"There's a difference, Lieutenant. You could have hit the canvas that first round. You kept getting back up. Tatum had a detached retina by the end of the night and never fought again. He had more points, but the way the bookies all saw it, *you* won that fight, you know that?"

"Yes ma'am."

One thing the old lady didn't know about that fight was that Frank had been in my corner. I would sooner die than get KO'd on the canvas with Frank watching. The last time Tatum knocked me down, the ref had wanted to stop the fight. The bell saved me. I stumbled over into the corner with Mickey and Frank there and threw up into the trainer's bucket. Frank put an ice mitt over my right cheek and popped my mouth guard back in. He looked me in the eyes. There had been no kindness or fatherly tenderness; nor was he cruel or mean in that moment, even though I would remind him of his cruelties and meanness for decades to come.

He wiped my face with a towel and brought my forehead to his. His eyes drilled into mine.

"You may not win," he said, "but for God's sake, you are going to fucking see this to the end. You're my son. Don't you dare quit on me."

I came out swinging.

As I got in the car and exhaled after my conversation with Alario's mother, I thought maybe I would rather she had gone into hysterics, thrown things at me, and cursed the Pittsburgh PD. Here she was with a boy on a slab, another in the dirt, and she's telling me she was an old fan of mine back from when I had a spark of something phenomenal in me. No, I didn't win them all. Never in the cards. But I still came out swinging. And every time the fights ended, win or lose, I was still on my feet, not on my hands and knees.

■ ■ ■

I called my little sister, who was finishing up her time at the district attorney's office and would soon become an analyst for the RAND Corporation in Georgetown. Getting her voicemail, I asked her to meet me up on Mount Washington with our father. Despite how Brady had encouraged me to "keep the peace" between me and Francis, I had a sinking feeling at sitting down with him alone. Without backup.

In January 1986, a newly divorced Frank Spenser, fresh from his hospital bed and his outpatient stint on the orthopedic rehab ward of the University of Pittsburgh, fathered a squealing, pudgy, pink, and perfect daughter named Francine with a hauntingly beautiful, shy, twenty-six-year-old volunteer nurse's aide named Shoshana Goyevsky. The question of my sister's conception and whether it happened while Frank Spenser was still attached to a configuration of rehabilitative pulleys and intravenous needles was the subject of much gossip, debate, and pontification by many of the good Orthodox Jewish houses and the not-so-good Mick Catholic apartments in the greater Pittsburgh area.

It had been especially scandalous since Shoshana was the eldest daughter of a popular Hasidic rabbi and was already betrothed to a promising yeshiva student who'd gotten his ordination from the Jewish Theological University in Manhattan.

Before Rabbi David Fliedelman could catch the train to cross the Hudson River with his master of divinity in hand, Shoshana Goyevsky had grown tired of love by postcard and enamored of the sad, gentlemanly goyim in bed 2305. Frank was the same age as her father but a world apart in terms of demeanor, attitude, wit, and confidence. Her father ran Temple Chevrei Tzedick, but Frank Spenser ran Pittsburgh, and that was far more thrilling for the little girl who had grown up seeing things from the women's side of the aisle with her head covered.

Meanwhile, Frank—emerging from a morphine stupor and flush with repentance and sobriety and the shock of losing his entire family before Brady even finished throwing his no-hitter of a doubleheader—perhaps clung to this introverted medic out of sheer desperation at the thought that nobody would ever love him again.

When Frank checked out of the hospital, Shoshana gave notice and turned in her scrubs. Within forty-eight hours, Rabbi

Goyevsky declared his eldest daughter dead in the classified ads, next to a post for Siberian-malamute crossbreeds in Squirrel Hill and an announcement for equestrian lessons on a rare as-yet unclaimed amount of available turf in Shadyside. Somehow the fact that Shoshana was less than 730 sunsets older than Kenneth Spenser never crept into Dad's mind, and if it did, it didn't bother him for long.

With less fanfare than was typical for his level of narcissism, Dad got married for the second time at the county courthouse with two prothonotary clerks as witnesses. He and Shoshana moved into that little shoebox apartment overlooking Mount Washington, and Frank Spenser screwed, laughed, lived, and screwed some more with that sweet little Jewish girl for three happy seasons of his bitter life.

But like all things in the Spenser family, a day of happiness and luck is followed by six days of grief and misfortune, and poor Frank fared no better. In agony from the effort of pushing for seven hours, lithe, olive-skinned, angelic Shoshanna developed a bleed in her abdominal wall before the doctors at Magee Hospital realized they'd miscalculated a canal birth over a C-section. On the third day after the girl was born, her mother, the rabbi's daughter, ascended to the "world to come" to be with the angels and submit to whatever fate heaven had in store for those who had the luck—or in most cases the misfortune—to love the deputy commissioner.

Crippled with guilt over his own self-fulfilling prophecy, the rabbi, known for dramatics and affectations, ended his tenure at Temple Chevrei Tzedick with a .410 shotgun through his mouth. In one of life's little ironies and in another demonstration of the effect of Frank's avalanche of shitstorms on the rest of us, rookie patrolman Kenneth Spenser of the Metro Division took the unfortunate call to his quasi-step-grandfather-in-law's suicide. Under the gore in the rabbi's study, Ken Spenser found a framed

Technicolor picture, reddened with age, of a young, clean-shaven Rabbi Goyevsky holding an infant Shoshana. In an inexplicable twist of sentiment and light fingers, Patrolman Third Class Ken Spenser liberated that photo from the crime scene and placed it in the nursery of his baby sister, perhaps wanting her to know that she had a history and came from somewhere other than us.

This left a grieving, limping Frank with a bundled, suckling, wailing nine-pound burden to carry up his own version of Calvary. How he didn't end back up in the bottom of a bottle before the dual funeral—Shoshanna and her dad committed to the earth together—was anyone's guess.

Two weeks after putting a slug in Danforth Washington's back, handbags and ankle-length dresses still hanging forlornly in Frank's wardrobe, he was prepared to tender his resignation as the deputy inspector of Metro Division in order to carve out a more normal life for this little blob that Shoshanna had left behind. Then Papa Mickey drove over one day. He faced Frank for the first time since my father had given my mother a concussion and nearly busted her jaw.

He admonished my father, told him what he honestly thought of him: how Frank had failed as a man, failed as a father, and how Mickey would be damned if he was going to sit idly by and watch Frank fuck up another child's life. He let my father know that he had kept from killing Frank over the years not out of deference to his daughter's wishes but out of shame—shame that he hadn't stood up for her when the bruises first started coming; shame for the denial our whole family was expert at; for the fact that Frank was, from the moment my grandfather pegged him, a loser sporting a cop's badge and thus everyone danced a royal charade around him. Shame at the fact that we were all enablers to the magic show he put on of being Supercop.

Mickey didn't want to hear Frank sputter on about how Shoshana had turned him around, reminded him of goodness, and dared him to love another completely and selflessly. He threatened to go to the commissioner as well as the papers with a laundry list of Frank's indiscretions and abuses over the last twenty-odd years if he did not immediately sign guardianship of Francine over to him, even though Mickey had no real blood claim to his adopted granddaughter. But by the time Mickey finished crucifying Frank in the headlines, he wouldn't be able to get a job as the night security guard at Woolworth's. He gambled on Frank's ego and narcissism—successfully. Frank Spenser folded, and with the help of a family-law specialist who had been Mickey's protégé in his youth, my grandpa won out at preserving the innocence of Francine Shira Goyevsky-Spenser, for a time.

Soon after Francine was moved into my grandparents' guest room, Frank went back to the only thing he hadn't fucked up: being a cop. From the time Francine was a month old until my grandmother's passing, Mickey and my grandmother fed her, clothed her, and entertained her. Everything from dolls to puppet shows to a mutual love of the symphony and entertaining her transitory fascination with Argentine ballroom dance. They cooked her breakfasts, laid out her clothes, corrected her homework, and, when she was twelve and a half, took her to the feminine products aisle of the local Walmart.

Upon Grandma's passing, Mickey enrolled her at Shady Side Academy as a boarding student. When she made the polo team at Shady Side, my grandfather groomed and saddled her horse faithfully through four championship years until she graduated as valedictorian in 2004. When she made all-conference her senior year at Yale in 2007, Mickey spent the greater part of his profits from the gym on a lovely chestnut mare that Francine dubbed Siren. Then Mickey passed in his sleep, weeks after Francine walked the stage the second time at New Haven, this time in 2009 with an accelerated juris doctor degree. Francine

Spenser, orphaned once again at twenty-four, was involuntarily brought back into obligatory contact with the man who had produced 50 percent of her DNA helix.

Up until Mickey's death, my mother had practiced daily indifference to Francine—a defensive measure, probably for the sake of her own sanity and not wanting to bring the clusterfuck that was my father back into her life. She'd regarded Francine as little more than a legitimized bastard that she was forced to encounter any time Fran visited or interacted with my grandparents. After Mickey died, however, Mom was faced with the reality that the daughter of her ex-husband was not going to magically disappear from our lives unless she could cast a spell to remove the absolute and unconditional love Mickey and the rest of us had bestowed on her for no other reason than she truly was our sister, no matter how unexpected, unwanted, or unwelcomed she may have been.

■ ■ ■

No replies from Fran, and no follow-up text. I took a pull of hooch I kept in a flask in the glove compartment and sat in silence in the Mustang for twenty minutes.

I didn't want to go back to the gym and deal with the ever-mounting sexual tension between the Spenser and Samuels-Hewitt residences. So I went to see Pop alone. I crossed the river to Mount Washington.

You enter LeMont through a narrow walkway only a few steps long that separates the bar—sorry, lounge—from the restaurant. About three steps in, you can tell you're breathing rarefied air. Here is a restaurant that doesn't smell of food. No rich, bright sauces or tangy garlic scents. Instead, it smells of money and privilege and power. And expense accounts—*big* expense accounts. The snap and crackle of American Express cards sliding through card readers is louder than the waiter-helpful chatter. The issue of how good the food is here *is* no issue. People come for the twenty-four-carat view and the starchy atmosphere.

Every Thursday night in the lounge, without fail, retired deputy commissioner Frank Spenser would sip a club soda while the councilmen put away liquor and brandy and flirted with waitresses young enough to be their daughters. Back in the old days, Kenny was all of eleven when Mom first started sending him out to pick up Dad from the LeMont. Driving her old green Buick and carrying a fiver for the doorman to look the other way as Kenny came into the bar, Mom would smoke three Newports as she sat in the car, waiting for Kenny to fish Dad out from the toilet. She had vowed even then to never enter a bar to look for Frank unless it was to identify his corpse.

It felt weird to walk into this place and *not* see the old man propped against the wall in the men's toilet, with a perplexed steward ready to hand you a mint and brush your shoulders if you would just drag your piece-of-shit father off the property, thank you. The same guy still works the bathroom, over thirty years later. And Dad graduated from being pissed in the stalls to sitting at the bar and drinking club soda and pretending to enjoy it.

One of the councilmen saw me and caught the head bartender's arm. "Deborah! Holy shit, get a round on me! Pittsburgh's finest just walked into the bar!"

My father looked up from his corner, locked eyes with his youngest son, and there was a genuine smile on his face. I never knew the bastard was capable of being happy. Can't recall a memory of him smiling when I was a child. Didn't even know the sonofabitch still had teeth.

He shook my hand. "Tom."

"Francis."

"Want to grab a booth? Have you eaten?"

"Starving."

The headwaiter came up in all his livery, a regular Alfred Pennyworth. He took my service cap and rain jacket. "Scotch and Coke, Lieutenant?"

"You know me well, Girard. If you don't mind putting the scotch and a few of his scotch friends in a highball glass, and leave the Coke in the can, please."

Girard raised a smug eyebrow. "One of those days, sir, indeed."

I couldn't get over the look of genuine contentment in my father's face that I was sitting across from him. It almost shamed me. My hatred, I mean, *almost* shamed me. I just needed to look into that one dead eye to recall what he really was. Still, I managed a smile. "I cannot remember the last time I had dinner here with you."

He chuckled and offered me a cigar. The lounge of the LeMont was one the last places in Pittsburgh you could smoke indoors other than the Greyhound station with the rest of the druggies and hobos.

"We had just brought Allie home from the hospital." I smiled at that memory. "Of course, we were seated in nonsmoking."

"God, almost four years!"

"Yeah."

Girard and his apprentice reappeared with the triple scotch and menus.

Dad indicated his forlorn club soda and lime. "I'm good. Feed the lieutenant."

I eyed the menu. "I'll have a steak sandwich, rare, with horseradish, tavern fries, and, um, . . . ah, hell, let's get a few of the crab cakes too and maybe me and the old man will split them."

I wolfed down the meal as I went into detail about what Brady and I had so far about the guns. He leaned forward in his chair, taking notes in a pocket reporter's book he carried that had a battered, frayed leather cover. I had to hold back a slightly amused grin as I spotted a faded edge of my sister's kindergarten photo taped to the back cover and knew somewhere buried in the pages were yellowed sports-page clippings of me and Brady, a more recent shot of Franny driving a goal between the posts on the polo fields at Yale, and one of Kenny rushing as a twenty-year-old in the pouring rain in the Army-Navy game. People all over the world now had photos in their phones, but my old man carried the concordance of his children's achievements from a lifetime ago in his Perry Mason pocket binder.

I could detect puzzlement as he wrote, and it both pleased and perplexed me to see him stumped on this. It was concerning that the one thing in my father's domain he was 100 percent constantly sure of, to the point of narcissistic arrogance, was cop work, and this was severely troubling him. I had lived through him handling serial killers, kiddie rapists, kidnappings, and dismemberments, but in this moment, his face took a dour, mournful countenance I had never known him to have. He was tired. And he looked (could it be?) concerned that I was out of my depth.

He was keen to change the subject. "It's good to see you having some appetite. You've always been bigger, huskier, but you look like you've dropped a lot of weight in a short time."

I took one gulp from the scotch and let the fire burn my stomach.

"Tom, I heard you had another rough patch this morning."

"Yeah."

"What's with the blues? You have court today?"

"Just court with Judge Kenny, so to speak. And I paid my respects to a victim's mom."

"You could have sent Marco for that."

"Ha!" I tore away at a roll from the basket on the table. "Marco and I had a bit of a tiff. We girls aren't getting along."

"I hear there's a woman in your life."

I glanced up. His tone wasn't facetious. "She's more of a friend. Just someone going through some rough stuff that I'm helping out."

"You're helping *her* out? Heh. Ain't *she* the lucky one?" He sipped his soda. "Your mom called on me a few days after the girl had moved in. Rose stops by every other month or so, brings a casserole, makes sure I'm using more underwear than just the top two sets in the drawer, brings pictures of the little ones. Don't look at me like that. Nothing sinister. We're old people, Tom. And we share three children together. We talk is all. We talk about you boys, the grandkids." He smiled as if he were recalling a historic moment, like meeting the president. "Sometimes we play cards for pennies. We have coffee, and a month to a month and a half later she comes with another casserole. She told me what you did for the girl. Saved her life."

"I wouldn't go that far."

"Tommy, you did. She was hemorrhaging. If you hadn't been there . . . Couple docs over at County let the mayor know, too. They wouldn't stop talking about the cop who kept watch over the girl from Homestead."

I avoided his eyes and instead looked out the window at the Pittsburgh skyline. "You would have done the same thing too, Frank. On the job, I mean. You're a good cop. Always were."

"But?" he asked. In his head he was probably playing connect the dots with the similarities between Claire's degenerate ex-husband and the former antics of Frank Spenser in his heyday of womanizing, alcoholism, and that brand of child abuse that all good Irish Catholics refer to as parenting and discipline.

I thought about what Alario's mom had told me about protecting people from themselves.

"No, Frank. No 'buts' tonight. I'm too tired to fight. How about tonight, we're just two old cops having dinner?"

"Sounds good to me, son."

I turned away from the window and didn't so much glare at him as feel sad for him. I heard the eagerness in his voice, how much he wanted to believe it, how much he wanted the word *son* to mean something.

"'Son' just feels forced, Frank."

"But you are my son."

I let out a braying hyena laugh at that. If a record player had been going somewhere in the LeMont, the needle would have scratched and shrieked to a stop. Familiar faces turned and shook their heads at both of us. *Those fucking Spenser assholes.*

"Francis, that's what's so fucking funny, or tragic, about it all. You're such an intuitive cop, and you don't even fucking realize what you're saying. You didn't just find me in front of the bar. I've *always* been your son. But I can count on one hand the number of times you've actually *been* a dad."

Before Girard could come back with a refill on my triple Scotch highball, Frank Spenser, who would rather be shot full of holes than break down crying in front of all his buddies at the LeMont, pulled a near obscene roll of twenties out of his pocket and dropped it on my place setting.

"For your dinner. Your dinner for one." He lightly touched my shoulder as he stood by the chair. Then he clapped his hand on my back, once, twice, gently, before stepping past me.

I knew that all these years he'd wanted for me to stand up when he did that, and hug him. But I couldn't.

"I'm pocketing the difference, Francis. I consider it collecting asshole taxes."

Five seconds later, I looked around and realized I was talking to no one.

He was gone.

■ ■ ■

I came back into the gym about one in the morning. Charley was in his spot next to Papa Mickey's empty stool. He didn't get up and greet me, so I went up the stairwell. Claire's light was still on, and her door was open, the jazz music on.

"You really look nice," she said to me when I stood in her doorway.

"Hey," I said. "What's the matter? Can't sleep?"

"I napped a bit this afternoon. Got up around seven, helped your mom close up. She and that one older trainer . . . Respottek?"

"Yeah, old Repo was my cornerman when I fought semipro. He's been with us since we were kids."

"We sat telling stories about you. Ha—they told. I listened." She came over to the doorway and gave me a gentle kiss, then another. She looked me over approvingly. A twinkle came in her eyes, and she looked all over again and delicately ran her fingers up my jacket. "Very . . . very handsome."

I had splashed on some Nautica when I was getting dressed up for the Kenny Spenser tribunal, and she burrowed into my neck.

"Mmm, you smell good too."

I kind of slid back to my door, fumbling with my key. "Umm, it's the uniform. You could put one of these on Randy Quaid and he would look dashing."

"Are you trying to be a good boy?" She laughed and leaned into my chest.

"It's been a horribly long day. Let me shower and get four hours before Marco and I have to be back in the office with our three fresh dead bodies."

She backed up, obviously disappointed but not miffed. One fifteen in the morning is not the hour I get playful.

"You could come over like last night if you want. Pajama frumpiness rules in effect." She held her right hand up, Boy Scout style.

"Okay. I might just do that."

I showered till the water ran almost tepid and threw on my academy tracksuit sweats against the nastiness of the chill seeping through the old building.

I stood in her doorway and watched her sleeping peacefully. Despite the cold in the drafty building, I shucked off my clothes with a childlike glee and crawled in next to her, felt the warmth of her back against my stomach. I slipped one of my arms over hers and was asleep before my head hit the pillow.

■ ■ ■

Sunlight spilled through the window. I heard Charley barking, conversing with the morning customers.

"You're naked, Thomas Spenser."

I let my eyes adjust and took stock of Claire. Curled up on the window ledge beside the bed, she had her arms hugging her knees as she gazed out at the Pittsburgh skyline. The original Mickey's had been parallel to the city streets of Melwood, but when he expanded the building and added the apartments, it added sixteen feet of height, which provided a fantastic view.

She was wearing a tartan pajama top—one of mine—along with pink socks and no panties. I had to peer closely for that last bit of info, and before she whacked the side of my head with an open palm, I saw a slight, trimmed tuft that confirmed she did not get her ginger shade from a bottle. She climbed back into the bed with me. As I reached to stroke one of those pale thighs of hers, I leaned forward to kiss her. For this I was rewarded with another whack across my skull. Then she took my face in both her hands, kissed me deeply, and wrapped her legs around my waist. Because I was a man, and all men are horny assholes, I tried to readjust so that our mutual nakedness could somehow meet. She cuffed me with my third skull crack in a thirty-second time frame.

"You Irish Ashkenazi hornball."

"Oh, come on, just three minutes."

"Really, what are we gonna do with the next two minutes and thirty-seven seconds?"

I grinned and pulled back to regard her. "My brother wants you to come to dinner tonight."

"Really?"

"Yeah. You've been bonding with the girls so much; I guess he wanted to see us together for himself."

"What do you mean?"

"Aww, honey, everyone was talking about us before *we* were even talking about us."

"So, what, your sisters-in-law and your mom are playing matchmaker?"

"Yeah. Didn't you think it was odd that a family full of self-righteous Jews and pretentious Catholics didn't blink twice at the fact that we were technically shacking up?"

She tapped her knuckles against the dividing wall.

"Technically. The wall keeps us chaste." She took on the accent of a downtown Irish priest. "The Holy Ghost is in the insulation, laddie!" She pursed her lips, mimicking a stern face, and then broke into insatiable laughter.

She calmed down her hysterics, and I stood up and smiled. "Pick you up at six?"

She smiled back at me and pulled me down for a long kiss. "It's a date."

I straightened. "No, it's my family. One night with them, and you might pack by morning."

"Tom." She sat up and pulled the blankets around her. "Really. All joking aside. What do you expect all of this to lead to?"

"Does it have to lead to anything? We're friends. I know what you've been through. I'm not asking for anything."

"I'm a thirty-three-year-old unemployed music professor living above a gym owned by some blatantly dysfunctional—yet extremely sweet—Irish Jews. One day I'm going to have to leave here and reenter the real world."

I had no reply to that other than to shamelessly try to get her to wrap those legs around me again. She coyly refused but made out with me all the same. Finally, in mock exasperation, she guided one of my hands down between her legs and began to gently swing her hips and shift against my wrist. I wanted her right then and there—but all the same, I listened to her softly repeating my name and telling me she'd never felt wanted like that before.

There was something so chaste and trusting in her voice—virginal, like we were sixteen in the back of my dad's Cadillac. I almost pulled my hand away like one would after scalding themselves on a brazier. Her free hand shot forth and clenched my elbow in a vise grip, and I felt slightly thrilled and slightly cheap as she used me as a means to her "end." When it happened, she squeezed my arm, closed her eyes, and bit down on my shoulder to keep the morning crew from hearing her pleasure. Her body shuddered once, twice, and she slumped back against the bed, gasping.

She arched and stretched and tried to pull me back into bed to fulfill what I had been longing for every night since she had been under my roof . . . and then my fucking phone buzzed, and the beautiful daydream that had begun our morning was lost.

I had to pick up the call; it was Brady getting back to me, and I wanted to meet up with him as soon as I could. Teasing me horribly, she stripped bare naked and walked to the shower. By the time Brady finished what he'd had to say, she was dressed and doing her hair.

I ran down the hall, got shaved and dressed, came back, and left a mug of hot coffee on her counter, hoping she would interpret it as it was meant: that I had missed our mornings together, those halcyon moments when I didn't even know I was falling for her, and I would much rather the rest of that day be spent tangled up in her.

CHAPTER 10

I met Brady at Primanti Bros. The original one, on the strip. Primanti's runs twenty-four hours, and their menu is the same for breakfast, lunch, dinner, or the munchies. Seven o'clock in the morning, he came walking in. Brady was a mess on his day off. He looked like he was trying to pass as an honest blue-collar worker in his Carhartt jacket and faded jeans. But his boots were too new, his pants were too clean, he didn't have that Pittsburgh kegger belly, and he was clean shaven.

Even to the blind vagrants, he looked like a cop in a Carhartt jacket.

"What the fuck, Tommy. You not go to bed yet or something? I don't think we ever met at seven in the morning unless one of us was about to catch an ass whooping."

"I need to talk to you."

"Shoot."

"I met with the wise man on the hill the other night."

"Yeah?"

"Something's not sitting right about your cop angle."

"What do you mean?"

"Pop rolled with the biggest rat fuckers of the rats in his day. Ever since he turned in his shield, he's been rabbi to the mayor. Different mayors get elected; Pop is still in the back seat, telling the driver where to go on the map."

"Go on."

"Brady, Pop was the one who fucking finagled you into Internal Affairs! He was your inspiration to go into IA to begin with—ever since he first took lead over there a few years after he got hurt, nearly a ten-year run as the head of Internal Affairs himself. What happened on every other cop job we have ever worked, pulling someone who ended up being dirty—ever since then, until now?"

Brady stared into his coffee mug. "Pop had word of mouth. He had a lead, a thread, a snitch. Something."

"It wasn't even just Internal Affairs. Pop ran the snitches like nobody else. Mellon bank on Broad gets hit, Pop has a snitch coming in the door before closing time. The guy slinging bad product back in 1995, thirty ODs across the city, Pop had three different crews giving him tips because they know a bad batch is bad for business. As long as he has been a cop, he's always been playing chess while everyone around him played checkers! And last night the fucking old man looks at me like I was speaking Sanskrit. I'm telling you, Brady, he was fucking floored!"

"You mean about the stolen guns?"

"No, about my off-the-books mansion in the Caymans. Yes about the guns, you tit."

"Maybe he's just getting old, Tommy."

"Don't let the gimp and that dead eye fool you. Motherfucker's older, but he's not dumber."

"You're saying this is, whatsit, subterfuge?"

"I'm saying whoever set this up has no idea about the rabbi. Someone may have paid off a custodian for twenty minutes in the evidence room—I don't know. But I don't smell dirty cops if Pop's nose doesn't twitch."

"You're avoiding the elephant in the room. Go ahead and say it, wise-ass. Pop's nose isn't twitching because he is involved somehow."

"Naw, fuck that. Would he be living above a hardware store in fucking Dormont if he had any spare bills? Cheap fucker takes the bus anytime he's not riding with the mayor. Mom brings him fucking casserole dinners still, and they're divorced going on twenty-eight years. The only bling I've ever seen him sport is the

Irish wedding band he still keeps on his right hand. That and his retirement watch. Unless he's Scrooge McDuck just swimming around in his millions in a vault somewhere, I don't think Pop is behind anything except how to politically spin the shit once it reaches city hall.

"But no. I think Pop's got a fiend in him that he thinks he can beat away with AA meetings and living like a pauper and being the consigliore to the mayor. He lives for that Thursday-night shit because it makes him look like a big shot. He was good police, but he and I have that Spenser touch of shit to anything else that's good in our lives. Pop is smart enough, but he isn't lucky enough to mastermind a caper."

Brady paused when I said that, looking thoughtful. "I can't even ponder Pop being bent. What's that make you and me and Kenny but three whelps of the biggest hypocrite in Pittsburgh?"

"Shit, Brady, whether he's crooked or he ain't, he's still the biggest hypocrite in Pittsburgh."

"How do you know? Like, how you know in your heart, for sure, it's not him?"

"I got the drop on him once in my life. I would know if I had it again."

"If you say so."

"Plus, one more thing."

"What's that?"

"Pop has spent the better part of thirty years trying to gain back my approval, showing what a God-fearing, law-abiding, wouldn't-harm-a-mouse new man he is. This is counterproductive to that logic."

We both looked at each other, not wanting to say anything. Brady spoke first.

"You're living in Papa Mickey's gym, and I'm making Velveeta sandwiches on week-old Wonder Bread for my lunches so that my cafeteria money goes into the kids' piggybanks. If either one of us is crooked, I swear to God we are the two cheapest fucking crooks on the planet. Even by Jewish standards."

"Why don't you start throwing that twin ESP bullshit at me now and tell me what's on your mind—or, as you would say, the other elephant?"

"Kenny? No. I know our brother. And so do you, Tom, even if you pretend not to. Kenny's been jumping through his own asshole since he was eighteen, hell-bent on making a name big enough to erase the memory of Pop. You know, the way Pop was, before then." That's how we referred to *it*—the night Francis Spenser was taken out by one of his own. All things in our lives prior to April 20, 1985, was "before then."

Brady looked at me with eyes just as pained as that day in 1985. "Fuck, Tommy, why'd it have to be you that day?"

"The same reasons I know it's not you now. Kenny doesn't have the stomach. You have too much heart. And I was always short on brains."

"Yeah, your dick was always more your compass. Tommy Spenser, Mr. Self-Deprecating, Woe-Is-Me, Not-Enough-Brains. What bullshit. Problem with you, my friend, is your balls, brains, heart, and cock play chess every day to decide what you're going to do when you roll out of bed."

"Brady, I want to know that whatever I bring you on this, you will back me up, hell or high water, no matter the target. No matter what I find, what goes before the grand jury, you have my back."

Brady extended his hand. "You've had a credited balance with the house going on thirty years. It's time for the house to pay off. Till they put me in the ground, Thomas. Partners, brothers, bandits. We came into this world kicking down the door, and so help me, we'll go out that way too."

Once again, in our family's lexicon, speaking in "cop" was synonymous with love.

■ ■ ■

I gazed at the insides of Alario Washington's corpse. You work enough in Homicide and Narcotics, you can wolf down a Primanti Bros roast beef with fries and coleslaw on top without bringing it back up in the coroner's office.

As I watched the doc do her work, I kicked myself for not bagging three more sandwiches for me, Mom, and Repo for lunch. As for Claire, the professor had two hands and a fully supplied refrigerator. She could make herself a nice soup stock in between violin lessons. Although I was falling for her, I didn't like the fact that a whole subconscious list of errands came with those feelings, and I tried to head them off. Save your life and put your abusive husband in cuffs? No problem. Get you lunch? Fuck it, you've got two feet and a purse.

The coroner's office had a new doc. Katya "Bones" Czaervich. Her accent sounded Balkan. Cute, from what I could tell under the surgical mask and scrub cap. Short. Maybe five feet zip. Smart, but not sassy. Bleeding academic, though. Confident but not condescending. I was enthralled as I watched her hack away at Alario the way I would tinker with the engine of the Mustang. Her scrub cap was personalized, slightly amusing: the red-and-gold logo of Manchester United's soccer team against a black-and-blue grid pattern my collector's eye recognized as their 1993 jersey.

"Judging by your accent, I'd have figured you more for Eastern Europe football, Doc."

"Hell no, Lieutenant. Giggs will bloody tear you apart."

Her blue eyes were the color of her scrubs. Peering at the organs, penlight in hand, she looked up at me, caught me looking at her. "How long, Lieutenant?"

"How long what?"

"How long have you had cancer?" She tilted her eyes up and

nodded toward me. As if to say: "Yeah, that motherfucker in the room. You can't miss him."

"Excuse me, Doctor?"

"You are, how they would say, checking me out? You think women don't do the same?" She was holding up Alario's heart to the examining light. She spoke to her tech, who transcribed everything even though I was sure a mic was recording as well. She continued her presentation to me as if she were a teacher at show-and-tell.

"Look, your estimation of the TEC-9 is accurate, even without ballistics. Puncture holes suggest nine-millimeter automatic. If we do a cross section of the heart, you will find a stitched pattern of the bullets; split it down the middle, two rows of four, equal in impact and length. This is indicating automatic feed, at extremely close range. No more than a foot from the target." She looked up at me. "Were there powder burns on his clothing?"

"Yes. No—what? No, I don't know. Doc, how the fuck do you take a look at me, behind scrubs, dressed just like you, and determine I have cancer?"

"The same way you could tell if I was or wasn't a murderer, Lieutenant. I, like yourself, have what your policemen call 'the eye.' The notorious Spenser boys are not the only smart people in Pittsburgh." She placed the heart in a big metal pan hanging from a chain attached to the ceiling like the duck coming down on the Marx Brothers show.

"I'm assuming cancer because the way you hold your right arm indicates a very recent surgery. Not the rotator cuff, not resection of muscle, not a bone setting, but removal of tissue. So, I'm guessing the doctors at Pitt Oncology removed as much as they could without having to put you under. Fist-size lump, non-malignant, but highly inconvenient under the right armpit, and from the way your right arm slumps, I would say they had to dig into the deltoid toward your back as well.

"You've been sweating since you came in. Since I know you're a veteran homicide cop who has seen enough bodies in his lifetime, and my assistant keeps the exam room at sixty-five degrees, I can assume you have the world's worst flu or you are currently experiencing withdrawal. As far as your treatment conventions, I would say, given your career and your lifestyle, you have foregone radiation and chemo and are on a regimen of painkiller cocktails. But by the generally obvious tremors and the appearance of extreme fatigue, I would guess that in the last three weeks, you have tried to come off cold turkey. From the apparent non-atrophy of your bicep, you have been engaging in some form of physical rehabilitation."

She walked over, lifted up my right arm, and palpated gently over the scar. "Whatever you have been doing, it is not normal post-op physical therapy. Much more physically intense. How am I doing so far?"

"Keep going. I'm trying to figure if you are legit or if my brother is behind the funhouse tent, whispering to the gypsy."

"You've dropped perhaps twenty pounds in the last four weeks. You asked for size large scrubs from my technician, and they are practically sliding down your backside. Your eyes and the burst vessels near the tear ducts indicate a deficiency of iron." She peeled back my sleeve and examined my wrist. "Bilirubin levels seem normal to low abnormal, skin is speckled with some jaundice but not mustard yellow, which means you are a drinker, but you haven't done thus far irreparable damage to your liver." She put two fingers onto my jugular the way you would put a suppository up your cat's ass. "Pulse is slightly high, indicating stress, and most likely you are clenching in pain. How big was the mass when they ultrasounded you?"

I showed her with my hands.

Like she was reading braille, she placed her hands down to my abdomen. Her eyes closed and she tilted her head, cocked and alert as if she were waiting to hear a hasp of a cylinder slide home, spinning the dial, trying to crack a safe. This chick was listening to my fucking cancer with her hands. If old Alario weren't lying on a table, showing the world his breakfast goodies, I would have been supremely turned on by the sexiness of her intelligence and how confidently she assessed me.

She let go, stepped back, pulled down her mask, and looked up at me for a second. "There's still time. Please seek the oncologist unless you want to end up on my table, Lieutenant. The tables at university are much warmer."

"Thanks, Doc. What made you choose pathology?"

"A low curve in regard to patient satisfaction. I am told my bedside manner is well over par." Then, without so much as a blink, she raised her mask, immediately steered around, and went back to the business of the late Alario Washington.

She scribbled furiously on the paperwork and passed it to me. "Wrongful death. Multiple close-range penetrating trauma to the vascular organs with firearm. He was dead before the first bullet exited. Would not have mattered if the EMTs caught him as he was falling. However, take a look at the scene photos. See how the body is lying, facedown? And how the arm is cocked awkwardly? One bullet lodged in the neck shows spinal cord clearly severed. A man is shot like this, his arms immediately drop to the side." For effect, she tightly grabbed each of my wrists. Then she brought both my hands to waist level and flung then away, downward.

"I estimate the shot to the neck severed the spinal cord but was not fatal. This was immediately followed up with, if not simultaneous to, the second shooter's multiple entry wounds to the torso. Pectoral muscles perforated. His arms would not have broken his fall. They would have sought gravity's laws and fell to his sides. Just like yours did now." She tapped the photo with her pen. "I cannot account for that arm sticking outward like it does.

No sign of fracture, and lividity on the body concurs that he fell face forward, flat."

"Doctor, what if the victims were wearing backpacks and the shooters picked that one arm up to recover the bag? Would the arm lay like that if someone finished pulling a bag off their shoulders?"

She looked up and extended a cleanly gloved hand. "Then I would say, Lieutenant, touché. You and I both score a point today, no?"

■ ■ ■

Mandy was a lovely lady. I had no idea what she saw in my brother Kenny. He was brash, stubborn, and condescending. But he was also very political when he had to be. When he wasn't surrounded by cops, he might be mistaken for a math teacher or a lawyer in the grocery store. But he was a damned good detective in his time; he knew the streets and corners. He had a good run in SWAT as the Metro commanding captain, was tactically minded, never lost a hostage once his team was called, never lost any civilians taking down a criminal, but went back to Homicide after I took two bullets in the 1999 PNC robbery. I know he did it for him, not for me, no matter what he said. I could catch a bullet anywhere else in Pittsburgh, even if I were writing traffic tickets.

He had made a risky gamble taking me onto the team fresh out of the academy, but no one seemed to remember the ten robbery shootouts he took me on where I didn't get a scratch. If it had been one of the other Irish, Polack, or Black cops getting shot, it would have been just another day at the office. But Kenny was seen like Superman when he ran SWAT. If Superman couldn't even keep his little brother safe, then what the fuck good was he?

Back to Mandy. She was tall, blond, Polish, some unpronounceable last name like Zeblyzewski. Seriously, her last name was Valchyzk—pronounced "Vowel-chick." She was studying to be a schoolteacher when they met. One of those big-haired "yinzer" Polish Hill Pittsburgh girls growing up, but she was very lovely and kind and seemed to balance my brother out. There was a bit of an age gap between them; Mandy was nineteen around the time Brady and I hit puberty. Still, not as bad as the distance between Frank and Shoshanna, and my mom welcomed Kenny's wife from the moment he brought her home. They were married the December before she got her undergrad from Washington & Jefferson.

She didn't make my brother take off the family yarmulke when he married her, didn't make him go to all those fanatical Pre-Cana classes the Catholics make you do, but he did it anyway, for her. She was the one woman in the world who could knock him down a peg or three, and their family was happy, for the most part. They had four kids, ranging from ages two to ten, all daughters. Thank goodness for that. The world needed fewer Spenser boys growing up to be cops. The girls all had Catholic names: Mary Frances, Ann, Tricia, and Theresa.

After the kids fussed, played, terrorized one another, ate, and then slowly retreated upstairs for bed, I helped Mandy clear the table while Kenny made small talk with Claire in the other room. I had done this for years because I loved Mandy very much and enjoyed what she had come to call our "girl talk." Her view of me was pretty much opposite to the rest of the family. I think everyone else had looked on me as a foster case since Samantha left with the kids, and the cancer issue plus my up-until-recently lack of career ambition was whispered about cautiously in the Ken Spenser household after "little brother" left for the evening. But Mandy never looked on me with pity. If I set myself ablaze with gasoline and matches, Mandy would say that the colors red, yellow, and blue looked really good on me. It wasn't her bullshitting anyone—it was just Mandy.

"How are you feeling, Thomas?"

"I have my days."

"Kenny says you're busting heads in the new task force."

"I wouldn't say that much, but the city sure has given us plenty of work."

"You get along good with Clarissa," she said, calling Claire by her full name. She was like that with people she adored. She called my dad Francis John for years, which always made me feel, yet again, like the odd one out in our family; Brady and Kenny and their families had a relationship with Frank that I couldn't fathom and tried to ignore. My brothers had reached across and made peace—heck, even Rose—but I had been holding out, the guerilla fighter in the jungles, like you read about in the eighties, who didn't get the message World War Two had ended and was still running around some remote part of the archipelago, stockpiling for battle for decade upon decade upon decade.

"We're just really good friends. We get each other."

"That's good. Thomas, I know all the girls are fussing over her, and everyone really likes her, including Mom, but you need to work on you for a while, okay?"

"I know, sis."

"I just know your nature. You take care of everybody else in the world until you are ten feet into a six-foot ditch." She sipped her tea. "Then you can't climb out."

"I know."

"You're like your mom in that way. Marco's wife called me around lunch. Said the new bones down at the morgue did a thirty-second clinical on you?" Marco's wife and the Spenser girls would have the CIA cleaned up in about a week. Intel travels fast.

"Yeah. My new primary care provider is the city deputy coroner," I laughed.

"Thomas. Everyone else is beating around it; I am just going to come out and say it to you. As Mandy, not as your brother's wife. Get back to the oncologist and buy yourself another fifteen to twenty years. Or even, who knows, you might go completely into remission again. Kenny will cover the child support if you have to take a sabbatical from the force. We would not leave you flapping in the breeze."

"I'm not gonna put my hands into your husband's pocket. We have a good profit from the gym still left over. I'm fine. Money isn't what's scaring the shit out of me."

"Not being on the job?"

"The job has kept me going."

"You need something more, Tom. And that brokenhearted girl out there isn't the answer either. She needs to remember what it is like to stand on her own two feet."

"Then how come Ma and you and Sarah and Inez have all adopted her?"

"Because we are helping out a woman in need. And it makes you happy that we do. More people love you than you know, Thomas Francis." She took my hand in hers. "You don't have to put yourself into the grave with this just because you are Frank Spenser's son and you lost a wife who was, let's face it, in the end, a selfish hypocrite and a bit of a bitch. Are you going to be laid up for a while? Yes. Are you going to be sicker than you have ever been? Probably. But there's a chance you will live. A good chance.

"Look at what happened with your father. You think he did that all on his own? How's a man stop his whole habit of character and do a complete one-eighty to how he's been living his whole life? He had to have asked someone for help along the way, if not God. And you're too godda— too darned proud to ask for help. I'm not going to guilt-trip you with your kids. Everyone else has already done that. Tommy, don't do it for us—for me, for everyone else who loves you and are too contrary to open our mouths—either. Do it for you. When God wants you home, He will call you."

"Or a southside banger will put a Glock 20 in my head."

"Don't disrespect my house with that cop talk. Quit being a cynic. Look at what God carried you through. You don't think Kenny still struggles that you took two bullets on his watch? That was back before any of the girls were born, and I still see that look come across his face when you come into a room."

"Kenny cares about what's in the walls of Fortress Spenser right here, and Brady's crew and Ma. Kenny doesn't have much use for me except when bodies hit the pavement."

"Your brother loves you very much, Thomas. You're all he ever talks about. He's so proud of you, and you don't even see it. You know what he said to me the other night when the news was on? He sits there and says he wishes he could walk away from all of this—Pittsburgh, the police, the city—and take the girls, settle for some quiet life. You know why he said he won't? Not your mom. Not your dad. Not Brady. Not the kids. None of that. He says to me: 'I don't want Tommy to think I quit on this city.'"

"That and he's got city hall in his sights."

"And who do you think he wants as right hand to the throne when he gets there? Here's a hint, superstar: it's not Brady."

"What do I know about politics?"

"What have you been doing the last fourteen years? Running into bullets for your big brother, as always. When he makes it, in five or ten years, then you just trade that badge for a briefcase."

"Boy, Mandy, you're something. Are you sure you're not the real rabbi?" I laughed again. "Ol' Amanda Valchyzk. You're something, all right."

■ ■ ■

Claire wrapped one hand around my arm and took my forearm with her other as we walked into the stillness of the gym. It was maybe 11:30. She softly broke her grip on me as we got to the narrow catwalk.

"Are you coming in for a bit?" she asked upstairs with an eager smile.

I thought about what Mandy had said to me. "You know what, it's been a long day."

"Not even to sleep?"

"It's been a long day, Claire."

"Tom, I jus—"

"I'm not gonna gear myself up, Claire, if that's what you're going to say. You're my friend and my neighbor—not my caseworker, and not my wife." It was a mean verbal snap, I will admit, but it needed to be said. "You're coming over and digging through my shit and snooping in my place, looking for a project, and there's plenty to work on of your own stuff."

She clenched her jaw, and her mouth went tight. A single tear ran down her cheek. She crossed her arms and looked away from me. "I was going to say I just wanted to be near you."

"Claire, I'm sorry I got out of line, but think about it. We're living on top of each other. If we were dating, like normal dating, there'd be breaks and nights alone and stuff, right? I like having you around. And I like holding you all night. But I'm trying to get my shit together. And I need time to adjust."

She got herself composed. There was a wary glare in her eyes when she met my gaze. She started to turn toward her door, but I caught her sleeve, gently, and she paused. For a second, I thought she was going to snap her arm back, or smack me, or yell. But she didn't.

"I love the way we are together. I love that you look out for me and try to take care of me. Let's take things as they come, okay? I am just grateful that you're here."

She nodded and then gave me a small peck on my cheek. I've had racier kisses from distant, elderly aunts.

"Goodnight, Thomas."

The symptoms for Percocet withdrawal are almost the same as when you are addicted. The only difference is that in the withdrawal process, you are more agitated. I had another night of horrible sweats and chills, throwing up, goose bumps, and tremors. I dragged myself down the hallway to the toilet. *Come on, trooper, five more feet.*

I didn't make it. Vomit, white wine, and my sister-in-law's best veal cutlets and linguini splattered on the tile.

Please, God, Claire—do not come over. Don't you fucking come over. You stay right in that bed. Don't you fucking knock on the door. I don't want another in the Clarissa Samuels-Hewitt lecture tour.

I stood up and grabbed a towel to mop up my accident. I stared at the lid of the toilet tank. *Fuck it.*

I took the lid off and flipped it over. I pulled off each remaining ampoule that was taped to it. Then, holding each one over the toilet, I cracked them open and dumped them. All fourteen ampoules' contents went into the shitter. I hit flush. I brushed my teeth for about five minutes until my gums started to bleed.

I took a shower, got into my characteristic cozy academy sweats, and made tea in the kitchen. I sipped the tea slowly, medicinally. Then I grabbed the rest of the meds and went out behind the building with Charley where the trainers and our one janitor set the trash out for the garbage man.

There was a burn barrel, a fifty-five-gallon drum where we burned leaves we raked from the small yard next to the maintenance entrance. It was about a quarter filled with leaves.

I threw the three pill containers in and followed them with crumpled balls of week-old *Pittsburgh Tribune-Review* pages. I emptied a bottle of barbecue propellant into the barrel and lit a match. In the short time since my shower, I had managed to soak myself in sick sweat all over again; however, my mind had never been clearer.

Charley looked up at me quizzically. Why were we burning stuff at two in the morning?

"Had to be done, pal. Had to be done."

I gently tried the doorknob on Claire's place. To her word, it remained unlocked.

I walked in and knelt next to her bed. I softly touched her shoulder. She lifted her head. Drowsy, confused, she looked at me with momentary shock.

"Thomas, what's wrong? What happened?"

"I just wanted you to know in case you were looking again, like being helpful or concerned or anything, that I burned it all."

"All what?"

"The stash, the drugs, the Percocet, the Demerol. Everything's gone. Even that gag bottle of Ibuprofen."

She hugged me. "Oh, baby, you're soaked in sweat."

"Kind of a rough night."

She asked, "Do you want to stay?"

"It makes me feel weak if I stay."

"You're no weaker than I was the day you brought me here. Sometimes people just need to stay away from trouble. And they need help doing it."

"I'll stay above the sheets. I'm freezing to death one minute, pouring in sweat the next."

She pulled back the blankets anyways. Her outfit for the night was some sort of berry-colored couture pajamas that were supposedly made by Victoria's Secret but managed to cover every square inch from her throat to her toes. As I took this in, she giggled in self-consciousness, fully awake now. “Never had much need for the thin sexy stuff. Wasn’t exactly the love boat in West Mifflin. Especially during NASCAR season.”

I lay closest to the doorway, and she curled up behind my back. I started, helplessly, to cry. “I didn’t dump it all just for you.”

“Shh. Shh. I know, Thomas. It would be quite silly if you did.”

“I’m not going to die in this fucking gym on my kitchen floor, Clarissa.”

“I don’t want anything to happen to you, Thomas. I want you to be well.”

I felt her fingers massaging the tension from my neck while her other hand inattentively played with my short-cropped hair. She brought her face next to mine, in profile so that our cheeks touched, and I felt new tears running on both our faces. She kept kissing my cheek, my neck, my ear. Then her kisses got more urgent, and her fingers were pulling at my sweatshirt. I rolled over to face her, and her mouth instantly covered mine, and I felt the warmth and playfulness of her tongue. By the time I got out of my shirt, she had kicked her legs and thrashed her pajama bottoms off, and she hugged me with her limbs fiercely. Her arms went around my neck, and she kissed me again.

More shyly than she had pulled off her bottoms, she opened and slid out of her shirt. It was arousing as she pulled herself up level to my chest and pressed against me, the softness and warmth of her body and the smell of being that close to her. Her legs and calves were strong, and they wrapped me possessively. Her chest pushed against me with eagerness and longing.

Despite my having seen her naked twice before, tonight I could tell she was self-conscious about her body—her hipbones were prominent under the skin, and there was a time I could probably count her ribs with my fingers, but the comfort of the last few months had put fullness into her face, an easiness into her posture, and as she had been busying herself with jogging and experimenting on the machines in the gym, her arms were toned and her stomach had a slight definition to it. She didn't look anything like the trembling cadaver in the turquoise robe anymore. Her eyes, though, still held a bit of the pain. I traced my hands over her warm legs, ran my fingers over her stomach, held her in my arms, and kept on kissing the spot on her neck that felt like pure comfort when I inhaled the scent of her perfume and hair.

I kissed her again and again, warmly, sweetly, and foreplay for us was just smiling, the eye contact, more kissing. I tried to be gentle, but as we started, I felt her body tense up. I hoped the tears I saw now were happy ones, or only plain tension. As if she knew my thoughts, she nodded reassuringly. I was almost afraid to be completely on top of her, she seemed so light.

After a bit of settling in, there was just gentleness and rocking back and forth. I heard her pace her breathing. Exhale, sharp exhale, long inhale. She kept running her hands up and down my back.

When it was over, we retreated back to more kissing, and I lay on my back while she adjusted herself against me, my chest once again her pillow.

We fell asleep intertwined with each other. But at that moment, I wasn't thinking of the woman I was falling in love with; running through my mind was Mandy's kind but firm warning.

CHAPTER 11

Saint Luke's Church usually opens at nine on Saturdays. There was a wedding at eleven, so there was no morning Mass. The pews were trimmed with ribbons and flowers. I had only been inside Saint Luke's for weddings and funerals, but the priest knew me like family.

Father Jay Scott Newman had known our family since Kenny was born. Most of his guidance to the Spenser family took place at the kitchen table of mom's house. He counseled my mother during the hard years, befriended my father after Dad was out of the hospital and on the wagon, and prayed at my bedside after the 1999 shooting. What I liked about him was that he didn't try to sell you on God.

"Thomas Spenser, in the flesh. And look at that—you didn't catch ablaze when you walked into the rectory!"

"Hello, Father." I shook his hand.

"What brings you here in your blues? Not carrying bad news for a parishioner, are you? Or are you hoping to crash the wedding today?"

"I was told I should always dress my best when I'm in court." I nodded to the crucifix. "In front of my judge and all."

"What's in the bag?"

"Irish lemonade." I pulled out a bottle of Tullamore Dew.

"Tom, it's barely nine."

"Good. Then it won't be on your breath by eleven, will it?"

He laughed and grabbed two mugs from beside his coffee pot. "Okay. One. To celebrate the Halley's Comet appearance of Lieutenant Tom Spenser in my parish and he's not burying someone or on the arm of a bridesmaid. Do you come for me to hear your confession, boy-o?"

"Thirty-five years of a Spenser boy's confession would have you miss the eleven o'clock wedding, Father."

"Indeed, my son. So, I once again venture into the dark, multidenominational country of Irish Palestine to cater to my flock in the Rosencoff-Spenser family. The last time Thomas Spenser came near this church bearing gifts, you and Brady had just shot a red-spotted woodpecker with a BB gun, saying you'd thought it was a pigeon. And you were both trying to give me your entire baseball card collections if I would bury it. You said, I believe, that without my blessing, it would be buried with your sin on it. I honestly believe you were worried more about that than the fine for shooting such a bird. Who, or what, did you shoot now, my son?"

"Myself, Father."

"Quite ambulatory for a self-inflicted wound."

"I'm on the needle, Father. Needle, pills, and booze. I know, in part, it wrecked my marriage."

"It doesn't excuse Samantha's infidelity."

I nodded in acknowledgment. "I had it under control for a few years, but my cancer is back. I don't know if I just used that as an excuse to start again, though. I'll lose my job if it keeps up. I'm scared, Father. Scared of dying. Scared of going on living like this. Living in fear. Scared of the emptiness I will feel when I sober up completely, scared of getting sick on chemo. Scared of hope. A while back I met a girl in a bad situation. I helped her out of it. I have love in my heart for her, Father, but I know I have to heal things about me first before I'm good for anyone. Plus, it seems like her life is laden with sadness, and I think I've had just about enough of that in my world. But I still feel responsible for her, Father."

"A foundation built on water is not a foundation, Thomas."

"Yeah, yeah, I know. I know what I have to do. What I ought to do. Mostly I'm scared."

"Have you sought professional treatment for the addiction?"

"Quitting isn't the hard part, Father. Waking up to this life every day and acting like I have a reason to continue is."

"Thomas Francis, you're a good man. A fine policeman. Whatever burden you carry in your heart, the Lord sees all. The good and the bad. There is no dialectic love when it comes to God."

"Then without the police. Without this woman. Without the children or my family. I need purpose."

"Do you remember that night you confronted your father? I came to your home the next day and asked you why you did it. You looked up and said to me: 'Because I prayed to God to stop it, and I wanted to get His attention for a change.'"

"Yes, Father. I more than remember what I said."

"Tom, while I do not condone violence, I saw a goodness in you. While what you did was brutal and shocking, it was necessary; you did what you did to protect your mother. You had purpose in you then, my child. You still have purpose. You need to give yourself peace and forgive your dad. Above all, you need to forgive yourself."

"I've had so much pain over the years, Father. How do I walk around without the burden?"

"Tom, know this: Neither God nor the devil has laid that burden you carry in your heart. You alone put it on your shoulders. And you are the only one who can let it go. I know what kind of man you are. Your family, your children know what kind of man you are. Now you need to see it."

He stood and extended his hand to me.

"I have to get ready for the Kaczynski wedding. I would tell my Catholic patrons at this point to say a few Our Fathers and Hail Marys, but for you I will just say stay out of trouble. As for your lady friend, I will just say this: Wherever there is someone in pain, and you approach them with goodness in your heart,

God smiles on that. Only you can judge whether or not your involvement in this woman's life will bring her grief. You cannot go wrong in God's eyes as long as you continue to err on the side of goodness. I will pray for you both. Take care of yourself, Tommy."

■ ■ ■

Four days later, I heard the phone ring at Marco's desk. "High-Value Target Task Force, Sergeant Escardo."

A few minutes later, he knocked on my doorframe. "Boss."

"What's up, Marco?"

"You want to go kick down some doors for old times' sake?"

I put down my glasses and looked up from my crime scene photos. "Who rang?"

"Patrol unit on northside found a few of Razor's old captains running around. They're freelancing ever since Razor got killed. Picked them up in a stolen car with two forty-five calibers in a compartment under the seat. They had put bogus plates on the hot car and installed one of those special compartments for the pistols.

"Snopes has them in the box right now. These two fuckheads couldn't wait to start talking. We have locations of three stash houses, and Judge Scanlon just signed off on the warrants. I guess they're trying to rid themselves of the competition, but the DA is talking about cutting a deal that they walk if the houses pay off. You want us to go one-on-one, me and Snopes, and have Detective Simmons lead the third?"

Although Snopes was the most senior detective, Simmons was better in house raids and takedowns, and we all knew it. If anything, Snopes would stick with us on raids while Simmons flew solo. Plus, we had dubbed this the "designated survivor" plan—all four lead detectives would not engage in a tactical operation on the same day at the same time; one would always be in headquarters. I pointed to the whiteboard and showed Marco he'd forgotten today's rotation on the roster for HQ was not me but Simmons.

I put on my vest and grabbed my blue raid jacket, PITTSBURGH POLICE MCU stenciled in yellow letters on the back.

"No." I pondered it. "No. Instead of raiding three, we'll all-out siege one. It's Monday morning. They probably haven't put out distribution yet, so two of the houses probably don't have a stash to hold. Give me the overlays. I want to see activity."

My gamble paid off. From our bird's-eye-view surveillance in the last six hours that Snopes and company had been questioning the suspects, we saw two of the houses had few cars and even fewer people going in and out. The third house was busier than a Best Buy the day after Thanksgiving.

"That's got to be where they're cooking and distributing from. Now I want confirmation. Call Taradash and my sister at the DA's office. No deal with those assholes. They were about to send us on a snipe hunt. The other two are fucking decoys." I grabbed the photos and headed for the interview room, boiling with rage. I did a cursory glance at the scumbags' arrest folder for five minutes in the hallway.

Demetrius Chesworth, twenty-one years old, had already done three years at Shuman for second-degree murder knocked back to involuntary manslaughter as a fifteen-year-old. Released with a sealed record at eighteen, junior sociopath tries to turn over a new leaf in the Marines. Lasts exactly thirty-six months, pisses hot on a urinalysis for cocaine and meth, comes back to Pittsburgh with a chip on his shoulder and a less-than-honorable discharge, starts back into the drug game as a soldier for the Washington family.

The hate in his eyes was boilerplate. I've seen it on every person I have ever cuffed who thinks I grew up on the other side of the Fort Pitt Tunnel just because I wear a tie and press my khakis.

I laid the photos out in front of him, and his eyes widened. He clearly hadn't realized our surveillance was this keen, and he knew his deal was in the wind.

"Which one is the house, Demetrius?"

"Man, who the fuck are you?"

I slam another folder down. "Six months ago. Your first order of business after coming back from Guantanamo Bay Windward Barracks was to take the last of your GI money and go on an epic bender in Atlantic City. But you took the train over to New York, and you raped an underage girl in Queens. Made bail and never showed up for the court date."

"Man, that was some bullshit! She was hooking and looked twenty-one! It was consensual!"

"Not according to the law of New York State. The good people of the five boroughs as well as those above the Hudson consider your little caper a class E felony. Looks like they still wish to pursue charges against you, and they are jus' delighted that Patrolman Suzcyk and crew found your raggedy ass over yonder in Oakland. I have the extradition papers right here. You'll be dodging dicks in Rikers this time tomorrow." I handed him a red Sharpie marker and pointed to three photos in front of him. "Work with me and I will do everything in my power to broker a deal with the Queens prosecutor. Which one is the jackpot?"

Eyes seething with more hatred, he pointed to the "superstore," then picked up the marker to circle the doorway points on the building.

I picked up my walkie-talkie. "Border Patrol, Drugstore Cowboy."

"Go for Border Patrol."

"Suspect Alpha confirms it's the Macy's Parade."

"Roger."

I picked up the extradition papers and signed them, then buzzed the uniforms back in to take him away.

"*We had a deal*!"

"I don't make deals with kiddie rapists. I said I'd do everything in my power. I have no power in New York City. Don't drop the soap, asshole."

I hurried down to the team locker room, where Marco and Snopes were already suiting up in their SWAT gear.

"Tommy, look, about that day at your place . . ."

"Ain't nothing. We were both wrong. Because each of us thinks we are always right."

He put his hand out to me. "Am I still a Spenser, boss?"

"Bitch, you're more Spenser than me." I embraced my partner and clapped him on the back.

"Let's do this."

"Marco, you stay on my back this one."

"What?"

"I mean it. You grab hold of the belt loops over my Irish ass, and you don't let go."

Marco regarded me calmly. "Your call."

"Fucking right it's my call. Notify the SWAT sergeant. I want their full day shift and their standby shift coming in. We roll in sixty minutes."

"You'll probably be calling some guys in on overtime."

"They love this shit." I loaded my M4, and Marco grabbed a twelve-gauge bullpup shotgun—a chopped-down version of a regular shotgun, fitted with a tactical grip in place of a shoulder stock and an additional grip attached to the fore-end. This makes it a superb breaching device as well as a great close-quarters weapon.

For a moment, I turned and almost expected to see Kenny there in a jumpsuit, throwing the huge, black hockey bag of takedown gear over his shoulder, with his little brother—me from twelve years ago—trailing dutifully behind him out the door.

"Believe me, they love it."

■ ■ ■

The stash house we hit was an abandoned shipping warehouse three stories high with a two-floor sub-basement.

"Pittsburgh police, search warrant!"

One of the SWAT kids had the battering ram, but with a ram there is always a chance they can still work the door as a defensive weapon against you, even if you have some poor bastard smooshed back behind it. I preferred to blow the door. A small charge on the hinges, and that bitch becomes flying splinters. Our guys sitting on the curb told us there were no little ones, no civilians in there. Blowing the door, plus smoke through the windows five seconds before the door blew, would be highly effective.

I nodded to Marco, and he ran up with the plastique, peeled back the adhesive strip, and stuck it to the door. Every guy on SWAT backed up about ten feet while still drawing a bead on the doorway. Stash houses usually have more firepower in them than Fort Knox.

I loaded a round in the "blooper" gun and fired an M203 canister of red smoke through the window with the velocity of a shotgun burst. There was confusion, cursing, and a few sporadic shots returned out the window. When the red smoke reached eye level of the window, I nodded to Marco. He clicked the button on the breaker charges.

BOOM.

SWAT went in first. Then the glass in the upstairs storefront window broke, and a blue fireball rolled out.

"*Fuck*! They're burning it, they're burning it! Put that shit out!"

Two more SWAT guys ran past me with fire extinguishers for just this thing. Marco and I nodded and followed them. I heard each two-man team yell as they cleared each room—then a surge in gunfire. *Aw, shit.*

The radio on my shoulder squelched. "Lieutenant, we got two men down in the stairwell!"

Fuck.

I ran to the stairs. Neither guy was dead nor dying. SWAT is usually so heavily armored that the most they get is the wind knocked out of them and a few cracked ribs unless the bangers were lucky and hit one of my guys in the throat. Or if it's just Murphy's fucking luck, like the day I went down. Marco and I had to split up until we knew all the SWAT guys were safe.

"Marco, go downstairs with the search team. I'll clear high with these guys."

Marco nodded and ran.

When we got up the stairwell, it was bad. SWAT guys don't get armored legs, and that's where both were hit. Some asshole was holed up in the room facing the street, and I guess he wanted to go out with fireworks. The SWAT sergeant was a good guy, but he was slowly letting the scene go to shit. The stack men—the guys behind the two point men who had taken the barrage of gunfire—had panicked and fallen down right where their wounded were instead of fighting through and clearing each room. Every cop will throw themselves over a wounded buddy, no doubt. But leaving him there and running another twenty feet and stopping the threat while your buddy is still lying there bleeding, that's the important part. You need security on the objective before you start breaking out the Band-Aids. Unless you want more people to get shot and die.

I grabbed one of the concussion grenades from my vest and heaved it into where the wannabe Al Capone was shooting from. Without waiting for the first to blow, I threw a second one, and followed it up with a flashbang. The healthy guys from the clearing team who were shielding their wounded buddies from the blast popped up after the flashbang went off, dutifully clearing the room. I heard two shotgun blasts hit our perpetrator, and he thudded to the floor.

My two firefighters ran in and fanned the room with their portable hoses.

My ears were ringing. I looked down at our shooter. Half his face was smoldering. Concussion grenades are supposed to be nonlethal, but two in a row will fuck up your day for sure. And it's a really bad day if someone puts a flashbang and shotgun on top. I did a quick assessment of his wounds. He took the shots point-blank, but he was wearing Kevlar. No hard plate, though. He was bleeding slowly, and most likely internally. I reached for a pulse and saw his chest move. "He's still breathing! Have Doc bag this asshole!"

My radio crackled. "Boss, basement is clear. We have four perps down. Marco is hit; I say again, Marco is hit."

I grabbed the hand mike on my radio. "Is he alive?"

"Roger. He's alive and stable. Took two in the shoulder. Don't think it nicked any arteries. We have pressure on the wound, and he's talking to us."

"Get him over to Mercy West. Any of the perps alive?"

"One is. Gutshot, but he might make it."

"Put him in the car with you guys and go. Don't wait for EMT. We have a guy really fucked up here plus two SWAT with leg wounds. Get Marco and the gutshot guy over to Mercy. If Marco's conscious, make the gutshot your priority. I don't want some IAD bullshit saying we let the dealer bleed out."

I waved in "Doc" McClusky, the field medic, and he quickly went to work stabilizing the perp. The field medic was really our team sniper, but he had been an 18D medical sergeant in Iraq and Afghanistan before joining the department. Using him was a lot quicker than sitting around with thumbs up our asses, waiting on ambulances. He cut away the guy's vest and started plugging the wound with Kerlix.

I grabbed the SWAT sergeant by his tac vest and shoved him into an empty room. "What the fuck was that?"

"You're out of line, Lieutenant! Get your fucking hands off me!"

"Is this fucking amateur hour? Since when do we camp out on our wounded before the building's clear? Or were you trying to kill all of them?"

"You're a heartless fuck, Spenser, you know that?"

"Yeah, but you're standing here talking to me and not still fighting for ground from the stairwell, are you? Where the fuck is your head, Sergeant?"

"You're one to talk, you shitbird. I'm sure they left behind some Oxy for you to snort up. Or why don't you poke around the downstairs rooms. Maybe one of the Black *brothas* has a beat-up wife you can take home for your pet project."

Fuck this guy. I was on top of him in seconds. I broke his nose and was ripping the Velcro panels of his vest open so I could gut punch the sonofabitch and make sure he felt it. But it was a hot scene, and I should have been a lot calmer. A wild dog forgets where he is fighting sometimes—and who's surrounding him. Three SWAT guys tackled me off of him. The sergeant stood up, aimed three or four hard kicks to my side and one for good measure to my head. But I think he pulled that one; my lip split open, but no teeth flew.

Then his gloved hand reached down to me. The playground

fight was over, and we were two cops again that were glad we at least got all our men out alive.

"Shit, Lieutenant, those perps got us good, didn't they?"

I stood up, spit out blood, and smiled a wild, blood-spattered grin worthy of the Joker. "Fucking drug dealers, Sarge. They think they're ballers." I went downstairs and talked to Tori Snopes. He didn't say anything or mention the state of my bloodied face and red drool coming out of my mouth; he simply raised an eyebrow and adjusted his black, collegiate-looking, horn-rimmed glasses as they pored over the bodies and the evidence.

"How are you, Snopes?"

"Better than you, I would reckon. You look like you just fucked a cheetah and the cheetah asked to get on top."

"How's Marco?"

"He seems stable. We have a slight problem, though."

"What's that?"

"Well, we're doing recovery of sensitive items at the moment, and we cannot account for Marco's assault weapon. He left here with his service pistol and his little pansy-ass gun you all clown him about, but the bullpup shotgun that he signed out from the armory before the raid—it's gone."

"What?!"

"Well, the circumstances of how he was hit. He was in a hand-to-hand scuffle with one of the perps, who surprised him and knocked the shotgun away by the barrel. Then the perp drew a thirty-eight and shot him near point-blank in the vest. It went through, but the vest stopped the rounds from striking arteries and killing him. Perp was shot by SWAT, but one of his associates fled the building and was apparently wounded."

"And you didn't pursue this?"

"Boss, this just fucking happened!"

I ran out of the building and frantically looked around for

a blood trail. My adrenaline was skyrocketing as I realized this fucker could wax me at any second. Then I saw him, facedown. White T-shirt, blue jeans, gang colors on his head, bare feet, not even time to put his shoes on when we hit the place. Marco's weapon lay a few feet from him.

With my rifle trained at his head, I rolled his body with a solid heave of my leg. He was clearly dead, had three solid shots to the torso with what must have been rounds from the SWAT officers. I turned and looked back to the building. No one had followed me out.

In a moment of complete insanity, my instincts working faster than my brain, I grabbed the shotgun and heaved it into the dumpster of the industrial warehouse on the opposite side of the fence from where we were. The dumpster was full of construction material and insulation rolls, and the rifle thudded but did not make a metal-on-metal sound.

I wanted to vomit and faint as I stood there over the body, hands on my knees, waiting for Snopes to come out there.

"Any luck?" he asked as he emerged with Doc McClusky in tow.

"Just a downed perp."

"Buddies must have picked it up getting away from us. Shit. We'll do a stolen-items report. Fucked-up shit happens in a raid. Sounds cynical, but at least it was a shotgun and not one of our fully automatic specials."

"I hear you."

Snopes reached and gently touched the bottom of my chin, studying my cuts and injuries. "You really need to read Dale Carnegie's *How to Win Friends and Influence People*, Thomas. Your popularity in this department isn't exactly pep-rally levels of wonderful."

"Ha. That's why I have you around."

Doc McClusky pulled me aside.

"Boss, why is he on his back but there's blood pooling from his chest wound on the ground like you found him on his belly?"

"Because I searched the body."

"Yeah, that's what I'm getting at."

"Fuck are you saying, Doc?"

"I think I'm saying it, Tommy. You roll cowboy with Marco, the two of you in the car, that's one thing. But when you roll out with the boys, you're responsible for all of us. *All* of us. And I'm not going to prison for a narcissistic functioning junkie who wants to play the game dirty."

"Fuck you, Doc. Go back with the EMTs. This is my fucking crime scene."

The guy who took the brunt of my concussion grenade and two in the belly ended up dying on the scene. After the two SWAT troopers had been rushed to the hospital along with Marco, the remaining EMTs, with nothing to do but bag the dead guys, tried to look me and the SWAT sergeant over, but the good sergeant told them where to fuck off. McClusky didn't even look my way.

The docs at Mercy wanted to look at me too, but I brushed them away until I knew Marco was all right. It took Samantha driving across town with her medical duffel bag that looked like a pararescue commando's load-out kit. After twenty minutes of yelling back and forth behind a curtain, I let my ex-wife shoot a whopper of toroidal into my cracked ribs and tape me over my torso with a Kevlar-esque vest of medical tape and gauze, like I had tuberculosis in a J. D. Salinger novel.

One of the concussion grenades must have been too close range for comfort because midway through Samantha's treatment, I passed out. They monitored me for traumatic brain injury for twenty-four hours.

■ ■ ■

At 2:30 the next morning, after I self-discharged out of the hospital, there was a slew of yellow caution-tape rolls around the warehouse and just one bored patrolman in a cruiser out front, listening to his radio and probably reading a porno mag.

I had come back from the precinct and parked my Mustang half a mile away. I wore my black thermal undershirt from the night of the sniper raid, my blue jogging pants from the academy, and my dad's black, knit Army watch cap. If I was caught, I had zero explanation, but I had no intentions of getting caught. Over my shoulder I had a small, forest-green duffel bag that would perfectly hold the bullpup and two towels to wrap it in, keeping it from knocking into my sternum while I ran.

I did a passive trot up to the front of the building and peeked around the corner. Nothing in sight. Patrol car still there, one officer, interior light on. No porn, but he was reading. Looked like a novel.

I boxed widely around the other warehouse and came up from the far side of its rear parking lot toward the dumpster. Pulling myself up, I dropped into nearly the same spot I had launched the shotgun that afternoon. I suppressed a shit-eating grin as my hand grasped the foregrip, trying to dissuade the feeling that I had committed about three crimes in the span of the last eighteen hours. Unauthorized possession/theft of a city officer's firearm, trespassing, and tampering with a crime scene immediately came to mind.

I hopped back out of the dumpster and heard the ominous sound of two pistols being cocked in unison.

"Find what you were looking for, Detective Spenser?"

I swear, if I'd had any water in me, I would have pissed a river right there. My instincts and near decades of training told me not to let go of the shotgun.

I swung around and faced my would-be killers.

It was them. Blue coveralls. They were wearing 1980s-style white goalie hockey masks. Unfortunately, tape covered their wrists, and they had dark clothing covering bare areas below the neck, so I couldn't tell if they were Black, White, yellow, brown, or Martian. Everything else was covered with dark makeup, the way Batman blackens his eyes under his cowl.

What the fuck are they doing here?

"Hey, fuckers. You're under arrest."

They both laughed almost hysterically through voice distortion filters in their masks. "How the hell are you going to explain being out here at a crime scene, stealing your partner's shotgun?"

"Maybe I had an inkling to go back out and look again."

"Without any sort of backup? Dressed like a cat burglar? Not even telling the cop up front you're having a peek?"

"So, you assholes are fucking cops?"

"We are simply good citizens. Doing what you refuse to."

"Outright murders, you mean? How about I sink to your level of justice? How about I send one of you straight to fucking hell?" I checked the chamber of Marco's bullpup and aimed it center mass at the fuckhead on the right. "Now, you fuckers may have the drop on me, but I'm damn sure taking one of you with me. And if they find my body alongside one of yours, it won't be long at all before they find the other one of you. The Pittsburgh police tend to frown when you kill one of their own."

"Big talk from a man who let his own partner get shot today."

I pointed the barrel down between the guy on the left's legs and pulled the trigger.

BLAM!

The majority of the buckshot missed him, but five or so pellets lodged in his shoe, and he went down swearing. He kicked off the shoe. His partner took an unaimed shot at me that ricocheted off the dumpster and zinged into a tree, helped his buddy to his feet, and they both ran for it.

My heart pounding in my throat, I rolled under the dumpster and braced myself there as I heard the uniformed officer run past. He was pursuing them, not me. I heard seven more shots, then him screaming into his radio for backup. His car came to life, and the siren wailed away.

Good, I thought. *They left him alive.*

I looked at my luminescent watch and counted off the longest five minutes of my life. When I heard sirens miles in the distance and was sure the backup cars were chasing the route the cop had followed, I rolled back out from underneath the dumpster and wrapped the shotgun in the towels. I spotted the shooter's shoe on the ground and grabbed it up before I beelined for the escape route in my head through the back pathways that would get me to the car past a minimal number of streetlights.

■ ■ ■

Behind my mom's house is a vacant lot near a set of train tracks that no longer runs passenger trains through that part of Pittsburgh. Near the tracks was a defunct junction box. Before the crack of dawn, I dug a hole near the junction box, unloaded and stripped the shotgun down into its separate components, wrapped it in oilcloth, sealed it in a weatherproof bag, and buried it. I then spent the next half hour with a shovel and a trowel, smoothing over the area and re-embedding rocks and turf to make the ground look natural again.

Again, I knew I was crazy. But something in my brain, even back then, told me that this was going to be a game of dirty pool. A cop with no ethics could use that gun, planted illegally somewhere, as motivating currency to force one of Razor's associates to give up even more information on the crews and end this fucking thing. But I had not been prepared to be made by the two murderers who had lit the fuse on this whole goddamned deal. And now I had evidence and no way to explain how I got it. I was a mess of nerves, trembling, about to vomit, and more than anything I needed a fucking hit.

CHAPTER 12

At 6:30 Wednesday morning, nearly thirty-six full hours after the raid, I came into the apartment. My ribcage was on fire, exacerbated by my nighttime antics. And I had flushed every last bit of pain medication. *Fuck.*

Careful not to get Samantha's tape-work wet, I filled the tub with water so that it just reached my waistline sitting down. Twenty minutes into my soak, I heard Claire knock.

"Okay if I come in, Tommy?"

"I'm in the tub, but sure."

"It's been all over the news. I was worried." She came down the hall and eased the door open. She covered her mouth to stop a scream when she saw me. The worst thing was the SWAT sergeant had kicked me on the same side the surgery had been on. The fucker's love taps had left dark welts of black and blue running from my ribcage across my arm, all the way up to the side of my face.

"Naw, this was . . . this was a misunderstanding." I fumbled for a cigarette. On the rare times in my life that I got the shit beat out of me outside the boxing ring, lighting up a Marlboro after the ass-kicking somehow made it more acceptable in the world of manhood. The cigarettes were stale and nearly green with age, but I choked a few puffs of nicotine out while Claire seated herself on the closed toilet seat and studied my injuries and my posturing, one curious eyebrow raised.

Surprisingly, her next move was to snatch one of my foul, bad-luck mementos out of the pack and press it to her lips. She leaned into my Zippo lighter, and as I snapped it open, she inched forward those fractions of centimeters, the tip of her cig touching off the flame. For a second, she averted her eyes to the door as if we were both in junior high and her mother were going to come through the entryway in a housecoat, ready to smack her behind the ear with a wooden serving spoon—an old favorite corporal punishment of my mother's.

"Kenny's wife called and told me Marco was in Mercy Hospital. I wanted to come down to see you yesterday, but your mom said . . . your mom said that it'd be better to wait to hear from you. That if it were something serious, the department would have notified us—I mean, her."

"Yeah."

"I would have gone with Mandy to visit Marco, but it's weird. I didn't want you to think I was making this, me and you, something it's not. Trying to be a Spenser wife groupie."

"You're friends with Inez and the girls. You had every right to go."

She took a puff of her cigarette, then ran her eyes over my body. "Jesus, you look like shit. Sweetie, you flushed and burned everything, too."

"I would rather have this pain than the other." My lies were getting so that I even believed them.

"Can I do anything for you?"

"Yeah. Dump the three bottles of scotch in the pantry. Down the drain, not in the trash."

She knelt down so she was eye level with me. "You're sure?"

"Right now, I don't need a drink. I need to sleep."

She picked up a washcloth and started to gently scrub my back, above the line of tape, massaging my shoulders. "I've missed you tonight."

I know she wanted me to say I missed her as well. But the truth was I didn't even notice her in the room. My mind went back to Monday night. Running up that hallway. Breaching that door and taking down the shooter. It wasn't suicidal; all I kept thinking the whole time was how much I didn't want to die, and now I pondered the electricity of how alive I had felt since it happened. A month ago, I would have paid the bastard to take me out on his rampage. But what kept coming back to me was the talk with Father Jay about purpose.

"It's already six thirty. Come to my place," she said. "I'm out looking for work today anyhow. My bed's bigger. You can pull the shades tight, sleep all day."

"Naw, I'll see you tonight. Maybe for a change I'll make something for you. I'm only gonna sleep a few hours anyhow. There's something I have to do today. Hey, Mandy and my mom . . . well, the whole family wants you there for Thanksgiving in a few weeks. Let's both go, okay? Together."

"Okay." She leaned forward and kissed me, taking care to avoid my split lip. She smiled sweetly at me and raked her fingers over my hair. "Sweet dreams, my detective."

I heard her pouring out the bottles in the kitchen, and then she was gone.

■ ■ ■

At 9:30, I felt like I was going to the principal's office. I nodded to the doctor's receptionist. Maybe she could see the meekness in my eyes; I wasn't ushered out or told that I wasn't welcome. I sat in one of the chairs and read a tattered copy of *Time*.

"Doctor Tolliver will see you now, Detective."

Tolliver's office had these overstuffed leather armchairs that always reminded me of some cigar-club gentlemen's lounge. In chairs like that, it's easier to take news that you don't have long to live. Tolliver had a rather good poker face, too. Maybe he had chairs just like them surrounding a green felt table in his basement game room.

"The prodigal son. What brings you back, Lieutenant?"

"I've been clean for almost a month. Clean as in not self-medicating. Dumped that G-pack of Demerol you gave me, the one from summer. I took six ampoules over a period of six weeks. Flushed the last fourteen. Stopped the Percocet cold. Watching my drinking. No binges. Flushed or burned all my pills. What you see is about a good month of withdrawal. The new reaper over at the city morgue diagnosed me as a junkie from across a fucking room while she was cutting open one of my crime vics."

"I have to hear you tell me, Thomas."

"I was disrespectful, and manipulative, and awful to you."

"That I don't care about. You think I don't get ten or more patients—or their loved ones—cursing me out each week? I want to hear you tell me something that lets me know I'm not wasting my time."

"I want to live."

"You want to live?"

"But—and here's the thing—I'm not out to get a script or a fix from you. I know I need to start treatment, but I can't have so much radiation that I am knocked on my ass and can't work either. Do that to me, and I think I'll just dive back into the pills."

"I agree."

"Can we contain it for a while? Like, fight the fire from growing instead of trying to drench the whole forest? At least till I knock this case?"

"The drug murders? That's your guys running it?"

"Yeah."

"I know coming back in here was uncomfortable for you. And I think it's bold that you dumped your whole stash. But you're making yourself sicker, too, going on the route of absolutes. If you are hooked on painkillers but having withdrawal and anxiety attacks, then denying any sort of antianxiety medication is only going to exacerbate your withdrawal symptoms.

"It's a vicious cycle, Tom. These crackheads we put in detox, you think we just stop everything going into their system at once? They would die! You're a smart man. Leave your ego out of the equation. Take what I prescribe you but take it *per the prescription*. I'm going to put you on Ativan for the withdrawal anxiety, and I think you need to cycle your sleep as well. I'm going to up your Ambien just a bit."

"Wouldn't you refer me to the rehab clinic from here?"

"No. I'm not going to run you through the embarrassment ringer any further. If I take your case back on, I will be your unilateral doctor. Cancer meds, sleep meds, anxiety meds. Anything short of you growing tits or needing a proctologist, I'm your man. You'll have one-stop shopping. And having one doctor, one source to go to, means your scripts can be monitored better." He paused. "Should there be any temptation for backsliding on your part"—he tore two sheets off the script pad, proffering them to me—"you might be tempted to abuse the Ambien. Find someone you trust to ration them out to you one or two at a time."

I thought of Claire's supergluing those pill packs one by one. "Fuck, Doc, I don't want to die just yet."

"It's progress from our last visit. Welcome back to the land of the living, Tom Spenser."

I swung by the county coroner's office as she was about to close that day. Her assistant had already packed up.

Doc Czaervich was out of her scrubs and wearing blue jeans, a purple, LL Bean–style checkered shirt, and a pair of practical but extremely tiny Salomon urban combat boots, like the special operators in Delta Force wore. The footgear made perfect sense in her line of work; she was standing for long hours in the morgue and needed supportive footwear similar to what those troops wore for endurance marches over the mountains of Kingwood, West Virginia. Still, it made her look more like a hiker's guide than one of the finest pathologists on the Eastern Seaboard.

She greeted me with a half smirk, half surprised look of piqued curiosity. "I do not think we have an appointment, Lieutenant."

"I'm one hundred percent positive we don't, Doctor. But I need your help."

"My assistant is not here. Can it wait until tomorrow?"

I surreptitiously looked around the room—rather stupidly, as obviously there was nobody there. "Is your lab recorder turned off?"

Her eyes narrowed with the slightest hint of mischief and childish excitement. "Of course."

I reached into the green duffel bag, revealing the shoe that had been left by one of the shooters. "There's trace amounts of blood in there. I need you to type it and run it against the DNA database for our high-profile Narcotics and special-task-force officers in the department. Particularly our undercovers in the Special Investigations Unit."

"You're asking me to commit multiple federal felonies without a warrant. Thank you, no. I am not going to jail."

"Listen, goddamnit. This is definitely under exigent circumstances. One of these assholes tried to take a shot at me the other night."

"Then have the chief of the Special Investigations Unit sign off on it."

"I can't. I-I-I . . ."

"I am not a stupid shit, Lieutenant. You were up to no good and somewhere you weren't supposed to be, no?" She gingerly took the bag from me so as not to get her prints on the shoe. "I will run this against AFIS and CODIS registries. I will say you 'found' it at the crime scene."

"That's not really even a lie considering it was right next door . . . just twelve hours later."

"Sweet fucking Christ, I don't even want to know." She looked away, searching for an idea, then turned back and focused sternly on me, a governess dressing down an insolent pupil. "Anyone in your task force that has worked in deep cover or has been on an interagency assignment with the Bureau or somewhere in the civilian federal government will more than likely have a swab on file that cross-references with their cover identity within the AFIS database, and they will be eliminated by default when I run the sample."

"You say civilian federal government."

"Yes. The only one I cannot access in the initial run is military. The DNA swabs, say, that you and your brothers did when you entered your military service are sealed unless you were ever charged with a crime connected to your service."

"Okay, that's fine. The people I'm looking to rule out have all worked on a federal task force at one point or another."

"I will make this absolutely clear. If anyone comes to me asking why I am hitting the AFIS and CODIS database over"—she looked at the contents of the bag in absolute disgust—"four drops of blood on a fucking shoe, I am throwing you right under the bus."

"That's fine."

"Also, I cannot guarantee a successful sample. DNA scrapes from dried blood on filtered paper under optimal laboratory conditions are tricky at best and require labor-intensive protocols and multiple extraction steps. You're asking me to pull evidence off a shoe that's been kept in a smelly gym bag."

"I'll roll the dice and take my chances."

"Tell me what I'm looking for and why this is so important to you."

"Doctor–patient confidentiality?"

"Well, since you seem hell-bent on making yourself a corpse on my exam table sooner than later, I will allow it."

"I think the shooters are cops, and they tried to take me out the other night. I managed to get off a round near one of their feet. It was pretty much a ricochet. I was just trying to scare them off."

"If they were actively trying to kill you, why didn't you engage with deadly force?"

"As I said, I wasn't in the realm of legality myself, and I don't want to rope you into any more trouble than you already are just by talking to me."

She bit her lip and looked at the bag in her hands, then up at me again. "If I can do it under the radar, I will match the state and below files as well. But I am not promising anything."

"Just say you'll try."

"I will."

"Thanks for giving a shit, Doc."

"Lieutenant, from what I hear, you've been walking off the edge of a cliff for so long that you are in for a hell of a fall once you look down. Perhaps this bit of aid on my part will just ensure you have enough cushion for an open casket."

■ ■ ■

"Speed! Audacity! Precision! Speed! Audacity! Precision!"

I'd heard Coach Repo chant this mantra daily to the fighters as they struck the heavy bags and sparred with each other. I heard it every single morning. I heard it in the evenings as I was getting ready for bed when the last classes wrapped up shortly before 9 p.m. It was my lullaby cadence; it was my morning reveille.

"Speed! Audacity! Precision! Speed! Audacity! Precision!"

It was the same mantra by which he coached me and Brady a little over twenty years before, when he was working at the gym part-time while he was a US Customs officer at Pitt Airport—when we were barely out of grade school and putting on gloves for the first time.

"Speed! Audacity! Precision! Speed! Audacity! Precision!"

I skipped rope in the corner as the fighters worked out in three-minute drills. The gym stank of perspiration and exertion. The automatic round-timer chime had long replaced the old-school fighter's bells from the movies, and on the final sound of the "bell," Repo dismissed the fighters for the evening. Then he came over and appraised me as I measured one of my biceps with trainer's tape.

"Looks like some decent muscle is coming back there, big guy. That woman of yours must be feeding you well. I'd say you've got about fifteen pounds back overall, from what the scales say, and the bicep is even better in muscle volume than it was before the doctor pulled the lump. What do you say? You ready for a scrap?"

"As long as you don't pull any punches, old fart."

I looked down at Repo's right foot. He had a bandage going from mid-calf down into his sneaker.

"The fuck happened to you?"

"Ahh, I was hanging something overhead for your mom earlier today." He pointed to a new sign underneath the Mickey's marquee that said Spenser Brothers Properties, LLC. "Didn't have a spotter, slipped off the ladder. Lucky I just rolled the foot."

"You know, I hit a suspect the other night with a ricochet in that same spot," I half-joked. "Maybe I should go get a pair of scissors, see what's under there."

"You are always fuckin' running your mouth too much, kid."

"It was just grab-assing, Coach. You know I'm your boy."

We climbed into the ring and both pulled on headgear and chest protectors as well as gloves.

In sparring, you never go one hundred percent all out. The objective is honing technique, not hurting your teammate. Repo brought me to my senses with a quick, friendly pop to the right ear.

"So, it's London rules, huh?"

"Nothing in London rules about being a daydreaming little bitch."

He followed up with a pummeling to my midsection, but it was still at about 50 to 70 percent of what he could really do. "How's your case coming?"

I feigned a right cross, then a left jab; he countered with an uppercut, which I blocked. I hammered on his abdomen, making sure my momentum and force matched his, and continued to counterpunch him into the corner. Blocking both his attempts at crosses, I sent him down for a five count. He sprang back up with both gloves at eye level.

"The suspects are a lot like you, Repo: very disciplined, all about speed, audacity, and precision. But I will catch them fucking up sooner or later."

"Like you're fucking up now?" He smiled like a used car salesman who had found a sucker on the lot first thing Saturday morning.

"Huh?"

"First lesson I taught you, Tom. Balance."

I was standing with both feet back. Repo took one swing with everything he had to my diaphragm, and while I was gasping for air, he nailed me with a left hook and knocked me clear on my ass. To add insult to injury, or perhaps to humble me a bit, he counted off just like a real-life referee would to ten. I never made it off my knees.

"Speed and precision, Tom. You're so arrogant the audacity works itself out."

I coughed up a wad of phlegm onto the mat, wheezing and dry heaving until I caught my breath. Repo laughed as one of the trainers tossed a towel up. In turn, he threw it squarely at my face, signaling that I could clean up my own mess.

"It's *sparring*, you crazy old fuck! You never go full speed."

Repo shook his head, kneeling, not patronizing or smug but

nearly pitying. "Son, that's not how I taught you. We always did the kill shots at full speed. Even in practice. Because in the real fight, you don't win if you're going in passive."

"Repo, I'm thirty-five fucking years old. Who the fuck am I facing off in the ring with, professionally?"

"It's not about if you're competing. It's you." He patted my shoulder with one of his gloves. "You're fighting everyone and everything, Tommy. So long as you're under this roof and you're working with me, I'm not having you taking hits half assed." He reached down, helped me up, and we took off our gloves and shook hands for the evening.

"Hey, Coach."

"Yeah, Tom?"

"I never saw you coming. You still got it. Even with one lame foot."

He cracked a wry grin. "Not bad yourself for a recent ex-pill addict who's fighting cancer. Just think of how much better you'd be with all that bullshit flushed out of your skull."

■ ■ ■

Snopes and I were in the task force's surveillance room, talking to two technicians about something we'd acquired earlier in the day. Up on two giant monitors was color video from the Fifth Avenue pavilion heist.

All the typical surveillance had been shit—either the traffic camera footage was too grainy, cameras had been broken and not fixed or updated, or surveillance just wasn't recording at those early hours.

Then, of all people, Darnell Washington himself summoned me to a bedside meet in his hospital room with Mike Taradash along for the ride. Darnell looked scared, like a test bunny about to get a virus injected into him. I wondered if the Washington crew had targeted him as a snitch. But he didn't ask for protective custody as part of the offer. He literally just wanted to walk—or, in his case, roll—out of the hospital a free man with no charges for anything before the night of the jazz club shooting.

He asked for an immunity deal in exchange for the information he had. Surprisingly enough, he refused the standard defense lawyer that the Washington Syndicate had on retainer, a class A scumbag of scumbags that made the Manson Family look like the Amish. He didn't have any lawyer, not even a public defender.

"What do you got for me, Darnell?"

Darnell shifted gears. He smiled brightly, sinisterly, a Nubian Cheshire cat. From beneath his sheets, he produced an iPhone 5, the newest on the market, turned it to the video mode, and hit the play arrow.

Mike Taradash and I watched in silence.

It was footage of the Fifth Avenue pavilion robbery, as if an action movie were being filmed in real time. The couriers were coming out of the building in the rain, with minimal people around, just as I had envisioned it in my head.

Sedan pulls up.

Two shooters exit.

Couriers have backpacks on, as we predicted.

Shooters are wearing mechanic's overalls and hockey masks. Again, same 1980s-style goalie masks that cover the entire face. Just like the night I saw them. Under the coveralls, they wear sweatshirts with hoodies pulled over the back of the head, hiding hair or skin features. Their hands are gloved, and the gloves are secured by duct tape to the wrists.

TEC-9s and shotguns spray bullets, but their shots are measured and don't hit anyone but their targets. Couriers go down, shooters get backpacks.

Back in the sedan.

Car takes off.

People on their way to work are still lying down in the puddles, screaming and crying. They finally get up and look around—it's over.

"Why would they literally sign their own death warrant and shoot themselves in the foot filming it, Darnell?" Snopes had asked while we were gathered in the hospital room.

"Bitch, you the college-educated motherfucker! Ain't you ever heard of psychological operations? Getting in the enemy's head and fuckin' with them?"

Taradash said, studying the video, "This is all wrong. This may have been filmed by someone they knew, but this isn't a production piece. This is too surreptitious. Look how these guys are doing this. Executed flawlessly. This guy with the camera . . . it's amateur hour. He's filming like a tourist. Something is off. The event is filmed like a third party—someone else—didn't know it was going to happen. But for some crazy reason, they had eyes on the target area."

"No," I said. "I know what it is."

Everyone turned and looked at me.

"Someone else had the same idea. Someone else was staking out the area. They were filming to study the routes. Whoever that someone is, maybe they were going to hit those guys, and this other crew just beat them to it."

Taradash stared at Darnell. "That's what this is, isn't it? You formed an alliance with some crosstown scumbags, and this was their peace offering to get into business with you?"

Darnell looked at Taradash with the same cocky look Razor gave me in the jail weeks before. "Here's the deal. Take it or leave it, but it expires in ten fuckin' minutes, White boy. You and the Jew here are too smart to say no to me. We keep all our business away from the market district and downtown. We don't sell over three grams a pop. We don't sell to kids. We stay away from all those nice, lily-white subdivisions. Just one little thing, though."

"What's that?"

"That million-five. That shit needs to find its way back to my ownership. I know yawl can't give me back the brown sugar dragon. Hypothetically speaking, if there was brown sugar to give."

This time it was Mike Taradash's turn to lose his professional decorum.

"You want the City of Pittsburgh to 'disappear' *one million, five hundred thousand dollars* from evidence holding because you have a grainy sixty-second video that shows nothing but two faceless guys in painter's jumpsuits shooting two other guys, *and* you want us to passively turn a blind eye to your continued future felonies? Have you been using your own product in here?"

"Mike, let him walk. Say no to the money and the dealing bullshit, but let him walk."

Taradash and Darnell looked at me with the same expression of shock. "Tommy, have you lost your mind?"

"I mean it. Let him walk. Let him try to run Razor's crew from a wheelchair. Better the devil you know than the devil you don't. He's got another few months in here anyway. But it's a conditional release. He has no contact with the Washington crew until the day he is released. I am talking zero. No visitors, no calls, no fucking cards or flowers. Let's see how long he lasts at the top of the garbage heap when we release him back into the wild, looking like the biggest piece-of-shit rat-turd motherfucker out there."

Taradash turned to Darnell with a rather triumphant smile. "Now it's your turn to take it or leave it. We'll give you eleven minutes."

In the task-force surveillance room, the technicians verified the video was authentic, the metadata was legit, and it was filmed on the day of the robbery in that location of Fifth Avenue.

Back at home, I sat on my couch, playing and replaying

the disc for hours on end. I studied the individual movement techniques, the way the shooters brought the weapons up, the way the shotgunner put the weld of the rifle stock up against his shoulder with familiarity, as if he were in a trap shoot. I studied how the fellow with the two TEC-9s moved with the dual automatic pistols like they were extensions of his arms and methodically sprayed into both targets, but his bullets didn't skip anywhere near a bystander.

I thought of the flow with which Marco and I moved through the Wilkinsburg stash house. These two guys were better than we were. They had an invisible rhythm to their pace, and without even a glance at one another, each knew where the partner was at all times, like opposite ends of a compass arrow. They managed to control the scene, control the small crowd, and they got what they came after and fled, gone, feet on the pavement to back inside the car in under fifty-five seconds.

Now we had another piece of the puzzle.

What we could establish about the shooters: They were six feet to six-five. Relatively in shape—they moved quickly; they were once athletes. They executed meticulously with military-grade skill—some paramilitary, police, special operations, or similar training. They trained as a team. They didn't target civilians if unnecessary, so either the girls in the jazz club were a fluke, a mistake, or there was more to that story.

I wondered if the girls in the club pulled guns of their own. I wondered, even more coldly, if they shot the girls first to get Razor to give up the location of the product.

Jesus Christ.

CHAPTER 13

In the days since we'd first become intimate, Claire and I spent in the bedroom those hours that one or both of us would have been cooking or preparing the apartment for the other's company. During that wild and whirlwind time, any attempt at companionable intimacy at first got obscured by a physical and sexual brawling that bordered on addictive. It was as if we had been together for so long in our minds that our bodies had to catch up for every night we had wanted one another.

I'd come off work on a Wednesday, and we would sleep and screw, get up and take walks downtown, then come back and get delivery, and repeat it all over again until I had to pick up a shift Friday. During the occasional golden break where I got four days off in a row, we would go twenty-four hours of just pizza and Hunan wok in our pajamas. We'd put on parkas and fleece caps and go to the roof of Mickey's gym and hang our feet off the side of the building with a carton of Gray's Papaya hot dogs in between, people-watching from the top of the building until it got dark. We'd make rum toddies and mix them with hot cocoa until we were either too cold or too horny to be out in the snow anymore, and then we'd clamber down the fire escape back to our apartments.

In the mornings, we'd go outside and run the trails of Schenley Park, come back, and swipe bacon and pancakes from the downstairs kitchen. Down the hatch, sex, shower, more sex. When she visited me on my breaks at work, we'd hit up halal and falafel trucks by the police station and throw a blanket in the limited recesses of the Mustang. After my shifts, we were connoisseurs of carryout sushi on the couch, followed by several bottles of wine and a full-on workout of intercourse that predictably ended with both of us sprawled naked on the queen bed in her apartment.

Despite the fact we were both loving it, I wanted to dial things back a bit and have a proper "date." I didn't want to lose that tenderness and chivalry we'd first had together. So, I set a real going-out date for us, the night before Thanksgiving.

As I was preparing for Claire to visit, my cell phone rang. My ex's number. I pressed the receive button and cheerily greeted Samantha. We had a snarky but humorous way on the phone with one another.

"Hey, gold digger."

"Hey, asshole. How's Marco doing?" It had been three weeks since the shooting, and Marco had been convalescent at home. Slightly weak, with complaints of fatigue and flu-like symptoms.

"He's good."

"Look, I know this is sudden, but Allan's sister-in-law had her baby early. Monica had to have a C-section. He's flying up to Andover tonight to help his brother out with the other kids. Since it's Thanksgiving, he will probably get raped on airfare, so me and the kids are staying here. Would you like TJ and Allison for Thanksgiving with your mom?"

"What about you?"

"I was gonna volunteer for a shift so someone could go home early."

"Forget that. You're family. Come eat with us. I'm sure my mom would love to have you."

"It wouldn't be weird?"

"No more or less weird than anything else in our history. Claire is going to be there."

"Are you guys together now?"

I paused at that, realizing we had spent nearly the last three weeks of nights together consecutively—as well as intimately.

"Not sure. She keeps me company; I make her laugh."

"Oh, by the way, I got a message on my service from your mom. She said Coach Repo was feeling a little under the weather, fever and such. Worried his pneumonia is back from last year again. I'll drop by the gym with a bottle of amoxicillin for him. Do you need a casserole or a side dish for tomorrow or something?"

"Well, since you can't cook for shit, I would say no."

"Fuck you, Tommy Spenser."

"Okay, darling. You have a nice day too. Love you, mean it, kisses, *mwah*."

"Bye, asshole." She was laughing as she hung up.

■ ■ ■

Claire brought something special over for the evening: her violin. After the waiters set the table in our private room at the Moroccan restaurant, one of the few of its kind in downtown Pittsburgh, she played her rendition of Vivaldi for me for twenty minutes. I watched in astonishment, fascinated at how she played, with her eyes shut, her shoulders and head and arms moving in rhythm to the notes—as if she were caressing a lover. To say it was beautiful would be corny; it was just lovely. No better word.

We didn't talk much as we ate by candlelight. The dish was lamb shawarma. Shortly after Tommy Junior had been born, I was "volunteered" by the governor for a CPATT tour, which meant assisting the Civilian Police Assistance Training team in Iraq, six years before Baghdad would once again fall, this time to ISIS. I was immersed in Arabic and mentored a police special response unit in Hillah for nine months. I never forgot how those humble cops welcomed me into their homes and served, laid out on newspaper, heaping piles of shawarma, cucumbers, tomatoes, and rice that we would all pull by hand from the pile. I stopped corresponding over the years after I learned over half of them had been killed since then; the rest were either dirty or running for their lives.

Claire sipped white wine from a stem glass while I nursed a ginger ale. She was dressed beautifully, as always. She had done herself up for the evening, a turquoise, long-sleeved blouse with a black silk cravat, a black skirt, and pantyhose. Her hair falling in waves to her shoulders, she had once again pulled her magical trick of taking hours with makeup in order to appear like she needed none at all. If she was disappointed that I had gone blazer and jeans with an open-collared shirt instead of a suit, she didn't say it.

I couldn't wear a suit on a date with her just yet. A suit made me think of the night we met, with me covered in her blood.

The conversation was not forced but not totally easygoing or natural, either.

"Is Marco going to be at your mom's tomorrow?"

"No, Inez said he is still pretty doped up and hurting. He's just resting and taking his happy meds for now."

A police siren wailed its Doppler effect as it sped down the street. I pretended not to want to get up and run to the window. The ubiquitous Pittsburgh p.m. liquor store robbery. Or maybe a hooker got punched around and robbed at knifepoint.

"Is your dad coming?"

"Yeah, you know, auld lang syne, new year on the horizon. Maybe the fucker won't disappoint us in the next year. Peace, love, happiness, goodwill . . . and lots of alcohol. At least for his sons."

She smirked and pointed to my glass with her knife. "You want to put some fire in that? You don't have to be a teetotaler tonight just for my sake."

"No, actually I'm all right. Listen, Claire. My kids' mom is going to be there tomorrow. Apparently their plans fell through.

Allan, her husband, had a family emergency, so Samantha is coming with the kids."

She processed that, then shrugged. "I guess I'm okay with it if you are. I mean, you guys have been divorced for years, she's remarried, and we're . . ." She paused and regarded me as if I were supposed to fill in the blank.

"Having dinner," I said with a smile.

She looked down at her plate. "Tom, what am I to you?"

"Aw, c'mon, Claire, don't get all pensive."

"It's a fair question."

"I think we've had enough earth-shattering events in the last few months as it is. Do we have to label it? Can't we just be near each other and that's enough? A couple weeks from now, you could be touring the world with another orchestra, and you'll forget all about your little Pittsburgh cop."

She bit her lip and averted her eyes from me. "I could never forget you, Thomas."

I walked her back to her door when we were done. She kissed me lightly, then pulled me closer, more hunger in her mouth. This time I was the one to gently break the kiss. We stood together with my forehead pressed against hers, in a loose embrace. I wished her goodnight. She gave me a quick kiss on the cheek and went inside.

After a moment, I pulled on the door handle—and her hands were on me, ripping off my shirt. She pulled my Glock out of its holster and dropped it into Sarah Spenser's old cookie jar, giggling as I hoisted her up onto the dinette and she obligingly hiked her skirt back. To my surprise, she didn't have on any underwear.

I felt the warmth of her mouth on my ear as she wrapped me in her legs.

"If you didn't come over, Lieutenant, I was going to break down that door to pull you over here by force."

Unlike the sweet and shy interlude of our first night, this episode contained all the romance of a rendezvous at a dockside bar's service entrance. She bit at my shoulders, dug her fingernails into my back, and screamed with delight when she reached the height of her pleasure. I finished and nearly felt like I had blown the cartilage out of my knee, and we crumpled to the floor with her pantyhose still twisted around my back and one of her flats in the recesses of my jeans. She playfully jumped up and pulled off the rest of her clothes, beckoning me with one finger toward the shower. I was surprised that we both had the energy for another round after all that, but we made love again until finally the mammoth-size water tank in the basement ran cold.

Toweled off, we lay on the queen bed in her room, exhausted from the effort. She nudged me in the ribs and asked if I still had those smokes on me. I obligingly pulled the pack out of my drawer in my apartment and walked back to the room naked. Reaching for the matches next to the scented candle at her nightstand, I lit one for her, one for me.

"Jesus, I should probably get a birth control script. We're doing it so much I might get pregnant."

"Ahh, so that's how you're working your way into the family, you little minx," I teased.

"You worthless shit!" she cried with mock horror and elbowed me a hard one in my ribs, forgetting she was now resting on my bad side. Astonishingly, they still ached from the night of the SWAT raid weeks before. I howled so horrifically that Charley started barking down the hall. She was half-crying, half-laughing as she ran into the kitchen to wrap some crushed ice in a terrycloth dishtowel. She held it against my ribs, sputtering apologies all the while.

Then, out of nowhere, she was kissing me and climbing on me, and the fire in my ribcage faded to oblivion as I felt her settle down on me. It was thrilling to look up at her for once, as she rocked herself back and forth, every thrust harder than before. She collapsed against me when she was done, and bastard that I was, I was already falling asleep when she whispered, "You're a good man, Thomas Francis Spenser, whether you know it or not. And I love you with all my heart, too, whether you know it or not."

■ ■ ■

I woke up feeling flushed and weak but didn't think too much of it; Doc Tolliver had warned my system was still playing pinball. Perhaps my exhaustion had something to do with my getting laid more in the last forty-eight days than the previous forty-eight months.

Around sunrise, I gently crept out of Claire's wing of the upstairs and tiptoed, naked, back to my studio, having retrieved my Glock from the cookie jar. I drank two cups of coffee and nearly a quart of orange juice, trying to pull myself out of my weighted stupor, like a hangover without any alcohol. In desperation and an attempt to get some ballast in me, I cracked two eggs in a frying pan and threw in a handful of green peppers and shredded cheese.

After eating, I grabbed a book off the shelf—*not* one of my Chabon specials. Instead, for the next three hours I revisited the manic paradox of Joseph Heller's *Catch-22*. It felt good to sit down for those hours and zone out. I could not recall reading anything in the last six months other than case files.

With the gym empty for Thanksgiving, I heard Claire through the apartment walls—making herself a light breakfast, talking to Charley as he waited for something off her plate, and singing showtunes with the confidence and shamelessness of a veteran performer of the stage. She tuned her violin, short yet blaring notes on the morning calm, and I could almost picture Charley at her feet like the trademarked RCA puppy, tilting his head in acknowledgement or disapproval.

I had almost gone back over to have breakfast at her place, but it was pleasant to sit in my own home and listen to her, and it felt slightly voyeuristic, as if I were hearing her for the first time.

That girl, singing a tad off-key, loves me.
That girl in the other room, talking to my dog, loves me.
That girl, slightly burning her eggs, loves me.

She never wore shoes inside, no matter how cold the floors were; thus I was forced to place her proximity in the building by the cheer in her voice and the low, hushed pleasantries she made with my dog.

That girl, fixing her violin, loves me.
Me.

Around 10:30, with a general malaise and pain I couldn't quite put my finger on, I had taken three Advil and soaked in the tub for a good hour before throwing on khaki slacks, a white shirt, a crimson necktie, and a tweed hunting jacket. When we met on the catwalk, Claire looked lovely as ever, wearing her trademark turquoise in the form of a plaid skirt, a long, cream-colored blouse, and a teal-and-berry-checked ascot. The blue peacoat finishing it off made her look like a prep-school girl late for class. Her hair was brushed back and wrapped in a black silk scarf. On this snowy day, she almost looked Orthodox or Hasidic.

We both were quiet on the drive over to my mom's. Still, she took my hand off the gear shift and held it in both of hers, wrapping her fingers in mine.

Thanksgiving in the Rosencoff-Spenser kicked off around 11 a.m., as it has dating back to when my grandparents were still alive. A small platoon of Spenser children came pouring into my mom's house and ventured to the backyard with soccer balls, footballs, and a substantial number of toys. Secondary outfits were a must as the first hours of play usually resulted in an abundance of mud or grass stains.

My dad was there; holidays are neutral zones for the sake of the grandchildren, so it wasn't too odd to have Samantha there with our kids as well. She was brushing our daughter's hair and smiled at me and Claire when we entered. Tommy Junior latched on to my leg the moment we walked in. Dad was holding court with the littler kids, telling them some cops-and-robbers story, obviously tuned down to a G-rating for the sake of his audience.

I hugged his shoulders as he hunched over in the leather armchair. "Happy Thanksgiving, Commish." I gave Samantha a post-divorce European peck on the cheek. She shook Claire's hand and welcomed her into the home as if she were still my wife. It was just habit.

Claire was almost immediately swept up by the women and girls. Mandy came out of the kitchen, already blanching with the fervor of a few cocktails, and squeezed my hand, leaning slightly toward my ear.

"You bad boy," she whispered, planting a playful kiss on my ear.

Amanda was always a bit too forward in her sex appeal, especially when she got a couple glasses of wine in her, and she often teased us choirboys that she knew we would have relished the thought of her in our "spank banks" as teenagers. I quickly dispatched the horny adolescent at the back of my brain and moved a good foot and a half away from her lips and perfume. I thought about her squeezing four kids out. I thought about her taking a shit. Anything to dispel the impropriety of my sister-in-law having just put her mouth—and tongue—on my ear within mere feet of my ex-wife and my new lover. Mandy made it a passive-aggressive habit of telling Kenny, in such form as she'd just shown, that she was *Mandy Fucking Spenser*, take it or leave it.

"Maybe you ought to stick to Shirley Temples the rest of the day, Miss Mandy. What did she say?"

"Nobody has to say anything. It's written all over your faces. That girl is on a fairy-tale high when she's around you. I thought you were going to be more careful. Just don't do the usual Tommy Spenser wrecking ball, okay?"

In the kitchen, Mom was boiling potatoes, checking pies, and basting the turkey like a mad laboratory scientist. Of all the ladies except perhaps Mandy, she was the best cook. But that was beside the point. Anything my mom did, she took over and made it her own. She could be as passionate about completely redecorating a house from top to bottom or consecutively reading her favorite series of books. Mom always had a project. Today's project was Thanksgiving.

Brady came in last, with Sarah and their four little ones in tow—four boys to Kenny's four girls. Tommy Junior and Allison were the happy balance.

The golden rule on holidays was no casework or shoptalk. This left the Spenser boys to start drinking rather early and retreat to the couches for football on TV. West Point was playing Penn State, and as always, we were cheering for the academy cadets. Kenny had started for four seasons with the academy as an all-conference running back and was seriously scouted by the NFL—who would have paid back his tuition to the Army—up until the summer after his graduation where he shattered his pelvis on his fifth jump in airborne school. He knocked out a Harvard master's in public policy while in a half-body cast at Walter Reed, and at twenty-three, with degrees from Harvard and West Point, Kenny found himself medically retired from the Army.

Never one to accept defeat, Kenny channeled his energy into being a cop. When the Pittsburgh police medical staff nearly laughed him out of the exam but gave him a probationary waiver, he marched into the academy and challenged the top candidate to the running track. The candidate thought it was a sprint. Kenny ran 26.2 miles, a full marathon, till his feet were bleeding. The star Pitt cadet collapsed after fifteen miles and nearly sustained brain damage from critical levels of dehydration. Thus began the legend of Ken Spenser. He still wore his West Point ring proudly, on his left hand, before his wedding band even. I'm sure Amanda had some pissed-off, liquored-up words to say about that not-so-trite, not-so-little insult behind closed doors.

Even with Dad, Kenny, Brady, and me all within five feet of each other, no cop speak was going on. We looked like meerkats observing the kids and the women. Every now and again, Claire would walk over to us, nestle in the space between me and the armrest of the couch, give me a soft kiss on the cheek, and spring back up to help shepherd the kids to some other distraction of toys or coloring books or whatever Disney DVD Mandy was playing for them in the dining room corner on a laptop.

After about an hour of this, Dad set down his glass of club soda and clapped his hands together. "I can't bite my lip anymore. Tom, Kenny, talk to me about what progress you're making."

Nearly as fast as the Flash, Mandy came around the corner from the kitchen, flour clinging to her cheeks, proffering a rolling pin in his direction as if she were going to hurl it like a throwing hatchet at his balding head. "*Francis John*! You know the rules."

Dinner was jovial and happy. The kids were extremely chipper, inquisitive, and well behaved. The smaller children were climbing and fussing over Claire, and she didn't seem to mind. Mom sat off of Kenny's right, with Mandy on his left. Claire sat across from me and tickled my shin with her toes. Due to the musical chairs of everyone settling in, Samantha came to the table last, inadvertently seated to my right, and we all laughed about the mix-up. Giving my hand a light squeeze and biting her lip, she gave me a smile and nodded kindly.

Brady was next to Claire, and Sarah was across from Brady. The little ones were in sequential age order on down next to Pop, who looked like he was holding counsel with some well-behaved, well-dressed Caucasian Smurfs. Every Thanksgiving since the divorce, Dad had deferred the head of the table to Kenny and happily took a seat at the kiddie end, tasked, as he was wont to do since he first became a grandfather, with feeding the tiniest of the Spensers. Brady's youngest son was six months old, a leviathan of pudge, baby vomit, soiled diapers, a head that seemed like it had been dropped absently at an angle on top of his neck, and eyeballs that never stopped taking in the world around him. The act of watching my old man fumbling around the intricacies of feeding and rocking his youngest grandchild while at the same time entertaining the other nine was a feat in itself.

Mom was in her element, moving back and forth around the table like the perfect hostess, hugging and kissing on the cheek each of her boys and her daughters-in-law. She didn't kiss Claire but squeezed her shoulder warmly.

I allowed myself one scotch and let the fire seep into my belly as we made small talk after dessert and coffee. Claire had resumed her spot next to me, cuddled on my shoulder, and tried to delicately dispose of the rest of my scotch, but she made a grimace like a kid raiding her parents' liquor cabinet when she sipped it.

Family stories went around. Dad and the boys and grandkids tried to have a bit of a rugby scrum in the backyard, but now the snow was coming down ridiculously hard. Mom coaxed them back in one by one with hot cocoa and spiced cider. I put on my parka and walked Charley around outside before he fell into an inevitable stuffed coma that would likely last till Friday. Then I lit up one of the Havana-cured stogies my dad had slipped me and stood there in the snowfall, marveling that everything I loved in the world was under one roof.

Suddenly it felt like someone had cracked open a pressure valve in my skull. My brain was pop rocks fizzing in soda water. My balance started to sway. I felt a sharp pain in my chest and attempted a stagger toward the back porch and the kitchen. I didn't make it. I pitched in the snow, face first, and my last awareness before it went black was of Charley's alarmed bark echoing on the cold air.

CHAPTER 14

I woke up in the bedroom that had once been mine and Brady's, wearing a pair of my dad's pajamas that had somehow stayed in the bottom of a wardrobe for twenty-five-plus years. *How many of the Spenser males were enlisted to get me up the stairs?* I wondered. Samantha was there, and the door was shut. Claire was in a rocking chair in the corner of the room, and I could tell she had been crying. Everyone else was outside the room; I heard murmurs in the corridor. Samantha's pararescue medic duffel bag was propped open and spread across my upper thighs, essentially pinning me to the bed. She even had a portable oxygen canister in that thing. With one hand, Samantha pressed a stethoscope to my chest; the other hand was cupped over my forehead.

"Hey, Doc. Are you gonna have to pull the plug?"

She closed up the medical bag. "I called Tolliver. I know you don't want it, but I gave you a half dose of what you were taking in the Demerol G-pack and some Midazolam to bring you back around. I gave you a script for some more Ativan to take the edge off the withdrawal. You have an awful fever still. At one point, you were delirious and almost 106. That's brain damage at that sustained temperature, buddy. We wanted to call an ambulance, but you were slurring and swearing about the hospital. Brady and Kenny had to ice-bathe you. When we found you in the snow outside, you were twitching, almost in a seizure. I thought it was a heart attack at first, and then your . . . your *friend* told me about how you had stopped all your medication at once."

"Do youuuuu thinkkkkk . . ." My words were mush. A 45 rpm record on 33. *Was it the aneurysm? A stroke?*

"No. It has nothing to do with that *other* case we discussed.

Or your collapse after the raid at the drug headquarters. This was just fever and withdrawal. You're having trouble talking right now because you've got Versed and Demerol in your system. That's as much dope in you as if you'd just gotten your wisdom teeth pulled."

"I'm sorry, Tommy. I'm so sorry." Claire's face was pale, blanched, with albino-pink lines tracking inside the whites of her eyes, and her cheeks were streaked with tears. She was an exhibit of guilt and remorse.

"*You* keep quiet," my ex-wife snapped at Claire. "*You* have no business to say anything right now. Who the hell do you think you are? You don't have any medical background! He could have died. Don't you know that cold withdrawal like that, it makes some people suicidal? You were the reason he did, weren't you, Miss Know-It-All? You probably confronted him, and he dumped all the meds; is that about right?"

Claire weakly nodded.

"You've got a lot of fucking nerve being all sanctimonious and self-righteous about the father of my children, considering not too long ago he was elbow-deep in your blood because your piece-of-shit husband decided to play wall ball with your head! So, this is how you thank him? By guilt-tripping him into doing something that could have killed him?"

"Come on, Sammy, that's enough," I croaked from beneath the blankets. But in my hoarse, scratchy, weakened voice it came out "Cahm-ahn, Sammmeee, tharsahrnuff."

"I didn't . . . I didn't think he would—"

"No, *you didn't think* is right! Did you talk to anyone else in the family? No. I'm one of his physicians; did you talk to me? No! Did you call a substance-abuse expert? No! But because my ex-husband adores you, you think that gives you the entitlement to tell him how to live his life? Why don't you just go back to whatever rock you crawled out from under and quit leeching off his family?"

Claire's mouth opened, but she did not speak. She looked to me, I guess shocked that I hadn't spoken up for her.

Fuck it, I was tired and thirsty and achy and sick—and to be honest, a little done and through with dramatic gestures on her behalf.

She calmly stood, collected her coat and other things, and I heard her protest in the hallway as my siblings and in-laws offered her a ride. She said she would call a cab. I heard the front door slam and the crunch of her shoes in the snow. Five long minutes later, I heard a car slow down outside the house, a door slam, and she was gone.

I went back to sleep and practiced some of that ultimate Spenser denial.

■ ■ ■

When I woke up, it was 9:30 in the evening. Sarah and Mandy, who I guessed had stopped drinking after the fiasco, had already taken their kids back, but Brady and Kenny were well into three-quarters of a hangover and shitfaced drunk. Traditionally, the Spenser boys got hammered, watched sports, and slept on Mom's couch through Black Friday shopping, thereafter binge-watching athletic events and marathons of *Mad Men* and *The Wire*, ultimately facing the morning light on Saturday with a vampire's abhorrence.

I felt too much like shit to join in this part of the holiday tradition. Mom was bundling up and farewelling TJ and Allison, and my kids came into the room to tackle me with hugs and kisses, asking if Daddy was okay. I reassured them I was fine, grunted with exhaustion as I heaved myself off the bed, and walked with them and their mom to the door. Samantha gave me a hug and looked at me for a moment.

"I was hard on Claire. But what she coerced you into doing was quite dangerous. Call Tolliver. He wants to see you tomorrow morning." She paused and brushed my cheek with her lips. "Thanks for dinner. Backyard drama aside, it was nice to be around your family again."

I watched the kids bound after her in the snow, two brightly bundled Oompa Loompas fussing and laughing, and it made my heart easy to know that parts of my life were not as dysfunctional as they had been a few years back.

My dad was still standing out on the porch, chain-smoking his stogies. I threw on my coat and shoes and joined him. He passed me an unlit one and snapped open what I recognized as my Zippo.

"Gave us all a scare."

"Yeah."

"Samantha and Claire both mentioned you dumped everything cold."

"Yeah. That was stupid, wasn't it?"

"Well, it's admirable. Your heart was in the right place. It was just as bad for me. I had to detox off the alcohol . . . and all the pain meds I was on at the time." He managed a chuckle. Then his face turned grim, and he looked forlornly, distantly, at nothing. "Took my eight-year-old son beating me into the ground to go cold turkey." Then he took another drag on his cigar, and I saw a slight mist form at the corner of his eye. I knew he was thinking of what came after the beating and the rehab. I knew he was thinking of Shoshana. The second woman to—all too briefly—bear the title of Mrs. Francis Spenser. The closest thing Dad ever had to salvation.

I sat on the glider chair on the porch, the metal covered

with snow and ice. "That was the scariest night of my life."

"Mine too, Tommy. Mine too."

"You want to talk about the case now?"

"No, I'll just sit here a bit with you. Now and again, it's nice just to not talk."

I studied my father silently, and for a time, there wasn't any hate or sarcasm or snappiness. We were two cops who happened to be father and son. Two men who still couldn't tell the women they loved most that they loved them; two men who didn't want to lose their children even though they had already lost them, a hundred times over, before that night.

"Sometime tomorrow I'll come by your place and tell you all about it," I reassured him, promised him. "Do you need a lift home?"

"Naw, I'm good. I'll call a cab. Don't want your mom driving in this shitstorm. You go home and look after that sweet girl."

"She's probably mad as hell at me."

"I think she's more scared than mad, Tom. You did what you did out of love for her. That's a lot of weight on her shoulders if things had gone wrong with you tonight."

"She wasn't there when I became an addict, and she didn't put a gun to my head to get me to stop either."

"What made you stop?"

"Honestly?"

"Yeah, honestly."

"Fuck, Francis. You know better than me. After a while it feels like you're already dead. Everything just gets numb. You pop one pill, have one drink, and you're numb until you need another. When Marco and I took down that stash house the other night, I knew I would rather be alive. I thought at first it was the rush of kicking down the door. Being back out with the SWAT guys. But it was more than that. I felt like my life mattered again. Even if I turned the corner and took a bullet in the eye, for that bit of time, my life mattered again. And when everyone was bandaged up and the bad guys were cuffed or body-bagged, I knew that my life still mattered. And for the first time I could remember, I didn't want it to be over.

"A doctor told me the other day that there was still time. She didn't know how right she was. For three years it's felt like I either want to die or want to get so wasted that I forget about living. The last month or so—it sounds like some Dr. Phil shit, but I'm tired of being Tommy the burnout. Maybe helping that girl made me realize there's a lot of good left in me. Or maybe it just made me grateful for how much I still have in my life. Claire . . . she has nothing, but she doesn't complain, and she doesn't lose hope."

Dad stubbed out his cigar and met my eyes. "When it comes to being a sonofabitch, you may think you're a bastard carbon copy of me, Tom, but you've got the good parts of me too. The difference between you and me is you're not afraid to take action to fix what's broken."

"That's not our only difference, Frank."

"Oh, I know that, Tommy."

I looked down. Charley had ventured over to my father and was curled up at his feet.

I rose from the glider and ambled over to stand quietly next to my father. I remembered when once I thought he was a giant, the biggest man in the world. Now we were the same height, and I realized that while he was not the titan I had envisioned as a toddler, he was also no longer the monster I had made him out to be for the better part of three decades.

"It's good having you here, Pop."

We gazed out at the street I had grown up on, taking in how many years had passed between two men. He put his hand on my shoulder and held it there for a long time.

He ambled down the small stack of steps and looked up at the house from the sidewalk, the home that thirty years ago was his—listening to the laughter inside of his two eldest sons, probably wondering at what point it had all started to go horribly wrong.

I said goodbye to him, went back inside, and changed into my clothes, newly fresh from the dryer. I hugged my mom farewell. Charley happily jumped into the passenger seat of the Mustang as I headed out. Dad was still standing there on the stoop, looking up at the top floor, as if he were waiting for my mother to lean out the upstairs window and tell him after nearly thirty years that it was okay to come home.

■ ■ ■

It was around 10:30 when I got back to the gym. Charley wandered off to some dark corner or whatever rope toy he had tucked away. The lights were on in the gym, and there stood Claire, all one hunded and five pounds of her, in a sweatsuit, wailing away on the Red Man.

Red Man is what we call our MMA dummy, a giant Frankenstein of red duct tape and padding that somehow resembles a humanoid in a fighter's crouch, about to grapple. Filled with sand and other ballast, he weighs a good 250 pounds, and in my fighter days, Papa Mickey would run Brady and me around the track, taking turns with Red Man over our shoulders in a fireman's carry. Well, not necessarily running. More like an agonizing stumble. We'd be soaked in sweat and sore for days, but, man, did our grandfather make us think we could do anything when we ran the track with Red Man on our backs.

In his retirement years, Red Man hangs by a metal O-ring bolted through the top of his head on a steel threaded rope running up to the rafters, linked at a swivel secured to the ceiling, and that's where I found the poor bastard, suspended at eye level of his opponent, taking hits that were probably meant for me.

"When you do a hook, don't use the base of your palms to connect. You'll fucking break your wrists like that," I advised, slightly amused, slightly aroused at watching little Claire Samuels-Hewitt acting like *Million Dollar Baby*.

"I don't want to talk to you. Go away." Side kick to the dummy. One-two punch. Uppercut. Jab. Side kick. Roundhouse. One-two. Straight knee kick to the dummy's groin. Had old Respottek been throwing in some jiu-jitsu lessons for Claire when I wasn't looking?

"Come on, Claire, I couldn't help what happened. It's not like I fricking staged having an incident just to make things awful for you. No one was conspiring against you. Samantha was a bit rough around the edges, but she was scared for me."

Her gloved fists hammered Red Man until I thought his head would split and sand would fly everywhere. She was cursing and wheezing as she pounded away. The hardest thing to learn for a novice boxer is to pace your breathing.

"Claire, you can beat the hell out of the dummy till your wrists break. Have at it. It's not going to change the fact that what happened today happened. You can be pissed at me till Christmas, or you can get ready for bed and let me hold you. It's been a really messed up evening."

She stepped away from the dummy and stomped over to me. "You've got a lot of nerve giving me demands after throwing what I requested of you, out of *love*, back in my face. Along with that bitch who married you."

"Hey, that's not fair! I didn't say that shit to you today; she did!"

"Yeah, you're just peachy now. You're fine as long as things are going your way! What about the next time when things *aren't* going your way? Say a cop gets killed? Or someone innocent gets killed? And your case isn't making progress? Or Samantha cancels a visit with the kids? What then? Huh? What then? *What then*? Is it back to the drawing board for Tommy? Or *back* to the *same shit*!" She started swinging haymakers at me, teasingly at first, but then she capitulated to full anger and her punches were chopping through the air at nothing. With the poise of a lifelong dancer of this particular art, I effortlessly backed away so that she appeared near clownish in her approach, as if she were swinging at an invisible man standing between us. Finally, after about fifty more seconds of this absurd two-step, I stepped forward, caught her gloves, and subdued her in a bear hug, as we both clumsily tripped onto the canvas floor.

"Calm *down*!" I ordered.

"Get off me."

"Are you going to calm down?"

"*Get off me*!" She thrashed her body, and the look in her eyes simmered. In one instant, she brought the force of her hips up against mine and arched with her shoulders, carrying my weight with her and flipping us both over in a junior varsity wrestler's move so that she was on top of me. She ripped the Velcro flaps off her gloves.

Next thing I knew, she embraced me, her mouth finding my throat, my chin, my lips, covering me in kisses, massaging my tongue with hers. I threw my jacket off, picked her up as I had done when she was wrapped in blankets and hospital pajamas just a few months ago, and this time carried her over to the elevator. She didn't stop kissing me even after we stumbled through her door.

■ ■ ■

I lay next to her in her apartment the morning after, running my fingers over her smooth, pale back. Her snowy complexion was a blanched contrast to the warm amber and auburn curls of her hair. She slept serenely in the predawn, diffused light just before sunrise. One eye opened up in profile, her head in the crook of her arm, and a twinge of sympathy swept over me as I noticed the lingering trauma of her ex still between us, the ghost in the room—because in the first moments, her eye widened and assessed me with fright and unfamiliarity, a sniper behind her scope.

Then she blinked, twice, three times, and it was like a switch had been thrown and a new pilot was at the controls. The arches of a smile came to the corners of her mouth, and she lifted her head, her sleepy green eyes tenderly regarding me as my fingertips traced over the wine-colored pinpoints of freckles adorning her back and shoulders.

"Don't you ever rest?" she asked.

"I did. I just seem to always wake up before you."

"I love being here with you."

"Funny for someone with a hell of a fucking right hook last night."

She snuggled up against me, and her bare skin against mine was warm and welcoming. As had become mutual habit, she rested her head on my chest, and my fingers tousled her hair, careful not to pull.

"Tommy?"

"Yeah?"

"You know all that crap, about stopping the pills and stuff, it's because I love you, right?"

Before I could answer, in that perfect cocoon of relaxation, my cell phone chirped on her nightstand. A vaguely familiar Pittsburgh number was on the screen, yet one not plugged into the phone as I was not used to calling its owner but rather her husband.

"Lieutenant Spenser."

"Tommy, it's Inez. Marco is at Mercy. He collapsed yesterday.

He's got a staph infection from the gunshot wound. He's got a really high fever and I am scared to shit, Tom!" Staph infection because of a puncture or a gunshot was rare but in many cases fatal. I sat up abruptly in the bed and felt Claire rise next to me, concern sweeping her face, keeping her head against my shoulder, perhaps to assess what was going on or simply to stay near me. I switched the phone to speaker so she could hear.

"Inez, honey, why didn't you call me when it happened?"

"I didn't want to ruin your time with your family." I thought of the drama that had ensued at the Rosencoff-Spenser house yesterday and felt a pang of regret that we hadn't encouraged the Escardos to come over. Maybe one of us could have identified that Marco needed help. Maybe he and I could've shared an ambulance, as it turned out.

"Where are you now?"

"Right next to him. Tom, they had to induce a coma to stave off the fever and infection. He's all on tubes and oxygen. I'm really frigging scared."

"I'll be there in thirty minutes, Nez."

■ ■ ■

Claire waited outside the ward while I scrubbed in and put on a mask and went in with Inez. Marco looked pathetic lying there like that, stripped down to his shorts, tubes and machines snaking and beeping all around him, and paler than I had ever seen him. His jet-black hair that he was so proud of (we teased him for having an Eddie Munster peak) had been shorn off completely to attach EEG electrodes. He was breathing on his own but was nonetheless intubated, and Inez's face was streaked with tears, evidence of a night with no sleep.

She stood and clutched onto me as if to avoid falling off a

cliff. I gently guided her back to her chair, and she squeezed Marco's hand and said in Spanish, "Your big brother is here." I almost broke into tears myself at that.

I sat and stared at my partner. He had gone downstairs on my call. If he died, it was on me.

As if reading my thoughts, Inez said, "He's a grown man, Tom. He made his own decisions. This isn't your fault."

Save for the humming of the machines, the hiss of his oxygen mask, and the beep of his EKG monitor, we sat in silence. I watched his chest rise and fall, an accordion valve. *If it isn't my fault, on my call, then who the hell's fault is it?*

An hour went by, and Inez eventually fell asleep in her easy chair, as close as she could possibly be to her husband, holding his hand through a rubber glove.

Mercy West had its own wing for those held under arrest. My dad's initiative, back in the '80s. Three retirees from the force worked in shifts as supervisors to the green hospital rent-a-cops, some of them lifers but a good smattering of Pitt and Duquesne and CMU criminal justice majors. Frank had also managed to squeeze out of the city budget a mix of transit police and regular Pitt PD into the guard force too, collecting some sweet overtime checks.

My first impulse after seeing Marco was to go into the room of the stash-house-shootout survivor, stick my gun barrel into his wound, rotate the angle of the pistol toward his heart, and pull the trigger, sending him straight to hell. But painting the walls red with that motherfucker wasn't going to bring Marco around any faster. Still, I decided not to go into his room with live ammo.

I met Claire in the hallway, un-holstered my pistol, and, out of view of nurses and orderlies, slipped it into her handbag. I gave her a soft kiss on the cheek and hugged her tightly, letting her know I would be no more than fifteen minutes. Then I walked toward the transit cop who was moonlighting on hospital security. The jawline, forehead, and eyes—plus the slight fuck-all demeanor I had at the moment—pointed to the fact that I was Frank Spenser's kid. Even with all that, I relinquished my badge to him. He took a perfunctory look at the credentials, blanched a bit at my promotion status since we had crossed paths last, nodded at me, waved me through the metal scanner, and handed me back my badge and ID, gesturing down the corridor with his chin.

"Room 503, Lieutenant. You'll find the scumbag you're looking for."

The scumbag had his attorney there. Not some wet-behind-the-ears public defender, whom I would at least admire for the necessary sewage slogging all lawyers in public service have to go through at one time or another. This guy, Taylor Jankowitz, was to most of the district attorneys a scumbag among scumbags. If there were high-profile murders in Pittsburgh, you could bet Jankowitz and Sawyer Law Firm was backing them.

Taylor had played baseball as a catcher for Kiski prep when I was a catcher for Central Catholic a lifetime ago. When the other was at bat, we would pass our time insulting and making sexual comments about the batter's female relatives. Spring of 1994, I said one too many times what I wanted to do to his younger sister with my tongue, and Jankowitz turned around and swung the bat at my head. The rivalry and the stakes had only climbed higher in proportion since that day.

"Holy fucking balls; 7 a.m. and Tom Spenser is sober."

"Fuck you, Jankowitz. I would have been here earlier, but your mom was offering freebies on Liberty."

"Quite witty and unoriginal there, lad."

"I need ten minutes with your client."

"Not without me in the room."

"You want me to come back with a subpoena?" I passed him

my notepad and my cell phone. "Nothing I say with him in there, or him to me, will be in my testimony. No recording devices."

I lifted my shirt to show him I wasn't miked.

"He's already facing attempted murder for Marco. You know it may become murder one if Marco doesn't make it; that's why you're here right now. You want to cut a deal? You let me talk to him, right now, and I will do an on-the-record letter of advisement to the DA to attempted murder. Think of that. Twenty years versus the killing agent in his veins. Otherwise, you're gonna have to go toe to toe with fifteen highly decorated SWAT officers testifying that at the crime scene he said he hoped that little spic was dead."

"So, the moral empire that is the Spenser family would stoop to blackmail and perjury?"

"When one of their own is dying, they sure would."

"Five minutes. I hear a peep from my client or you so much as give him a dirty look, and I will have you in cuffs on brutality charges by lunch."

I walked into the room. "Hello. I think you know who I am."

His name was Marlon Davison. He had a long rap sheet of battery, dealing, prior burglary, assault with a deadly weapon. In the hospital bed, he looked a lot younger than twenty-six. In the stash house, he'd exuded an air of arrogance, even after being gut-shot. Now he was scared. He had been through four surgeries and had a good portion of his small intestine removed.

"Who took out Razor? Who took out Darnell? Who killed Alario? Who is making a power play?"

He clicked the self-administering morphine pump. "Free enterprise, nigger."

"Who. Took. Out. Razor?"

"Razor was bad for business, gettin' too careless. Struttin' around. Front of the po-lice. Full of hisself."

"Were you one of the triggermen on Razor?"

"Naw, man. Outside talent on that. Out-of-towners. Came an' . . . an' went."

"My partner is in the other room. My family adopted him when he was twelve. He may die in that room."

"All in the game, right? Us against yawl. People die. Yo' partner, there's a reason he become a cop instead o' selling insurance."

"Aren't you the philosophical fucking atypical gangster?"

"Just telling it like it is, Officer. Nothing personal."

Maybe it was the smugness and arrogance in his tone. Maybe it was the fact he was trying to legitimize his argument at the price of one of my best friends dying in the other room. Or perhaps it was the reminder of the hazy line between being a cop and a convict.

I swung my arm back like I was about to throw a fastball and brought my fist down onto the bandages. Hard as I could. Harder that the blows that cracked Chris Tatum's eye socket when I was nineteen. I clapped my other hand over Marlon's mouth, and he howled into the heel of my palm. His eyes teared up with immeasurable physical pain, and he made some more muffled screams into my hand. I kept the hand over his mouth and applied pressure with my other hand to his larynx.

"Tell that scumbag lawyer of yours a single word, and I will cut your dick and your balls. Let you watch yourself bleed out from the gash. Then I'll take you out toward the airport, one of those little farm towns. Dump you at a pig farm and let the pigs tear away at you while you're still fucking alive, you little thieving nigger junkie scumbag. My brother in there dies, it will be worse. Much, much worse. You ever suggest we have any sort of commonality with each other again, I will kick out every last one of your teeth. Get better, asshole. I want you healthy as a horse when they put you in the death chair. Yeah, that's right. You can die in the state of Pennsylvania even if the cop survives, and I will be there on the other side of the window, watching you choke out your last, pitiful, worthless breath."

I almost wanted to vomit at my own words, picturing the gory outcome I had painted in his imagination, acknowledging the line I'd crossed. I would never do it, not even to a murderous, drug-dealing psycho. But he didn't need to know that. And it worked. With his eyes bulging and none of the arrogance of fifty seconds ago, he nodded.

I opened the door. Jankowitz looked at me and with a mixture of confusion and indignation entered through the door and looked in on his patient gasping for air, monitors and alarms going off the charts. Two nurses ran past me.

"*I'll have your fucking badge, Spenser*!" he screamed over my shoulder.

"Get in line."

I didn't look back.

CHAPTER 15

Claire took my hand as I walked back to her. We didn't speak in the car ride to the gym. She followed me into my apartment, dropping her purse and coat. I retrieved the one remaining tucked-away bottle that had been mine and Marco's from above the stove, the one that hadn't been dumped. I downed three shots before she gently pushed the bottle aside and hugged me, guiding me to the table to sit. At first it was just choking sobs, but I soon let out a wailing cry into her shoulder, loud and painful, blackened with grief.

She clutched my shoulders. "Listen. I know you've had shitty things happen, and I know Marco is a brother to you, and I know this sucks, but do not go down this road. I am not going to find you on the floor again in your own puke. I am here for you. I *love* you. We can get through this."

I tried to regain my composure, but the tears opened back up. We sat for a long time at my kitchen table. All at once, I was exhausted. I cleaned my face up at the sink and felt like I didn't want to cry anymore.

She exhaled audibly and brightened a bit. "Do you have to work today?" We both looked at the clock on the breakfast counter. It said 10:15.

"I should, but Doc Tolliver told me to take it easy. I think if I went in now, I would start rounding up shitbags to throw in an interrogation box and beat out a confession that they had anything to link them to the guys who did this to Marco."

She chuckled as she put the bottle away and replaced my glass with orange juice. "I don't believe one word of that, Tommy. I think even if someone put a bullet in me, you would not do that. You may be lacking a lot; you may downright loathe some things about yourself, but what I don't see is you breaking the law to get what, or who, you're going after. That invisible line that separates you from the scumbags and the pushers and the murderers that you put away—*that* is a line that Detective Tom Spenser doesn't cross. That is your redemption. And I have a feeling—just a feeling, after being around everyone yesterday—that your father didn't cross it either. For all his shortcomings, all his sins, and the collective shit that has gone down between all of you over the years, that is one thing the two of you have in common that you, Tommy Spenser, don't hate about yourself."

She was sitting on the couch now, kicked back against the cushions, a bit self-satisfied. She looked how I looked working a witness when I knew I was right.

Oh, my dear, sweet, naive Claire, I mused. *If only you knew about the shotgun buried behind Mom's house. If only you knew about every single time I went over to fuck my source to score ten hits of Oxy. If only you knew how many nights I left Samantha alone and crying when all she wanted was for me to open up to her about my demons and let her in, but I just walled off and became more of an asshole. And you have the sweetness and innocence to look at the mountain of shit that is me and speak of redemption.*

"Clarissa Samuels, you have missed your calling. I have been told by more than one person lately I could use a good shrink."

Claire wordlessly pulled my pistol back out of her purse and surprised me by dropping the magazine from the handgrip and racking back the slide to take out the round in the chamber. She professionally tilted the barrel to ensure no remaining rounds were lodged inside, then balanced the gun steadily in the palm of her hand. With her other hand, she thumbed the single round back into the magazine housing and slid it across the table. She offered the now-empty gun grip-first, like an instructor at the firing range.

"My dad, he knew his way around a gun. Contrary to

everyone's opinion around here, I'm not totally the worthless ingenue in distress."

I retrieved my gun. "Thanks."

"How many more raids do you plan on going on in the near future?"

"Why do you ask?"

"I'm just worried about someone trying to hit back at your family where they can. Damn near all of Pittsburgh knows your family name and its connection to this company. I would sleep a little better on the nights you're not around if I knew where your mama kept that shotgun of hers."

I gazed across the room into the eyes of a woman who either was no longer scared of things that went bump in the night or was putting on one of the best acts to pretend she actually was that woman. Either way, it was an impressive turnaround compared to the trembling, sobbing mess I had first brought in here. I kissed her on the cheek and went back to sit with Marco.

■ ■ ■

Visiting the hospital brought back bittersweet memories.

After Brady and I finished SOFTIC at Bragg, we were augmented to the Long Range Surveillance Detachment (LRSD) of the 313th Military Intelligence Battalion.

The LRSD folks are as unconventional as conventional line soldiers can be, so it was a nice transitional assignment to prepare us for what we would be doing and the independent critical thinking required when we would return to join 20th Group.

The LRSD guys were pissed—not just at two outsiders coming into their ranks but also because they had all done a two-week INDOC selection to be considered for the team, and here their det commander had just cherry-picked two nasty Guardsmen to come along. So the team had us go through their own internalized version of an INDOC—but far worse because you usually run a thirty-two-man platoon through an INDOC to see who will quit, and it was just two of us against all of them. They ran it like a frat-boy hazing, thinking we'd beg to quit.

Then Brady ended up holding the record stalk and fastest run time of any LRSD scout in the division's post-Vietnam history. While two teams were tracking Brady, I took out their radios and spark plugs from their Humvees, disabled their transaxles, and skinned my knuckles pulling out the coolant plug at the base of their radiators. They caught me about forty-five minutes before Brady finally gave in to the megaphone requests of "The exercise is completed; can we all fucking go home now?"

Before General Whitmeyer made the rest of the INDOC cadre walk the fifteen miles back to base after a good dressing-down concerning "never judging a soldier before he performs," he offered me and Brady a ride in his truck. We shook his hand and chose to walk back with our men. That sealed it for the chickenshit rivalry and marked our acceptance into the team.

Two weeks later, we were patrolling along the Albania/Kosovo border. Back in our rear support area one day, a truck with no markings pulled up, and out stepped two fellows in American woodland camouflage uniforms with no insignia. They had full beards and hair that went well past the close-cropped standards of the regular Army. Their commander told Brady to grab his rucksack and his weapon, and I didn't see my brother again for four months.

My brother had always had a knack for languages, and Russian and Yiddish were early-spoken tongues around my maternal grandparents. Brady had absorbed languages in college, too, so a team of special operators from the clandestine operations branch behind the lines in the Kosovo campaign wanted to utilize this kid from Pittsburgh who could send a round through a flea's ass at 500 yards and who absorbed the Balkan dialects like he was atop the tower of Babel.

The clandestine operations branch comprised CIA operatives as well as current and former spec ops military. Brady was the sole guy on the roster with zero operational background outside of being a drilling reservist. No way were we telling Mom and Dad. He wasn't supposed to be in any sort of situation like that; at the beginning, we had both been assured we would be doing mostly observational stuff. But when the SF guys snatched him up, any previous promises were null and void.

On the day he faced the fight of his life, the two-man spotter/sniper team was just supposed to observe for a twelve-hour night shift, and they were scheduled to switch out by 0700 the following day. But a snowstorm changed Brady's fate. The extraction helicopters couldn't get in to pick them up, and at 0545, his spotter, a Special Forces buck sergeant, stood up to get a better position to radio from and immediately took five rounds in the chest.

Brady tried frantically to save him, using whatever plastic he could find in his pack to make a seal over the wound, trying to plug the holes with one hand while firing the spotter's carbine rifle with his other. At some point, all three of the radios had died, including the spare one on Brady's hip. There was no air cavalry coming in over the treetops, and there would be no big-ass A10 Thunderbolt Warthog laying down Gatling cannons to cut a path for him to flee. All the runways and helipads were blanketed in snow. He was alone. For sixteen hours, Brady held off against twenty to thirty Serbian regulars—at least, that was the number of dead bodies found later.

The poor sergeant bought it early, despite Brady's efforts. But it wasn't a remarkable feat that he'd tried to save they guy. It was what Brady did *after* the guy died.

He expended all the sergeant's ammunition first because the

M4 carbine had a shorter range; he was saving his .50 cal Barrett for the money shots he could make with the skill he knew the Serbs didn't have. Every time they tried to advance, he pushed them back. And they were lazy and foolish with their ammo, where he was precise. He had about eight fragmentary grenades between himself and what he'd salvaged off his spotter's body, and he threw out each one of them like he was still pitching a no-hitter at Central Catholic with me reading his calls on the other side of the plate.

When the sun went down, he had them. His Barrett had a nightscope; their weapons did not, and over the hours of darkness, he decimated what was left of that unorganized mess. The recovery party would later tell me that most of the dead Serbs had been headshots, exploded pumpkins across the snowy landscape, and the ones who weren't headshots had been center mass in the chest, the .50 cal round—designed for punching holes in tank armor—having blasted clean through, eviscerating those who caught Brady's fire.

During the firefight, they shot a rocket propelled grenade into his fighting position, and by a stroke of luck, it missed him and the spotter completely; but it blasted a tree wide open and sent shrapnel and splinters through Brady's vest, ripping open his right shoulder deltoid. Amazingly, it missed bone and arteries. After he ran out of .50 cal ammo, he bandaged himself, destroyed the maps and the communications gear, and rendered the Barrett unfireable with a thermite charge that melted it and the M4 rifle into a molten, twisted pile. He then hefted his spotter's body into a fireman's carry. By then he was only armed with his backup pistol and the spotter's pistol. Most of the regular Army was carrying the Beretta M9 sidearm at that time, but the SOF guys had opted for a blocky, chopped-down Glock version of the .45, preferring its stopping power. The Glock .45 is effective in an estimated distance of feet, not meters, so I'm guessing by that point my twin brother was making his peace with God and solemnly preparing to die.

Army intelligence assessed that over the course of that time until they picked up the signal of the tracking chip sewn into the cuffs of their trousers (a standard for all soldiers working in or alongside Spec Ops), my brother had covered over 225 square miles while evading the Serbs, all the time carrying his spotter's body. They estimated he moved at a rate of four to five miles an hour. That's twelve- to fifteen-minute miles in full battle gear, carrying nearly 200 pounds of dead weight. No stopping to break, no food, nearly no water. At some point that week, when he reached what he hoped was a friendly village, he ditched his uniform for the clothes I would finally see him in and stole a sled to drag his burden to the point where he was reunited with the quick reaction force that had been sent to look for him.

It was nothing short of amazing. When asked by his debriefing officer why he hadn't dropped the body to try to gain more ground and save himself, he said solemnly: "They would have put his head on a pole for his family and all of CNN to see. I would have used my last grenade on both of us before I let him fall in their hands. We don't leave someone behind, sir. *Ever.*"

I was summoned up to the joint special operations task-force headquarters when the medevac brought in one wounded, one dead. A crowd of about 200 support soldiers, special operators, and regular guys from my airborne unit were up there as moral support for, well, I guess me. Until the stretchers were side by side and they put the spotter in the body bag, I couldn't tell who was who. They were both about the same height, dirty, bloody, and had beards and haircuts well out of regulations.

Then there was a croaking sound, and a hand reached up, beckoning one of the pretty female medics kneeling beside him. The medic leaned close, her eyes brimming with tears, and she said: "Corporal Tom Spenser, if you're out here, your brother wants to talk to you!!"

There was a glorious tribal whoop. Even the stoic spec ops warriors he came back with were visibly shaken and holding back tears for their lost comrade, whom Brady had thought enough of to bring back with him. Brady was unshaven and starved, and his hair was filthy and no doubt riddled with lice. But no way was that SF commander letting us mosey out the back way. The team commander came over to my brother, Brady looking like a Holocaust victim at that point, twenty-five pounds and a lot of muscle lost off an already slender frame. His right arm was in a crude sling, and he smelled like shit. The Special Forces major kissed both of Brady's cheeks and the top of his forehead, wrapped him in a bear hug, and they both openly cried and wept on each other for the death of their friend.

I didn't leave his side for the next two days in the field hospital. His cheekbones were prominent, and a deadness in his stare combined with a frightful intensity I had never seen in the eyes of my twin. Over the next days, the medics bathed him, cleaned him, cut his hair, and dumped him back in our unit; he rode out the rest of that deployment as our unit armorer, stripping and cleaning weapons in the gun cage, though he had fought like hell to get back to being a shooter.

When the battalion ended its tour, we unceremoniously went through demobilization at a small Reserve center in North Carolina. By the time we saw our family again, his sling was gone; only the troubled, faraway gaze remained. He was the person I had been closest to all my life, but that brutal war in a faraway country had stripped my brother of whatever innocence remained in him at the age of twenty and replaced it with a hard bitterness and a lethal edge that I dared never cross.

In any other battle campaign, it would have been the Medal

of Honor and a ticker tape parade. But we were in a political gray area when it came to the campaigns in the Balkans, and little Johnny soldier boy from Pittsburgh wasn't supposed to be wasting the ethnic-cleansing Serbs on the front lines. So Brady's Purple Heart and Silver Star came in an official envelope from the Pentagon with a nondisclosure agreement to never voluntarily speak about what had transpired.

One day when Brady was getting ready to move to his and Sarah's new house after their wedding, I was helping him load things from an old rental locker. He had gone ahead of me in his truck, and I came across the medals and citations in the storage locker. There was an accordion file as well, with a blanket investigation—what the Army calls a 15-6—of the events surrounding his spotter's death and a full accounting and analysis for the battle as well as the circumstances of Brady's disappearance and days on the run away from those tracking him. There were Xeroxed copies of sworn statements given by those involved in rescuing him from the no-man's land.

For six hours, by the fluorescent light of the storage unit, I read about my twin, who even long before that day in Bosnia was the finest man I'd ever known. I didn't measure his strength by the intense conditions under which he'd fought, or the enemies he'd killed. There was something else to Brady—his humility, his heart, and his quiet dedication—that separated him from me and Kenny. I opened the hinged boxes that held the awards. The beautifully embossed, dark-blue leather clamshell cases each contained one medal, and a plastic film over each showed the medals had never been removed. I repacked the box and file as I'd found them and handed them to him the next day at their condo, saying nothing.

A few years later, we were twenty-three, and I had shot my first kill in SWAT. Brady and I went rip-roaring drunk downtown. We told ourselves it was celebratory cowboy shit, but really it was so I could drink away the image of the bank robber holding a pregnant teller hostage—neither of them much older than us, and I'd put a bullet in his right eye and sent a fist-size hole through the back of his head. It had felt like he'd looked right at me, coming out of the bank a split second before I pulled the trigger.

When we were finally both drunk enough that evening for me to confront Brady with what I'd found in the box that day and the lengths he'd gone to in order to bring his buddy back, he simply looked at me and said, "I imagined it was me instead of him. And I imagined how Ma would have felt just getting a knock at the door with no actual body to bury. And I decided if I couldn't find the strength to bring him back for his mom, then I couldn't face my own family, knowing I'd left him there."

That was just my brother for you.

■ ■ ■

When I looked through the window of the ICU ward and saw Brady standing vigil with Marco pale and weak and still breathing on machines, I wanted to go in there and hug Brady and let the both of us cry. But at the same time I didn't.

So we both stood our watch, him inside the room and me outside the window, praying for the fourth boy in the Spenser family and wondering if adopting him into our ranks had brought him under the curse of our family. Seeing the grief and pain in Brady's eyes, I didn't have the strength at that moment to go into that room and comfort him. Maybe I was morally weak. I love my brother, and I would never deliberately hurt him, but seeing him in a moment of humanity made me feel not so absolutely shitty about my own life.

Brady didn't have shit to prove to anyone. He never gave a shred of one evening to doubt, self-loathing, drugs, or remorse.

He knew exactly who he was and what he was capable of, and he still went home every night to the arms of a woman he adored and four boys who thought he hung the moon. My brother was free and confident and happy in all the ways I was not.

If you tied it all back to us growing up in that smelly old gym, it made sense. I was always the idiot taking direct hits to the face and head just to show how tough I was. Brady was an endurance man. I kept on breathing out of sheer spite, and Brady fought to survive. There was no moral dilemma in his motivations.

I pulled my phone out of my pocket and dialed.

"Hello?" The warmth of Claire's voice jarred something deep in my throat, and I bit back a choked sob. I didn't called her often; she was usually either ten feet away from my apartment or right next to me in my bed.

"It's me."

"I've been thinking of you. How are you? How's Marco?"

"Everything's about the same. Listen, I have to tell you something. The whole craziness of the day got in the way. But I heard you this morning, and I heard you when you took the booze away from me later. I haven't felt this way about another human being in an awfully long time. I love you, Clarissa Samuels-Hewitt or Clarissa Samuels or Claire Hewitt or whatever you want to call yourself. I love you, and I want to always live up to the man you make me feel like."

"Thomas, you don't have to live up to anything. You just have to be you. Just be you and keep on being kind to me. And one more thing, Tommy. Promise me something?"

I would promise her the whole world if that's what it took, and it wasn't just words. I wanted to give her the world. I wanted to give her my heart, and I wasn't terrified about it being torn to shreds. I more than loved this girl; I trusted her. In all the time I thought I was healing her and nursing her to health, she had been doing the same for me.

"Anything, baby."

"Take some of this love you're giving to me. Take some of it back for you. Give it to yourself. Because you know what? The guy I am in love with, he's a rather good man, he's a *great* cop, and he is a kind son and a loving brother, the best friend you could ask for, and an amazing father. But . . . he needs to look in the mirror and make peace with what he sees."

The tears streamed fiercely down my face as I sobbed up against the Plexiglas window. I wiped the mess with my sleeve. I nodded, even though she couldn't see me. "I will, Claire. I will. I love you so much. I want a life with you. I want to come home to you. I know we both met in the middle of all this ruin, but I want to build something."

"Don't cry, sweetheart. Don't cry. There's been enough tears for a while. Just come home to me. I want to look at you. I want to love you. I want to see you smile. God, Thomas Spenser, I want my arms around you right now. Goodbye, my love." She paused. "My heart. I will see you soon."

When I had composed myself somewhat, I pressed a surgical mask to my face and went into the ICU, clapping a hand on Brady's shoulder.

He looked at me with a sad smile. "Go home, Tom. I've got this tonight. Sarah's coming in to sit with me. We've got Frankie looking after his brothers."

My oldest nephew, Francis John Spenser II, my father's namesake, was conceived after Brady and I returned from Bosnia in 1997 and born six months after Sarah Costello walked down the aisle with the slightest bump showing in her gown.

I walked to the bed of our adopted brother, bent over, and kissed his forehead. A sick, yellow, plucked chicken. His chest rose and compressed robotically, and the hiss and beeps of the machinery was like something out of a science-fiction horror flick. The EEG scribbled on the screen, reassuring us that his brain was active and his body was trying to heal, but his pulse and other stats were so fucking weak, and he looked starved and scrawny in that hospital bed. His eyelids fluttered for a moment, and he opened them. There was a hint of a smile under the plastic and rubber of his mask.

I bent over again and squeezed his hand. "Hey. Hey, you asshole. Don't try to talk—you've been intubated. You go back to sleep, okay? Brady's right here."

He weakly nodded, his eyes already heavy and floating with the medicine high he was riding. I let go of his hand and left the room without looking back at Brady.

■ ■ ■

When I got back to the gym, it was 11:30 p.m. The entire Friday after Thanksgiving had been lost in a slideshow of hospital rooms, panic, grief, and exhaustion. I was weak as I climbed the catwalk to our apartments, struggling with one foot in front of the other, no alcohol or codeine to blame it on—just grief. Grief and shock and sadness. I opened the door to my place and started to put my stuff down, but then I decided against it.

I grabbed a box and picked several pictures off the wall. One with me and Samantha holding the kids, one with my grandfather proudly standing between his three grandsons in their police uniforms, one snapshot of my dad in my corner when I was twenty, our eyes locked together as an out-of-focus Repo sealed a cut over my eye. The cameraman had captured a son and a father, and for thirty perfect seconds he was being the father he was supposed to be, rooting for his boy, advising him, guiding him and coaching him, even if he was leaning on a cane supporting the shattered leg his son had years ago left him as an indelible mark. My eyes, gaze, and posture were all focused on the man to my front, and when the bell rang, I came out swinging. I won that night, for my dad.

I packed these and as many clothes as I could fit into a few more boxes and duffel bags, got my twelve-gauge shotgun and my four other pistols from the locked cabinet, and retrieved the $22,000 I had in a cigar box in the dresser. I was done with that apartment. My grandfather had died there, my marriage had died there, and *I* had nearly died there.

Carrying all my stuff, I opened the door of Claire's apartment, to her surprise and bewilderment, and told her that was the last night we were living there. We would buy and make a new home together.

That night was beautiful, even though neither of slept a wink. We cuddled in bed and talked excitedly, like little kids on Christmas Eve, of what kind of house we wanted. Claire cried as she talked, happy tears of relief staining her face and the pillow, the relief of not having to dread the future. We weren't going back to a repossessed property in which she had suffered and endured insult and abuse; we weren't going to keep living in this bubble, trapped in our own self-pity and grief.

As I held her tightly and asked her to be my wife, we sobbed and cried in our mutual joy. I already knew Father Jay would forego the ritual of all the Catholic Pre-Cana classes and obligingly marry us in a quiet, unassuming, and brief ceremony at his rectory. Claire was so close with the girls that I knew Mandy or Sarah would gladly stand for her as a witness. My witness would not be my partner, who was still in the hospital; nor would it be either of my brothers, who would gladly do it but then shake their head behind closed doors, thinking that I was losing it or rushing into things.

Francis John Spenser I, my father, would stand for me as my best man because he knew the roads I had journeyed down, the dark, bleak nothingness that lay at the bottom of my heart, that no-man's-land of contempt, pain, forgiveness, and redemption. My dad would stand at my side, knowing full well that I would not be a perfect husband or even the ideal husband but that I had lost too much already and wasn't going to wait one more day while the world slipped away from me. Maybe I was finally admitting that this was my dad and the fates were not going to send me another one. Or maybe I just chose him because he was long overdue for my forgiveness.

Even if I did not perfectly execute every single one of my vows to Claire, I knew in my heart that I would honor her and keep her safe, and that was much more than she had known in an exceptionally long time.

The next day, we put a security deposit on a three-bedroom cottage in Scott Township, minutes away from the kids and within the thirty-minute commute to my headquarters required for law enforcement of the city of Pittsburgh. One room would be for us, one room for Claire to work on her music, and the last room for the kids. Allie would take my old bunk bed.

The next week was a happy blur of plans, moving boxes, and phone calls. We packed out the apartments, rented a truck, took the meager bit of furniture out of the two studios, and moved into our cozy ranch house. In a matter of hours, Claire picked up where she had left off in the loft apartments, going about with paintbrushes and rollers, decorating each room in pastel hues, bright and welcoming and soft.

As soon as the county courthouse opened Monday morning, we registered for a marriage license, and then I had a long talk with my mom and dad about my plans. Claire told her folks over the phone, at some points yelling, at some points giggling, and at some points downright in tears. I wanted to get on a plane with Claire and meet her parents face-to-face, but she assured me it was better this way because they would either attempt to talk sense into her or insist on something more formal and extravagant, and she would be faced with the humiliation of none of the friends she had lost showing up to share in the day. The way she saw it, she was in her thirties, no longer daddy's little girl, and she was done making decisions based on other people's feelings.

I dropped by Samantha and Alan's house. Alan warmly congratulated me, while Samantha said nothing but strained a smile nonetheless. At the end of the visit, she came up and pressed something into my hand. It was my grandmother's wedding band and diamond, originally given by my mom to Samantha to pass along to our daughter one day when she was old enough. Samantha felt that it was more appropriate to give it to us. She assured me my grandparents would want to pass along to me and Claire the love and wishes of their nearly seventy years of happiness together. She kissed me on the cheek, hugged me for a moment, and out of Alan's hearing said, "Don't make this one regret loving you."

Charley, despite all the adoration he'd shown Claire, defiantly tried to stay at the gym with my mom and the staff. We couldn't coax him out from beside Papa Mickey's stool. Finally, I scooped him up in my arms, and we left for our new place.

We were married the following Saturday, but thanks to my parents, it wasn't the tiny gathering we had originally planned for in Father Jay's rectory. Instead, we revisited the atmosphere of the recent Thanksgiving celebration at my mother's house. We stood in the living room I had grown up in, and Father Jay skipped Mass and the lecture of a sermon and the overdone cliché of 1 Corinthians 1 and united us in marriage. Mandy had a beautiful floral arrangement made for the bride, a bouquet of white roses specially sprayed and tinted turquoise, Claire's favorite color.

Claire wore the same color of ribbon in her hair. She defied a divorcée's modesty with a white dress; she was starting over.

Brady, Kenny, and I were all in our blues. Even my father had broken his out of mothballs and stood next to me in his uniform and decorations, the patriarch I remembered from my childhood, a former king taking one last ride through the villages. He handed my grandmother's rings to me, and I put them on the hand of the woman I adored. Her happiness beamed through joyful tears, those expressive green eyes shining with eagerness and hope.

To think this had all started on a night that began with drugs and money and guns and ended with Claire miscarrying and being sedated in a hospital bed. For one day, none of that mattered. I was surrounded by family who loved both of us, and I was marrying a woman who had seen my absolute lowest point and loved me anyway. We weren't two broken things; we were two people in love.

The ceremony was followed by a huge, specially catered dinner feast; we'd talked my mom out of her usual authority in the kitchen. As I sat as the guest of honor alongside my wife at the head of the table, and my family raised their glasses to us, I knew that this moment was ours, hers and mine. We looked at each other over the candlelight and wineglasses, and I felt genuine contentment. I didn't see the battered housewife that had been thrown out in the cold. I saw my loving friend and companion.

Somewhere in that evening, I stepped out onto the front porch and empathized with my father's tinge of homesickness from the last time we were all together. Then my wife came out onto the steps, held out a welcoming hand, and gently pulled me back into the celebration of our family. A house that held a history of abuse, suffering, alcoholism, denial, and sadness seemed to transform, if only for one evening, into a place of lightheartedness and joy.

■ ■ ■

When Marco took a turn for the worse, it made sense that Francine, who knew about being taken in by strangers and being an outsider looking in, would take it badly.

Before they had tacitly reconciled after Mickey's death, my mother didn't have much to say about Francine Shira Goyevsky-Spenser. Marco had more weight as a family member than Francine did. My mom had consciously chosen Marco even as she unconsciously rejected Frank's daughter. When Mickey passed, Francine disappeared for months until, between the boys and my old man, we finally talked my mother into accepting her. But even Frank's recent attempt at a relationship of mutual respect with his ex-wife couldn't begin to inculcate Francine as a full-fledged part of us, an adopted daughter validated and welcomed under Mom's roof beyond major holidays.

Two weeks before Christmas, my partner's infection worsened. He'd contracted pneumonia, and his immune system deteriorated further as his lungs filled with fluid. Though Mom opened her home, Franny mostly lived at the hospital with Inez in those two and a half weeks. Both Inez and my sister held a cyclic twenty-four-hour vigil for their downed officer, wearing scrubs, masks, and gowns. Marco rallied, and we thought we were in the clear, ready to take him home at New Year's; but three days after Christmas, a bacterium spread to his brain.

He died the morning of December 29. We had all been living at my mom's in shifts, as a base of operations, and had tried to pass a happy Christmas/Hannukah for the kids' sake. I had been curled up on one couch with Claire's back spooned against me and two of Brady's sons intertwined on the opposite couch. Charley had slept on the stairway landing. Before dawn, I heard something I hadn't heard in my life—at least, not at the same time. It was the sound of my mother and father crying at the kitchen table at 5 a.m.

Suddenly I heard a howling scream from the backyard, rushed

to the screen door, and there was my little sister, swinging my baseball bat at a tree trunk, wailing in sorrow. As if she had now fully realized what it meant to be one of us.

Francine was born into tragedy, and she'd been shunned by my mom her whole life. She'd never had any true family but my grandparents, who had raised her because they didn't want another fucked-up Spenser kid in the world. The only two people she'd known as parents were already dead, and now her fellow misfit sibling had died. Marco, who'd gained the validity and acceptance from my mom that Francine had struggled for, was gone because of a bullet that was fifty-fifty meant for me.

"Marco, you clear low; I'll go up."

"Am I still a Spenser, boss?"

And that was what Francine was asking now, in our fucked-up rite of passage. It was her way of screaming to the sky: "Am I a Spenser now?"

And finally, she was answered. My mom crossed the lawn, gently took the bat out of Fran's hands, and finally embraced her—the daughter she'd always wanted but whom shame, injury, decades of spousal abuse, and pride had prevented her from accepting.

Marco had had two simple requests in the emergency documents that Inez and I opened upon his death. He had officially been Mom's ward since he was twelve. He'd paid the $700 fee in Pennsylvania for a name change and had Frank and Rose sign the official paperwork some years back, in the event of something like this. He'd just never filed it with the prothonotary. He was buried under his now fully legal name, and his headstone read: MARCO ESCARDO SPENSER.

His second request was that he be buried next to Papa Mickey. So we laid him to rest in between Shoshanna and Mickey, and I enjoyed imagining the conversation Frank must have had with the director of the Beth Abraham Cemetery. Once again, Frank had used his name to pull something off behind the scenes.

We buried my partner on New Year's Day 2013. Kenny, Brady, Dad, and I were all part of his honor guard. The police commissioner escorted Inez, as was standard protocol, even though she had hoped for me or even Frank to do it. The bullshit of political affairs was at play, and it was politics as much as tradition for the highest-ranking cop on the force to be at the widow's side.

Dad had obtained a special brace for his leg in order to withstand the weight and stress of standing at attention with Marco's coffin alongside the rest of us, and he didn't falter. Brady wept as he put his Silver Star and Purple Heart in Marco's casket. My finishing touch was to have the current SWAT armorer demill and retire my old SWAT sniper rifle, removing the firing pin and welding the components of the bolt action to make it unusable. I lovingly tucked it in Marco's lifeless, clasped hands, and we closed the casket.

At the cemetery, we folded the state flag of Pennsylvania, and Frank presented it to Inez, who wept freely. Frank held it together until he rendered the salute to the colors, did an about-face, rendered a salute to Marco's casket, and then stepped off on his left foot to pivot away toward the rest of the officers in the formation. Something ripped through him at that point, he started to fall, and both Kenny and I broke out of our positions by the grave and caught him, gently walking him over to an empty chair.

I kept one hand clapped on his shoulder as seven Pennsylvania State Police troopers (a tribute to our department from the governor) rendered final honors to Sergeant Marco Escardo, firing three blank volleys from their long barrel shotguns. I felt my father jump at each shot. I looked down at him, pitying the state he was in, just now truly seeing his frailty and helplessness. *Why, oh why, Dad, did you wait till now, till one of us was gone, to start loving us?* But I supposed that wasn't entirely true. I just couldn't see it until now.

I looked over in the seated crowd and locked eyes with my mother. Her eyes were clear, dry. She had cried everything out in private. She had suffered loss upon loss before this. Now her face to the world, as always, was an iron cloak wrapped in silk and lilies. Strength was both her weapon and her shield.

■ ■ ■

The next day, Frank turned in his paperwork. Without so much as a handshake, Frank left city hall and handed in the gun and badge that he had maintained as a reserve officer in the department. I guess he had been going through the motions for some time, and Marco's death was a slap in the face, showing him that while he was one of the most powerful men in Pittsburgh, he was helpless to protect those he cared about.

He refitted and did small repairs to the modest building that had been his home and property for nearly twenty-seven years, closed down his and Shoshanna's old place and the hardware store below it, and listed the lot for sale. He got rid of nearly everything he owned, save for a '78 black Monte Carlo. All the dapper suits he wore as special consultant to the mayor went to Goodwill. He removed all his medals, badges, and accoutrements from his uniforms, save for the one he wanted to be laid to rest in, and put them in a trunk for the first Spenser grandkid who graduated Metro. When we buried Marco, we'd buried the larger-than-life façade of Frank the cop as well.

Half of Marco's policy had been left to me, half to Inez. I tried to give the check to her, but she refused. So I gave Claire the Mustang and got a Hummer H3—loud, obnoxious, and obscene. Compared to my old Mustang, it felt like a limo. A chop shop that owed me a couple favors put in ballistic glass and Kevlar siding just like the CIA used in Afghanistan. It was out of practicality as much as vanity: there was a price on all the Spenser family's heads, according to my snitch who dealt freelance for a few of Razor's old crew.

Dad showed up at Mickey's on January 3 with a small duffel bag. Mom wordlessly handed him the key to Claire's old apartment, the security pass card, and the keys to the gym. No money changed hands; his room and board would be paid by his working for the staff as a coach. He dragged a twin bunk and a small end table along with some chairs out of the third studio and began to make the old spartan quarters his home.

At about 5:45 the following morning, he put his sweats on, grabbed a whistle, and started training the fighters as they came in. It wasn't the old house, but for Frank, he had come back home to stay, and he and Mom had finally agreed on a spot where he somehow belonged: not quite in her home, no longer in his own, but a détente somewhere in the middle.

CHAPTER 16

In early March, I was in the basement firing range of the headquarters building that housed Internal Affairs. The 200-meter tunnel, soundproofed and salvaged from a subway line that never got completed, was the only place in downtown Pittsburgh where you could fire an M21 sniper rifle indoors and conduct pinpoint accuracy in terms of verifying your optics and judging your trigger pull and weight. Given the tight quarters and potential for ricochet, the bullets utilized were half the powder weight, so I was furiously scribbling an algebraic formula from memory of the ranges at Fort Bragg to compensate for what would be a full powder load.

Wearing a pair of shooters' goggles and ear protection, Claire sat slightly over my shoulder with her eye on the spotter's scope. I had no idea why, but she loved these Friday afternoons with me when I took off early from the task force, and she would lie at my side as I tried to stay sharp. When I was sure nobody else was around, I'd let her take six to ten shots on the trigger, and her grouping could fit inside a nickel. I remembered reading about women in the Israeli Defense Forces being natural shots and instructors when it came to the sniper scope because they intuitively grasped the weapon in a gentler manner.

We lay side by side on a padded mat, and like two members of a sniper team in a hide location, her body was pressed alongside and overlapping mine, one leg kicked over my backside. If it weren't for the rifle, we could have been watching TV together in bed. Her spiraling red curls were tucked up into a PPD baseball cap. She was so close I could smell the cucumber-scented wash she scrubbed her face with, and my mind wandered to a memory of kissing her when she first cleaned her face in the morning, all mint toothpaste and cucumber melon.

She saw me daydreaming and playfully nudged my rump. "Come on, Captain. There's still more bad guys on your target."

Captain Tom Spenser. That had been my consolation prize for burying my partner. When they placed Snopes as my number two man in the rank of lieutenant, it bumped me up a notch. In my wardrobe at home, Frank's old railroad-track captain's bars were pinned on my blues. It choked me up that he had held on to them all these years for me especially; Captain Brady Spenser wore Kenny's old bars. We were all still numb from putting Marco in the ground, so the promotion had just involved me and Kenny and a few pulls from a bottle of bourbon in his office. No pictures, no reporters, no Claire in a Jackie Kennedy suit, wearing my mother's pearls. Our family was in mourning, not in the mood for a party.

Marco's shooter died during the night of January 14, and the security tapes were missing from the hospital. It hadn't been me, although I wish it were. I had been on a stakeout for forty-eight hours, watching Razor's old crew. Kenny was in Charleston, South Carolina, at a Homeland Security conference. Neither of us needed to ask Brady, though I knew that the man who had outfoxed a regiment of Serbian commandos would have no problem slipping past a couple retired cops in the middle of the night.

We originally assumed congestive heart failure, but my friend down at the coroner's office ruled it a homicide when she found neoprene fibers in the gangster's teeth and nostrils. Someone had to have cut a piece of neoprene, most likely from a wetsuit, and made a seal over his nose and mouth. In his drugged state, he probably made no struggle while the assailant held the seal for five minutes until his heart flatlined. A lovely bit of intrigue, and a far more peaceful death than the scumbag deserved.

I racked another round into the breech and let my breath out as I applied the slightest pressure on the trigger. I didn't react to my "spotter" reaching a hand up under my thigh and starting to massage there. She breathed a sweet kiss into my ear, but my scope held steady. The jacketed round flew out and split the paper right at the bridge of the nose of the "robber" holding a child hostage. I cleared the shell from the chamber, dropped the magazine from the weld, and put the weapon on safe. Then, playfully and laughing as I did so, I threw Claire over on the padded mat. She already had her goggles and earphones off. She pulled the baseball cap back and let her hair spill behind her, giggling as she hiked down her sweatpants and kissed my neck. I began to fumble at my zipper; then the PA system called my name over the loudspeaker.

"Captain Tom Spenser, report to the IAB chief. Captain Tom Spenser to the Internal Affairs Bureau chief, sir."

Claire pulled me back down in a hungry, long kiss and teasingly groped me once more, then began to rearrange herself. She handed me the PPD cap while I broke down my rifle and secured it back in the safe that housed the long guns for the precinct.

"Let me know what the doctor says," I told her as we walked arm in arm to the central lobby.

She kissed me chastely and cupped one hand to the side of my face. "I'll make dinner tonight. I've got lessons at five, but they should be gone by six thirty."

"I'm so glad you're doing a little bit of teaching again."

"To heck with that! Give me another year and you'll be a symphony groupie carrying my bags in all the classy towns!"

"I love you, Mrs. Spenser."

"I love you too, Cap'n."

I watched her saunter out toward the lobby door, twirling the keys to the Mustang at the end of her finger, the slightest bounce in her walk as she unconsciously wiggled her rear end. My mind drifted to whether I had an extra suit in my office at the task-force headquarters. Perhaps I could show up at our house clean shaven and well dressed, with roses, and we could put on some Van Morrison and finish what we'd started back in the firing range.

I went to the locker room and wiped the residue off my hands, the cordite of the M21 still in my mouth and nose. I popped a couple Vicodin and drank from the spout at the sink. My diaphragm felt hard again, and the tissue around where the doc had been zapping with chemo was tender, and ached. Against my better judgment, I took one more Vicodin and lodged it like dip under my tongue. Tolliver *did* say to take as needed. Finally, I splashed water on my face and headed to my brother's office.

Brady was growing a beard—it was slightly funny. I walked into his office and fell back onto the couch. None of the rest of us had beards. Even old Frank shaved twice a day.

I didn't jibe him about it because he looked like he had seen a ghost.

"What's up, muthafucka?" I said in my best Hank Moody voice.

He slid a folder across his marble-top desk. "This is the visitor's log to the county courthouse the day the TEC-9s later used in the Little E's shooting went missing. November 13, 2006. Look at who was there in item thirty-three."

I stared at the signature, futilely hoping it was a prank: Commander Kenneth Scott Spenser, PPD Homicide.

I met his eyes. "No. That cannot be right."

"Thomas, I checked the mileage logs from his precinct that day. He was there testifying in a bench warrant for a felon they had picked up in Morgantown. This is too much to be a coincidence."

"So, how did he get the guns?"

"Think about it. Some poor schmuck evidence officer sees an out-of-town dick come in, waving a bunch of fudged documents—the clerk thinks they're legit—and shouting about jurisdictional conflict. To avoid an ass chewing, he signs the guns over. My guess is Kenny sent the guy a certificate of destruction a few weeks later and burned the originals. The guy logs that the weapons were certified destroyed, and I'll bet Kenny found a backdoor way to get through their firewall and pull the original transfer records too. But I can't get the surveillance folks to pull anything off of the hackers in Special Investigations without a warrant.

"He screwed up in one place, though; he couldn't get around the visitors' log when you first come in. That's entered on a standalone computer, and they scan your ID. That thing is also printed and cc'd by personal courier to the circuit judge's residence every night at close of business. Post 9/11, they want a record of everyone who visits in case something happens—a shooting, bomb threat, whatever."

I slid the folder back. "I don't believe it. This is bullshit. I am not assisting you in crucifying our brother unless you have an eyewitness at the scene. Otherwise, this is all circumstantial."

"Tommy, you're the one who told *me* that I needed to back you up no matter what you found. Now you're shitting on me when I come to you with probably the hardest thing I have ever had to come to my brother with?"

I stood up, glaring at him with my mother's trademark look of indignity and reproach. "He's a good man, Brady. I'm not going to sit here and listen to you suggest he had something to do with these scumbags that put Marco in the ground. Fuck, what is the matter with you? Being in Internal Affairs too long turn you into a piece of shit too?"

Brady threw a punch. I savagely rolled him over the desk and began pummeling him with short, rapid, MMA-style punches to his face, arms, and neck. He wheeled back and planted one solid fist into the center of my diaphragm, hitting my tumor and stealing the air from my lungs for about fifteen awful seconds. I jerked up one leg from the floor and kicked him in the crotch. He staggered and fell back against his desk. One quick motion with his left arm, and he cleared his hip holster and was pointing his Desert Eagle .50 cal in my face. I stepped back from him and brought my .45 clear and up, and for a moment I posited that if one of us pulled the trigger, the bullet would fly right into the other's barrel.

The sound of the pistols' slides ominously racking in unison was the fitting finale to this incongruous scene; I was pointing my gun at the man I loved most in the world. I thought back to a lesson Frank taught us when we were six, with an air rifle: to never point our weapons at anything we didn't intend to kill.

Then came pandemonium. Three or four officers who'd heard the commotion burst in and drew their weapons on me. Some of the older—and a bit wiser—senior officers hollered at them to stand down when they saw who I was. Ed Peters gently stepped between me and Brady and wrapped his massive hands around the barrel of my .45.

"Sir, please drop the magazine and rack the slide back." He said over his shoulder, "Boss, you do the same. Both of you clear and holster your weapons." My .45 seemed a child's toy in his huge hands. "Go home, Tom. Whatever this is, you don't need half the force out there seeing it."

Brady was seething as he held the pistol on me for ten more seconds while I cleared and holstered mine. Breathing out slowly, he engaged the safety and holstered his own.

"You draw a weapon on me again, Brady Spenser, you better finish the job, or I better not see you coming."

"Fuck you, you piece of shit. You're the only scumbag cop I know that can make Frank Spenser look decent. Why don't you get a few more scripts of Oxy and crawl under a rock and die?"

"Go back to the sewers with the rest of your rat squad.

You want to take a badge from your brother? Take mine, you sonofabitch."

I unclipped my gold detective's badge and threw it at him. It banked off his forehead, but he didn't flinch. A steady pool of blood was forming at my feet, dripping from my jaw where he'd sucker punched me. A few teeth seemed loose and tender. Between him and the SWAT sergeant all those months ago, the Pittsburgh Police Department was handing me my ass in black and blue.

I stomped out of there, knowing it would get back to Kenny. I'd like to see how Brady explained that fucking incident.

■ ■ ■

I spent two hours hammering away on the bags at the gym and kept my cell phone off. I vaguely wondered if Frank would show up, but in a rather comforting turn of events, he was having a late lunch with Francine. It was dead at the gym. I had a couple medicinal shots of bourbon over at a corner bar after we closed up early.

At 6:25, I pulled up to my house—and as soon as I killed the engine in the Humvee and saw the front door hanging open, I knew something was wrong.

I drew my .45 and crept toward the main door. Then I heard a low, soft whimper. Charley was lying between the hedgerow border and the brick exterior of our house, moving slightly. A metal pipe lay next to him. Some bastard had beaten the shit out of him, but he was alive. I checked my poor pup over for fractures, and he yelped. Felt like his right hip was dislodged, and he was a mess. Pieces of torn, bloody denim showed he'd put up a hell of a fight.

As I waited for my phone to power on, I went back to the jeep and got my two-way radio out of the steering console.

"Any nearby units, any nearby units in Mount Lebanon or Chartiers Valley. This is Captain Thomas Spenser, PPD Major Crimes. I have a 459 and possible 207 at my house, 1330 Raven Drive, Saint Clair Heights, Heidelberg. Need an ambulance on scene, and page any nearby mobile emergency veterinary service. Someone attacked my dog and is possibly in my house with my wife. I say again, they have tried to kill my dog, and they are in the house with my wife. 1330 Raven Drive! All possible units, respond now!"

"Hang tight, Captain Spenser; this is Mount Lebo SWAT commander. Six minutes out."

Sprinting across the lawn, I threw a blanket over Charley and ran back to the Hummer, grabbing my vest and shotgun out of the trunk. I made sure Marco's baby Beretta was in my boot; the .45 was holstered in my back holster, and I shoved one canister of tear gas in the flap pocket in the front. Approaching the entrance, I racked a load into the twelve-gauge and rolled the tear gas can through the door.

Sorry, honey. You'll cough snot and puke, but you'll be alive.

Lastly, I pulled the breakaway panel on my tac vest to reveal a duplicate of my police shield embroidered in gold thread. I didn't want SWAT putting holes in me—or Claire if she was inside.

At the academy, they run you through the CS chamber so often that you get used to it. I had also been an instructor for them for five months after getting shot. After a ten-second count, when I knew the gas was eye level, I ran in, squinting and bisecting each room.

Claire's afternoon violinist student was trussed up in the kids' room, flex-cuffed to TJ's desk chair. I cut his cuffs, threw a wet cloth in his hands, and told him to cover his mouth and run for the door. I then texted Kenny and Brady: Prairie Fire—My House. Prairie fire was our code that some shit was going down and to get here ASAP.

The bathroom held a male's bloody clothes, the aftermath of Charley's attempted takedown. I continued my exploration with a knot in my throat. Was I about to find a rape scene in our bedroom? Nope, empty, and the bed was made. Claire's sweatsuit was folded neatly on the bed, and her wallet, purse, and keys were on the dresser.

I approached the basement door, barking into the radio attached to my tac vest, "Mount Lebo SWAT, where the fuck are you? Check your fire. I say again, check your fire upon arrival. I am in a blue sweatshirt, khaki pants wearing a PPD cap and a tac vest. My gold shield is in plain view. I say again: check your fire upon entering the premises."

"Hang tight, Captain. Four more minutes."

I cautiously opened the basement door and made my way down. The tear gas obviously hadn't reached here. I swung my rifle upon reaching the base of the staircase, and when I rounded the banister, the barrel zeroed in on my wife.

My poor baby. Claire had also been flex-cuffed to a chair. She was stripped naked and bloody. The black skirt and aquamarine blouse she had changed into for her violin lesson were crumpled in a corner, along with her pantyhose and underwear. Both her eyes were black and blue. Her mouth was split; there was a laceration on her left cheek, and her lips were puffy. I saw blood running out of her ears. The fucker must have been whaling on her for hours.

Only one scumbag I knew could have been so vicious—and he had nothing to do with Razor's crew.

Jake Hewitt stepped out of the corner of my game room. He was dressed in a wholly authentic-looking Mount Lebanon police uniform, and my mind went fuzzy. I could have cried at that moment. All those nights soothing Claire that he was a worthless failure who had run away to Seattle with his tail tucked between his legs. All that reassurance that he was a gutless coward who would never come back. And there he was, like a chess master, or Kilgrave from *Jessica Jones*, waiting for the perfect moment to strike.

I suddenly wondered if a Facebook friend of Claire's had a public photo on their profile from our wedding. I wondered if Hewitt had saved up enough to hire a private investigator to research our family. I wondered if anyone on Claire's side had been dumb enough to post our wedding announcement in the newspaper. I wondered if he had collected the parts for the phony Lebo PD uniform piece by piece from sellers on eBay or if he knew the delivery shifts of the dry cleaners contracted by the police force.

I wondered also what else he had in store for us.

It struck me then that this was no simple kidnapping or robbery. A premeditated murder was about to happen. He would put on my tac vest after he'd killed us. Just loosen the straps a bit to fit his frame. And when SWAT hit the place, he would step out of the shadows like a first responder and disappear in the mayhem. Dressed like that, I was sure he had meant to kill Claire's student as well.

"Drop the shotgun, Detective."

For all the efforts he'd put into his costume, he hadn't brought his own firepower. I recognized the Sig Sauer in his hand from my personal collection. Kenny had the pistol custom made when I left SWAT, an Irish flag stamped on the slide with the CCCP flag of the old Soviet Union on the opposite and a Star of David in the middle. If our family had a coat of arms, this was it.

I kept my gaze on the pistol. From the recesses of my brain, a fact I should have immediately remembered flared to the surface, and once it registered with me, I was completely calm. Calmer than when I'd breached the door at the cookhouse and covered those injured SWAT guys. This day was going to end badly for Jake Hewitt. Yet he still had his hands on Claire, and I couldn't risk anything until I physically got her away from him.

"You're a bit incorrect, fuckstick. It's detective captain now."

He grabbed a length of Claire's hair and pulled her head back near his. "Drop it, or I kill this little whore right now."

I laid the shotgun flat. Upon seeing what appeared to be my supplication and surrender, Claire bawled like a helpless child.

"Drop your issue piece too."

I held the pistol grip of the .45 between thumb and forefinger and gently set it next to the shotgun. I didn't know if he had any hidden weapons, and I didn't trust myself at two meters on a quick pistol draw when my wife was both hostage and bait. He was completely focused on her at that moment, and that was a dangerous place for his mind to be and a dangerous time for me to choose bravado over tact.

"What do you want here, Jake? I don't have any money in the house, and if you're here for your ex-wife, well, you're not doing too good a job of respecting the merchandise," I mocked, gesturing to Claire's mass of bruises.

You fucking demon. The things I am going to do to you, Jake Hewitt. A legion of vultures will be picking your bones in hell for this.

"I'm sorry, Tommy." Claire was a picture of catastrophe again, and it broke my heart to hear her ask for forgiveness. I should have gone with my gut instinct and put a bullet into the back of this motherfucker's head back in September, back when Marco had him in the interrogation box. We should have just thrown him in the Aliquippa River. My wife wouldn't be beaten and flex-cuffed naked in our game room if I had been a bit more like Brady as opposed to Kenny.

Hewitt threw a small sack down in front of him: my getaway

fund, now up to just over $26,000. "You're a bad liar, Captain. I'll take the one you have stuck in your boot, too. My wife told me all about your backup piece."

"Oh yeah? She tell you that she faked all her orgasms for the ten years you were married? And how a stripper couldn't find your micropenis with the Hubble telescope?"

The steel toe of Hewitt's faux police boot cracked against the side of my face, and I felt an explosion in my left ear. The wounds in my mouth that Brady had put there earlier poured out fresh blood, and I tasted bits of brown, congealed blood that had just started to scab over.

Again, feigning my submission, I laid Marco's piece in front of my shoe. All those bullets in front of me, and there I was, in his eyes helpless.

"You're gonna die *after* she goes. I know you called for backup, and I know I have a small window. But you're going to watch this worthless little whore die first. You're going to die knowing you failed her." He pointed the gun to her left kneecap, and his index finger rested on the trigger. A near inaudible click told me he had disengaged the safety.

Claire began to scream hysterically. "Jake, Jake, I'll do anything you want! Don't hurt me anymore! *Please*! Please let Tommy go! I'll come with you! Please don't hurt Tommy. He's been nothing but good to me! *Please*, Jakey, *please*. I'll go with you. Just don't hurt me. Look at me, Jakey, look at me, please don't hu—"

Hewitt smashed her mouth with the butt of his pistol. More blood flew.

That was the last time I would let her hurt by letting him live.

"There's one thing I don't lie about, Jake Hewitt," I hissed.

"What's that, motherfucker?" he said, placing the barrel back on Claire's patella. My hands lowered ever so slightly. Whatever was going through his mind, he couldn't hold the gun on me and Claire at the same time.

Three feet to the shotgun—now or never. I kept eye contact with him.

"The day before my kids visit, I take the bullets out of all my weapons."

He managed a patronizing smirk. "A decorated homicide and narcotics cop not having his gun ready to fire at a moment's notice? Nice bluff," he said, and squeezed the trigger.

Click.

Claire reflexively spasmed and screamed, waiting, like Hewitt had been, for the crack of the firing pin striking the round and the slug taking out her knee. Then her eyes turned to me as the knowledge registered on her face. There had been no gunshot, and her knee was in one piece. Hewitt's eyes widened, and he racked the slide back, hoping to eject a jammed round and chamber another, but the slide locked to the rear, showing the magazine was empty and nothing was in the chamber.

Amazingly, at that moment, Claire's eyes settled into the calm she had appraised me with that morning after Thanksgiving.

"I love you," she whispered, barely a choked murmur.

Hewitt began to move toward the three weapons in front of me, the only ones in the entire house that had ammunition.

"Get down, Claire, *now*!" I shouted and grabbed the shotgun, kicking the other two pistols behind me.

She twisted on the legs of the chair, to the right so that she and the chair fell away from Hewitt, exposing him completely.

I delighted in the panic that crossed Jake Hewitt's face as I pulled the trigger. His left knee exploded into a cloud of blood, bone, sinew, and pink mist. The remainder of his lower leg hung there for a millisecond, as an afterthought, as the full weight of him collapsed against my game room bookcases. Down on the floor and still bound to the chair, Claire shrieked, inching up against the wall.

I leveled the shotgun at my waist. "Is this what you were going to do to my wife, Jake? *Your* wife? The woman you vowed to protect, honor, and cherish? *Till death*? You're lucky, Jakey-boy. Just hang in a few more seconds. Time is up."

I chambered the pump again and aimed at his right foot. He was screaming uncontrollably, and his face was already a sickening gray.

Don't go into shock just yet, Jakey-boy. I'm just getting started.

I sighted in on his right boot, pulled the trigger, and his toes flew, blood and gore spattering up high enough to spray the bogus police shield he was wearing. I racked the slide again and with the next shot took off his right hand. He howled above the sounds of the police sirens outside.

I grabbed a folded blanket off the top of the dryer and placed it around my wife's shoulders. With a strap cutter from my tac vest, I cut Claire's cuffs and her feet bound to the chair and helped her stand, wobbly from the circulation being cut off from her extremities.

She stood up, hugging me and sobbing.

"Run," I said. "Run, and don't look back."

She covered her torso and privates with the folds of the blanket. Then, trying to salvage the remnants of her dignity, she knelt and looked directly into the eyes of her ex-husband. Something left her gaze as she studied him. She brought Marco's tiny Beretta eye level to him. He spat at her, dark blood mixed in with a steady black drool. The shredders I had loaded in the twelve-gauge were designed to pierce standard-issue Kevlar. At this close range, even without precise aiming, pieces had already ripped into his guts, spleen, and liver.

I gently pulled Marco's pistol out of her hand and slid it into my front pocket. "Go outside, baby."

"I need to see this, Tom."

"No, you don't. Run outside and lie down next to Charley. Keep your hands out and cover him with your body. It's going to be a madhouse with the SWAT team, and I don't want you taking a round."

It hurt my face like hell, but she kissed me and broke out of my arms to make her way to safety. She closed the basement door on her way out.

I chambered another round and blew away his left ribcage. Viscera started to slide from the gaping hole, a thickened stew pouring out of the pot. Red bubbles foamed now, trying to compensate for the collapsed—shredded—left lung. "I'll see you in hell, motherfucker," he croaked, nearly hissing, and his eyes started to blacken over, two onyx stones. I was sure at this point he was blind from the shock and blood loss shutting down his brain.

I racked the pump of the twelve-gauge one last time and pointed the barrel at his face so that the front sight post was digging into his cheek. The hot barrel sizzled against his cheek.

"That's all right, Jake. I'll race you, though—you go first," I said.

I smiled and pulled the trigger.

All at once I went numb. My ears were ringing from the close-quarters shots. But there was something worse in my head than the report from the shotgun blasts and the mutilated corpse of the would-be killer in the corner. I slumped back into the chair that Kenny and the boys had bought for me as a wedding gift. It was a lovely, chocolate leather chair like in Tolliver's office or the Harvard club.

I let the shotgun clatter to the floor, pushed the heels of my palms against my eye sockets, and let out a scream, crying for my Claire, crying for her pain, crying for my dog.

The pain in my abdomen throbbed, and I felt bile climb up in my throat. My eyes closed in a fog of blackness. I realized that I was experiencing a seizure. That was the last thing I remembered.

CHAPTER 17

I woke up in Saint Clair under an oxygen mask, hooked up to monitors. My clothes had been sheared off, and I was naked except for a papery exam gown. When the door opened, I saw armed Pittsburgh police outside my room. I'm talking riot-level armed.

Samantha was to my immediate right, and Claire to my left. Without even thinking about it, I reached out and squeezed both their hands. Claire's face had become bluish and yellow with faded bruises, and with a jolt I realized I had been out for much longer than one evening. My mouth was dry and crusty, and the small pitcher Claire held to my lips with a bendy straw felt like heaven. I was surprised when Samantha opened a small wrapper and handed me a fentanyl lozenge as I swished the ice-cold water in my mouth. Fentanyl was hardcore shit, practically legalized heroin. Still, I took it under my tongue and let it dissolve. Samantha grimaced as she reached underneath the gown and deftly detached my catheter.

Claire paid no attention to the medical necessity of Samantha's work. She smiled at me through tears of relief, and Samantha graciously exited the room, giving Claire a cryptic nod as she dimmed the lights and shut the door. Claire, wearing a robe and pajamas, delicately climbed up, careful not to unnecessarily shift me, and settled in the bed, covering my cheeks and lips with kisses and tears.

"I was so worried about you."

I wanted to ask, "How long was I out?" but the fentanyl and whatever cocktail of drugs was in my IV caused my words to sound like "Hahhh lunnngg."

"It's been ten days, baby."

Ten days was an awful long time to keep a battered woman with lacerations and no broken bones. I pointed to her. "You eh-kay?"

She smiled through tears. "Yes, sweetie. I am okay. I'm not a patient. I've just been staying here next to you, in a little bed they brought up. I was only in the hospital for three days, but I've been back to gynecology for checkups. Dr. Tolliver's wife just wanted to monitor us."

"Huh? Tolliver wiive? Us?"

She brought my hand to her belly. "I'm three months pregnant, Thomas."

How? How did neither of us know? Had life been really that full-tilt crazy that even with all my cop insight, Frank and the boys, and the bloodhounds that made up the current and former Spenser wives, none of us noticed? She had filled out a bit, but I'd figured it was stress, the emotional toll of Marco's funeral; some people take comfort in eating. For me, it had been OxyContin and Demerol and Percocet—though, amazingly, I stayed within the orders of my scripts after Marco. Drugging myself up would have shamed his memory. I had wanted to feel every bit of anger and grief, stone-cold sober.

Horrific images of her with Hewitt in our basement flashed through my mind. They hadn't been having a tickle fight. Belt lashings, welts, kicks and bruises, clocking the side of her face with the pistol.

"Baby eh-kay? Baby hurd?"

"No, the baby is fine. I covered my belly as best I could when Jake was . . . was attacking me. That was why I went to the doctor that day after visiting you at the shooting range. I took a home test but didn't want to tell you till I knew for sure." She leaned over and kissed my lips several times more.

I brought my hand attached to the IV around her shoulder

and pointed above her ear hidden in her mountain of curls. "You eh-kay? Shrink? Psthychatrith?"

She laughed through her tears. "No, baby. No psychiatrists. He's dead. It's over."

My tongue didn't feel so full of cotton anymore. "*Whafuck* is wrong *wif* me? My head . . . pounding."

"Maybe we should wait for the doctor." Her demeanor changed, her body stiffening slightly. She kept holding me but looked downward, away from my eyes.

"Babe," I said, although it sounded like "Bay." "Tell me. You're scaring me. *Whaaas* wrong?"

"Tommy, you had a brain aneurysm that burst. You died four times in the ambulance ride over here. They zapped you with the paddles until the defib charge unit went out. Then the EMTs put a needle of adrenaline straight into your heart. One of the medics straddled you and kept doing chest compressions until we got you to the ER. Five more minutes' difference and . . ." Her words dropped off.

I reached up and felt the padding and bandages on my skull. In one swift motion, I pulled them off my head. My hand felt a bare, shorn scalp with a few days' stubble and an ugly centipede of sutures forming a fresh scar in a curve beginning at my right temple and going behind my ear.

The door opened, and Brady was standing there.

He crossed the room and handed me my gold shield. When I refused to look him in the eye or accept the shield, he laid it on my chest and leaned in.

"As of today, Internal Affairs has cleared you, but given the gruesomeness of the crime scene and your subsequent impairment immediately afterward, the district attorney's shooting team and their internal investigations unit are still going to hold an administrative hearing. I don't blame you, little brother. If that bastard had Sarah like that, they wouldn't be able to identify him from the sludge at the bottom of my storm drain. So, you *are* going to look me in the eye and thank me for covering for your ass. You *are* going to respectfully answer any inquiries from internal investigations. You *are* going to show me the fucking respect of my position and authority in this matter. And you *are* going to remember that I did this—not for you, but because I love those kids, and because I love Claire. Or I will make sure you're retired with a medical and the only work you're doing is mopping up boxers' bloodstains after Frank has smoked his fighters."

Claire's grip tightened on me, but she didn't intervene in the argument. Brady didn't even blink in her direction.

"Look me in the fucking eyes, little brother, and tell me you understand."

My next words came out garbled, but my message was clear. "Fuck yourself, rat king. *Seven nurr eighhht* minutes doesn't make me your little brother any more than that rat shield in your pocket makes you my superior. And that fucking Silver Star and Purple Heart you got, Captain America? That don't make you a fucking hero to me. I would have saved the last bullet for myself. Look in the mirror and realize all you're doing with your life is living a shred of a moment in time when you were badass. Ancient fucking history."

He straightened up and attempted a grin and a chuckle, but I saw agony in his eyes; I had hurt him dearly. What was going on here? All three of us at one another's throats—me at his, him at Kenny's. He chuckled again and buttoned his blazer.

"That's how you would have played it, huh? Tommy Francis Spenser. So in love with death. Too bad, you almost got your wish. Pending Internal Affairs' complete review and a blessing from Special Investigations, you will be reinstated as task-force commander, but I am under orders from the acting commissioner not to let you run point on any raids or conduct patrols of any kind until the doc clears you. Your lieutenant will bird-dog in the field for you. If those terms aren't clear enough, I can hold on to that badge—"

"Captain Brady Spenser, *sir*. The only time you ever touch my badge again is if I am under arrest or in a casket. Do *you* understand?"

He walked toward the doorway, then turned back, and I clearly saw the shame and pain in his eyes, deeper than when he had farewelled his sergeant in the Bosnian morgue.

"In case you were wondering, I headed over as soon as I got your text, and I rode with you and Claire in the ambulance. I'm glad you're okay. Oh, and my official title is deputy inspector now, *Captain*."

Just as suddenly as he'd appeared, he left. Claire nestled back against me.

What the hell does he mean, "acting commissioner"?

"What's going on with you and your brother?"

"I can't tell you."

"Can't, or won't?"

"Can't."

"Well," she said, stroking a hand along my cheek, "you're quite lucky you are lying here with a hole in your head. Otherwise, I'd have to be pissed off."

"Charley? How is he?"

"They had to do surgery on his hip. He's fine now. Your dad is taking care of him back at Mickey's. He looks a little stupid with a cone around his neck and a quarter of his body shaved, but . . . he's going to be fine."

I went back to sleep, feeling her face against my neck and her body against mine. When I woke again six hours later, it was the middle of the night. Next to my gurney was an easy chair that converted to a cot, and Claire was curled up in it. I felt filthy, despite the best efforts of the hospital staff, and when I pushed the call button, the nurse came and helped me shower with the use of a plastic cap over my skull incisions. Before reconnecting my IV, she changed me into pajamas, along with a fleece robe that was so comfortable and warm that tears of gratitude welled up in my eyes. I then grabbed a walker near the bedside and balanced on it with one hand while I rolled my IV cart with the other into the hallway. Two SWAT guards were still there, and one of them broke from his post at the door to walk alongside me.

"What's with all the excess security?" I asked the SWAT sergeant. Ironically, it was the same guy I'd taken a roll with when I raided the stash house, the same day Marco had been shot.

"We're at defensive posture. Word got out on the streets about that deal at your house with your wife's ex and the hostage situation; then people spread news quickly that you were incapacitated. They knew the task force took a hit." He paused and looked straight at me. "The commissioner is dead. He was shot the Monday after you went down. At an elementary school, greeting kids. Coming back to the vehicle, his detail was ambushed. Five cops shot. Three in ICU.

"The mayor appointed the deputy as acting commissioner. Your brother Kenny took over for him as Metro deputy. Brady went up to run Special Investigations. Ed Peters is acting commander of Internal Affairs. Your new lieutenant, the colored fella"—he meant Snopes—"took the task force until you're one hundred percent. So, with everyone in your family in the spotlight, the bosses put us on overtime to watch you and the missus. You guys are like the Kennedys now."

I let that sink in. All of that transpired in 240 hours. Ten days. I might as well have been asleep for ten years.

"That's a bad analogy. The Kennedys are all dead or died in office."

"I meant, you're famous."

"Well, fuck, I don't mind famous, but if we're going chronologically, that makes me Teddy, the dipshit."

I was already winded. We had only walked about eighty feet.

"You need something, sir? Feel like turning around?"

"Yeah." I reached up to rub my scar again, and I felt the odd surgical plate that covered where they had drilled. The bone in my skull would fuse back, but the plate was a protective cover until it did.

I sat down in a wheelchair by the nurse's station. "She's going to want to go back to our house in the morning," I said, meaning Claire. "When you come off shift, I want you, personally, to take her to my mom and dad at Mickey's. I want her at Mickey's or my mom's until I can walk out of here. I'm sure they probably have patrol cars at both buildings, but I want a couple of our undercovers with eyes on too. Call Ed Peters and tell him. Get a message to him without using the hospital switchboard. Use a payphone or your cell. He's got clout to get a few people over there without it going under my brothers' noses."

I borrowed a pen from him and wrote a number on a scrap of newspaper at the visitor's area. "This guy. Tell him I want him as her attorney. Claire isn't to talk to the police about what happened without him there. Nobody from Special Investigations talks to her either without her lawyer and my PBA rep. That includes Inspector Brady Spenser."

"You want Taylor Jankowitz as her attorney? Isn't that a conflict of interest?"

"The last clients of his that my partners or I shot or put in cuffs are dead. When you're bleeding in the middle of the ocean, you want a shark on your side."

I didn't tell the SWAT sergeant that if Brady's suspicions were correct and our eldest brother was dirty, I wanted the advice and confidence of the best defense lawyer in Pittsburgh. I'd use the mostly boilerplate cover of the IAB investigation of the Hewitt shooting to get a feel for Jankowitz's skills, and then I would confide in him when I felt he was stable and/or slick enough. Claire would be pissed about being "jailed" at Mickey's, but after what had happened with Jake, I didn't want her going back into that house without me.

At the crack of dawn, Jankowitz came into my room, and the SWAT sergeant, in his patrol-duty blues and free of his SWAT tactical gear, took Claire home. She shot a wary glance over her shoulder, as if she were leaving me in the room with an axe murderer. I gently waved her out, and she mouthed "I love you" as she pulled the door shut.

Attorney Taylor Jankowitz sat across from me.

"Tom Spenser. The only guy who could get a hole in his skull and look prettier for it."

"I need us to stop this little professional pissing contest we've been having. Whatever your shortcomings, you're not a conspirator to murder. The commissioner is dead, and I think your remaining clients in the Washington crime syndicate killed him."

"What are you offering me, Tom?"

"Redemption, Taylor."

He sat there, poker-faced, and calmly turned and looked out the window.

"So, your wife's ex . . ."

"Yeah."

"Lots of holes in him for self-defense."

"Perhaps."

"Sounds like you need a lawyer, my friend." He broke out a yellow legal pad and a pen. "Tell me everything that happened from the time Mrs. Spenser—Clarissa, I mean—left you at the firing range."

■ ■ ■

The neurosurgeon was an affable man, and his presence would have been otherwise reassuring and welcome, but when he said I couldn't ever box again, I wanted to vomit. Not that I was planning on stepping into the main event ring at the edge of forty, but per his instructions, I couldn't even spar with the kids at the gym anymore. Any hard impact to the skull would risk a brain bleed or a cerebrospinal fluid leak. If he had his way, I would have probably been retired from the force at that moment, but for once I appreciated that the family name worked in my favor—special accommodations were being made, along with the fact that we were on high alert.

I was still on the bench for at least a month or two of rehab, but I wore out my attendants with three to four sessions daily. Although I could walk fine, I still needed a wheelchair when I became exhausted.

After the first week fully conscious, I went home from the hospital. I hadn't been cleared yet to drive, and Claire was adorable as she steered the tank-like mass of the Humvee around the neighborhood. Our destination was my mom's house. Everyone would be there to greet us, save for Brady. I couldn't drink because of some of the post-op drugs, but that was probably a blessing too. My body had detoxed from alcohol during those ten days I had been under. Truth of the matter was I wanted food, not booze.

As my father helped me out of the Humvee and into the wheelchair where I had been ordered to rest in between my rehab sessions, I saw tears in the corners of his eyes and a protective tenderness that I had never known from him. I had shrunk more in the hospital on liquid diets and IVs, and I was light enough for my dad to lift me like a baby. Claire had wrapped my head with a fleece watch cap from my military days so that my ugly puckered scar wouldn't freak out the kids. Amanda had tears in her eyes as well as she crouched down and hugged me. My mom looked at me with the relief that only a mother who's had a child at death's door could contemplate. Sarah Costello Spenser gave me a peck on the cheek, but I saw in her eyes that we needed to talk. Soon.

Spheres of matzo the size of polo balls appeared in tureens of chicken broth garnished with chopped green onions. I went to compliment my mom, but her slight smirk and a blush on Claire's face told me that my wife had concocted one of my favorite childhood dishes. Fresh hot loaves of crusty French bread from Rosenbloom's bakery helped us wipe the bowls clean. The main course was a "kosher" Moroccan couscous, meat heavy, to include chicken, merguez sausages, and lots of lamb. The final piece of the evening was a three-tiered chocolate cheesecake from Cheesecake Factory in my favorite blend of Snickers and peanut butter.

My body wasn't used to any of it, and I'd probably puke it all back up within an hour, but it was a hell of a homecoming, nonetheless. We talked, reminisced, and laughed for hours. I rubbed at the stubble of two and a half weeks' beard growth and noticed Sarah across the room, staring into a cup of hot cocoa, disengaged. I motioned for her to come over.

"What is it, Tommy?" Her face wasn't unkind, but I could tell that she and Brady had talked at length about what had happened, his suspicions, and my reactions.

"Can you still do a razor shave?"

"You want me with a straight razor, at your throat, right now?"

"Better you than Brady."

She got her upper body under my right armpit, helped me up the steps to my mom's room, and sat me down at the vanity. A few minutes later, she came in with a metal bowl into which she emptied a steaming kettle of water. She massaged my face with a hot towel and worked lather around the beard. Taking the straight razor that had been my father's when he lived here, she inserted a new blade and began to work the edge back and forth across a leather strap. Then, like a Mafia assassin about to render a kill, she grabbed my chin from behind and placed the blade at my neck.

The blade gently scraped at the stubble as she worked, and for a while she was silent, the only sound a tinny clacking when she rinsed the blade in the metal pan. It was intimate but not sexual; I had never felt anything for Sarah Costello but a brotherly love. Yet my asking her to do this, something I knew she did for Brady near daily, was on some plane familiar and loving, with a level of contrition and apology on my part. As my head was tilted back, our eyes met; though Brady and I were not identical, we had each other's eyes. She looked away first, snapping back into reality and rinsing the blade.

"My husband loves you, you shitbird."

"I love him too, Sarah."

"Then what's your problem?"

"I love Kenny as well. I have to give him the benefit of the doubt."

"You think there's a valid reason he was there the same day the weapons went missing?"

"I have to believe there could be."

She was silent for a little longer. I felt her thumbs trace along my chin line, feeling for spots she'd missed. She scraped another swath from where my dog-tag chain touched my neck, the razor running back up to my jawbone.

"He wanted me to tell you he wasn't avoiding you tonight. He's working a double, and quite frankly he didn't think you'd want him here."

Now was my turn to be quiet as she walked in front of me,

shaving my face, cheeks, moustache line, and chin. Not a single nick. She soaked another towel in a new batch of steaming-hot water, squeezed it out, and wiped it across my face, letting it rest there for about a minute as I inhaled the steam. She turned the chair around so I was facing my mom's mirror again. My cheeks were sunken and my eyes heavy with stress and fatigue. Yet her twenty minutes with a razor and some hot water had made me feel more human, more alive, and more present. She knelt beside me, and our eyes met in the mirror, as if we were greeting our doubles who were jailed in super-max security through a window.

"However mad you get at him, don't ever bring up Bosnia again. You haven't been there in bed next to him the last twenty years. He wakes up screaming sometimes. Or it's cold sweats when he thinks he's back in the bushes and the Serbs have attack dogs tracking him. Or sometimes he's just weeping in a ball on the floor. You're not the only one in this family with demons."

"Sarah, I promise that despite what happened at headquarters, I love your husband as much as I have since the day we were born. But ever since Frank . . . went away, Kenny has been the man keeping this family together. If it comes down to it, I will put the cuffs on him myself, but it will be because I am sure, not because Brady told me to."

"Okay," she said, brushing my cheek with her lips and putting my fleece cap back over my skull. "Let's get you back to your party."

If Kenneth was guilty of a criminal conspiracy to transfer weapons to the street echelons of the Pittsburgh drug scene, he didn't demonstrate any signs of guilt or neurosis that night. He was the perfect political superstar at the top of his game. I might have an angle with Amanda, but she would never side against her husband, even if he was guilty as hell. I told myself to enjoy my party and sleep on it, but the devil in my (newly drilled) skull couldn't resist. I rolled my wheelchair onto the back porch and, against my doctor's orders, lit up a stogie from a box of Cuban cigars Frank had procured for my homecoming.

Kenny soon came out on the porch with a gin and tonic, an unlit cigar between his teeth. He borrowed my Zippo, and for three whole minutes, neither of us said anything. Finally, I spoke.

"What have you gotten me into, Ken?"

"I don't know what you're talking about, Thomas."

"Ken, don't bullshit me. I know, goddamn it. I know that you were at the courthouse in Morgantown the same day those TEC-9s from the jazz club shooting and Fifth Avenue Plaza originally disappeared. Tell me you're not tied up in this."

"Tom, having that stroke or whatever it was has messed up your brain. I don't have a clue what you are talking about."

"You were at the Morgantown courthouse the day those weapons ceased to exist on paper. I'm not a fucking mongoloid, Kenneth! I know what you did!"

"So frigging what, Tommy? You know how many times I've been to the Morgantown courthouse the last twenty five-odd years? At least once a month! Homicide testimony. Kidnapping testimony. Interagency-task-force testimony. A dead whore's body is on the state line two-thirds in West Virginia and a third in Pennsylvania? All sorts of shit! So, some guns are missing on a day I'm there, and you paint me as dirty?"

"I'm not talking to you as a cop. I'm talking to you as a brother. Have you gotten yourself into something we can't get out of? I see the genius of it. Or at least the mad-scientist part. Unlicensed guns that were supposed to be out of the system years ago, distro them to the right people, and let the gangs go to war with one another, killing off the competition. You were the SIU director. You knew all the players, all the dealers, all their stash houses. You were tipping them off to one another, in the hopes that they'd kill one another off. Then what? You run for mayor, with the legacy of how you cleaned up the city intact?

"I know you didn't kill the commissioner. You're not that heartless, and you loved him like a surrogate father. But now your little pawns aren't satisfied with killing each other. Now they're going after cops. They're connected to the same shits who put Marco in the ground. You toasted a man you helped put in the dirt."

"Tommy, do you honestly think if I had something to do with this, I'd turn those guns loose to a bunch of shithead gangbangers? You honestly think that little of me? You can't fix this with your baseball bat. And you don't know what you're talking about. You're going to come across to anyone of substance as a crazy person. You just went after your other brother in the middle of Internal Affairs headquarters with about forty decorated witnesses. But you're also hero of the month for taking out the scumbag that tortured and beat your wife.

"Make no mistake, buddy, I can bring out all the reprimands I never filed, all the substance-abuse history, all the suicidal, self-loathing shit you ever involved yourself in, and at the end of the day, it will be the delusional ravings of a cop riddled with guilt and PTSD from failing his dead partner." He stubbed out the cigar and flicked the rest of it into the shrubbery. "I'm doing good things for this city, Tom."

"You of all people should know, Kenny, being Frank's eldest son, that the good never makes up for the horrible shit you've pulled."

"If the day comes for a reckoning, I will take as many of those bastards with me before I die. I've made peace with my decisions, and I knew full well the consequences of my actions, Thomas. If you had solid proof, you would have come at me by now. You really gonna do this just to fill the craving in your guts to be the hero? You gonna put Mom and Dad up in the courtroom, or on the witness stand? You gonna subpoena Mandy, who you love almost as much as Claire? I don't think so. Fifty bucks says you end up at the bottom of a bottle of Oxy before I ever come close to getting cuffed."

Tears streamed down my face as he turned toward the door to walk back inside. "You were my hero, Kenneth. How could you do this to me?"

He came over to my wheelchair and playfully cuffed one of my cheeks, then bent down and kissed the top of my head through the fleece hat. "You never needed a hero, Tommy. You're better than that. You're braver than that. We're never going to speak of any of this again. Whatever you think about me, whatever you think I've done, we've still got a job to do. Are you going to fall on your sword and be the martyr, or are you gonna help me finish this first?"

He left me out there on the porch without hearing my reply. I don't know how long I sat there, but the next thing I felt was Claire gently wrapping a blanket over my shivering shoulders. She wheeled me back inside, into the deserted kitchen, and drew no attention to the tears flowing down my face. She sat down at the Formica countertop and gently took my hand.

I cannot tell you how much I loved my wife in that moment, and how grateful I was for her quiet kindness the rest of that evening as she pulled the shutters on the doors separating the kitchen from the dining room. Using my fatigue to explain my disappearance, she quietly protected me from the rest of our guests, and I heard as she farewelled each family member one by one until my mother was upstairs asleep and my father had long since gone back to Mickey's.

She came to me, her coat and scarf on, car keys in one hand.

"Claire, I . . . Something bad, it's—"

She stopped me with a kiss. "It can wait till tomorrow, darling. Let's get you home."

"Thanks for tonight. Keeping everyone entertained when you saw I was hurting."

"Don't ever thank me for something like that, Thomas. I'm your wife. For once, you need to let someone take care of you."

I swear I was asleep before she buckled me back in the Humvee. I don't know how she got me in there, and I don't remember getting back to the house, and I don't remember her getting me out of the 4x4 or my clothes.

When I woke the next morning in our house, it was so peaceful that I imagined the last two weeks had all been a horrible dream. I reached over and touched my wife on the belly, where a new life was beginning.

Claire's eyes opened, and she put one hand over mine. "Good morning, Cap'n."

"Good morning, Mrs. Spenser."

"What do you want to do your first day home?"

I grinned. "Nothing to do with work."

She smiled back. "Good answer."

CHAPTER 18

A month later, I sat in court for my administrative hearing to return to the force, awaiting the judge's return from recess. Snopes approached my table and looked like his best friend had died.

"What do you have for me, Tori?"

"The night you and Marco hit the poker game, your tip was from Kenny, wasn't it?"

"Yeah."

Snopes bit his lip, looked down at the table, and slid a manila envelope over to me. "I pulled these a few weeks ago from the traffic camera files. I did a search of a square mile in all directions, and then I did a more detailed search four square blocks in the vicinity. The time frame is within twenty-four to forty-eight hours before you guys hit the bar."

Sure enough, there was a picture of Kenny in an unmarked car, and then a closer one of him surreptitiously walking past the bar.

"Well, that means nothing. He could have been doing a hasty recon, getting eyes on the site to verify the info from whoever gave him the tip."

Tori Snopes looked me dead in the eye and shook his head. "I didn't want you to see this one until the day you were officially back on duty. This is from the hardware store's security footage on the street parallel to the bar. The camera above their loading ramp faces the bar's back entrance. We never had a need to pull their footage because all the suspects were either arrested or dead, and we'd recovered the heroin."

He played a video on his phone. It showed Kenny jimmying the loading door of the bar, with a small satchel over his shoulder. "How much would you bet that inside that pack is two kilos of black tar heroin and Kenny planted it there to make it look like those guys were the shooters, or at least bought the dope off the shooters?"

"Tori, I hear you, and it makes for a hell of a fucking mystery novel, but I need to find a smoking gun. All we have him on is breaking and entering. Shit, a cop jimmying a lock? That might just be illegal search!"

"Are you saying all this because he's your brother?"

"I'm saying this because I want whatever charges there are to stick."

■ ■ ■

Due to Francine's relation to me and Mike Taradash's long history with all of us, they both had to recuse themselves from the departmental investigation regarding the homicide of one Mr. Jacob Hewitt.

Claire had given her statement earlier in the day and held her own against the ambitious deputy district attorney, Andrea "Andi" Cartwright. Miss Cartwright did not like any of the Spensers and thought we were monopolizing the law enforcement wing of Pittsburgh; she was making it her mission in life to expose some corruption or malfeasance on our part. Jake Hewitt getting shot to bits was like a birthday, Christmas, and Easter all in one for her.

Judge Daniel Rhogen came back in, devoid of robes but wearing a smart, black, button-down waistcoat over long, white shirtsleeves. He motioned us with a wave of his hand to sit back down as we popped up to the bailiff's call to rise.

"Where were we?" the judge asked, not cheerful but mildly pleasant for post-lunch.

"Your Honor, Captain Spenser is making a mockery of these proceedings. The fact that he has hired the highest-profile defense attorney in the tri-state area strongly suggests he has a matter of criminal malfeasance to obfuscate from this court," Cartwright said.

Taylor Jankowitz stood. "Objection, Your Honor. Detective Captain Spenser's record of service is stellar, and there is nothing in the crime scene or witness statements that suggests any criminal wrongdoing was committed by him or Mrs. Spenser on the day in question. Captain Spenser is completely within his rights under castle doctrine to have utilized deadly force in a matter where the offender severely beat the captain's wife, tried to kidnap two civilians, and committed felony animal cruelty."

"Allegedly, Your Honor," Cartwright said.

Jankowitz turned to the DDA with a nasty glare. "I'm sorry, Madame Prosecutor, I didn't know you were Jake Hewitt's defense counsel. Say what you want about me; there's some sewer jobs even I won't take."

"Fuck off, Counselor."

The judge banged his gavel and leveled his own dirty look at the DDA. "Miss Cartwright, you are lucky this is a hearing and we are not in open court. You will not ever use that vulgarity in front of me again. This is not a frat house. One more remark like that, and I will jail you for contempt."

Andi Cartwright stood her ground, unruffled by the judge's threat. "Your Honor, approach the bench?"

"Both of you." Judge Rhogen waved his hand.

Jankowitz spoke first. "Your Honor, my client has no interest in the privileged information regarding any of my cases in the alleged Washington family syndicate, nor does this incident in which he and his wife were involved connect to the Washington family, living or deceased, in any form. There is no conflict no matter how the DDA wishes to spin it. He hired me for the express purpose of defending against what the DDA is trying to accomplish—scapegoating him in some conspiratorial pipe dream. This is a case of a husband defending a wife and his home, plain and simple. I should hope Miss Cartwright's family and pets need not be beaten within an inch of their lives for her to agree with this."

"All right, Counsel; that is uncalled for. I am dismissing the DDA's motion to dismiss Mr. Jankowitz as Captain Spenser's counsel. This is a procedural formality and not a trial, and Captain Spenser is cooperating willingly. Does the city have anything else to enter as evidence before I make my ruling?"

Cartwright used her silver bullet. "Your Honor, the detective's ex-wife gave a statement that he removes the ammunition from all of his weapons before his children visit, save for the three he uses for duty. He knew the weapon Jake Hewitt held was not functioning. This is a cold-blooded assassination of a rival lover."

Judge Rhogen reddened at that statement. "Counsel, you are testing my patience. There is no evidence of premeditation on the captain's part. Jake Hewitt entered the Spenser residence illegally and with intent to do harm. He took two people hostage and beat Captain and Mrs. Spenser severely. Captain Spenser could not risk his wife's life with the possibility that Mr. Hewitt may have found ammunition elsewhere in the house and loaded it in that pistol before Captain Spenser entered the house.

"I have the recommendations of the Special Investigations Unit and the acting commissioner. They have no grounds for arrest. This is the textbook definition of a clean shot, and you damned well know it. I am ruling the shooting was justified. There will be no referral to the grand jury. This case is dismissed with extreme prejudice. Captain Spenser is free to go, with the City's apologies. He is reinstated to active police duty within the parameters of his medical recovery and doctor's orders."

The gavel banged.

"Miss Cartwright, you had better think twice before you

attempt to tarnish the reputation of an officer who has stood before my bench for fourteen years with an impeccable record of service, arrests, and integrity in the line of duty."

Cartwright stomped over to me and shook a sheaf of papers in my face. "You have everyone fooled, you scumbag hotshot, but I *know* what you are. Taradash and your sister won't always be here to clean up your messes for you. One day I am going to find you in a mountain of Oxy, and you'll have let another cop—or a kid this time—die on your watch, and I am going to be fucking thrilled to put you in orange pajamas and *bury you* under the fucking prison."

"Get away from my client, Counselor."

Cartwright chuckled. "A match made in heaven. You two fucking ghouls deserve each other."

I couldn't help myself. "Madame Deputy District Attorney?" I said, smugness emanating from my voice.

She spun around from the doorway. "*What*?!"

"Sometimes you have to let a wolf go to catch a bigger wolf."

She softened, tilted her head curiously at me, and walked back over to us. "What are you offering me?"

I waited until Rhogen and his bailiff as well as the clerk stenographer had cleared the chambers and it was just the three of us in the courtroom.

"Razor Washington and his colleagues' murders. You know as well as I do those weapons used were once impounded police evidence. And you know as well as I do there was a limited chain of custody on those weapons. Only about ten people between here and Morgantown, West Virginia, have the total authority to transfer or destroy them."

"And I know one of them has the name Spenser. If you're saying what I think you're saying . . . Are you willing to wear a wire?"

"I'm not a rat. And I am not going to turn him in just yet to Internal Affairs either."

"So, what exactly are you offering me?"

"I think I know how me and Marco came to Razor's that very first night." I motioned to Jankowitz. "If I can get you a meet with the Washington crew's enforcer, and you hear it from him, like real testimony, would that be enough to secure a warrant to take down Kenny?"

"You aren't going to wear a wire, but you would let a drug-dealing killer testify against your brother?"

"Yes."

"Let's take it to the DA."

■ ■ ■

District Attorney Mike Taradash took all of this in and then stared at me from across his desk for a long time. He smoked a Havana-cured cigar and extended one to me. His gold Citadel class of '87 ring gleamed under the green banker's lamp on his desk.

"This whole thing is tainted, tainted. All of you . . . *all of you*—except for Andrea, Snopes, and Ed Peters—are going to have to recuse yourselves once we bring him in. Before I go into the dockets. Brady too. And your sister was clerking in my office. Frank can't be anywhere near it either."

We wired up Cartwright and put her in a bulletproof vest. We did the same to Jankowitz. They were both miked and rigged with wires. Franny, Snopes, and I had earpieces. We chose the ball field over by Wilkinsburg as the meet location again, as it was considered territory of the Washington gang. This time, we didn't notify Wilkinsburg PD that we were coming. I was sure they were still out for blood and blamed me for one of their best patrol sergeants getting killed.

We had Franny slightly out of pocket, in the batter's dugout with my shotgun. Franny also had a concealed weapons permit and carried a Ruger .380 LCP in her handbag. Snopes was off near the access road with a spotter scope and a set of night-vision-capable binoculars; he would interdict anyone trying to come down the road to interfere with us or hit us by surprise.

Beyond the outfield, past the fence and behind a set of floodlights, Brady perched with a sniper rifle. Ed Peters was next to me with an MP5 assault weapon on a sling across his chest and a bullpup shotgun at the ready. I had a bullpup of my own and my chopped-down Recon .45 combat pistol in my right hand, with my thumb on the safety and my finger resting above the trigger guard.

All of us were in civilian clothes. None of us had our badges or even a shred of legal documentation. If this went sideways, all we had were the surveillance and wiretap warrants on Mike Taradash's desk. We had absolutely zero legal jurisdiction to be in Wilkinsburg without probable cause.

Around 2:30 a.m., a grayish-silver Mercedes S-Class with blacked-out windows pulled up, thumping DMX. They were courteous enough to dim their lights as they drove up so as not to blind us.

Helped by three of his minions, Darnell emerged from the rear passenger side and ambled over to us on a cane. He and I sized each other up, almost begrudgingly, and then he extended his hand. Not wanting to escalate an already tenuous situation, I took it with all the enthusiasm of picking up a turd barehanded at the dog park.

"You too good to shake my hand, Officer Tommy?"

"I'm surprised to see you back from the dead is all."

"Same goes for you, nigger," Darnell said. "I was already ordering flowers for your fucking funeral."

Jankowitz spoke first. "Darnell, this is Deputy District Attorney Andrea Cartwright."

Darnell glared at me. "This a fucking sting? This a fucking setup?" With his good hand, he reached inside his coat and pulled out a Desert Eagle—similar to Brady's (and Razor's) but tricked out, gold plated, ridiculous looking, and aimed center of my forehead.

Ed Peters brought his bullpup to hip level and aimed it square at Darnell's groin. "I wouldn't do that if I were you, homeboy. Look over at your driver."

Darnell glanced over one shoulder. His driver had dropped his own pistol and was trembling, wetting himself, Brady's red laser dot from his sniper rifle in the center of his chest.

Ed continued, "I give the signal, and it's happy birthday right here, right now for your boy over there. You fuck with me some more, or any of the rest of us get hurt, it's the rest of you in rapid succession. Now have your man pick up his gun, and everyone else's, and pass them over here."

Darnell grudgingly lowered his pistol and handed it to me. "You heard the man."

"Tell us what we want, and you'll get these back, and we all go our separate ways."

"What do you want, Officer Tommy?"

"Were you tailing us the night I arrested Razor? The first night. On Diller Avenue."

He let out an exasperated sigh. "No."

"But you were there to take him out."

Another exasperated sigh. "Man, am I gonna go to jail about what I *wanted* to do?"

The deputy district attorney looked at me, then at Darnell, and shook her head. "Not if you tell us what we need."

"Yeah, we was gonna roll up on him. But you three cops

got in our way big-time. You kind of did us a favor setting him up. 'Cept fucking *this*"—he tapped his chest where his gunshot wound had been—"kinda fucking sucked. Plus, whoever took out my foot soldiers too."

"Wait, what do you mean, we three cops? It was just me and Escardo in our patrol car. And we didn't set up shit."

"Aw, c'mon, Officer Tommy. I ain't gonna throw any shade on you, but if we all bein' honest here, admit that that other cop planted that shit."

"Darnell," Cartwright said urgently, "what other cop?"

"The big man!" He pointed to me. "His big brother! Big Kenny!"

My blood ran cold. "Kenneth Spenser planted the drugs and money in Razor's car?"

"Yeah, player! And then when we saw him do that shit, we called the tip in, and you guys pulled up and collared Razor. We didn't think he'd make bail so soon. But, you know. It cost me some blood, but still. The king is still the king, as they say."

"But you didn't have anything to do with Razor's hit at your club?"

"Bitch, if I did, do you think I'd get myself shot in the process?"

"Good point. What about the commissioner? If we're going to strike a deal, I need to have the names of the guys who took out the commissioner. Right now."

"What the fuck are you talking about, Officer Tommy? That wasn't my boys."

My fingers tightened around the bullpup. "Don't play games with me, fuckhead. I have all of you now, right here, minimum five years on weapons charges for threatening officers of the law."

"Tom, look at me. *Look at me.* You just took out our major supply when you hit that stash house. We were *rebuilding*. Why would we take a shot at the head of the department and draw the heat back on ourselves?"

"How about Detective Sergeant Hamilton outside the first stash house? You gonna tell me that wasn't you as well?"

"It was my guys, yeah, but they was on they own. And whoever those psychos were in the masks took care of them already. The three who did that are the three who got shot to shit at the Penn Hotel and the garage."

"That's too easy. You're lying."

"Bitch, if I wanted to lie, I would have relied on those dead fools' anonymity and let you wander with your thumb up your ass some more. All you knew was a car shot at you. You never caught them. But now you know they killed Hamilton and they died in November, so they didn't ice the commissioner. I just closed a case for your punk ass just now. I didn't give the orders on Hamilton *or* the commissioner. Around the time you raided the stash houses, a bunch of fools was trying to freelance, looking to make a name."

I heard a loud scream from the baseline area. *I know that voice.*

The radio on my hip cracked to life. Snopes's voice. "Tom, three o'clock. Movement."

I saw Franny. But something was wrong. She had her hands above her head. A figure clad in a black hood, fatigues, and a tactical vest was crouched beside her. "Snopes, try to follow!"

"Got it, boss!"

There were three successive shots, then the barking, clapping blast of Snopes's shotgun.

"Boss," he gasped over the radio, "he's . . . he's got her. I'm sorry."

I wheeled back and shoved my pistol in Darnell's face. "Get on your knees, motherfucker."

"Ain't me, dawg. He isn't with us!"

"Get on your fucking knees."

Darnell dropped to the ground, screaming, crying, clutching

my legs. I kicked him off and braced my boot on his head. Ed Peters said something and tried to pull the shotgun out of my hand, but I still had the pistol. The deputy district attorney was trying to body-block Darnell. Jankowitz grabbed her and pulled her away. Then the rest of Darnell's crew piled back into the sedan and floored it in reverse, with Jankowitz giving chase, trying to yell some sense into them.

The sedan proceeded about fifty feet. And exploded.

The DDA, Ed, and I were all knocked on our backs. The impact of the blast threw our weapons away from us and even busted the strap on the one Ed had across his chest. Jankowitz had been decapitated by the explosion.

Darnell staggered to his feet and picked up Ed's shotgun, aiming it at me and the deputy district attorney. I motioned for Ed to run and held the DDA's hand, closing my eyes, thinking of Claire, wondering what our new baby was going to look like—if it would have her smile, her red curls.

BOOM.

Ed, the DDA, and I blinked at each other in shock. Then we looked at Darnell. Or what was left of Darnell.

He was slumped over on the ground, a bloody, gaping hole in his neck, blood foaming and spurting. I thought the shot had come from Brady, but I looked over at the floodlights and saw him coming down the ladder pegs two at a time.

I looked back just in time to see Kenny and Respottek—clad in matching dark overalls, the white hockey masks pulled up to show their faces—emerge from the darkness, raise their weapons, and pump more rounds into Darnell. They had Franny's weapons with them as well.

They also had Snopes, along with his shotgun. Obviously they had tried to pursue whoever took Franny, then circled back when the car blew. They dragged Snopes up, wounded but alive, and Kenny tore Snopes's jacket into strips of fabric and applied first aid to his gunshot wounds.

I heard Franny screaming in the distance. The engine of a 4x4 revved to life and sped away.

I picked up my pistol after a brief search and held it on my brother. My other arm used Ed's shotgun as a crutch to push up into a sitting position. Ed held the backup weapon he'd retrieved on Respottek.

"Repo, you fucking scumbag," I snarled.

He couldn't even look me in the eyes. I thought of the chant from the boxing ring. *"Speed! Audacity! Precision! Speed! Audacity! Precision!"*

Exactly how he and Kenny had hit their targets.

I looked up at both of them, and sure enough, hanging on combat slings across their chests were the two TEC-9 automatics that had sent us on this snipe hunt in the first place.

"You fucks. You did this?" Ed snarled, looking like he could pull Kenny's skull open with his bare hands.

"Not tonight we didn't. We followed Washington to see who he was meeting with, see what was going on."

"Bullshit. You followed us to kill Washington and any witnesses."

"Ed, I swear to God, that wasn't *us*. Somebody else rigged their car!"

The four of us all regarded each other in surprise. Even poor Snopes, trying not to bleed to death, had a *what the fuck* look on his face.

We were still trying to come to terms with everything that had happened in the last thirty seconds when a crater appeared in the middle of Repo's chest and he was eviscerated by one of the deadliest shooters in the Bosnian conflict—and someone who had loved him since childhood. In those last moments, Repo was conscious enough to lock eyes with Brady as he dropped to his knees and pitched forward in the grass, not far from the man he had just killed.

"You motherfucker." Brady raised the rifle and sighted the scope on his older brother. This close, Brady hardly needed the scope.

"Brady, buddy, it's me. It's Kenny."

Kenny looked Brady in the eyes but continued, with almost mechanical motions, to apply pressure and fashion a battlefield dressing for Snopes. He sat him up and had the DDA continue to hold her hand on the wound. Brady, disgusted, spoke through gritted teeth.

"It was *you* who took the weapons. You had this planned years ago. You put Tommy's task force together so you could take the credit for whatever successes they had. So you could create your legacy for mayor one day. You set up Tommy and Marco on this goose chase. It was you and Repo who hit the jazz club. You planted the heroin at the poker game. You two at Fifth Avenue. You had Repo suffocate the survivor from the SWAT raid while you were at the law enforcement conference because it would draw the heat away from you.

"You were behind everything. And you send your little brother, coming off of a couple-years-long narcotics bender, because you think you can bury the cases in his fuckups and no one will ever find anything? You used us, you fucking filthy piece of shit. Our brother Marco, who was just as much a blood brother as any one of us. He's dead because of you, you cocksucker!"

"Brady, listen to me. I will answer for all of that later. We can rationalize you taking out Repo just now—you took out a suspect who was wielding a weapon, yeah? Matched the description of the killers? But my weapon is down, brother. You do this now, you shoot *me*, you take out your own *brother*, that's cold-blooded murder, plain and simple. Brady, it's not the Army, it's not

Bosnia, I'm not armed—you pull this trigger, you are not a cop anymore; you're a vigilante. *You are a murderer*. You are just as bad as me. Whoever did this, they just grabbed Franny. They are going to *kill her* if we don't find them and bring her back home."

While Brady was considering this, others in the group had already made their minds up. Ed Peters kept his shotgun trained and approached Kenny, pressing the barrel against his head. Brady held his hand up, and immediately Ed raised the barrel away.

"He's right." Brady looked sick at that concession.

"Are you fucking serious, boss? He just as much admitted to being the killer!"

"Give me twenty-four hours to get Franny back. Then you can put him in the fucking gas chamber for all I care."

"Let me come with you," Ed and I said, simultaneously.

"Get his statement first," Andi said.

We all turned around. The DDA had a gash in her forehead, trickling blood, but her voice was steady and her eyes resolute.

"I will do a blanket emergency action authorization that will cover this . . . this . . ."—she waved her hand—"this mess for tonight. But we take him back to the station. Get a full confession. To everything. Then he can help you find your sister. But you keep a gun in his back at all times when he is off police grounds. And yes, cuffs stay on. Ostensibly this will look like Jankowitz had me meeting with some of his clients to cut a deal and one of the vigilantes set off the car bomb and got the drop on us. That should at least be what the press runs with until we can find who has your sister."

Ed turned Kenny around and snapped the cuffs on him. "I respected you. You're a fucking piece of shit."

"Ed, we have to bring him through the station. Let him have his hands in front. He's not going anywhere."

Ed looked at the DDA for confirmation, and she nodded.

I handed Franny's pistol to the DDA and left Franny's shotgun near her feet and Snopes's shotgun next to him, within arm's reach. The rest of us gathered up the remaining weapons and prepared to bolt.

Thinking fast, Brady cut Repo's body armor away with a survival knife he had carried since Bosnia. Repo had regular street clothes on under the coveralls, and Brady cut the coveralls away as fast as he could with Ed helping him roll the body out. Now Repo just looked like a poor schmuck who had wandered into the kill zone instead of being an accomplice.

Reading what my brother had in mind, I took Repo's discarded coveralls and spread them open, throwing his body armor into the center. I then unloaded and cleared his and Kenny's TEC-9s, as well as the hockey masks, and piled them on top.

As I was doing this, I glanced up to the DDA, realizing that up until thirty minutes ago, she was still out to get the Spenser brothers in her crosshairs, and presently she was armed to the teeth. At that moment, she was holding leftover strips of Snopes's T-shirt to her own injuries trying to stop the blood from running down her face. She glanced away, shook her head at nothing in particular, wiped away more blood, then turned to face me. Her face aglow with the inbound police lights as well as the flames, she nodded and weakly gave me a thumbs-up to continue—followed quickly by a middle finger from the same hand.

I wasn't thinking at the time that I was obstructing justice, tampering with evidence, and pretty much committing perjury before the fact by dumping the evidence into Darnell's vicinity; I was thinking Kenny and Repo were my family, and I was protecting them. Tying the coveralls into a hobo bundle of sorts, Brady sprinted over to where Darnell's car was still cooking off secondary explosions and heaved the bundle into the center of the blaze.

Ambulances and squad cars started to pull up on the scene.

The DDA motioned for us to go while keeping her arms firmly wrapped around Snopes, applying pressure to his wounds. Brady, Kenny, Ed, and I beat it through the woods to where Kenny's car was still parked. The DDA was already pulling out her phone and putting in a call to Mike Taradash to expect this goatfuck.

■ ■ ■

Mike Taradash was not a man to scream or get overtly angry, but as he took Kenny's statement, his eyes held a deathly cold glare, and his lips pursed and hands clenched while Kenny rattled off names, dates, caches of supplies, weapons, vehicles, and targets he and Repo had accumulated. I got sick and threw up in a hallway trash can three times.

We had walked Kenny in through the task-force squad room with a jacket covering his cuffs, but there was already murmuring about what was going on.

When Taradash was on a bathroom break, I turned the camera off and latched the door, sitting across from Kenny.

"Looks like I owe you fifty bucks, little brother." He had a deflated look of resignation, but something about him was content, at peace.

I pulled out two of the cigars Frank had brought over for my welcome-home party from the hospital, and we lit them, sitting there, reminding me of when Taradash and I sat there the night after SSG Hamilton and that poor girl had gotten killed at my stakeout.

Wait.

"Where are you going?" Kenny looked up at me quizzically as I jumped to my feet.

"I'll be right back."

I motioned for Sergeant Simmons, the last one besides me in the task-force chain of command who wasn't dead—Marco—or wounded—Snopes—to continue Kenny's interrogation with Mike

Taradash. Then I ventured over to police headquarters' main building, down to the basement morgue to talk to the forensics techs. What was left of Darnell and his buddies were on four tables in Dr. Czaervich's lab, and the coroner and her assistants were trying to reassemble the other three from the car like a set of bloody tinker toys that had come without instructions. I tried not to look at the fifth body, still covered with a sheet, the huge red stain betraying the crater Brady had made in the chest of someone I had loved like family, someone I had once called my friend.

Not a friend anymore. A cold-blooded killer, I thought.

What's the difference? something inside of me asked. *You have pulled the trigger on people.*

People who were trying to kill me.

Jake Hewitt would have something to say about that.

Poor Taylor Jankowitz was already in a drawer somewhere, with his head reattached as well as the coroner's assistant could manage until the morticians had a crack at it. At least he wasn't blasted into pieces or dissected in full view. He would rest quietly, if not peacefully, until being prepared for his funeral. I imagined that event: his wife, kids, and mistresses all coming together in the chapel at Shugar's Funeral Services.

Dr. Katya Czaervich was gleeful as a twelve-year-old on Christmas morning. She shucked off the arm-length gloves coated with gore into the red safety receptacle and talked to me while scrubbing at the sink.

She was back in the wares in which I had first met her, blue scrubs and cap, and I suppressed a grin at noticing those Delta boots once again, this time covered with clear plastic rain bags. She pulled off the mix of cute and kick-ass quite well. (What I had incorrectly assumed to be a Balkan dialect was most likely East German, if her scrub cap—white and printed with bold-type phrases like ALLO, GUTEN MORGEN, TSCHUESS, MACH'S GUT, ABEND—was any indication.)

"If you want to flirt with a girl, Captain, you could just bring me flowers, no?"

I smirked and dutifully held up my left hand, showing my gold wedding band. "Not in the mood this morning, Doc."

"I know. And from what I hear, you have a family member in the wind. I am so sorry."

"That's all right. At least now I know why we never got a hit back on the DNA. Respottek was in the service just like most of us, but before they started doing DNA swabs. He never got in trouble and had never worked in law enforcement anywhere else outside of Homeland. Nowhere had any sort of biological sample of his on file except private healthcare."

"Correct. Sadly, and I hate to use such a clichéd phrase, but we didn't know what we didn't know. However, I have some good news that may get you started in the way of a lead. The residue from the car bomb is a nitramine-based explosive called RDX." She motioned for me to look at a slide under a compound microscope in the small lab adjacent to the autopsy bay. Not sure what I was seeing, I peered at small, crystallized flakes surrounded by what could best be described as tiny dots the color of ash.

"RDX. Where do I know that from?"

"You should know it very well. It's part of the makeup in the linear-shaped charge that your SWAT teams use for breaching steel doors. And it has a long history with the military. You know it as a part of the most commonly used explosive, a frequent tool of the conventional infantryman and paratroopers: Composition 4, or C4."

"Paratroopers and Seabees—erm, you'd know them as naval construction engineers."

"Yes, even modern commercial civilian engineers would still have a small window of use for C4, although HMX and Dynex are the most common for building demolition and structural supports, and Dynex is usually used for clearing boulders and larger rocks—"

I grabbed Doc Czaervich by both shoulders and planted a smooch on her cheek. "Doc, I think you just saved my sister's life."

Her eyes widened with surprise as I rushed out of the room and took the steps from autopsy and the coroner's office two at a time.

I pulled my smartphone out of my jacket. "Brady, grab your long rifle, grab me an MP5, some tac gear for both of us, and meet me by Kenny's car. I'm going to go pull Kenny out of the interview and tell Mike Taradash what we're doing. I think I know who has Franny. No backup, or she's as good as dead."

CHAPTER 19

We put Kenny in a bulletproof vest, and I took the cuffs off him. No way was I giving him a firearm, but I did give him a taser and a launcher gun modified to deliver nonlethal beanbag rounds. I didn't think he would use it on either of his brothers, and if he did, we were all going to jail anyway.

We pulled up to Stafford Demolitions Inc., a sprawling warehouse between Greentree and Carnegie and close to Parkway Center Mall that used to be a paper mill. It was nearly 7 a.m. People weren't rolling into this part of the industrial park for work yet, so we had a window of time to finish this.

A blue 2006 Ford Explorer was parked diagonally out front. It looked like the rear passenger window had been kicked open, and there was blood on the shards of glass. A trickling line ran to the warehouse door, to a bloody handprint on the concrete next to the doorframe.

Brady chuckled. "Franny."

I nodded, gritting my teeth, fighting tears.

Kenny looked perplexed. "What?"

Brady, not even looking him in the eye, said, "Didn't they teach you anything at West Point, you stupid fuck? It's evasion and escape 101. She's leaving markers for us to follow. It couldn't be any more obvious if it was breadcrumbs. More importantly, she's leaving us a proof of life."

Brady knelt next to the palm print and extended his own hand over the red fingermarks. His hand was much larger. "Look at the size difference, dipshit. If we surmise that this asshole took Franny, and we know his own daughter is long dead, then we know whoever left this handprint of blood isn't him. It's got to be Franny."

Kenny nodded cautiously. "What if he's got this place booby-trapped? Like he did the car?"

This time I was the one to answer.

"No, this is all cinematic. He wants impact. That car bomb didn't go off randomly. He did it exactly when I was out of the kill zone. He wants us to suffer like he did. Whatever he has planned for Franny, he wants us to live to see it."

Brady looked at both of us. "I'm going to find a spot to engage him. I'll take him out with a base-of-the-skull shot. That way if he has a switch rigged to blow something, he won't be able to trigger it. You two move in and try to get Franny. It doesn't look like there's many exterior light sources, so we have a tactical advantage before full daylight. If you can find the power, kill it, and I will take him out."

I grabbed a piece of rebar lying by the door, winced, and shoved the door open with it. Nothing went boom. We proceeded in as if we were stacked in a SWAT team; Brady broke away, and Kenny and I were back on the hunt like so many years before. We kept following Franny's droplets of blood.

We came to a cleared area in the warehouse and found a pile of crates set up in pyramid fashion. Toward the apex sat Franny and Esther Stafford's dad. Stafford had a gun trained on Franny. Fran looked otherwise okay; she didn't seem beaten or tortured. However, a vest with about fourteen sticks of Semtex and TNT completely covered her torso, and an oblong silver box the size of a brick was attached on her chest. Wires protruded from it, and a series of numbers on a display spun in sequence, like a slot machine. Beside the numbers was a keypad, like on a touch-tone phone. More difficult than a timer. Enter the wrong numbers on the pad, and she'd go bang. Enter the right numbers and she'd live. The worst ATM pin code you could ever imagine.

"Drop your guns."

"Mr. Stafford, listen."

"I don't want to hear it. Drop your guns."

"Sir, that's my baby sister up there." Typical Kenny, the used-car salesman with a million-dollar grin. "How are you, Franny?"

"Fuck you, you piece of shit! I had my earpiece in! I heard everything that went down!" Franny's eyes carried a repulsed venom I had never before beheld. There was nothing Kenny could do to redeem himself.

"Now, now, Franny. You see, Mr. Stafford, sometimes families fight, but deep down they still love each other. And I don't want anything bad to happen to Franny, just like I know if it was your little girl in that vest, you'd do anything for her."

"It *was* my little girl, you arrogant *fuck*! Your brother killed her!"

"Killing my sister isn't going to bring her back. I thought like you. I thought going around the city and cutting off the heads of the snakes would root out the evil. But snakes just keep springing back up. But look at my sister there, sir. She isn't a snake. She isn't evil. She's trying to do good for the people of this city. She is a good woman with a good heart, and she's the type of woman that your daughter aspired to be. Killing her isn't going to do anything for your daughter's memory but shame it and send your soul straight to hell."

"I'm *already* in fucking hell!"

I had the MP5 red dot straight in the middle of Stafford's chest. Brady's red dot was between Stafford's nose and his lip, which meant the bullet would blow out the base of his brainstem. But instead of a kill switch, Stafford had a more sinister improvisation.

He had Fran on the boxes so that if he was shot and no longer holding her and the vest, she would lose her balance. The weight of her body would pull out the detonation cords as gravity did its job. A failsafe mechanism in the vest would trigger a backup detonator, and my sister would be red mist on the warehouse walls before Brady could get a second round off or Kenny and I could move.

"You know what, sir? If you want a hostage, take me."

Stafford and I both stared at Kenny.

"Wha . . . what?"

"Take me. We will let my sister go. We'll get the news crew down here, whomever you want to talk to."

"I want an apology from the *acting commissioner*!"

"Because you killed the old one that day at the school, didn't you?"

"You're fucking right I did!"

"You killed him, and you shot all those cops, and they had nothing to do with that night. All of this started because of me. So, take me." Kenny spoke softly into his earpiece: "Brady, as soon as Fran is out of the blast radius, you end this."

"Kenny—"

"That's a fucking order." Kenny dropped the beanbag shotgun on the floor so that it clattered loudly. He unclipped the taser from his belt and laid it down as well. Taking off his West Point ring and wedding band, he handed them to me. I quickly shoved them in the cargo pocket of my tactical vest. I teared up involuntarily as he bumped my fist with his and gave me a wink and began to climb up the crates.

I kept the red dot fixed on Stafford's chest. Stafford, true to his word, unbuckled Fran from the vest but kept his gun trained on her head, finger on the trigger. The grieving father also held a small plunger detonator in his other hand that would blow the three of them up if Kenny tried anything. I nearly bit my lip bloody with anxiety, my eyes focused on the fifteen feet of cord between the Sharpie-size detonator and the vest being moved from my sister to my brother.

After Kenny had the vest buckled on him, Stafford put the detonator in his pants pocket, then started the four-digit spinning dial back up again, signifying the vest was once again a live bomb.

I motioned to Fran to begin her descent. Bawling incoherently, she climbed down and threw her arms around me. I crouched down with her behind a pylon and whispered, "Run, honey. Run for the door. Stay low. *Now.*"

Once I heard the warehouse door slam, I hissed into my throat mic as calmly as possible: "Brady. Do it now."

"Kenny's going to die."

"Brady. *Do it now.*"

"I . . . I can't."

"Do it, Brady. Do it!"

I saw the red dot on Stafford's head disappear. Brady had taken his gun sights off him.

"I'm coming down and calling the negotiator."

I flipped the safety catch on my MP5 and brought the sight up for a target. If Brady wasn't going to do it, I was. *Goodbye, Kenny.* My index finger started to apply pressure on the trigger. *Squeeze. Breathe.*

Nothing. *Click.*

FUCK!

I had been so amped up and stressed getting Franny back, running on no sleep, and finding out my brother was a mass murderer, somewhere in all that I had ignored the muscle memory basics of chambering a round on my third weapon of the evening

Stafford, hearing the trigger strike on nothing, knowing he'd been played and that no audience was coming, began to bring the gun up to engage me.

I racked the slide, chambered a round into the breech, and aimed again. *Breathe. Breathe. Breathe. Squee—*

BANG!

My shot went wide and missed because Stafford was no longer in my crosshairs. Kenny, with one last tackle from his West Point glory days, slammed into Stafford with all his strength and knocked him from the pile of crates down to the concrete warehouse floor. Amazingly, the fall didn't kill either of them, nor did it immediately trigger the vest, but it did knock away Stafford's firearm, which I immediately—and perhaps stupidly—ran forward to grab.

I then saw my eldest brother grab Stafford by both shoulders, reach into Stafford's pocket, and pull out the detonator. He hugged Stafford close to his chest as he brought the plunger up to eye level. Then he turned to me and gave me that stellar politician's smile of his. He never heard my screams, my shouting, "NO"—that we had him, we could bring him in now, he didn't have to do this.

"Fifty bucks, Tommy!" Kenny shouted with a smile. "Drinks on me!"

He hit the button on the plunger, and the current went straight into the metal box. It bypassed any failsafe or controls Stafford may have had and immediately triggered the charge on the live blasting caps inside the box. Those blew as primary, and since they were at his heart level, I was sure that my brother and Stafford were dead in a millisecond.

The blasting caps triggered the larger sticks of TNT strapped to Kenny's chest. For a brief second, there was a nuclear-like pulse, and it felt like all of the air in the warehouse had been sucked out. I was blown back into the aisle I had just been standing in with Franny, and everything went murky.

I thought at worst I'd had another concussion.

When I came to consciousness, there was only a smoking crater of burnt plywood where Stafford and Kenny had been standing, and Franny and Brady were knelt next to me. Brady was doing something to my left leg.

He was applying a tourniquet.

SWAT was converging on the place. Doc McClusky took over for Brady and gave me an easygoing grin. "Hey there, boss. How's it going?"

"Aww, fuck off, Doc. You're loving this. Give me some goddamned morphine."

"No can do, brother. Your pulse is as shallow as a kiddie pool. Morphine would turn that pretty young wife of yours into a widow, and we can't have that."

"Kenny, Doc . . . where . . . Kenny . . . uhhhh . . . Where's big Kenny?"

Doc and Brady locked eyes with each other, and Franny leaned forward and held my hand, smoothing my hair back. I had no idea that the red mist on her face was arterial spray from what was left of my leg. "Kenny will be here soon buddy. You just stay put."

Doc looked up from what he was doing with an alertness in his eyes as he listened to the stethoscope on my chest. "We're losing him. Back up, Franny, honey. Go with Brady. I gotta get in there—"

Exhaustion swept over me, and in a panic I realized I was going into shock. It felt the same as when I had blown Hewitt away, and I worried that I was having another stroke. In the back of what few receptors were still sparking in my mind, I was sure I was slipping away from loss of blood. This wasn't such a bad way to go; I felt absolutely nothing. I heard Brady and Franny calling my name, but I had no way to get to them.

I saw my grandfather wearing a patient, kind smile—the

same way he would look at me from behind the ropes at my fights when the chips were down and I was losing, when he knew more than anything how much I wanted to quit and just have it be over. He would say something over and over to me, in all those matches over all those years, and I knew he was saying it to me now, repeating it over and over in Yiddish.

"*Shtey aoyf aun haltn feyting. Shtey aoyf aun haltn feyting. Shtey aoyf aun haltn feyting.*"

Get up and keep fighting.

EPILOGUE

I was having one hell of a year. Cancer, gunshot, concussion, aneurysms, seizures, strokes, and now amputation as the icing on the cake. Plus, a vigilante brother who conspired with my childhood coach in a series of murders across the city.

There was plenty of evidence in Stafford's workplace and residence to tie him to the commissioner's killing and the shooting of the five cops during my hospitalization after Jake Hewitt's attack. Kenny's suicidal takedown of Franny's cop-killing kidnapper spread like wildfire through the press.

HERO COP OF PITTSBURGH DIES RESCUING SISTER, AVENGES FALLEN COMMISSIONER.

Taradash sealed Kenny's confession, which would have gone to the grand jury. Kenny's involvement—his guilt—never made the papers.

And as far as the public knew, Repo had died as an innocent bystander in the middle of a gangland turf war. The fact that he and Kenny had always been masked and in coveralls while pulling off the killings made it easy to put the blame on Razor and Darnell's crew—and Razor and Darnell's crew were far from innocent babes themselves. I did not shed one goddamned tear about falsely attributing a few more homicides to them.

I felt the worst for the departed attorney Taylor Jankowitz, Esquire. That poor bastard was simply trying to right a wrong, clear his conscience, and maybe sleep a bit better at night. If there is a goddamn heaven, I hoped they let him in. He more than paid his debt in full.

What was left of our brother's body, and Repo, remained

in cold storage at county until the end of the investigation. To my surprise, Amanda requested—and the prosecutor's office granted—a postponement of the inquests, the evidentiary findings, pretty much everything until I came home from the hospital eight weeks later. Her argument was that she wanted the investigation complete and everyone debriefed, nobody jumping to conclusions, and, more importantly, the media far, *far* away from her and the girls. She had also delayed a funeral or memorial until she had all the final findings from the case, no matter how horrible or ugly they turned out to be.

We brought Mom and Amanda into the station for the official, classified briefing of what really transpired. Mike Taradash, Andi Cartwright, Ed Peters, and the acting commissioner were on one side of the table. Amanda and Mom were on the other. Brady, Francine, and I sat out in the corridor after each of us played our part. I was back in a wheelchair and wouldn't be fitted for a prosthetic until the burns on the stump that had formerly been my left leg healed completely.

Andi Cartwright came out first. She reminded me of the Greek myth of Sisyphus pushing the rock up the hill. Here she was, the firepisser hotshot out to clean up the streets, and in one night she had entered the moral ambiguity that was the orbit of dealing with the Spenser clan.

We had talked many times since I had been in the hospital and during my recovery. There were milestones of caveats that would come with her silence. This wasn't just about the greater good. She told me flat out if she ever caught me anywhere near a recreational bottle of pills again or up to any of my old "therapeutics," there would be no quarter and no mercy. She hated Taradash for leaning on her to drop her crusade; she hated the Old Guard for backing Kenny's legacy; she hated me and Brady for picking our family over the rule of law; but she still respected us for saving her. She held her gaze on us thoughtfully before speaking.

"In some twisted way, I feel like I owe them. Kenny and Respottek, along with the rest of you, saved my life. Seriously. There's no telling how that night could have played out. But I will never be okay with how *this* is playing out right now. They're *murderers.*"

I tapped a cigarette out of my stale pack of Marlboros and lit one.

Cartwright looked even more disgusted. "You know darn well there's no smoking in here."

"They're dead murderers, Andrea. And thanks to the late Mr. Stafford, most of the remaining Washington crime syndicate is dead." I proffered the pack to her. To my surprise, she took one and let me light it.

"That crap you told me at your hearing, about it taking a wolf to catch a wolf. Do you really believe all that horseshit, or was that some fluff you were telling me in the moment?"

"I think I'm particularly good at my job, and me being good at my job makes you able to do yours."

"There's something I want from you, Thomas."

"What's that?"

"I want Marco Escardo's shotgun from the SWAT raid brought to the evidence room sergeant by six thirty tomorrow morning, and I will grant prosecutorial exoneration to the person who took it."

I sat in my wheelchair wordlessly but felt the slightest hint of a smile lift the corners of my mouth.

"You think I'm an idiot? I knew it was you from the moment I saw the team inventory and his was the only weapon missing. I figured you were going to use it to frame Darnell or one of his foot soldiers into giving up the identity of the shooters. That was before you realized the shooters were people in your own family. That will teach you to racially profile." She blew out smoke in a fine, cone-shaped puff toward the window. "But isn't it a bitch that it turns out we are a bunch of sinful motherfuckers framing them anyway? And don't give me any condescending lectures about the greater good."

I didn't. "What are you going to do now, Counselor?"

"I don't know. But I am not sure practicing law in this town is the right call anymore."

"Who else is going to keep the wolves away?" I extended my hand. To my surprise, she shook it.

She turned away on her high heels, and they struck the corridor, announcing her departure like the formidable warrior she was. "Six thirty tomorrow, Captain, with that shotgun. Or I wheel you off in a squad car. There are ADA-accessible jail cells in county lockup."

I stared after her, terribly disappointed that Kenny hadn't utilized her, and people like her, to fight his crusade the right way before resorting to dressing up as extras from *HEAT* and going "guns akimbo."

Francine smiled and squeezed my hand. "I never thanked you for coming to my rescue, big brother."

I didn't look at my kid sister to avoid showing her the tears pooling in my eyes. "And you'll never have to."

We then heard accusatory tones, flat-out screams, and crying coming from inside the conference room.

First Mom came out, not looking at any of us, and stomped off toward the parking lot. She threw something in the trash as she exited the building—a shadow box containing Kenny's officer, detective, and inspector badges and department ribbons, to include his highest award, the Pittsburgh police Medal of Valor, for exceptional heroism. Kenny had earned that medal by going back into a hail of gunfire to pull a downed officer and a wounded civilian to safety in the PNC bank robbery in 1999. The officer ended up surviving with two bullets in his side and had recently married a woman named Claire.

Mom had been clutching the box all through the hearing. Brady wordlessly fished the display out of the trash, scraped some garbage away, and looked up at me.

"If nothing else, Frank or the daughters would want it."

Amanda emerged a picture of composed grief, a blond, blue-eyed Jackie Kennedy, all in black, lifting her head proudly, although in that moment she was anything but proud. She dabbed both of her cheeks with a tissue and smiled sadly at all of us.

"Thank you all, truly, for protecting me and letting me hear it from them, today, here. But I will not engage in any further hypocrisy. I will not participate in this lie that the department is playing at. There will not be a police memorial. There will not be an official funeral. There will not be an honor guard. No dress-blue twenty-one-rifle volley. He is going to be cremated and his ashes spread over his grandfather's grave."

"But, Amanda, people are going to wonder—"

"Brady, shut. The fuck. Up." Her eyes could have fired lasers into my twin.

All I could think was *What the fuck is left to cremate?*

I was the first to speak up after a long pause. "Come on, I'll drive you over to the funeral home." My right foot could still operate the brake and gas. "We'll pick out an urn."

Amanda nodded, and Franny gripped the handles of my wheelchair. The three of us ambled off, leaving Brady to contend with his demons alone, as always.

■ ■ ■

It was Doc Katya Czaervich who delivered my get-out-of-jail-free card. We stood in the empty lot behind my mother's house, in the predawn twilight, and she held a red-lens flashlight in one hand and my crutches in the other as I dug up the packed soil with a spade.

"You Spenser brothers are so fucking overrated," she said.

"Huh?"

"You have the entire city, the entire damned city, to hide this contraband, and where do you pick? Your mother's backyard. What a ridiculous, juvenile, shortsighted move on your part."

"Well, Doctor, I was really thinking of a place that an outside agency would need to get a warrant to search."

"Eh, I don't want to hear it. Overrated, and an insult to my intelligence."

I opened the weatherproof bag, reassembled the parts, wrapped the now fully functional shotgun in a cloth blanket we had brought with us, and set it down beside me.

I reached for a clipboard on the ground next to me. "Okay, Doctor Katya Czaervich, MD, chief pathologist of Allegheny County. By signing this document, you are attesting that at 5 a.m. today, this firearm was delivered to your possession by unknown persons and that you will immediately turn it in to the PPD evidence locker as it matches serial number WIN5693341909, the raid firearm of the late Detective Marco Escardo."

She took the pen and signed it. "With this signature I verify that you are certifiable and need inpatient care, Captain."

I tore the slip off and handed it to her. "Doctor–patient privilege?"

She smiled. "Until I see you on my exam table." She turned around with the shotgun and walked to her car; then she was gone.

■ ■ ■

One day that summer, Brady and I called on Mandy one last time before she left the city. We had not seen her since she'd interred Kenny's ashes at the cemetery, though she'd had Mom over privately and let the girls visit their aunts and uncles and cousins. We had salvaged Kenny's rings from the burnt waste of my tactical vest, had the jewelry shop that made the West Point ring fix the stone, and professionally cleaned both of them up. We knew she didn't want any tribute to Kenny the cop, but as far as we cared, Kenny the soldier's integrity was impregnable.

We'd both stayed in the Guard since Bosnia, Brady as a major in 20th Special Forces (18A) and I as a chief warrant officer three (180A), now remanded to a staff position after my amputation. However, we both decided that today would be our retirement, as a way of paying tribute to Kenny. I had taken a medical board retirement. Brady got an early authorization. We wouldn't get a full pension like if we had been full-time active duty, but at least our families wouldn't have to worry about deployments on top of us being policemen.

For the ceremony, we put on our Army green service uniforms, bloused into our jump boots, and donned ties and ribbons and berets. Mandy didn't come; we knew she wouldn't. Afterward, we drove over to the house she once shared with Kenny, the SOLD sign hanging forlornly out front telling me my brother was indeed gone forever. Brady had five slices of cake wrapped up in a Tupperware box, and I carried the small oak box with Kenny's rings. She smiled puzzledly at the door, let us in, and greeted both of us with hugs.

She didn't know why we had come. When I opened the ring box and set it on her table, she wept openly and ran to the kitchen. After a few minutes, she returned, pink teary rims around her puffy eyes but composed and smiling brightly.

"I'd thought they were gone."

"No, honey. He . . . he gave them to me, right before he climbed up there to get Franny. They were all banged up in the blast. We got them fixed."

She put the wedding ring to the side and clutched the West Point ring. Brady and I shared a momentary look of our own puzzlement.

"You dummies. All these years you thought the West Point ring was him rubbing it in my face that the academy was more important? You both were there; West Point Chapel was where we got married!" She reached inside her shirt and produced, on a gold chain, a three-quarter-size "sweetheart" version of Kenny's ring. With the fervor of a teenager putting on her boyfriend's letter jacket, she unclasped the chain and put Kenny's ring set beside hers, then restrung it around her neck, with Brady helping to clasp it.

"*These* were our wedding rings. Those bands were something your mother picked out. He always loved me." She openly cried some more but was smiling, and we hugged her from both sides, staying that way for quite some time.

■ ■ ■

Mandy and the girls got Kenny's full pension. That had been part of the deal to close the case. The commissioner, the DA, and Jankowitz's partner, Dickie Sawyer, who represented our entire family at no charge, worked that out as an agreement. It also came with a hefty nondisclosure incorporating that Mandy or the girls would never talk to the press or they'd forfeit everything.

Repo's family also delayed his funeral until I was well enough to accompany the body as it sat in a cargo car on an Amtrak to West Texas. I was met at the station by a second cousin, who shook my hand. I accompanied him to the funeral home for moral support, and though the body had been in cold storage for two months, it was still gruesome as the mortician lifted the sheet. The cousin nearly collapsed in the corner. He decided on a closed casket, obviously. Asked me to stay for the service. I told him I had to get back. Mumbled something about my wife expecting.

"You guys were like his kids. He'd do anything, no matter how crazy, for you boys."

"Sir, you don't even know how correct you are."

I allowed myself one exception and got drunk as a monkey in a whorehouse on the way home from that mindfuck. I was sweated out and sober by the time I reached Union Station in Pittsburgh.

■ ■ ■

Somewhere in the middle of all of this, they handed Brady the Special Investigations Unit. With a gold bow. On a platter. Since he was the one who gleaned the connection between the weapons and Kenny in the first place, they thought it fitting that he be the one to take up the mantle and try to make some good out of the total shitstorm Kenny had caused. You usually have to be a captain with twenty years in grade since the academy to rate SIU. Kenny had been an inspector for a decade before he got it. But I don't think people cared much about the time-in-grade requirement; they just wanted someone behind the desk who wasn't going to be a corrupt, murdering motherfucker.

Ed Peters took over Internal Affairs permanently and was promoted to a full captain. Snopes recovered completely from his injuries and went to my spot in Major Crimes as a lieutenant.

There aren't too many SWAT commanders running around on just one leg, but I fought like a bitch to get there. Prosthetics, medical boards, recovery from both the stroke and the amputation, an absolute shitload of an uphill battle. They tried to retire me early—several times, in fact; but thanks to mine and Kenny's rescue of Francine and taking out the commissioner's killer, my name carried some popularity instead of the notoriety of Frank's legacy.

Of course, if word got out about what Kenny and Repo had truly done, it would upend everything again.

I wear one type of prosthetic when running team drills or when SWAT is going on a mission, another type when walking or during a typical day at the office, and a third when I'm doing any type of distance running beyond three miles.

Since the surgery, my hands shake if I'm on the scope for too long, and some nights I wake up drenched in sweat, and it's only Claire's loving words and kind, soothing voice that remind me that nothing is coming through the walls to kill me. After an hour or so, my heart stops pounding through my ears.

We all thought Francine would get the hell out of the city and go back to the RAND Corporation in Georgetown. I really wouldn't have blamed her. But no. She's working on her own version of redemption now. I think she's trying to erase Kenny's sins, like Kenny had been cursed to try to erase Frank's. She's in victim advocacy full time now, not just litigation. Social work, too. We still have a close relationship; she owns Frank's old building, converted the bottom into her law offices and community legal clinic, and she and Claire are as tight as sisters. Franny is completely in love with her new nephew.

Before our boy was born, Claire and I took a road trip down the coast and celebrated what we considered our long-delayed honeymoon in Charleston, South Carolina. We spent a month down there, surf fishing on the beach, taking long walks in the historic city—as long as her swollen calves would allow—and watching Friday parades at the Citadel. In the evenings we had dinners at the Peninsula Grille or Hall's Chophouse and walked arm in arm like teenagers, admiring the sunset over the market town.

I had gotten an offer, and even considered, a job with the campus police at Citadel, but Claire knew I would not be happy going from where we came from to strolling around a campus with a sidearm and a nightstick, even if the assignment involved something as rewarding and noble as keeping cadets and students safe.

Still, we stayed in Charleston that whole month, through the remainder of her pregnancy, and she ended up going into labor while we were on a date downtown one night. We delivered at the Medical University of South Carolina and welcomed Mark Brady Spenser into the world.

Blessed with his mom's ginger curls, my expressive eyes, and his uncle Brady's cheeks, jaw, and forehead, there was no question even before he was born of who he would be named for—or, more importantly, who he was not going to be associated with *at all*.

It was as if we had woken up one day after the funeral and Kenny had been erased from the family. His West Point class picture that once hung in Mom's living room, along with his Army commissioning photo at Trophy Point, with Mom and Frank at his side, had disappeared, along with the wedding pictures of him and Amanda. Mom didn't speak his name anymore. I understood that was her way of punishing herself, blaming herself, but wasn't sure that was the best way to go about processing his loss. Kenny was dead, and he had done horrible things, but he was still her son. I still had the photo from Mickey's nightstand of the three of us at my and Brady's police academy graduation, with Kenny standing proudly, his arms around our shoulders; Mom was moving that over my dead body.

Word on the street was Frank had a heart attack when Kenny's corruption was revealed. Others said he went back on the bottle. Some of his bar buddies at the LeMont would tell you he swallowed a bottle of sleeping pills. One of his hookers from the '70s swears up and down she saw him throw his retirement badge in the Allegheny River. But Frank's too much a narcissist for any of that self-destruction. I'm not judging the bastard; I just know him is all.

When I came around in the hospital after losing my leg, Frank's was the first face I saw, and it told me everything. He didn't have to do anything more to punish himself or repent. Kenny had broken him. Frank's one redeeming grace for all those decades had been that his children were nothing like him. Perhaps in trying so hard to avoid becoming him, we had unearthed something even darker in ourselves. The one least affected by it was Francine. I pray to God she has a long, joyful, quiet life, and finds a way to unburden herself of this ugly self-loathing shit.

It took me forever to finally come out to the cemetery. God bless Amanda, she had put a brass marker at the base of Mickey's grave with Kenny's name etched on it in Hebrew. Although he had converted when he married Mandy, he was still Jewish by bloodline. Typically, Jews are *never* cremated, or the surviving family is strongly advised against it, and most of the time, ashes will not be interred in a Jewish cemetery; I had to chuckle at Amanda's middle finger to the rabbi who ran the cemetery, her last act before she had taken the four girls and disappeared out west of the city.

I heard leaves crunch behind me.

It was already November again. It was odd to think that the entirety of this tragedy had started over fourteen months before, and here we were now, forever changed, a part of us in perpetual grief, two less loved ones in our family—three if you included Repo—but blessed with our new son.

I knew it was Frank standing there.

I hoped he would not ruin the moment by saying something.

I hoped he would just let it be me and him, Marco, Mickey, and Kenny—together.

After some time, I heard tires grinding on the gravel, the sound of Sarah Costello's jeep with Brady at the wheel. It was sunset on a Friday, and Brady and I were the only Jews in Pittsburgh who would be anywhere near this cemetery. Brady pulled a long case out of the back seat and walked toward us with it slung over his shoulder.

He wordlessly drew three shotguns from the case when he got near the gravestone and handed one to Frank, one to me.

"Couldn't get blanks. Rock salt was best I could drum up."

"I don't think he'd disapprove," Frank said absently, staring at Marco's and Kenny's resting places. "We'll just aim towards the pond."

"Seven in each?" I asked, checking the breech in mine.

"Yeah."

"Should we do a count?"

"I was thinking a one-two?"

"Sounds good. Form up on me."

Brady was the base. I squared off of Brady, and Frank off of me. We then stood at attention, brought the shotguns up to port arms, and shouldered them at the ready.

Under Brady's quiet count, we shot off twenty-one volleys in bursts of three abreast, a total of seven times each, to give Kenny the hero's farewell that he had been denied.

Brady, Frank, and I cleared the chambers of the last shotshells and solemnly picked up the spent rounds at our feet. We then just as quietly put the rifles back in the sling bag, and Brady departed as unceremoniously as he'd approached.

I started toward the Humvee. Frank had parked the old Monte Carlo next to it.

"You coming, Dad?"

"Not just yet, Tom. You go on. I want to stay with the boys and Shoshanna a bit longer."

ACKNOWLEDGMENTS

For my editors over the past nine years. Has it really been nine? I am worse than Grady Tripp in Michael Chabon's novel. Jocelyn Gerwig, Virginia Diaz, and Kristen Hamilton, thank you for your support and your brutal honesty. You have made this book better than when it first started. And if it took nine years, so be it.

To my brother Bradley David Ellis, my father, Brian John Ellis, and my grandfather Simon Cohen: It was the best feeling in the world to breathe life back into the three of you for the pages of this book, if only for my imaginary little universe. It broke my heart for a second time when I had to say goodbye to you at the end.

Dad, in fiction I gave you a much more morally superior character than you ever had in life. It wasn't for your sake. It was for those you left behind.

ABOUT THE AUTHOR

BRIAN ELLIS earned his Bachelor's degree in Political Science from Pennsylvania State University and his Master's of Leadership Science from The Citadel Military College of South Carolina. He is a former soldier and paratrooper whose career spanned twenty-two years in the infantry, Signal Corps, and mostly airborne infantry or infantry enabler units, to include three deployments with the 82nd Airborne Division to Iraq, Afghanistan, and Hurricane Katrina. He served two more combat tours, in Iraq as a State Department police advisor and in Afghanistan as a member of the 42nd Military Police Group. Brian retired from active service in 2016 as a major. He currently works as an instructor and member of the commandant's staff at Virginia Military Institute. Brian divides his time between the suburbs of Washington, DC, with his family and working in Lexington, Virginia. *Redemption* is his first book.

www.ingramcontent.com/pod-product-compliance
Lightning Source LLC
Chambersburg PA
CBHW030626310726
48979CB00003B/895
9781646639632